# Calling Time

## by

### Sian M. Williams

The following novel is a work of fiction. No character contained within is a true representation of any person living or dead. All rights reserved. No part of this work shall be reproduced, stored in a retrieval system or transmitted in any form by any means, electronic, mechanical, photocopying, recording or otherwise without the prior written permission of the author.

sianscriptsinfo@gmail.com

# Introduction

'Calling Time' is a simple story, a romantic story. All of the characters are fictitious and are not intended to be true representations of any individuals living or dead but more of a representation of a cross section of people at all time in the modern world.

It is set in 1985 against a backdrop of Mrs. Thatcher doing her best and her worst; Bob Geldof lifting the world in a valiant attempt to unite everyone against the famine in Africa with his Band aid concert; singers and songs still well known to this day; fear created by terrorist bombs and a lingering cold war; and young people everywhere stepping into a working world of massive unemployment.

By moving Meg to a small island, I hoped to remove the influence of particular politics and world events to highlight the ongoing angst and self-absorption of young people as they leave the comforting arms of family and educational establishments with confidence, ambition and dreams of greatness totally unprepared for the realities and often disillusionment of adulthood.

This is Meg's story; she is 'everywoman' searching for food, shelter, love and self-esteem in a world that is not always kind. The people she meets on her journey of self-discovery provide her with many life lessons and open her eyes to the realities and responsibilities of adulthood. It is seen through her eyes, her thoughts, emotions and reactions. In life we don't always know what other people are truly thinking and feeling and often we get it wrong.

In 1985, long distant correspondence was through letters, cards and expensive landline telephone systems  Despite the massive technological advances in communication, misunderstandings and miscommunication are still a huge part of the rich tapestry of our lives today. The same mistakes are made as each individual strives to make sense of a changing world. Collectively, we slowly evolve emotionally, and history continues to repeat itself.

SW

# Acknowledgements

A huge thank you to Suzy Daniels for all her time, help and encouragement, to Helen Board for all her invaluable comments and commas; to Angie Boyle for the title, and for always making me laugh; to Tracy Pike for her wise words of advice; to Sharon Thompson for proofreading and to Craig for giving me the time to write. Thank you to all the wonderful people I am very proud and lucky to call my friends.

*The best thing in life is a true friend.*

*Be one*

# CHAPTER 1

*July 1985*

Sunlight streamed through a slit in the curtains and struck Meg's sleeping eyes, forcing her to wake. She groaned and hauled the duvet over her face, leaving a mass of soft, dark curls peeping over the top. She rolled over turning her back to the intruding sun and fell out of bed. She landed on the hard wooden floor with a thud.

Meg lay naked on the floor completely confused, and then it dawned on her with slow pleasurable memory that Pete was back. She filled with warmth as she thought about his surprise arrival the day before and the passionate lovemaking that followed. She peeped over the edge of the mattress to look at him, but his side of the bed was empty. Irrational panic gripped her.

The bedroom door opened and he appeared, fully dressed in jeans and a T-shirt, standing in the doorway holding a cup of tea and smiling at her. Her tummy twirled with desire as she looked at his tall, strong body, his face tanned by life under a desert sun, and his dark hazel eyes looking out from under a shock of thick brown hair. She could still hardly believe that he was here with her.

"Johnson, what are you doing down there?" he asked, laughing.

"Um, just looking for something," she mumbled climbing back into bed and modestly covering herself with the duvet.

"Here you go, sleepyhead," he said as he came to sit on the edge of the bed and ruffled the top of her head.

"Thank you," she said taking the cup and blowing on the hot tea, "What time is it?"

"Nine."

She groaned but grinned up at him over the mug.

"You're up a bit early for a Saturday, aren't you?"

"Couldn't sleep. Your curtains are too thin and you were snoring."

"Was not!" she said smacking his leg.

"Come on, it's a beautiful day."

Fully awake now, she suddenly leaned over to turn on the radio at the side of the bed with excitement. The distinctive voice of John Elton declared that he was still standing.

"You can listen to the radio in the car," said Pete.

"My interview should be on any minute!" she exclaimed and Pete laughed.

The end of the song faded out and the familiar voice of Sheila Richards, one of Meg's mentors and a local radio celebrity came on to chat easily about things in the news and told listeners that they would be playing more tracks from the Band Aid concert held the week before, which had raised a staggering fifty million pounds.

"Come on Meg. We've got things to do," Pete said with an edge of impatience.

"Wait, wait. Listen!" Meg sat up and turned the volume up.

Sheila's smooth voice brought the conversation round to local fund raising activities and introduced the story that Meg had covered about sponsoring a sheep. She had managed to get an interview with a famous author and included comments from a sheep called Uriah Heap. "Baaaa, baaaaa" came across the room from the tiny speaker and Pete fell about laughing.

"When are they going to start paying you? You've been doing this stuff for ages now and they still only give you petrol money. You're baaaaarmy." He found his own joke very funny.

"Don't laugh. I've sold that one to Radio Four."

She laughed with him, but inside she was deeply hurt. She tried to sound confident but she didn't really feel it; her stomach bubbled with nerves.

"I'm going to get a break soon. I'm sure of it. They've got an official traineeship coming up and they gave me a driving test a couple of days ago along with another girl who's just come down from London this week, but she's only done one recording. I've been there for nearly a year now."

She wasn't going to tell him until she got it, but she wanted him to take her seriously, and she wasn't very good at keeping things to herself.

It was nearly a year since she had first walked into the radio station and asked if she could have a day's work experience. Since finishing university she had applied for countless positions without success. Along with many of her fellow students she had been unable to use her degree for the career she wanted and was making ends meet with waitressing, and shifts at a call centre doing market research. Most of her friends had left for various parts of the country to sign on the dole or move back in with their parents. She didn't want to do either and so she had spent a lonely few months moving from one terrible flat to another, barely able to pay the rent.

Completely knocked and deflated by the stream of thank you but no thank you letters she had plucked up the courage to go into the local radio station and ask for a chance to gain experience. The Station Manager had eventually shrugged his shoulders and said she could spend a day seeing what went on. Determined to make the most of the opportunity she had asked questions, offered to help out wherever she could and volunteered to go out on the street interviewing people about their views on a new shopping centre. She had returned with the tape and after a kind producer, Rupert took the time to show her the basics of editing she set about trying to cut down the interviews into a beautiful flow of comments. It took her hours as she listened intently through headphones to the recording and tried to cut out all but the most interesting and amusing comments. Most of the time was spent cutting in the wrong place and then trying to stick the tiniest bit of tape back in where she'd cut off the end of a word or not left a natural breath and generally making a very messy job of it, but she stuck at it. Eventually, at eight in the evening, Rupert came up and said she ought to go home, but impressed by her determination he invited her to come back for two weeks experience. She'd been working for them ever since doing two or three interviews a week, improving her editing skills and helping with the production of shows for which she received fifteen pounds a week for petrol money.

Yesterday had been a good day; one of those special days, when it seems as though, at last, your life is beginning to make sense and things are falling into place. She had left the radio station feeling happy and confident. Rupert, had given her the thumbs up, indicating his conviction that she would be offered the official traineeship, and when she stepped outside, Pete had been waiting there to surprise her.

"A driving test? Is that so you don't run over any sheep when you're out and about as a roving reporter?"

"Ha-ha, very funny. No, it's for driving a radio show. Pressing all the right switches, fading in and out and all that."

"Oh God! Hope it's easier than operating an oven. Have they seen you in the kitchen?"

She threw a pillow at him and he grabbed her and started to tickle her until she was giggling and screaming for him to stop. He pinned her down on the bed, looked at her intently, and kissed her. It was a long, gentle kiss that sent tingles through her entire body and she pulled him closer but he pulled away and jumped off the bed. She felt another twinge of uncertainty niggling into her sense of perfection.

"Come on, get dressed. Let's get out of this dump."

"It's not a dump. It's wonderful and I can stay rent free, so it's perfect for now."

"Rent free, yes. I wonder what Tom wants in return."

"Oh don't be silly. He's an old friend. He doesn't have to pay for it as long as he's farm manager. He's glad of the company."

"I'll bet he is."

It didn't occur to Meg that Pete was jealous. She was so madly in love with him that she only worried about whether he loved her. Tom was always making passes at her, but it was almost a joke between them. She didn't want to spoil seeing Pete with a silly argument. She threw another pillow at him and ran to the bathroom laughing.

When she returned, Pete had gone back downstairs. Pulling on a pair of knickers she looked out of the bedroom window of the little farm cottage across the fields of golden corn and bright yellow oil-seed rape. She wriggled into a short denim skirt and rummaged in a drawer for a bra to match her pants before putting on a blue vest which hugged her body, accentuated her neat, fit figure, and left a slice of smooth, flat tummy on display when she moved. She dragged her fingers through her dark curls and attempted to make them look a little less unruly and glanced in the mirror on top of the chest of drawers in front of the window, grimaced and applied a little mascara to lengthen the dark lashes bordering her bright blue eyes. She poked the brush into her eye causing it to water and a great black smudge of black ran down her cheek. She swore and wiped it all off with a sigh.

She paused before heading downstairs, staring out over the fields to where they met with the sky, which was clear and blue in the July heat wave. On the horizon, she could see Tom's tractor slowly moving across the skyline. She loved living there, in the middle of the countryside but only fifteen minutes from town.

An old school friend, she had quite literally bumped into Tom, or into his car, when he had nearly run her over on the high street. It was a truly serendipitous event. Her flat mate was moving to another city for work, the lease was up on the house that they shared and they were talking about her options as to where she was going to live next. Deep in conversation they had stepped into the road in front of a black Land Rover coming out of a tiny side street. The driver, a young man with a mop of unruly, bright blonde hair stuck his head out of the window and yelled at them. Meg stepped back in shock and then shouted with delight when she recognised her old friend from home and they stood in the street chatting before hooting horns from cars behind made them move. They had gone for a drink and he told her he was working on a farm just outside the city and lived in a small farmworker's cottage with two bedrooms. When she told him what she was doing, he immediately offered her the spare room, rent-free as he didn't have to pay rent, and she was overjoyed to accept the offer. It meant she had been able to work at the radio station for the little they gave her in expenses without having to do as much part time work to cover her rent. She had seen it as a sign that she was doing the right thing, and on Monday, she would be proved right.

She felt a buzz of excitement and her thoughts ran on. Then, she would be independent, she could rent a flat and have somewhere just for her and Pete when he was on leave from his engineering job in Saudi Arabia. Deep down she'd hoped he would buy a flat for them, make some kind of commitment, but she would never suggest it. They'd been together on and off since they were poor students together, but she still felt that she didn't want to be after his money. A niggle replaced the buzz, a familiar feeling. Did he really love her still? Two years he'd been working away now. The first year had been wildly romantic and exciting. Lovely letters, phone calls, missing each other badly, the anticipation of seeing him again, whenever he was on leave and then the phone call last summer saying that they needed to talk and the arrangement to meet in Athens before a holiday of island hopping.

A sickening feeling flooded through her as she remembered that holiday. She couldn't bear to think about it. The relationship had been strained ever since and she had spent the year trying to get them back on track, but it was hard with a long distant relationship. They were still together a year later and she loved him deeply, but she didn't know how to move the relationship forward. She got on with life, had fun, and worked hard, but he was always in her thoughts. On the surface she appeared confident and carefree but inside she was struggling, losing confidence in herself in all areas of life. She ached with the longing to be with him, and was filled with joy whenever a letter arrived or he called her on the phone. He was the one. She loved him and wanted to be with him, but at the same time she wanted a career in her own right, she didn't want to be a Saudi wife with no life apart from playing Mah Jong and buying gold jewellery, did she?

Since last summer it had been different. He had become elusive. His phone calls were less often and she would wait getting worried and upset. She'd go down to the local phone box in all kinds of weather with a vast pile of coins to try and get hold of him, but more often than not he'd be offshore. More often than not when they did speak they would end up fighting with no chance of cuddling and making up and she would try to make amends in long letters. On one of his leaves earlier in the year he had gone on holiday with his mates instead of seeing her and although she had told him it was fine she had cried herself to sleep feeling the irretrievable gap growing between them but he didn't finish it and she clung on hopefully. Pete was growing in confidence as the money piled up in his bank account and his career was on an upward curve while she was struggling to make ends meet and trying to stay optimistic despite the continual rejections. Looking forward to Pete's letters, calls and visits home kept her going but she wasn't sure they shared the same path anymore.

She took a deep breath as she thought about the radio and then about Pete. "Please, please let us be all right," she whispered. Once she was independent, earning her own money they'd be on a more even footing, she decided. "Roll on Monday," she said to herself as she tied her hair up in a ponytail. She grimaced at herself in the mirror and ran downstairs.

Pete was standing in front of the stove cooking eggs and bacon. She went up behind him and hugged his tall strong body.

"What's that for?" he laughed. "Make yourself useful and pass me a couple of plates."

After breakfast, they stepped outside into the glorious sunshine. Pete's fabulous red Ferrari stood shining in the farmyard, incongruous with old barns and silo towers. They stood there admiring it, both hardly able to believe it belonged to Pete.

"Come a long way from that old Mini at uni, haven't we?" he said, and Meg's heart jumped at the sound of that 'we'.

They spent the morning in banks with Pete organising his vast sums of money. He told Meg he had to go to Devon on Sunday evening to meet his uncle and see about buying some property. He asked her to go with him, but she reminded him that she had to be at the radio station on Monday morning.

After a light lunch in a quaint pub by the river they hired a rowing boat and spent half an hour laughing as Meg rowed them round in circles and into trees overhanging the bank until Pete took over and pulling the oars with long, strong strokes took them smoothly back to the jetty. Afterwards, they sat on the riverbank eating ice creams and watching children feed the ducks. Pete seemed distracted and Meg felt uptight, wishing he would say something important about their future; wishing she could say the right thing. It should have been an idyllic romantic afternoon but something hung between them. He talked about his job, the long hours spent on rigs and the intense heat of Arabia and she listened, and soothed, and praised him. He took her to the radio station so that she could collect her moped and she drove along the middle of the winding lanes back to the farm, laughing as Pete followed behind, ridiculously slowly in his Ferrari, and beeped his horn at her.

In the evening, they had arranged to go out with Tom and a crowd of friends. Pete got on with them all. He was sociable and easy going, generous with his money without being flash and Meg felt proud to be with him. They met in a pub in the town centre, and gathered near the bar in the busy, crowded bar. Duran Duran came on the jukebox and a group of new romantics wearing flamboyant clothes cheered. Meg turned to look and they started to dance; the guys wore loose, white-sleeved, frilly pirate shirts, their hair was short at the sides with messy, bleached quiffs on top and they wore black eye-liner. The girls, wearing heavy make-up, were in brightly coloured batwing tops with padded shoulders and pencil skirts. When Duran Duran finished and was replaced by Sting and The Police playing 'Every Breath You Take', they downed their drinks and left the bar.

Meg and her crowd enjoyed some banter, laughing and joking, and then moved onto more serious discussions about the state of the country under Margaret Thatcher. Opinions were mixed on the handling of the miners' strike that had finally ended a few months ago and the desperate situation faced by the huge mining communities around the country. They moved onto football and the hooligans causing terror at so many games and the most shocking events at the Heysel Stadium with the wall collapsing and the terribly sad and devastating fire at Bradford City's Valley Parade Stadium that was caused by neglect. Meg had been involved in covering both events at the radio station and she enjoyed sharing informed knowledge of what had happened. Pete was winding Meg up and she was getting carried away with her passionate views. Tom lightened the growing tension by interjecting with,

"And did you know they have decided to stop the production of red telephone boxes?"

Everyone exclaimed in disappointment as if this was sadder than the plight of miners and the terrible events at football stadiums.

They moved onto TV, what was happening in the new soap opera, Eastenders and comparing it to

Coronation Street, then discussing favourites such as Only Fools & Horses and The Two Ronnies.

"How long are you over?" Teresa, a girl Meg played squash with, asked Pete.

"Another two weeks or so," replied Pete.

They fell into conversation, Meg went to the toilet and Teresa turned to Pete and asked him straight out.

"So, what's going to happen with you and Meg? It must be difficult keeping up a long distance relationship."

"Oh, we'll see."

"You men and bloody commitment!" she said.

Pete hesitated. He did not know these people well and he often felt like he was intruding on Meg's life.

"You have no idea how much I love that girl. She wants to make a career in radio or whatever and I'm in Saudi. Sometimes I miss her so much it hurts, but there's nothing for her over there and I won't stop her doing what she wants to do."

"Have you told her?"

"Meg knows I love her. We've come through a lot. We'll be all right," he said. He turned away and faced the bar, "What are you drinking?"

Tom, Pete and Meg stumbled back into the farmhouse and Meg made them all coffee and burnt toast.

"How did you manage that?" Tom laughed.

"It was tricky, I was looking for the sugar and then, well the grill was hot."

Tom and Pete just laughed. Tom finished his coffee and said he had to go to bed. He needed to be up before dawn.

They waited a while and then Pete drew Meg into his arms. His hand reached up under her shirt. She sighed with pleasure as he kissed her neck and throat and they proceeded to undress each other in growing passion and urgency. His hands massaged her erect nipples and she shivered with pleasure as he moved his head down to kiss and lick, enjoying her rising excitement. He laid her gently down and his fingers delved in between her legs stimulating her wetness and increasing in tempo as she gasped in pleasure, reached for him and directed him into her.

Breathing heavily, Meg clung on to him and whispered, "I love you." "I love you, too." he replied.

They gathered up their clothes and crept upstairs. Meg climbed into bed next to him and snuggled up hoping to take advantage of the loving closeness to talk. He mumbled something unintelligible and fell into a deep sleep with gentle snores emanating across the room. Meg lay awake feeling that all too familiar hollowness in her stomach. *What if she didn't get the traineeship? What would she do then? Everything depended on it. It was the break she needed to feel that she was on the right path, validated in her decision. She knew she'd chosen a difficult career path but then with unemployment at well over three million every career path was difficult. She couldn't go on earning no money and taking advantage of Tom's kindness. If only Pete would commit, give her some stability...oh God.*

They were both groggy as they drove up to the supermarket to buy supplies for a barbeque. Tom was finishing early and going back to work in the evening, so they'd planned to have a feast before Pete set off for Devon and Tom resumed his farming duties. As they set up the grill in the yard, dark clouds began to gather in the previously clear sky. The incorrigible British weather was playing its usual trick on would be barbequers and with the added effects of thunder and lightning the rain came down. Meg and Tom ended up standing in the kitchen watching and laughing hysterically, as Pete insisted that they must not let the weather defeat them. He stood outside in a wind-sheeter under a huge umbrella balanced over the grill cooking burgers and sausages in the pouring rain. Meg put on one of a collection of music tapes that a DJ at the radio had made for her with an eclectic mix of music from the seventies and eighties and she and Tom watched, laughing through the window as Pete slaved away, to the sound of the Eurhythmics', 'Here Comes the Rain Again'. In the end a pile of blackened, smoking, inedible meat remained on a platter as they ate the salads Meg had prepared and The Smiths played 'This Charming Man' in the background.

Pete came downstairs with his bag packed. He shook Tom's hand and thanked him, saying he'd see him in a couple of days. Moving out of Tom's sight Pete hugged Meg and looked down into her face from his six foot two height, with his deep brown eyes. They kissed long and hard and he said that he would call when he could.

"Good luck with the house buying," she said.

He ruffled the top of her head and grinned. She stood and waved as he drove off with a roar of power through the puddles and mud on the farm track. The usual empty hollowness of saying goodbye consumed her, and the fact that he hadn't wished her luck with the job.

# CHAPTER 2

Meg got onto her little white Honda 50 moped, fastened the helmet strap and whirred off to the radio station. The rain had cleared and it was warm enough not to need gloves. It was a relief after riding in the middle of winter. Despite being wrapped up like a mummy in scarves, a woollen hat under her helmet, layers of clothes, a coat and thick gloves, nothing could prevent the steady penetration of cold as she sat motionless on the small machine completely exposed to the elements, conveying her at the breakneck speed of thirty m.p.h. She often arrived to interview people in the surrounding villages with her fingers so stiff she was unable to work the tape recorder. Her face, like a block of red ice, was so numb that she could barely move her lips to speak. Trying to appear dynamic and professional, she felt like she came across as a bumbling fool with a speech impediment, until she thawed out.

Once comfortable, she was good at endearing the people she interviewed to her, and produced light, entertaining and often informative pieces. One of her favourites had been a ninety-year old man, who had just completed the making of a four-poster bed as his ultimate goal in life. She had been invited into his flat and edged through a hallway and along a corridor piled high with coal (he wasn't going to get caught out again by a fuel shortage) and followed him into a bedroom filled by a very substantial four-poster bed. During the recording, he told her that building the bed was actually his penultimate aim. His ultimate desire, he announced with a gummy smile while looking intently into her bright eyes with his watery pale ones peeking out from creased, sagging eyelids in a rather lecherous fashion, was to sleep in it with someone. She had wished him luck and backed out of his flat fairly rapidly. Hardly breaking news material, but popular with local listeners.

Today, with the sun shining, she made her way through quiet, winding country lanes to the main road and crossed into the city. She was happy and excited, full of anticipation of just reward and recognition for her perseverance. She had spent hours and hours learning how to edit recordings, drive shows, do research and prepare interviews. She had been in at five in the morning and often left late in the evening whenever she could. A couple of other hopefuls had come to the station for one or two days in the time she'd been there, but then disappeared. One of these, Debs had come from London the week before to visit friends and she had recorded an interview. They got on well, had been to the pub a couple of times, and Meg had given her help with the editing of the tape.

She parked her moped and rushed into the radio station full of expectation and giddy anticipation of being able to start work full-time and be paid for it. She met Debs at the top of the stairs.

"Hi, Debs!"

"Hi, Meg," she replied flatly.

Meg noted the tone and her immediate thought was that Debs had been told that there was no more work for her. She felt excitement, but prepared to hide her joy and find the right words. Debs spoke quickly, barely able to look at Meg, "Listen. I wanted to be the one to tell you. They offered me the er, the traineeship, er, in the pub on Friday night."

Meg froze. She couldn't speak. She stared dumbly at Debs trying to get the words to sink in and make sense. Debs mumbled another apology and ran down the stairs past her. Meg went into the office in a daze. Rupert was almost crying when she asked him what was going on. He hadn't been consulted; it wasn't what he wanted. She asked if she should go and speak to the managers. Embarrassed, he told her it would do no good and that she couldn't continue now there was an official trainee starting. The 'friend' that Debs had been visiting, and sleeping with, was the station manager's best friend. Meg didn't even know that Debs knew him What a fucking two-faced bitch! Meg had been so helpful and full of advice with the tape Debs had done for the station; she had actually helped her get the position. Her mother had warned her about people like that.

Suddenly, she remembered the engineer who had given them the driving test, Derek. He had taught

Meg many months before and she always had a chat and a laugh with him. During the test he had been moody and distant and had actually stopped the test half way through mumbling, "I can't do this." She had thought it was strange, but presumed at the time that he was too busy to be doing testing. Now she realised that she had been set up. Why was she always so trusting and naïve?

She picked up all her tapes, her notes, and her letters of thanks from listeners, shook everybody's hand, though they could barely look at her, and she could barely contain the burning behind her eyes. She went home with tears blurring her vision and her stomach churning as she rode back down the tiny country lanes, which only yesterday she had ridden down laughing, with Pete behind her. She felt embarrassed, humiliated, a failure.

Meg sat on the sofa in the living room of the old farm cottage and stared at the bare, brick fireplace and the faded, peeling wallpaper unable to move. So much for signs. She felt as if she had been kicked in the stomach and a strange lump lurked at the back of her throat. She was unable to think straight. Paralysed by shock, she just perched on the edge of the threadbare sofa in the sparsely furnished lounge with her eyes filling with tears that slowly brimmed over and rolled unceremoniously down her cheeks. Her hopes and dreams had been ripped apart.

The phone rang jolting her out of her catatonic state and it was Pete.

She asked if he was coming back that night. He said he couldn't make it, and she couldn't bring herself to admit to him why she desperately needed to be loved and hugged.

"What are you up to, tonight?" she asked, trying to sound normal.

"Oh, just going out for a bite to eat and a drink."

There was something in his voice.

"Are you going with Uncle Ray?"

"Um, yes. He'll probably be there. Look I've got to go, I'll call you tomorrow."

She muttered a weak goodbye and slung down the phone. What the bloody hell was he doing? She knew there was a woman involved. She knew him too well. But who?

She tried to forget about it, tell herself she was imagining things because she was upset, but she couldn't. She phoned him back.

"What are you doing, Pete?"

"Meg, stop being silly."

Meg had been here before with him. They'd broken up over it years before. She thought they didn't play stupid games anymore.

"Pete," she felt her voice cracking.

"Meg, don't let's have a row. I'll call you tomorrow."

She slung the phone down again, kicking herself for not playing it cool.

She went to the front door and looked out across the corn-filled fields stretching as far as the eye could see; glorious in contrast to the blue, but now the gold seemed to have faded. She loved living there, but now the beauty and the peace only made the hollow wrench in her stomach stronger. She went inside and found a bottle of wine and a packet of Tom's cigarettes; she didn't smoke but it seemed like a good time to start. She sat in the chair staring into space drinking steadily and puffing tobacco until the tears began to roll down her cheeks. She thought of calling someone, but the truth was that she was embarrassed. She didn't want to tell anyone. She hadn't had any support from her family for choosing to work for nothing and she had not proved them wrong. She looked at the pile of Monday issues of The Guardian in the corner of the room and felt sick. She drank some more wine and began to sob. She held her face in her hands as the tears streamed down her cheeks, her chest heaved and her nose began to run.

Finally she stopped. Feeling light headed from the wine and cigarettes, she breathed in deeply, grabbed a tissue to blow her nose and picked up that morning's copy of the paper. There were pages of appointments and she began circling possibilities. Then she stabbed angrily at the paper with her pen. She had applied and applied and applied to jobs and received a corresponding number of rejections. She struggled to turn the huge pages of the broadsheet, folding and bashing them untidily until she reached the small ads on the travel pages. She needed to get away, to escape. The call with Pete was the last straw. She had kept going, determined to succeed, hoping and wishing and praying for things to fall into place. She needed to sort her head out; start again, refreshed and suntanned. Beating the paper into some sort of shape, she looked through the last minute get away offers. She realised that however cheap they might be, she didn't have enough money. Then she spotted a small ad from a travel company.

'Reps required urgently for Greek island resort.'

In desperation she called the number.

When Tom arrived home stinking of silo and dying for a beer she greeted him with a cold can and the news that she had an interview for a job in Greece.

"Excellent," he said, "we'll go to the pub to celebrate, and then you can sleep with me."

"We'll go to the pub," she replied with a small smile.

Tom drove them to the pub up the hill in the tractor, stopping off to pick up their friends. Brian, Bill and Josh, who were neighbouring farmers, clambered into the trailer hooked onto the back of the tractor laughing and joking. The pub was in a tiny village next to a huge, ancient windmill, which stood silhouetted against a twilight sky. They sat outside looking over the valley with sheep scattered here and there over the slopes and got drunk (or in Meg's case, more drunk) on cider. She was made to confess what was going on and they commiserated loyally, slagged off the radio station for her and then gave her practical advice on how to seduce managers and stab people in the back. They made her laugh and relax a little bit, but her stomach still gnawed with pain and confusion.

When they got back to the cottage, Tom tried to persuade Meg to go to bed with him, asked her why she was wasting her time with Pete, and passed out on the sofa. It was a bit of a ritual.

# CHAPTER 3

The interview was in a house in London the following day. Two women, who she discovered were originally from Greece with dark hair and olive skin, directed her into a room and left her sitting on a sofa while they answered telephone calls in strong London accents and then shouted to each other in a strange language which she presumed was Greek. The elder of the two, Athena, a very foreboding looking woman with a stern manner and immaculate appearance, eventually came in and sat down opposite Meg. Meg sat looking keen and alert, ready for questioning. Athena stared at her intently and asked her if she wanted the job. Meg, knowing that she should probably be asking many more questions, said that she did, and after explaining briefly how much she would be paid, Athena told her when to be at Gatwick and to look for the company sign. When she left, Meg realised that she didn't even know where in Greece she was going.

With time to kill, having thought the interview would take much longer, she walked aimlessly through the streets of London in a befuddled daze. Half of her was just pleased that she had actually been given a job and with noisy buses, lorries and cars spewing thick exhaust fumes into the air around her she felt excited about going to relax in Greece under clear blue skies. The other half hoped that by some miracle the radio would realise that they had made a mistake or Pete would say something to stop her from going.

She found herself in Camden High Street and passing a small arcade she saw a sign for fortune-tellers. Intrigued, and desperate for guidance in any form, she wandered in. A number of small shops on either side of the small passageway had bohemian looking men and women reading cards or palms. A tall, thin man with dirty blonde hair stood leaning against a doorway. He caught her eye and beckoned to her. She followed him, feeling suddenly very nervous, into a tiny room and he asked her to take a seat. She sat on a small, wooden chair and he sat opposite and asked her to hold out her hand. He held her hand gently in his and then looked intently at her with large, almost luminous, green eyes. She held his gaze with sudden intense anxiety; her heart was beating fast and she felt her outstretched palm become clammy. He started to talk in a very soft, unhesitating monotone. He said that she must be careful because she attracted many men with her bubbly personality but then pulled back and left them wondering and unsure about who she was; a knot formed in her stomach as she struggled to admit that this was true. He told her that he could see a ring, a gold ring; he could see the Middle East. Her heart lurched. He continued, telling her that she would live in the Middle East and have property at home and abroad. A flood of joy engulfed her. He said some more, but she was fixed on the image of the ring that he had seen and in a blur of shock she paid him, thanked him, and left.

By the time she got back to the farm she was laughing at herself for wasting good money on the reading. But it was really weird that he had mentioned the Middle East and a tiny glimmer of hope remained. Perhaps Pete would finally ask the question, stop her from going to Greece, and make plans for their future together.

Pete called just after she got home.

"Hello," he said softly.

"Hello," she replied feeling unsettled and unsure.

"Are you all right?"

"No, not really," she answered honestly. " Did you have a good evening?"

"It was all right."

"Who were you out with?" she blurted.

She had planned to stay cool and not ask any questions, but she couldn't help herself. She heard Pete pause and then,

"I went for a drink with a girl from the estate agents."

Meg's heart clanged.

"Right. Was she nice?"

"She was all right. Bit boring. It was nothing, Meg."

"Good, so why couldn't you just tell me?"

"I didn't want to upset you. Uncle Ray encouraged me to go, to improve business relations. I didn't want you to get the wrong idea."

"Thank you. Now I've got the wrong idea because you didn't tell me. I'm going to Greece the day after tomorrow."

Pete kicked himself. Now what was she doing? He didn't know what to say.

"Oh. Right. Oh, what happened with the radio?"

"I didn't get it."

"I'll come down tomorrow."

"If you want."

"I do want. I'll see you tomorrow. I love you."

"Yes, I love you too."

Pete put the phone down and banged his head with the palm of his hand. He knew he was in the wrong and he didn't know how to put it right. He decided to do nothing.

Now Meg was determined to go. She didn't allow herself to think about anything apart from packing and getting things ready. Everything was too much and she was running away. She concentrated on making a list of things to do and spent the next day rushing around without stopping to think.

She bought Tom a bottle of good whiskey to say thank you, and they sat on the doorstep of the cottage in the warm, late afternoon sun before he had to go back to harvesting work. They hugged and Tom kissed her on the cheek before saying, "Take care, sort your head out and let me know how you're doing."

Meg smiled while tears pricked the back of her eyes. She turned to him and said, "You take care, Tom. I'll probably be back next week knowing my luck! Have a good harvest and thank you for having me."

"Hmmm, I didn't, did I? Missed your chance there."

They both laughed and Meg watched him with great fondness as he strolled across the cobbled yard lighting up a cigarette as he headed for his tractor. Then she turned and went in to check her rucksack and finish packing up all her things, as she waited with growing anxiety for Pete.

Pete arrived at about eight, awkward and unsure of himself. Meg felt the familiar leap of her heart when she saw him. God! She loved and wanted this man, but the hurt turned to stubbornness and she chatted away brightly about the job in Greece as if it was exactly what she wanted to be doing. He believed it and felt he couldn't stop her. He led her upstairs to the bedroom and they kissed, and stroked and caressed each other's bodies. When he finally entered her she wrapped her legs around his body and pulled him deep into her, wanting the moment to last forever.

With her head resting on his chest and his arm around her, they slept for a couple of hours.

At three o'clock in the morning, he drove her down to the airport. He knew he'd let her down and she refused to talk about it. He had expected a long talk, where she explained how she felt and told him what he had done wrong. He would have said 'sorry' and everything would have gone back to normal.

They stood in the sterile expanse of the airport terminal. A few tired, silent holidaymakers carried their luggage across the floor to check in early before the throngs arrived. Meg checked her bag containing her purse, her passport, and an easy read novel for the hundredth time and slung the strap of the satchel over her head onto the opposite shoulder.

"Good luck. Let me know where you are," he said.

'Please ask me to stay, ask me to marry you. Beg me not to go.' she thought.

"I'll call you as soon as I can." Is what she actually said.

With a kiss and a hug she walked away with her heart breaking and tears burning at the back of her eyes.

'What the hell am I doing?' she asked herself once and then refused to think about it.

Pete stared after her feeling strangely lost and confused.

# CHAPTER 4

The charter plane was packed like a Greek train minus the chickens and goats with eager holidaymakers sharing egg sandwiches and crisps and after three and a half hours of screeching kids and bickering couples Meg stepped out of her tattered dream and into a nightmare.

Preveza airport consisted of one very long runway in the middle of a large tract of flat land. There was a small hut, which constituted arrivals and departures, check-in, passport control and baggage check, a low fence running round the edge of the field from the hut was the only boundary. Thus, the departure lounge was effectively a field. It was a military airport on the mainland and only three charter flights had the franchise to use it.

She was not welcomed by anyone looking for the new rep, but merely briefly acknowledged and hustled onto a coach as another young woman, slim and pretty and about her age, but looking decidedly tired and harassed, fussed and struggled in the rising heat, to round up those passengers who belonged to her group.

All on board and the rep, Alison, stood up in her shorts and baggy T-shirt and tucked her straggly hair behind one ear as she lifted the microphone to her unsmiling mouth. In a bored monotone she went into a not very welcoming welcome speech explaining that there were three resorts and would those people booked for each resort please be ready to get off at the right place. She then explained that there was a causeway to the island, which they could cross as long as it wasn't time for the swing bridge to open, to allow vessels to pass through the channel. It wasn't, and the coach made its way onto the island via the bridge and the narrow causeway. After the interesting and informative introduction, Alison sat down next to the driver and lit a cigarette without a word to Meg, who sat uncomfortably self-conscious, in the seat behind, feeling like a fool. The driver turned on some music and Madonna sang out 'Holiday'. A few of the younger, more exuberant passengers joined in. Meg didn't feel like she had much to celebrate.

They drove across an expanse of flat land with sparse greenery, by-passing the main town of Lefkas bearing the same name as the island, and made their way along a fairly decent road towards, and then along, the coast. On this journey, Meg failed to take in the beauty of the gleaming sea to her left and the changing landscape to hilly and mountainous on the right. She was slightly overwhelmed by the heat at the airport and very intimidated by the lack of welcome and organisation upon arrival. It was a sign of things to come.

Alison and her boyfriend, Larry had been on the island since the beginning of the season in April. It hadn't occurred to Meg that starting near the end of July was odd and these two were leaving that very day in the height of season.

Given what they obviously knew and she was yet to discover, they did not fill her with fear, but their advice to get vitamin c tablets, watch out for someone called David, pronounced Daveed, and their obvious desire to get away from the island 'a.s.a.p.' worried her slightly. She couldn't understand it. The resort that they worked in, Vasiliki, was at the far end of the island, which ended in a long peninsula. It was a windsurfer's dream. Delicious white sand which stretched away into the distance against a bright blue sky and met tamed rollers, which rose and crashed away from the coast and slid up the beach making it easy for people to paddle out and surf safely back in.

Alison handed her a useful list of Greek phrases written phonetically and with English phrases to make them easy to remember (Parakalo – please – parrot claw) and they left her alone, at a table on the beach, while they sorted out the new guests. She watched a group of young teenagers try, with little success and lots of laughter, to windsurf on the learner board at the top of the beach. A young English guy with wavy, sun-streaked hair and a deep tan went through the instructions, showing patience only with the pretty girls. Alison and Larry came back for her, and she trailed along behind them, in the increasing heat, like a lost puppy to various makeshift buildings as they got on with things without any explanation.

The day wore on with Meg feeling more and more isolated and unsure of what she was meant to be doing. Eventually, they said they were going back to Lefkas town and she climbed into the back of a jeep and sat wilting as they drove back up the length of the island to the main town. They showed her a small square with the hospital, a long, low military type structure on one side. The chemist and the bank were on the main street amidst other old, low-rise shops, cafes and houses. Everything was busy and disheveled; narrow streets filled with old cars, trucks and jeeps with horns blaring were lined by peeling, once white washed, low-rise buildings. People, a mixture of tourists and locals, young and old, hustled with each other and the traffic in the intense mid-afternoon heat.

She trailed around after the miserable couple, who barely spoke to each other let alone her, and eventually took her back to the bank where she got the chance to change most of the little money she had into drachma. Outside the bank, they introduced her to the man in charge of the company on the island. He was a Greek man related to the two women who had interviewed her in London. His name was Spiro, which made her want to laugh as she thought of the character from 'My Family and Other Animals'. He was short, bald, bulging and frenetic. He seemed very excited and pleased to see her and welcome her. He said good-bye to Alison and Larry dismissively, and told Meg to follow him. Meg politely said goodbye and they said goodbye without looking her in the eye and then Spiro hurried her away and into the street where she followed him to a battered, odd-looking, white car.

Spiro clambered into the driving seat of the tiny car, barely squeezing his large stomach in behind the steering wheel and indicated for her to get into the passenger seat as he lit up a large cigar. As she struggled to get the seat belt to work, he blew out a cloud of cigar smoke and set off with a blast of his horn and a blast of exhaust fumes into the traffic. He talked very fast, non-stop English mixed with what she presumed were profanities in Greek which he yelled out at other drivers, pedestrians, goats and chickens, while continuing his conversation with her, puffing on his cigar and flicking the ash vaguely in the direction of his window.

He explained that she was to be in charge of a small resort called Nikiana. The girl who had been there, had left, though he didn't give a reason, and of course, Aleeson and Laary were leaving and they were bad, lazy people, no good, no good.

They drove fast out of the town and along the winding coast with the sun going down behind the mountains. They went straight through Nikiana, which he indicated briefly, and seemed to consist of just a few buildings right next to the sea. He said he would show her the island and then they would have some dinner before he took her to her accommodation and she could start work the next day.

She tried to remain calm and ask sensible questions, but in truth she was in shock and as he never paused for breath, she didn't have a chance to speak much, even if she had thought of the wisest and most interesting things to say.

They drove along curving, narrow roads, which became rough tracks the further up they went, and the further up they went the greater the view of the surrounding sea and the tree-covered hillsides strangely silhouetted in the twilight.

They couldn't go all over the island because apparently there weren't roads all over the island. The road began to descend but Meg had no sense of where she was, and it was now quite dark, and there were no streetlights or any signs of life.

Just as her unease was beginning to grow, they came round a corner and headed towards a cliff edge. The moon came into view, huge in a clear, star filled sky, sending a sparkling path across the surface of the sea and illuminating a small bay below. It was a glorious picture, which she mentally photographed and never forgot. At the bottom of the cliff road, they pulled up on the edge of the bay and Spiro marched over to a wooden shack with a couple of tables outside, which turned out to be a taverna. There was no one else there apart from the owner and a couple of waiters. Spiro was greeted with much arm slapping and winks in her direction and they were led to one of the tables adorned with dim oil lamps, set on charming, clip on, plastic covers in blue and white check which immediately reminded Meg of last summer with Pete. Pete, where was he now? What was he doing? Was he missing her?

They sat at the table looking out across the beach to the waves gently lapping at the sand. It was without doubt a most relaxing and romantic setting. A couple of glasses of wine, the charm and flattery that only the Mediterraneans can get away with and Meg, pushing away any misgivings, felt relaxed and hopeful that she had made a good decision. Meg realised she was very hungry as the waiter served them with course after course of delicious local dishes. Tzatziki, tahini, souvlaki, tarama, kalamari and the most wonderful selections of seafood she had ever enjoyed.

They left the restaurant and made their way back up the cliff road. She felt at ease and warm from the wine, though she was sensible enough not to drink too much and remained alert. She let Spiro do all the talking, at which he was very good, and he had persuaded her that the island was amazing and that everything was straight forward and under control.

They drove back through Nidri, which was bustling and bright with holidaymakers strolling between shops and tavernas, and then onto a quiet stretch of road with trees going steeply up the mountain on one side, and down to the sea on the other. It was dark and winding. As they came round a bend, Spiro suddenly turned into a hidden entrance above the sea. In the headlights she could make out a two-story building built into the rocks. He explained that this had four apartments, which she would be in charge of and suggested they go and meet the people staying there. She followed him trustingly down some steps and onto the front terrace where about ten people were sitting around some tables.

And there the bon-homie disappeared! Spiro introduced himself and they bombarded him with a string of complaints and demands. They had been told they would be staying in luxury apartments with a private beach. They had told the rep but after the first day, they had not seen her again. The water didn't work properly, the electricity kept cutting out and so on and so on.

His response? He introduced Meg as their new representative and disappeared. All sense of well being deserted her. She felt as if she was facing a pack of baying wolves and there were no trees to climb. She took a deep breath and managed to calm them down, listened sympathetically and suggested that it was too late to do anything that evening but they could make a list and bring it to her the following day and then she would sort things out. She said how pleased she was to meet them all and looked forward to seeing them the next day. They were not happy.

She left, shaking slightly. Spiro was waiting at the car, puffing away on a cigar. He said nothing and got in, so she got in and asked what they should do. He shrugged, his earlier bon-homie disappeared and he gruffly told her he would take her to her room now. They drove down a long and winding hill to the edge of Nikiana and she noted that one of the complaints had been that it was supposed to be a two-minute walk from the village. Over a mile up hill in the blazing sun was not a pleasant prospect.

He pulled up outside a group of one-storey chalets built with a varnished pine finish. In the dim light, they looked quite attractive with a small verandah running around the edge. Spiro gave her a key for the door of the room nearest the front with the number one on it and said he'd meet her in the bar opposite, at eight in the morning. She looked opposite and could see that there was a building but could not see any lights or sign of bar life. It was only about eleven o'clock but she realised she was exhausted and more than anything she wanted a hot shower and some sleep.

She took her bags and went into the room that was small and clean, with an en-suite shower room. Two beds with thin mattresses took up most of the space and apart from two bedside tables there were no cupboards or wardrobes or even drawers. She hadn't been able to tell anyone she had arrived, and wondered if anyone cared.

England seemed a world away, though Pete was never far from her thoughts, and she felt hollow as she missed him and couldn't speak to him. Why hadn't she talked things through with him? She was so tired she decided to shower in the morning. She got ready for bed and set her alarm clock. She lay down on the thin mattress and started to think about where she was and what she was doing, but fell asleep.

A persistent, low buzzing noise woke her and it wasn't the alarm; it was still pitch black outside. Mosquito. Aah! She hated them, feared them, and their sneaky buzzing just around her head made her really upset. She'd forgotten the bloody repellents.

Unwilling to wake up properly, she covered herself with the sheet, but it was too late. The ominous silence left her fearful of its whereabouts and then, sudden buzzing in her ear made her leap out of bed and switch the light on. The offender was hovering in the middle of the room; she slowly lifted a shoe and tried to keep her eye on it as it moved erratically here and there. Intent on keeping it in sight she caught her knee on the end of the bed and collapsed in acute agony. Rubbing her knee and biting her lip in pain she looked around and saw the mosquito had landed on the wall, or was that another one? She limped towards it, and with a hopeful aim, smacked the shoe against the wall and a splurge of red appeared on the white surface.

She went back to bed, her ears alert to any sound, and eventually fell asleep again. She woke to the alarm feeling as if she had slept for about two minutes. She didn't even experience the confusion of waking up in a new place and taking a while to remember where she was.

# CHAPTER 5

When she stepped outside after a lovely hot shower, it was already very warm. The sky was a hazy blue and now she could clearly take in her surroundings. Her chalet was part of a group of four rooms built in a square with an entrance to each room on the outside wall. She walked round to the back and saw that there was an identical structure with four more rooms on the other side of an open area. In the middle of this small piece of land stood a large outdoor shower with a rickety surround made from branches. Apart from the rustic shower it all looked newly built and quite charming.

She went back to the front and crossed the road to see the building opposite was white and square looking with seemingly two stories at road level. There was one door on the roadside at ground level and some wooden steps at the side leading up to another floor. On the other side of the building there were a few steps going up to a door and then more steps going down the other side to the beach revealing that there was another floor below. There were no signs to indicate that there might be a bar inside.

To the right, the road went up and round a corner towards Nidri and the accommodation she had been introduced to the night before. There were a couple of small buildings well off the road on the right hand side. To the left was a stretch of rough undergrowth forming a small ridge above the beach for about fifty metres with no buildings and then there was a short stretch of road with low buildings on either side. All the buildings were similar and it was impossible to tell if they were houses or shops.

There was nobody to be seen, no cars, no life, just the lazy fig trees and the promise of more heat.

She wandered over the road and made her way up the steps at the side of the building and she could see through the glass door at the top into a small unnamed bar. From there the steps went down the other side to a terrace and more steps from there led onto the beach. White sand and varying shades of blue water stretched away and she enjoyed a moment of serenity. It was so pretty and peaceful.

She pushed open the glass door and stepped inside the bar where there was no sign of Spiro. She was quite relieved; she needed a coffee and to get her head together. The bar felt new with bright, whitewashed walls adorned with a few local ornaments and a number of round tables on a clean stone floor. At the end of the room were plate glass patio doors opening onto a balcony. On either side of the narrow parapet were more steps leading onto a terrace below. A couple sat quietly at one of the small, round tables drinking coffee. An older man sat near them reading 'Hunt For The Red

October' by a new author called Tom Clancy that Meg had vaguely heard of from book reviews on the radio. Behind the bar counter stood a wiry, fair-haired man in his early thirties with slightly hunched rounded shoulders, a ginger moustache and a dour expression, wiping glasses. Meg smiled brightly and asked for a cup of coffee in slow English, followed by a 'parrot claw.' She wasn't sure if he was Greek or not. He didn't return her smile, but poured some very dark liquid into a tiny cup and handed it to her silently, along with a glass of water.

She sat up on a stool and thanked him, though she had been hoping for a large mug of steaming, milky coffee.

"I'm Meg, the new rep," she tried, holding out her hand. He gave her a cynical look, shook her hand lightly and said, "Michael," before continuing with the slow, methodical glass wiping. Meg sipped the strong coffee and watched the people in the room wondering if she should speak to anyone, but decided to wait.

An hour went by as she sat quietly watching the people and listening to their conversations. She asked Michael for an orange juice and continued to people watch with growing trepidation.

As more people came in and spoke to each other, it became apparent that they were all not happy and this had given them plenty to talk about. Some were whinging; others were making sick jokes about Tenco and concentration camps. The mix of couples in their thirties or forties or older with no children around all looked fairly tanned and healthy. They seemed to be thriving on the camaraderie of shared stories about the water in their bathrooms running out in the middle of a shower or the water stopping all together forcing them to use the outdoor shower.

She could feel herself going hot and cold and it wasn't the coffee and orange. She decided to remain anonymous for as long as possible.

At ten, Spiro bustled in with his signature cigar, signalled to Michael, gestured for Meg to follow him and made his way out onto the balcony overlooking the beach and terrace below, not looking at anyone else. She followed him out, clutching her glass of orange juice. Michael brought coffee and water to the table without saying a word.

Without pausing, Spiro told her that this was her 'office', and that she should be there from eight in the morning every day to look after the guests in Nikiana. There were twenty-three people including the ones up the hill. They were all leaving the following day and a larger number of people were arriving, so he was arranging more accommodation, but he couldn't tell her where that was going to be.

She tentatively asked him some questions and discovered that there was a small taverna at the other end of the village and a small shop. In Nidri, there were lots of restaurants and water sports and trips around the island. There were buses, but he didn't have a timetable. There was no information about the rest of the island provided for holidaymakers and no entertainment organised or on offer.

"There is a beach," he stated waving his cigar towards the beach behind him as though Meg might not have seen it. He took a sip of the water and stood up, taking a folded sheet of paper out of his pocket.

"I have to go now. I see you later."

"Wait. What about all the complaints last night?"

"They are leaving tomorrow."

"But the new people will have the same problems, won't they?"

He gave her a disparaging look, his dark eyes glinting with annoyance, handed the paper to her, which was a list of the new guests, and walked off quickly with his head down.

She sat there dumbfounded, looking out at the beautiful calm sea and the long, lazy beach curving round to a small headland, wondering if she should just run away. She didn't have time to think too long.

"Hello, are you the new rep?" said a female voice behind her.

She turned round and smiled at the woman standing there.

The voice belonged to a plump lady with bleached hair and black roots, wearing a little sun top and a mini-skirt with short, fat, red legs sticking out of the bottom. She wore no bra and Meg found it difficult not to be distracted by the seemingly live animals bobbling about, as the woman expressed herself with lots of hand movements.

"Yes, hello. I'm Meg."

She smiled brightly and held out her hand, but the woman ignored it.

"Good. I'm Barbara and I think you should know that this holiday has been a complete disaster for me and my family."

"Oh. I'm sorry to hear that. What seems to be the problem?" Meg's heart began to race but she remained calm.

Barbara went into a tirade of complaints and then her husband appeared behind her to join in and he was equally verbal. Meg didn't have a chance to respond, even if she had had anything useful to say. As she was speaking none too quietly another two guests joined Barbara and her husband in the list of horrors that they had all experienced.

She discovered that they were staying over the road as well, and that she had been very lucky to have a hot shower as the tank only had enough water for one or two showers at a time. Therefore, either late at night or early in the morning were the only times you ever got hot water and sometimes there was no water at all. They had all resorted to using the large open air shower in the middle, which explained the 'Tenco' references she had heard earlier.

After Barbara and co, had had their say, Meg apologised and said that she was horrified and that she would certainly see what she could do. They left unconvinced, but obviously got satisfaction from having a punch bag to vent their anger on.

In the course of the day, guest after guest identified her and went through the same general list of complaints. The main problem, she realised, was that all of them had been told that they would be staying in luxury, air conditioned accommodation. She kept smiling and sympathising and even went over to look at the accommodation with one very distressed couple to share helplessly in their upset. She found it difficult to fully empathise. As far as she could see, the island was idyllic. The accommodation was basic, but she bet that air-conditioning was a rarity on the whole island. Having hitched and camped around Europe a few years previously with Pete, perhaps her expectations were not as high.

She finally managed to get away as they all made their way down to the beach and joined others lying in the sun on towels or cooling off in the sparkling sea. She went back to the bar and ordered some water from Michael, who had been joined by his wife, Lorraina. She was dark and slim with pale skin. They were locals but Michael's fair hair and blue eyes plus the very pale skin on both of them surprised Meg. They looked at her with dour expressions and a cynicism as if to say 'How long will you last?'

She decided to sit up at the counter and persevered with light conversation, even though they only just about responded. She felt that she would need some allies, if she were going to survive, and that they too suffered from the rudeness of unhappy people. They ran the bar smoothly, but people were looking for ways to express their frustration.

At about four in the afternoon, with her face aching from continually smiling, she decided to escape and go for a walk.

She had been told to start in the bar at eight in the morning and didn't know when she should finish or if she ever did finish, so she actually felt guilty leaving.

It was still very warm as she made her way towards the village. On either side were small, basic looking bars and odd-looking residences with one storey fully occupied and furnished but the beginnings of a second floor left unfinished. Greek men with black trousers and white vests, sitting, smoking and drinking at small tables, seemed to be shouting at each other, and then laughing. They stared at her, as she walked past and exchanged comments, but they didn't feel intimidating. They were relaxed, open, and alive, compared to the uptight moaning holidaymakers she had been meeting all day. Sitting on wooden chairs outside a few buildings were old ladies dressed completely in black, their dark hair with strands of grey held up in tight buns above their tanned, deeply lined faces. They sat alone, watching the world from their doorsteps with sewing or crochet on their laps.

She came to one building that had boxes of water and Coca-Cola outside. There was no sign, but she hoped it might be a supermarket. It was. Inside, the tiny space was crammed with a disarray of food and household goods. She asked if they had a telephone and when they looked at her as if she was mad, she went into an elaborate mime of using a telephone. The shopkeeper laughed and led her behind a huge stack of boxes to a contraption that looked as if it dated back to the early twentieth century, but it was a working telephone attached to a meter. The relief she felt and the sudden, desperate need to call Pete, surprised her.

She dialled the number of his parents' house and it rang and rang. Meg felt panic rising inside and then someone picked up. It was his older sister. She was pleased to hear from Meg and her voice was kind as she told Meg that Pete had gone away with some friends and no, she didn't know when he would be back, would she like to leave a message? Meg realised she couldn't even leave a number and said, 'no thank you, she would call again.'

The pit in her stomach opened up and she wanted to cry. She paid the exorbitantly high amount for phoning in the daytime and managed to go ahead and buy repellants, water, coffee and a kettle. She was now really beginning to regret her rash decision. What on earth had she been thinking? She could have been with Pete now enjoying his leave, sorting out their future together. Did they even have a future together now? Had she effectively finished it by rushing off to Greece?

With her purchases, she made her way back down to her room. On her way, she passed some of the people she had met in the bar, and, despite their strained acknowledgement of her, the enemy, she smiled with great warmth. They did not respond with smiles and launched into more complaints.

As she got to her room, someone called her name in a shrill voice. She turned to see a small lady aged, she guessed, about fifty, with neatly styled, black hair and a smart blue dress, waving at her from across the road.

"You, come telephonee."

Confused, her immediate thought was that it was Pete, but then she realised that that was impossible. She went across and went in through the small door in the front of the building that led into an apartment. In the hallway she picked up the phone. It was Spiro to tell her to be ready to go to the airport in the morning at half-past nine and to check that the guests were ready to leave. She put down the phone and smiled at the lady. She smiled back but seemed to be mocking her. Then she said,

"You too skinny, come, eat."

Meg looked at her in surprise, not sure whether she should accept, but she was very hungry. She laughed shyly and followed the lady, who told her that her name was Callista.

It was a tiny apartment, a small kitchen, big enough for one person to stand in, with a cosy lounge/dining area beyond. A closed door led to, she presumed, one bedroom and a bathroom. Sitting at the table was a large, middle-aged man eating with his fingers and watching a loud TV in the dark, cool room. He was wearing a vest and trousers with braces. He looked up and nodded at Meg before turning his eyes back to the TV. Callista pointed for her to sit down on the other side of the table.

She did as she was told and Callista brought a plate of lamb and potatoes. It had strange but enjoyable flavours and remembering that she hadn't actually stopped to eat all day, Meg was very grateful and ate with pleasure. They managed to make a little conversation, and Callista indicated that she was in charge of the chalets. Callista chattered away in Greek to her husband, who responded in monosyllables.

Meg smiled and ate, but then she felt a little uncomfortable so she said she had to go, and stood up. Callista took her to the door, still smiling at her in a slightly mocking way. As they reached the door, Meg suddenly dared to ask if she could give the phone number to her family. Callista did not speak very good English, so it took a while of pointing and gesturing, but she finally understood and, said yes, and wrote down the number on a scrap of paper.

After washing in boiled water from her newly acquired kettle – there was no hot water in her bathroom – she changed and went back to the bar. She borrowed a pen and paper from Lorraina and put up a clear notice to remind people when the bus would be departing for the airport the following morning.

She tried chatting to Michael and Lorraina again, and though they were still not particularly friendly, she did find out that Michael was Callista's son. He and Lorraina had a winter home in Athens, and came home to Callista's to run the bar in the summer. Meg took her drink, and her novel, which she thought she might read, down the steps from the balcony to the terrace below at the edge of the beach. The light was beginning to fade as the sun went down on the other side of the island, and she watched the changing colours of the sea as it gently rocked onto the sand. It was a truly beautiful setting. She never opened her book. The terrace began to fill with guests. It was their last night and they were going to drink. Drink and complain. The relatively small group of people had all got to know each other and there was a sense of unity in time of disaster. Their friendships were not based on having shared a great holiday, but because they had been drawn together in adversity.

Meg looked at the perfect beach and the gentle sea. A soft breeze fluttered the leaves of eucalyptus and fig trees. Around her, the stories of their disastrous time were repeated and expanded. Someone even compared the situation to being in the war. A thin, slightly pathetic man with a quiet, mousy wife had probably never had so much fun. They were quiet and dull and would probably not have made friends easily in different circumstances, but they had become part of the group with the shared experience. Meg felt a little bit sorry for them and had listened sympathetically when they told her how they had been told they would be in luxury accommodation earlier in the day. However, after a few drinks the man became boring and loud, revelling in the litany of complaints. Suddenly, he began to insult Meg as if she was responsible, and she repressed the urge to tell him exactly what she thought of him. Instead, she said gently,

"Well of course, I am sure you will all be complaining in writing when you get home and asking for your money back."

He huffed and blustered, but it set the others off into a discussion about all the different bodies they would be complaining to and contacting and took the attention away from Meg.

She looked around at all the people relaxed and comfortable in shorts and T-shirts, drinking, smoking, laughing. It was late evening by now and there was no need for jumpers or sweatshirts in the balmy climate. Most of the guests had the relaxed, healthy glow of a week or two in the sun with nothing to do, apart from Mr. and Mrs. Mouse, who were red, and peeling, and covered in mosquito bites.

Meg tried to change the subject and asked them what they had done every day. It soon became apparent that they had formed a routine. Breakfast in the bar, sunbathing and swimming, a snack in the bar followed by a siesta or more swimming and lazing, and then dinner in the taverna at the end of the beach and back to the bar. Before they could allow any feeling of enjoyment to slip in, they started to complain about the food at the taverna. It was all strange fish and they didn't have chips!

She laughed out loud, and luckily, they thought she was laughing at the incredibility of no chips. She waited for a complaint about the beer, but it didn't come.

She got up and went to the toilet. On her way back, she met a couple in their twenties, not much older than her coming into the bar. She had seen them earlier, but they had not spoken to her.

"Still smiling then?" asked the girl in a Yorkshire accent.

Meg grimaced and shrugged.

"What else can I do? Have you had a good time?"

"Well we have to agree the accommodation and set up is not what we were expecting, but it's a great place and the weather has been superb."

"It's actually been hilarious trying to get a shower and listening to all the old gripers," added the guy.

Meg laughed.

They told her that they had not spent much time in Nikiana. They had taken the bus to Nidri most days and walked back when it was cool, it was only an hour's walk.

"There's loads going on in Nidri," the girl added.

"I'll have to check it out. How often do buses run?"

"Every hour on the hour," said the girl. "And they are spot on. I suppose the island is too small for them to get delayed," she laughed.

They offered Meg a drink, but before she could reply, busty Barbara who, it turned out, was there with her husband and her father, came rushing in from the terrace.

"Quick, can you come and see my Dad. He's got this swelling on his leg and he's going all funny."

Her voice was slightly slurred.

Meg followed her on to the terrace. A few people were crowding round the old man, who was lying back in a swoon, moaning about the pain in his ankle. Meg took a look. He took off his sandal and rolled off his sock to reveal a veined ankle and a gnarled, scabby foot. Meg grimaced, it did look a bit swollen, but then she glanced at his other leg and realised it was a perfect match. She got him to put the sore leg up on a chair and asked his daughter to get him some water. She told the others that he was all right, probably just a reaction to a bite. She didn't have a clue really, but she was pretty sure he was just a bit drunk and attention seeking. The other guests, who had been overly interested in their drunkenness, were just as easily convinced that they didn't have to spoil their evening and went back to drinking and adding this disaster to their list of complaints.

Meg felt strangely responsible. She stayed with the family while the man had some water and then he suggested a brandy might be what he needed. After smoking a couple of cigarettes, drinking the brandy and having a slurred attempt at charming Meg, she thought it would be safe to leave him. As she stood to go, he suddenly fell forward with a groan and appeared to pass out.

Barbara gave a little scream and yelled at Meg to do something. Get him to a hospital or something. Despite not being convinced that it was genuine, Meg felt she had to show concern, worried that if he died in the night it would be her fault. She went into Michael, who said he would take them to the hospital in town in his van.

They had to half carry the old man, who had come round from his fainting fit well enough to groan and complain loudly, because, of course, he couldn't put any weight on his ankle. Meg practically rolled the very drunk Barbara and her husband into the back of the van and sat the old man in the front between her and Michael. At a frightening speed, he charged along the coast road and down to the hospital in Lefkas town.

The hospital was old and echoing with a feeling of dirt despite the strong smell of disinfectant. She had visions of waiting for hours and was worried about costs and insurance. The large entrance hall was surprisingly quiet and their footsteps resounded on the grey stone floor. They went up to the reception desk and Meg indicated the man. The girl at reception said nothing, but pressed a button and pointed to some long benches lining the wall where they were to wait. After a short wait, a very efficient, pleasant nurse came to see what the problem was; her soft-soled shoes smacked gently along the empty hallway.

The old man began moaning and groaning dramatically as she looked at his leg.

She stood up and spoke seriously, in good English. "You'd better come with me. I have just the thing for this condition," she stated. She indicated for him and his family to go in front then she turned to Meg and said, "I know exactly how to deal with this."

'Oh God!' thought Meg and sat down next to Michael to wait anxiously in the eerily empty reception area.

They returned two minutes later with the old man looking very pale. He had miraculously stopped limping and was holding his bottom. The nurse held up a huge needle and syringe behind his back and she winked and smiled at Meg.

"It's okay, no need to pay."

Michael and Meg exchanged glances and she suppressed the need to giggle. She wasn't sure what the nurse had said but Barbara and family were very subdued on the journey back. They thanked Michael and Meg awkwardly and staggered off to their rooms. Meg finally got to her bed at four in the morning. No time to think. Alarm set, repellents on, sleep.

The next hopeful, excited holidaymakers were already on their way to the luxury destination they had saved all year for, and she had to face them in just a few hours.

# CHAPTER 6

Meg sat in the bar sipping coffee, waiting for people to wake up and come over with their luggage. She had checked with as many guests as possible that they knew what time the bus was leaving. Most did, and she just hoped that she didn't have to go chasing around, waking everyone up. Luckily, by nine she had checked everybody off the list and waited, with the jaded, finally quiet group, for the bus to arrive.

At the airport, they all made their way into the check-in hut. Some said goodbye; the northern couple wished her luck; Barbara, the old man's daughter, gave her a sheepish sorry and thank you; Mr. and Mrs. Mouse assured her that they would be complaining, and the rest ignored her.

The plane they were to catch, landed soon after, carrying the next lot of tired but expectant punters. Meg watched them all blinking in the sunlight as they made their way off the tarmac and towards the waiting coaches. A dark man about thirty with short curly hair swaggered over to her from another bus.

"Hi, I'm Daveed," he said confidently. He ran one hand through his hair with open fingers and offered her the other one as his eyes ran over her body.

"Hi, I'm Meg, pleased to meet you."

'I don't think.' She could already sense why Alison and Larry had warned her about him.

His eyes narrowed slightly as he realised she hadn't giggled and blushed as most women did.

"Right, that's your bus over there. Here's the list of people staying at your resort. Check them all off and take them back. They have a welcome drink at Michael's and then you take them to where they are staying."

A welcome drink, blimey.

She rounded up her guests, most of them tired from the early morning start and an uncomfortable charter flight. The group consisted of a number of families with young children. On the bus, she decided to give a decent introductory speech as opposed to Alison's version. At least she could set off on the right foot, even though she was dreading the reactions they would have to their accommodation. Maybe if they liked her, they wouldn't be angry with her.

Standing at the front of the coach, she held the microphone up and launched into her planned words of welcome, looking out at a sea of strange faces and wondered how she was ever going to remember all of their names. A man near the front leaned forward and indicated that the microphone was not on. 'Shit' she thought, 'so much for my radio skills'. She found the switch, apologised with a nervous laugh, and started again. She tried to give them a cheery speech with a couple of jokes thrown in that got a couple of titters and then she sat down feeling like a twit and very nervous.

# CHAPTER 7

The bus stopped outside the bar and she led the way inside, while the bus driver piled up bags and cases at the side of the road. Inside, Michael had put out glasses of cheap buck's fizz and plain juice. Everyone helped themselves and sat down around the bar chattering pleasantly. So far, so good.

Meg explained that she would take them all to their rooms group by group. Looking down her list, she realised that four people were without specified accommodation. She prayed that Spiro had it all under control and called out the names of those staying across the road.

About twenty men, women and children of varying ages, shapes and sizes gathered up their belongings. She checked their names, tried to remember them all, took them over to the chalets across the road, and gave them keys for their designated room. She hoped that at least first impressions were good before they realised that there was a problem with the water. There was no immediate reaction from any of them, as they gladly went in to unpack and sort themselves out.

She wandered slowly back looking up and down the road. Still no sign of Spiro.

She went back inside and pretended to be doing paper work, literally swapping two sheets of paper over and over and giving the impression of studying them carefully. She glanced up at the remaining guests. Three families were going up to 'the hill' accommodation, the name given to the place she had visited on her first night. She presumed they didn't have to walk up there with their luggage.

There was a tall, confident looking woman in her mid-thirties with highlighted blonde hair styled in a chignon, she was wearing a smart pencil skirt, a top with padded shoulders that was tight fitting and flared over the waist and shoes with high stiletto heels. Looking as if she was dressed for a business convention rather than a relaxing holiday she sipped her drink elegantly and cast her eyes over the other people in the room with disdain. She rested her hand on the back of a chair occupied by a young girl clutching a small backpack. On the next table were two men in their late twenties wearing T-shirts and jeans, smoking and drinking. One was talking loudly and making little jokes for the little girl. Presumably, he was trying to get the attention of her mother, but he was being ignored. He was well built with broad shoulders and thick strong arms from lifting weights. A slight paunch gave away a liking for beer and over indulgence. He had short, thick, brown hair and a good-looking face, but an air of knowing it. The other guy was tall and skinny with untidy black hair, a pleasant but unremarkable face, and an insipid bend to his lanky body.

The woman spoke to Meg. Her voice was falsely posh, thinly disguising a rough accent, and brusque.

"Can we please go to our rooms? I'm tired and I need a shower."

"Yes, of course I'm just waiting to hear that they are completely ready for you," Meg lied. "Please excuse me, and I'll just check with my boss."

Meg got up and hoped she looked as if she was doing something important and efficient as she left with her clipboard. Outside she looked desperately up and down the road for Spiro. His battered car was parked on the opposite side of the road, so at least he was close. Then she saw him coming up from the beach, hot and flustered.

Wiping his head with a handkerchief, he came up to her and said, "Right, where are the people for the beach accommodation?"

"I have four people without anywhere and the ones for the hill."

"What! Why, the people for the hill? They should have taken the bus there."

"I thought everyone was to come here first for their welcome drink."

"No, no!" he shouted.

"Okay. What shall we do?" She realised by the look of intense rage on his face that it was not a good question and immediately said, "Let me take the four to the beach and then we can organise the hill people. Perhaps you could take them in your car"

He looked at her as if she was mad and then unable to come up with a better solution agreed.

"Where is the beach accommodation?" she asked quietly.

He mopped his sweating brow and then grappled to light a cigar. Puffing furiously on the thick brown stem, he played for time and then brusquely replied, "I'll have to show you!" as if it was her fault.

He looked as if he was going to have a fit, so she went inside and said to the people based up the hill.

"I hope you don't mind waiting just a little bit longer. Please have another free drink and you will be taken there as soon as possible."

There were twelve people down for 'The Hill' accommodation, three families. They seemed to be quite relaxed and happy about having another drink. Spiro did not. She then asked Spiro if the beach place was near enough for them to carry their luggage. He looked completely flummoxed as he realised it wasn't.

He smeared more sweat off his head and mumbled, "Okay. I take the luggage and you start walking."

Meg looked at the blonde woman in her smart clothes and high heels and took a deep breath, "Melissa Giles and Lucy Frimpton?"

The blonde woman indicated that she and the little girl were the ones in question. Keith was the name of the body builder, and Aaron was the skinny guy. They followed her outside and she got them to point out their luggage, which Spiro then loaded into his car.

Meg behaved as if this was quite normal procedure and announced, "This way!" Before setting off down the road.

Spiro drove down the road and with relief, she saw him turn off about one hundred yards away. The two men walked with Meg and Keith chatted away about the flight and his other holidays abroad. Melissa tottered behind with her silent daughter.

It was hot.

They got to where Spiro had turned and followed a rough track towards the beach. Spiro had parked outside a one-storey, grey, unpainted construction mostly hidden from the road. It had a little verandah running round it and fig trees leaned over the roof. The beach lay just beyond. It looked quaint and homely from a distance but up close, it was dingy and unkempt.

Spiro unloaded the baggage, and was going to leave, but chignon Melissa stopped him, "Please show us inside."

She spoke charmingly but with an edge of menace and Spiro had to comply. There were two doors on the verandah each opening into rooms with en-suite bathrooms. In one was a large double bed and in the other were two beds with metal frames that looked like they had been borrowed from the hospital with thin lumpy looking mattresses.

Melissa announced that she would have the room with the double, but needed another bed for her daughter. Spiro was groveling and agreeing. He showed her where the extra linen and a fold-up bed were kept in a large wooden chest. It was the only piece of furniture, apart from the beds, in either room. Then he pointed out the view of the sea from the window. She wasn't distracted. She looked in the bathroom that turned out to be a small cubicle, a cold, grey, stone room with a showerhead and a hole in an uneven concrete floor. An unsavoury looking toilet bowl, with a cistern and chain up above, sat forlornly to one side.

Melissa began to complain bitterly and Meg was thankful that she had made Spiro stay. The two guys looked embarrassed and went through to put their things in the other room. Lucy stood by the door anxiously fiddling with the tie belt on her pretty dress. Melissa demanded to be moved and of course, Spiro said yes, yes he would see to it. Meg had to admire the way he managed to get away by promising everything Melissa wanted.

Meg and Spiro left and drove back up to the bar. An hilarious episode of ferrying luggage and people up the hill ensued. Luckily, the families left had all got to know each other. Children were playing together, and the adults were relaxed after two, (or possibly more), free drinks before lunch. Also luckily, it was impractical for Meg to go, as the car was full, so she said she would see them all later and impetuously announced that there would be a group dinner at eight that evening at the local taverna.

With Spiro disappearing round the bend carrying the last guests, Meg went back into Michael and Lorraina and asked with a grin if there was a Buck's Fizz left for her.

"Spiro is paying so why not?" said Michael. Did she detect a faint smile? He poured himself and Lorraina one as well.

Meg thought the bar would be empty now but as she sat down and sipped her drink, she saw a lady in her mid forties was sitting out on the balcony. Her heart gave a little jump. She hadn't forgotten any one, had she?

She waited to catch the woman's eye and as soon as she did, she smiled and the woman smiled back and came over to her.

She held out her hand to Meg, "Hello, I'm Sandra. I think you handled that really well."

Meg hadn't noticed her before, so she looked at her questioningly, and felt a little embarrassed. She was a tall, slender lady with an air of confidence. Her soft grey hair had been cut in a fashionable short bob and she had sharp, blue eyes.

"I'm the new rep," stated Sandra, "I'm here to coordinate all the resorts."

"Oh right," Meg felt intimidated by this statement but at the same time warmed to Sandra's ease and openness.

They both went to sit out on the balcony and swapped brief histories. Sandra had been working in the travel business for years but had been office bound in London for the last few and had needed to get away for personal reasons so she had taken up this offer.

Meg admitted that this was her first experience and although she hadn't really known what to expect, this hadn't been it. She felt reassured that she would have someone like Sandra to turn to instead of the hysterical Spiro who eventually returned, sweating and red. Meg expected a bombardment of abuse. Instead, he came over and beamed at Sandra; he was obviously still in charm mode for her.

"Good you two have met. Now I will take Sandra to the other resorts. We see you tomorrow."

Meg decided to take a chance while Spiro was in Sandra's presence, "I need pens and paper to do notices and let people know what is available."

"Okay you buy. Give me receipt.'

"And, um, who pays for my food?"

"This you pay for. You need advance?"

"Yes, please."

He pulled out a huge wedge of notes and peeled a few off for her.

"Okay, bye," he said abruptly and ushered Sandra out in front of him.

They left. Meg ordered a toasted sandwich with her choice of a ham and egg mayonnaise filling from the array of containers and watched as Michael spread the filling over two rectangular slabs of bread, which was then squashed and toasted in the grill. He wrapped the now thin and crispy sandwich in white paper and handed it to her. She took it back to her 'office' on the balcony with a bottle of water and took a bite. It was delicious, possibly the best sandwich she had ever tasted, but before she could take another bite, one of the guests from the chalets across the road interrupted her. It was Sarah, who had come on holiday with her husband and two children, and she was not happy. Meg decided it would be impolite to eat despite being ravenous, so she reluctantly pushed her sandwich to one side and listened.

There was no water and the room was too small for the whole family. She had been told that they would be getting an apartment big enough for four.

Sarah was a petite lady with lanky brown hair and small, brown eyes. She spoke very quickly, her voice one notch higher than normal and on the point of breaking. Meg felt awful as she gently explained that there was very limited accommodation. In her head, she was trying to work out how Spiro had managed to get four beds into any of the rooms. She knew that one of the chalets was still empty but she wasn't sure what plans Spiro might have for Melissa and daren't suggest giving it to anyone.

She promised Sarah that she would see what she could do. Then she tried to console her by describing the beauty of the island and telling her to join everyone for dinner that evening.

Sarah went away dissatisfied.

So did the young couple, Phil and Elaine, who were not as concerned about the room, or even the water, as they were about the thinness of the walls. She presumed it was probably inhibiting for their sexual activities and was tempted to suggest they waited until everyone was out at the beach but didn't feel she knew them well enough. She went through the same speech about the island and dinner and they left.

Sarah's husband, Denis, was the next one to approach. He was more easygoing, a levelheaded man, with a heavy build, a thick black beard and receding dark hair.

"I realise that this is not your fault, but my wife is really upset. If there is anything you can do I would be very grateful."

The way he said "I" Meg understood the grief he was going to get if nothing happened.

"Anyway, about this dinner. We would like to come what's the plan?" he added, smiling.

Meg didn't have a plan. She didn't even know where the taverna was, let alone whether they could cater for large numbers at once, but she said,

"Great! If we all meet here in the bar at 7.30pm I'll lead the way. Tell anyone you see." she smiled and for some reason shook his hand.

"Right see you later. And don't forget – anything you can do."

"I will do my best," she promised smiling at him.

She felt awful. She had absolutely no idea how she could improve marital relations for Denis. Her sandwich lay cold on the plate beside her, but she ate it hungrily. No sign of any other guests. She started to panic about the 'dinner'.

# CHAPTER 8

She headed down the road into the village. The same men were outside the bar so she smiled and shouted hello. They laughed and called her over for a drink but she shook her head and continued past the little shop. There were a few similar buildings further up but she noticed on the left, built a little way up into the side of the hill, very smart new looking apartments. The only sign of luxury she had seen since she arrived. A bit further on the right the thick foliage that lined most of the coast road stopped and an expanse of sandy track led straight onto open beach.

She followed the track and came to a large taverna at the top of the beach with an outside area at the front shaded by a roof on metal poles.

It looked very shut. 'Damn, siesta time'. She was very hot and sweat ran down the back of her legs. She wandered around the building looking for any sign of life. Gingerly she ventured round to the back where there were some smaller buildings and collided with a body coming the opposite way.

She stepped back in surprise and almost exclaimed as she took in his appearance and found herself looking into the deep, dark eyes of the most gorgeous young man. He had a small towel wrapped around his waist, revealing long, firm, brown legs below. A strong, lean, upper body and a shock of black wet hair, sticking up after he had rubbed it with the towel in his hand, made him look as though he had just stepped out of an after-shave advert. She guessed he was about nineteen or twenty.

He laughed, revealing straight white teeth and said something in Greek.

"Sorry. I, er, um I was just seeing if there was anyone from the restaurant here."

She spoke too quickly for him but he did speak English.

"More slow, please."

"Oh, sorry. I work holiday people, er Spiro?"

"Ah Spiro. We know Spiro. You work for him. Bad luck!" he laughed and she did too.

"I have problem," she said speaking in broken English very slowly and of course more loudly, as you do.

"Tonight I bring many people here. Is possible?"

He frowned, not understanding her.

"Tonight...I come to eat."

She demonstrated eating by pinching her fingers together and pointing with them at her mouth.

He interrupted her.

"Yes, yes, no problem."

"Not just me. Me and," she held out her fingers and indicated twenty, "twenty, maybe."

He frowned and bent his head towards his left then right shoulder looking up at the sky as if calculating.

"Maybe. You speak with boss. He come five minutes. You want water?"

"Yes please," replied Meg.

"Go seet. I bring."

Meg walked back round to the front and sat at one of the tables. The Adonis returned wearing shorts, and a T-shirt with 'No Problem' printed on the front. He handed her a glass of water with ice and sat down opposite her.

"Thank you," Meg said smiling.

"No problem."

He pointed at his shirt and they both laughed. Then he looked at her intently.

"You have beautiful eyes."

She laughed and thanked him.

"And a lovely laugh."

Meg smiled at him with one eyebrow raised and he grinned. Suddenly a large voice boomed out from inside the restaurant.

"Gregor!"

He jumped up and said, "The boss, wait."

He came back with a big, burly, darkly tanned, older man who spoke even less English, so with Gregor translating, she hoped they managed to arrange for her to come with lots of people at about eight and was assured that it was as his T-shirt said. She wasn't confident, but at least it was arranged.

On her way back, she stopped at the little shop to buy paper, pens, and other necessities and to try again to get hold of Pete. Her stomach was in a twirl as she listened to the ring tone. She gripped the scrap of paper with Callista's number on it, in her sweating palm.

"Hello?"

Hearing his familiar voice, her heart jumped.

"Hi, it's me."

There was a pause.

"Meg? Is that you?"

Why the pause? Why didn't he know straight away? Who else could it be?

"Yeh, it's me. How are you?"

His voice much brighter now, "Hi! I'm fine. How are you? Having a good time swanning around on Greek beaches?"

"I wish," she laughed. "I'm okay. It's..."

What could she say? Where could she begin to explain? Another disaster.

"It's great. Beautiful island. I've met some really interesting people. It's quite hard work though, very busy."

"Oh yeah."

"No really. What have you been up to?"

He went on to tell her he'd been down to the coast for a few days. His uncle had a large house right next to the beach where he had spent most of his childhood. Meg also had very fond memories of times they had spent together visiting his relations.

His Nan, who lived there too, was one of those wonderful women who despite being in her late seventies was always pleased to see you and took great pride in providing gloricus roast dinners, high teas with home baked cakes and scones, and full English breakfasts. He'd been out with his cousins and had had a great time. Then he had gone to watch some cricket with some guys from work who were also on leave.

"We had such a laugh. We went for a meal after and then onto a club where we managed to run up a bill of two thousand pounds mostly on champagne."

"Wow!"

She could feel him slipping away and didn't know how to draw him back. They had taken different paths. He was on the straight sure path of ambition, money, and success. She had lost her signposts and was on a winding detour, not knowing where she was going or what she was doing. She knew deep down that coming to Greece had been running away, but she had hoped it would make him miss her.

"I miss you," she tried weakly.

"I miss you too."

She grabbed onto those words and tried to make them mean as much as she wanted them to mean.

"I have to go. I'm on a meter and it's running very fast."

"Okay. Take good care."

"Um. I have a number if you want to ring," she blurted.

"Oh right. Hang on let me get a pen. Okay, go ahead."

She gave him the number and said goodbye as sweetly as she could. She left the shop with that hollowness again. Not enough said. A rift of miscommunication. Was he playing it cool because she had left? Was she too cool, unwilling to admit she had made a mistake? Deep down she knew that going to Greece was meant to have provoked a reaction; to somehow get him to realise that he couldn't live without her and make a commitment. It had backfired and there was no going back now.

Pete put down the phone and stared at the number. God, he did miss her. 'Let her get rid of her itchy feet and she'll be ready to settle down,' he thought. As long as he was in Saudi, he couldn't tie her down, she would never be happy with the constraints on women there. Couple more years of making good money and he could get a transfer. It was good that she was so independent.

Meg crossed directly from the shop to a small path, which led to the beach. She emerged from the shade of fig trees onto the soft white sand. It was not far to the water's edge even though the tidemark revealed that the water was out, but the deserted beach extended about half a mile to her left and she was about two hundred and fifty yards from the bar. There were no people along this stretch; they were all further down, not far from the bar. She began to walk back planning to tell as many people as possible about dinner. She came behind the beach apartments and saw Keith and Aaron stretched out on towels. There was no sign of Melissa and her daughter. She called out 'Hi" and they both sat up. Keith plumped out his chest a little as she approached, and said,

"Hi there gorgeous," in a voice which made her cringe.

She chatted to them briefly and they both said that they would come for dinner. Keith asked about discos and nightlife. She laughed and told him that Nikiana had very little, but Nidri was supposed to be quite lively. He was cocky and flirtatious.

"Well, what are you doing tonight? Why don't we go and check it out."

"Could do."

She thought 'why not?' She needed to find out what was on offer. Maybe she could organise a crowd to go, so that she was still doing her job.

Further down, was Sarah with her family. They had joined up with the other families with young children, and they were all playing in the sea. She spoke to Tim, a single father with two young girls, and he said that Sarah had told them all about dinner and they were all keen to go. The older lady with two teenagers sat in the shade reading. Meg remembered that her name was Charlotte and asked her how she was.

Charlotte was a large lady in her forties. Her extensive bosom protruded out over a rounded belly in her black and orange patterned costume, which she didn't seem comfortable wearing. Her brown hair with streaks of grey was swept up in a bun on top of her head. She was very well spoken with a calm, soft voice. She said they were fine as though they weren't but she didn't want to make a fuss. She too agreed to join in the dinner. Her sixteen-year-old daughter, Elizabeth lay asleep on a towel nearby, her pale body exposed to the sun. Her brother, James was strolling along the water's edge wearing rolled up trousers and a T-shirt, absorbed in finding shells.

Arriving back at the bar, Meg got a drink and prepared a notice about the dinner. She included mention of a trip into Nidri for anyone interested. She also put up a notice about bus times although she wasn't sure when the last one ran. Then she realised that she hadn't seen anyone from the hill accommodation. Should she walk up and check that everything was fine? What she really wanted to do was have a swim, cool down and relax for half an hour, but she daren't.

She set off up the hill. She passed the buildings on the right and saw that one was a residence of some kind. Another one that seemed complete and inhabited on the ground floor but bare breezeblocks forming the framework for an upper floor stood unfinished with no sign that any building work was on going. The other one was a bakery. As she neared, the delicious aroma of freshly baked bread met her with huge affection. She went to have a closer look. There were a couple of tables with chairs at the front. Inside was a small serving area and counter with a large area behind stacked high with bread and cakes and beyond that, ovens. A portly man with a round, smiling face greeted her and asked her if he could help her in Greek. She realised that she had already picked up some phrases from Alison's list and from listening to Michael and Lorraina when they spoke to each other. She understood but had no confidence to speak. She smiled and indicated she was just looking. He turned and picked up a small cake, wrapped it in thin paper and handed it to her. She took it, smiled, and got her purse out, but he shook his head.

"Entaxis. *Is good*"

She plucked up courage and tried a simple thank you in awkward Greek learnt from the sheet Alison had given her, 'a ferrets toe', and hoped he understood. He replied with something that sounded like parrot claw so she thought she must have said the right thing. As she turned to leave, she noticed stacks of honey by the door with Lefkas written on them. She hadn't realised this was a honey-producing island. She loved honey.

She left the bakery and set off up the road, unwrapped the small sticky cake and took a bite. The overwhelming sweetness flooded her taste buds. It was thick and a bit sickly. She continued up the hill wrapping the remains in the paper and put it in her bag wishing she had remembered to bring some water with her. The light was beginning to fade and heat was dissipating into warm balm. The mountain rose steeply on one side and tall trees lined the coast side, as the road moved away from the water and then back round towards it. It was a pleasant walk at this time of day. A few vehicles went past, mostly old and battered cars like Spiro's, a lorry heavy and rumbling, driven fast by an islander confident of the route, and a bus, too big for the road, gears roaring and brakes whining, as it rounded the bend. Stealing the silence for a few moments.

As she walked, her thoughts ran from apprehension at what mood these guests would be in, to mentally calculating how many would be going to the taverna and praying that the staff could cope with the numbers. Behind all the practicalities was Pete.

How had she sounded? Should she have said more? He'd only mentioned male friends, but were there women involved? Unfounded jealousy tipped her guts upside down. Why had he not known it was her straight away? She thought about being with him; the loving, fun times, and wanted him so badly. Then she remembered the times he had hurt her, the other girls that had led to them breaking up time and again throughout university. By the time she reached the accommodation, she was in a dark dither created by her own mind.

She drew a deep breath and went down the steps. Before she turned the corner of the building, she could hear laughter and chatting. She arrived to find all the families sitting on the terrace outside the rooms. They greeted her and she asked how everything was.

"We had a problem with the water, but Bill here managed to fix that."

She looked over at a small, smug looking man with a beard and glasses, swigging wine.

"The rooms are dreadful but there is a beach of sorts just below us if you don't mind jumping down and waiting for the tide to go out. We've got our duty free and we're fine!"

Meg told them about going out for dinner and they all agreed that that would be great. Full of relief she accepted a glass of wine and sat listening to them chat. They were laughing at the organisation and at Spiro. She felt uncomfortable, and although she agreed with them, she too was 'the company' and was not going to join in. She got away as quickly as possible and said she would see them later.

She walked quickly back down the hill, realising that she didn't have much time to change and go, and hoped they wouldn't be late. It was still very light and the cicadas whirred in the still branches of the trees lining the road.

She washed, again in boiled water, and went over to the bar to make sure she was ready and waiting for the holidaymakers to arrive.

Eventually, everyone was there apart from Melissa and Lucy and when she asked, Keith told her that they had decided not to come. Thinking no more about them, she led the others down the road. Keith came up beside her, and chatted her up along the way. She was pleasant to him but not in the least attracted by his false charms.

They arrived at the restaurant and to her delight long rows of tables were ready with glowing candles in glass pots, which wouldn't be truly effective for a while yet. The sea sparkled in the light of the slowly setting sun as the white surf swished up and back repetitively, with a slow and rhythmic shhhhh, beyond. Four young good-looking waiters in black trousers and white shirts, including Gregor, stood waiting.

The owner, Kostos, greeted her warmly. Everyone sat down where they pleased, new found friends sat close together, chatting and lively as Gregor gave out menus in Greek and English. The choice was extensive but it soon became apparent that chips were not on the menu and chips were required, children moaned and parents grumbled. Meg grabbed Gregor and apologising asked if there was any way they could do chips.

Gregor spoke to Kostos who looked dismayed. He didn't see what was wrong with his fried potatoes and nor did Meg, but she wanted to keep people happy and he liked the smell of money. This was a big crowd of people. He pulled Meg into the kitchen and she showed him how thin to slice the potatoes and then threw them into a sizzling pan of oil. Easy! She couldn't believe they didn't already know.

Kostos laughed and ordered one of his assistants to start slicing and frying. He grinned at Meg and said, "Next you show make Big Mac."

"Never," replied Meg, "I apologise for all holiday makers who don't appreciate fresh, lovely local dishes."

He looked at her quizzically not really understanding and she laughed, "Children happy, parents happy, buy more wine!" She rubbed her thumb over her fingers indicating money and he laughed. This he understood.

Everyone was happy. Delicious dishes were ignored, as most of the guests ordered things they recognised with plenty of wine. As a chef, Kostos may have been disappointed, but as an entrepreneur, he was not. At the end of the meal, he told Meg she didn't have to pay whenever she brought 'big group.'

During the meal, she barely ate as she was going round explaining dishes, trying to persuade them to try new things unsuccessfully and asking who might be interested in going over to Nidri. She was also trying to make it clear that she was not with Keith, who had made sure he sat next to her and was getting more tactile, the more he drank.

The waiters, with their limited English, flirted with the women and she spotted Gregor winking at Elizabeth, who was blushing and playing self-consciously with her napkin. She was pale and shy with a few spots adorning a plain face. Long straight mousy hair hung down over her shoulders and she was obviously enjoying the unusual attention.

Meg found out from Gregor that there was a disco on the near side of Nidri, which was not a nightclub and it was perfectly acceptable to take youngsters. The bus driver would stop for them, but they would have to get taxis back or walk.

The people from the hill were merry and happy to go back to their rooms for a night- cap. Sarah and

Denis, with Tim, the single father and another couple John and Diedre with their teenage son, Mark, decided that a family disco might be good fun. Mark was a young fifteen year old. He was quiet and unassuming and had sat with the other, younger children through dinner chatting to them. Charlotte and her serious looking son, James did not want to go but Elizabeth looked disappointed. Denis jumped in and offered to look after her if she wanted to join them. Meg was relieved she didn't have to take that responsibility.

Keith and Aaron were of course very keen, so after paying all the bills, those going to Nidri made their way to the bus stop in time to catch the last bus at ten. They all piled on and Meg went into one of her special mimes to explain disco. She pointed at the children and did a little jig saying, "Disco, disco."

The driver locked at her with confusion, so she repeated the same action. Surely disco was an international word? The driver watched with amusement in his eyes and said, "Again."

Meg repeated the actions and the driver burst out laughing, and as if he had only just understood, "Ah disco, disco!" Then he did a little jig in his seat before putting his foot hard down on the accelerator so that Meg nearly lost her balance. She laughed and grinned at everyone, her face going red, and they all laughed.

Everyone held on tight as the bus rocked and shook as it went round bends at speed before pulling up suddenly at the side of the road in darkness. The driver pointed to a path on the other side of the road and they all got out warily. Sure enough, down the path a short way, they could hear the thudding beat of loud music and came to a large pre-fab building with a small door in the side. A neon light above the door announced "Discotheque" in bright flashing letters.

The door opened into a small reception area with a desk, and a young Greek woman took the small entrance fee. She made no reaction to the ages of the children and they all went dubiously past her, up some stairs and into strobe lights and thumping music.

There was a bar to one side, a few chairs and tables and a large dance floor surrounded by mirrors, which was full of young, trendy Greeks shaking their bodies and staring at their own reflections as they moved to a mix of tracks by David Bowie, Queen, Bruce Springsteen. The youngsters got straight up and began dancing and playing around. The adults went straight to the bar.

A short while afterwards, Gregor arrived with the other waiters and some English looking girls. He waved at Meg and then joined the throng on the dance floor and began moving his body erotically and provocatively around the girls, keeping one eye in the mirror as Frankie Goes to Hollywood sang out 'Relax'. Meg smiled to herself; he was absolutely gorgeous and although he knew it, there was an attractive cheekiness about him and he exuded a gentle confidence rather than arrogance. The girls, in their early twenties, were dressed in skimpy flared skirts and strappy tops, their hair was tied up in high messy pony tails with thick bands or bows and they danced self-consciously around their handbags placed together on the floor. Meg couldn't quite relax even though the place felt friendly and safe.

The song ended and Howard Jones' 'Things Can Only Get Better' started up. Meg turned to chat with Tim and Denis but Keith appeared at her side and dragged her up to the dance floor. She danced carefully, keeping him at arms length, even though she loved to dance, and hoped the words of the song were true. At the end of the track she laughed and said thanks and moved off the dance floor leaving him to carry on dancing to 'Everybody wants to Rule the World' by Tears for Fears. Everyone on the dance floor joined in with the chorus in loud tuneless voices, not really knowing the words. Keith moved closer to one of the girls, who frowned and turned her back on him and he danced away pretending it hadn't happened. Meg turned away and kept her eye on all the children as their parents drank more and talked loudly to be heard over the music. Mark danced obligingly with the young girls a couple of times and played with Denis and Sue's eight-year-old son. Tim and Denis were then grabbed by their daughters and made to dance. It was a lively, fun atmosphere and they were good people, but she felt like she was working the whole time and it was impossible for her to relax.

Meg felt as though the DJ was mocking her as he played 'Don't You Forget About Me' by Simple Minds. Then the music began to slow and 'Against All Odds' by Phil Collins'; Spandau Ballet's 'True', followed by a classic heart jerker, 'I Want to Know What Love is' by Foreigner left Meg feeling very alone, and a deep sadness engulfed her.

Couples began to smooch on the dance floor and Meg saw Gregor was dancing slowly with Elizabeth, holding her close and moving his hand gently across her lower back and so she caught the attention of Tim and Denis. They took the hint and said it was getting a bit late for the little ones. Denis gathered the small children and Tim waited until the track finished before gently tapping Elizabeth's arm and telling her it was time to go. Reluctantly she smiled shyly at Gregor and said goodbye, her eyes sparkling with hope and desire. He smiled and said how sorry he was to say goodbye to such a beautiful lady and that he would see her soon. She floated out of the room behind Denis and Sarah. Meg went up to Gregor and pulled him gently to one side, "Be careful, don't break her heart."

Gregor laughed and said, "Meggie, Meg, you have to trust me!"

Meg laughed too, "No, I don't."

Gregor looked at her suddenly serious, "Really. She is lovely, sad, young girl, she need to feel beautiful. This I do, nothing more. Too young for me, I am good Greek boy."

He grinned at Meg and she laughed, "That's good to know."

Gregor looked over to where the English girls were standing talking to his friends, one of the girls looked over at him and gave a small smile and Gregor said to Meg, "Now, I have some older business."

Meg laughed and said, "Fair enough. See you tomorrow."

Gregor strolled over to join his friends and casually slipped his arm around the waist of the girl as he made a joke that made them all laugh. Meg went out to the reception and asked about taxis. The woman indicated outside and sure enough, a couple of scruffy looking local men were leaning on cars, smoking and talking. There was not room for all of them so Keith said to Meg,

"Hey, let the families go and you, me and Aaron will get the next one."

Aaron, who had barely spoken all evening, managed a drunken "Yeh," and slumped down on a tree stump.

Fifteen minutes later, there was no sign of another taxi. They asked inside and received a nonchalant shrug. They decided to walk. Meg didn't mind, she had drunk a fair bit of wine herself over the course of the evening and fresh air and a walk sounded appealing. The cicadas partied in the trees below a star filled sky as they made their way along the dark road, breathing in the cool and refreshing air.

It was a long walk but Keith was a good talker and even Aaron joined in as they chatted about life and swapped other holiday anecdotes. When they got back to Nikiana, Keith said he had a bottle of wine, which seemed to the three of them like a good idea at the time. Meg, feeling the need for company, sat on the step of the beach villa talking to them both and they came up with the plan of going to Nidri the following day so that Meg could find out what was on offer and maybe organise some trips. She felt that at least if she was going with some punters she wasn't deserting her post. Keith was talking and laughing very loudly, every so often he glanced towards the door of Melissa's room and then loudly shushed Aaron and Meg (who were not talking loudly) so as not to disturb 'Chignon Melissa'. Eventually Aaron crashed out on the verandah.

In what he obviously thought was a seductive, low voice, Keith switched to full on Mr. Smooth. He moved up close to Meg and stared at her.

"You know you have the most beautiful eyes?"

"So do you," replied Meg laughing.

Twice in one day, gosh! However, while Gregor was cheeky and lighthearted, Keith was slimy and false.

"No, I'm serious. I know it's corny but I feel as if I've known you for ever and even though we might never see each other again, wouldn't it be nice to share something we can always remember?"

Meg could barely suppress the need to giggle, "Keith, I think you're great and thanks for the offer but..." she could see his ego was not going to like rejection "I'm engaged and even though at this moment I'd like to forget that, I can't," she said with subtle melodrama. "I'd better go. See you tomorrow."

She tried to make her voice sound full of regret while inside she wanted to laugh hysterically. She stood up and began to walk away.

"Can't I have jusht one kiss?" he called after her. His voice slurred and he glanced back at chignon Melissa's door.

"No, sorry. See you tomorrow."

"Worth a try." She heard him mutter as she walked back down the empty road.

She raised her eyes to the sky.

"Dear God!"

# CHAPTER 9

She felt a little bit fuggy when she dutifully arrived in the bar for morning duty only a few hours later. The families, as she called them, arrived at nine and said what a good time they had had. Before making their way on to the beach, they asked her if she wanted to join them for dinner that night. She happily accepted the invitation and told them she was going to Nidri later and did they want to come. No, they were just going to laze and swim.

She wondered if Keith and Aaron would still come, but at eleven they arrived looking a little bit rough around the edges but lively and ready to go. Keith acted as if nothing had happened the night before and was still flirting and oddly jubilant. Rejection had merely spurred him on it seemed.

She waited until midday to make sure that there were no late risers with any problems. Charlotte came for breakfast with James and a very bright eyed Elizabeth. Charlotte said hello politely, and asked if there were any trips she could take the children on. Meg explained that she was going to find out and would let her know. There was no sign of the young couple; Meg presumed they would be making the most of the peace and quiet. She had some lunch with Aaron and Keith served by a cynical looking Michael and they caught the one o'clock bus.

The bus stopped in the middle of what was the main and only street. There was a long stretch of bars facing onto the beach and on the other side souvenir shops and small boutiques all selling vests and T-shirts with 'No Problem' splashed across the front in different colours. They made their way between two tavernas, where a mix of nationalities were enjoying lunch served by waiters all wearing traditional black trousers and white shirts. The beach was wide and long. It was not crowded but there were people spread out across the white sand, sunbathing, strolling along the edge of the sea or swimming. A motorboat pulling an inexperienced water skier sped across in front of the beach and opposite the shoreline, out to sea, was a tiny island. Beyond that, you could make out the outline of two or three more, rising out of the ocean like the backs of huge reptiles. The beach curved round forming an elongated horseshoe bay with the headland coming back on itself diagonally opposite them. A marina housed a large number of fishing boats of varying sizes and some expensive looking yachts sat quietly, in contrasting wealth. Meg took photos and made notes on the different excursions and the prices.

Keith suggested they all have a go at water skiing. He said he had done it before. It was something Meg had always wanted to try. She felt guilty about having fun, but persuaded herself it was all part of research. Keith and Aaron went down to the water's edge to watch the water skiers and Meg went over to a Greek man lazing back in a deck chair with a large wooden board next to him, which announced in chalk: water skiing, boat hire and island tours.

He was sitting in the shade of a large fig tree and as she approached he picked up a bottle of beer from his side and took a long swig. He was about forty, tanned and fit. He greeted her in perfect English with a strong Greek accent in a slow laid-back style. Meg made notes of all the prices on the board and he asked her why. He laughed at her response and said,

"Good, good. You bring everybody to Niko I have the best boats, the best prices. You want to try water skiing. You try now for free."

Meg jumped at the chance and found herself sitting in the water with a life jacket up against her ears and her feet being jammed into huge skis, which she was desperately trying to keep upright. Somebody passed her the rope handle and the boat started to move forward. She started to feel the tension of the pull and with all her might pushed herself up out of the water. She was up. She was up! She pulled too hard and wham! She was down. She tried to swim but the skis were heavy under the water and twisted.

"Relax, relax!" shouted the boat driver. She flailed her arms wildly and managed to get the skis in front of her. She was at least straight again. The rope was thrown to her and the driver shouted instructions for her to sit in the water with her knees up and apart and to hold the rope handle up to her chin with the rope going between her legs. Bad advice, very bad advice.

The boat pulled away again, fast. She started to move up out of the water but the pull was too strong. She let go of the rope and the handle flew forward smashing the inside of her thighs as it went through. Jesus! It hurt. She wouldn't give up though and the boat came back round.

"Last try, this time you do it."

She went through the same palaver getting straight in the water and was beginning to feel distressed, but calmed herself, sat back and held onto the rope again. There was no way she was going to let go of it a second time. She hunched up in the water, the handle close to her chest and let the boat pull her up and out. She was up; she wobbled, got her balance and felt the exhilaration of flying across the top of the water, the wind blowing through her hair, for at least twenty seconds. The boat started to turn; she lost her balance and toppled sideways into the boat's wake. She came up coughing and gasping, but thrilled. She was pulled ungracefully onto the boat and taking the life jacket off she saw her thighs red and smarting. Over the next few days, they were to turn black, blue, and varying colours of green, yellow and brown as the bruises came out. They also caused raised eyebrows and smutty comments about how she got them.

Keith and Aaron were laughing at her when she returned. It was Keith's turn to go next and she watched, impressed, as he swung smoothly up on one ski and slalomed across the wake of the boat occasionally holding on with one hand as he smoothed his hair back with the other. She exchanged glances with Aaron and he rolled his eyes and went off to get some beer. He decided not to have a go. Meg thanked Niko and promised him that she would tell everyone to go to him. She said she would be back to hopefully book a trip round the island for a large group. He smiled and shrugged and went back to his spot under the tree and picked up his beer.

They walked along the top of the beach looking at all the different tavernas, which were all virtually the same with blue and white checked plastic covers and small wooden chairs. Some played music and offered different specials but the menus all offered the same basics. Calamari, moussaka, stuffed vine leaves and Kataifi were announced in white chalk on blackboards at the entrances to all of them. Waiters called to them and gestured to empty tables. None of them was busy.

Meg felt she ought to get back so they made their way towards the bus stop. Coming in the opposite direction, she couldn't mistake the black curly hair and distinctive walk of Daveed. He was with a young woman, walking arm in arm. When he saw Meg, she wasn't sure who was more awkward. She felt like a schoolgirl playing truant and started to explain what she was doing. He stepped away from the girl and explained that he was looking at some new apartments.

"Boat trips?" he suddenly said, seeing a way to avert attention from his activities.

"I know some of the boat owners. I can organise a trip if you want."

Meg said that she had spoken to Niko.

"Nick the Greek!" Keith laughed at his own joke.

Daveed said that Niko was a crook. No, he knew how to get a good deal. Meg shrugged and said okay. She presumed he knew more than she did. She got on the bus feeling quite pleased with herself. She had a lot of information to share; she had taken some photographs and hopefully had a boat trip to offer. Aaron sat down first so Meg quickly sat beside him. Keith sat in front and turned himself to face her leaning over the seat.

"So, what's for tonight then?"

Meg felt uncomfortable. She felt that having said 'no' she was now a challenge.

"I think everyone is going out for a meal again in the village," she said, hoping that he might think that too boring, but he and Aaron agreed that that was fine.

It was about five when she tried the shower in her bathroom and, hoorah, there was hot water. She stood revelling in the water streaming over her body. She had arrived three days ago and yet with that odd deceit of time when you are away from home it felt like months. She smoothed shampoo into her hair and massaged her scalp trying to relieve the unabated tension in her body and mind.

Suddenly she sensed the water losing its heat and intensity. She played with the taps but to no avail. The stream of water reduced to a trickle and she was left trying to rinse out the remaining shampoo in the barely dripping cold water.

As she came out of the shower, she heard a knocking on the door. She wrapped her towel around her and opened the door slightly. It was Callista. She looked very stern as she said,

"Telephonee. Spiro, quick, quick!"

Meg threw on a T-shirt and shorts and ran over the road barefoot.

"Hello?" she said in a bright voice as she picked up the receiver.

A barrage of abuse came down the phone.

"You no good. You slut. Bad lady--" This was followed by a lot of Greek, which she presumed was not very complimentary and then, "You pack your bags. You are fired."

She heard him slam down the phone and stood in shock, tears welling up in her eyes as she put the receiver back down. Surely, that can't have been for going to Nidri. Her first thought was Daveed. What had he been saying? Was he trying to get in before she said something about him and the girl – as if she ever would?

The phone rang again. She didn't want to answer it. It wasn't her phone. Callista came in from outside and picked it up. She spoke in Greek and then,

"Yes. Okay."

She held the phone out for Meg.

"Hello," her voice not so bright now.

"Hello," came an English voice. It was Sandra and she didn't sound happy either.

"Meg. What's been going on? Where have you been today?"

"Sandra, I've been to Nidri for a couple of hours to find out about boat trips and things to do."

"Spiro is furious. We came down at about two o'clock and couldn't find you. Then we went to see the woman who complained about the beach accommodation, Melissa something. She told us that you have been doing nothing apart from getting drunk and sleeping around."

"What!" Meg was astounded.

"Sandra, I have not stopped working since I got here. I organised a meal for everyone last night and took a group to a disco near Nidri. I sat in the bar from eight until one today and spoke to nearly everyone. I then went up to Nidri to find out about trips and I haven't seen Melissa what's her face since we took them to their rooms yesterday."

"Okay, calm down I believe you. What did Spiro say?"

"He sacked me."

"Oh God. I told him to wait until I had spoken to you. Don't worry. I'll sort it out. We'll come down tomorrow."

Meg thanked Callista, and gave her a weak smile. Callista gave her a strange, knowing look and reached in her bag to pull out a packet of cigarettes. She offered one to Meg, who accepted, not knowing what to do with herself.

"My God, Callista. What is going on?"

Callista didn't say anything. Meg drew on the cigarette and blew out the smoke without inhaling. She did this a couple more times.

"I know my career history isn't brilliant, but sacked after two days is a record."

She blew out more smoke and Callista started to laugh.

"You astie micre pithike." *'You funny little monkey.'* She pursed out her lips and blew a couple of times imitating Meg.

"Like monkey," she said and laughed again.

Meg couldn't help laughing too, "I don't often smoke," she laughed again, tension broken.

She walked back across the road, the tarmac hot beneath her bare feet. She wasn't quite sure what to do. Did she still have her job? Did she care?

"Hi, Meg. Still on for tonight?"

She turned to see Denis and Sarah followed by their two children and John, Diedre and their son, Mark, coming back from the beach. Behind them were Tim and his girls. She suddenly felt self-conscious of her appearance - bare feet, no bra and still wet, unruly hair. They didn't seem to notice.

"Hi! Yes, yes I am. I mentioned it to some others. Is that okay?"

She felt trapped into looking like she was with Keith.

"No problem. Shall we meet in the bar again at about 7.30?" said Denis.

They were good company, safe and friendly. John and Diedre went past with a hello and see you later and their son, Mark gave her a shy smile as he trudged past with the swimming bag. Tim's girls stopped in front of her.

"You haven't brushed your hair," stated Ashley.

"I like your T-shirt," commented Samantha, the elder one.

"Come on you two," Tim said, giving her a grin and raising his eyebrows.

"See you later."

She briefly wondered why he was on his own. He was thirty-something, slim and good looking and kind and loving towards his daughters.

Back in her little room, she lay on the bed and wondered what had made Melissa say those things. What a cow! She had barely spoken to her. Maybe that was it; maybe she should have gone to see her in the morning. Maybe she was upset that nobody had asked her to the dinner. Damn, she should have gone to find her. With all these thoughts she didn't really understand how this explained the awful accusations.

She got dressed, pulling on a pair of high-waisted turquoise, cotton trousers, which were cool and loose and a white vest. She let her hair dry naturally, untangling the knots with her fingers. She had caught the sun on her shoulders; a deep red that she hoped would turn brown. She moisturised her arms and face and felt the skin drinking it up. A flick of mascara and she was ready. She was tempted to get completely shit faced, punch Melissa in the nose and get the next flight out, but for some strange reason she liked all the other people and she wanted to make sure they had a good holiday. She was also aware of how it would look if she arrived home after three days. It might seem like a million years to her, but back in England it would be three days. She got her pens and paper out and designed posters with all the information about Nidri and a request for names of anyone interested in a boat trip to one of the islands. She took them over to the bar about seven and asked Michael if she could put them up on the door.

When she had finished she sat up at the bar, ordered herself a large brandy and said 'cheers' to Michael and Lorraina. Michael and Lorraina both looked at each other and smiled knowingly.

The families arrived all in good humour and said they had found another taverna half way down the road. Meg had not noticed one on her journeys but it was great that she wasn't in charge. Keith and Aaron arrived and they all set off for dinner. This time Denis led the way to the small bar halfway along the main street where she had seen the local men drinking and chatting. It now had a row of tables outside and the proprietor came rushing out to greet them. Competition was on. Denis had gone wandering during the day and had stopped for a drink and asked if there were any more restaurants. The owner had jumped at the chance. He stood beaming and started fussing over everybody to sit down. He gave out menus identical to the ones from the Taverna, but it soon became apparent that he didn't have any of the things on the menu, but, he did have chips. He announced this with pride in broken English.

Everybody found this hilarious and then after a lot of questions, Meg managed to discover that he had just one main dish and chips. Everyone agreed it was worth a try. It turned out to be an incredibly tasty fish stew. They ordered wine and everyone was relaxed and full of life.

Meg had not been able to avoid Keith sitting down next to her and her discomfort grew as he lazily laid his arm across the back of her chair. She leaned forward self-consciously and turned to Tim who was sitting on her other side.

"Talk to me, please," she whispered under her breath.

He looked surprised and then glanced at Keith's arm and understood.

She turned her shoulder away from Keith and began chatting away to Tim about anything that came into her head. Keith left his arm on the back of her chair and she spent most of the meal hunched over the table, sitting as far forward as she could to keep away from his touch.

At the end of the meal, they split the bill and Denis suggested a nightcap back at the bar. They all got up and strolled down the road. Meg found herself with Keith on one side and Tim on the other. Keith controlled the conversation with his ability to talk about himself indefinitely and she and Tim responded politely. When they got back to the bar, Keith quickly asked Meg and Aaron what they would like and hurried to the bar. Tim ordered a round for the rest and Meg went with the others to sit on the terrace. She deliberately sat between Sarah and Diedre, but Keith came back from the bar and pulled up a chair forcing Sarah to make space for him.

Meg thanked him for the drink and then paid him as little attention as possible. She felt guilty because he had been good company going to Nidri but she had made it clear that she wasn't interested in anything more than friendship. Now she was anxious to avoid anyone coming to the conclusion, that Melissa was right and that she had formed a relationship with him.

Eventually, Diedre and John decided to leave and called Mark who was playing with the younger children. Aaron took the opportunity to suggest to Keith that they go up to Nidri. Keith asked Meg if she wanted to come with them and she refused as nicely as she could and they left. Meg breathed a silent thank you and relaxed.

Denis and Sarah's children came up with Tim's daughters, Ashley and Samantha and they began begging their parents to let them all sleep together. The parents all looked at each other. Tim immediately said,

"Well, I tell you what. If you don't mind, Sarah, they can top and tail in our room. Give you a bit of freedom."

Sarah beamed at him. Meg suddenly had a good idea.

"Listen, the room next to yours is free. I didn't dare offer it to you before because I wasn't sure if Spiro was going to move anyone in. If you don't mind them being in there, I'll give you the key."

"Won't that cause you a problem?" asked Denis.

"No, I don't think so. I'll have to tell Callista, the woman who looks after the rooms. If there's a problem with Spiro, I'll tell him you complained so much I had to do something!" She couldn't be sacked twice – could she?

"Great!"

Surprisingly, Sarah then added, "Thank you. Listen Tim, you stay here and have a drink. I'll sort the kids out and Mark will help keep an eye on them."

"Hey. Thanks. Are you sure? Shouldn't you check with Diedre before you get Mark to move in with a bunch of giggling kids?" asked Tim.

Sarah laughed, "Diedre's my sister and trust me. I think they'll all be very happy not to be sharing."

"Can I stay here for a drink as well?" asked Denis.

"Oh, no. I've got plans for you," said Sarah with a wink and Denis pretended to jump up and run.

They all laughed and Meg got the key from her bag.

The girls jumped up and down squealing in delight.

"Okay girls. Be good, come and give me a kiss before you go," said Tim.

Meg and Tim were left alone on the terrace. It didn't occur to Meg that Sarah was doing a bit of matchmaking by leaving her and Tim alone. He was so much older and had two children. He gave no impression of being interested in her in that way either. He was kind and polite with a dry sense of humour, which came out in odd bursts over the evening and he laughed as though he surprised himself. There was something subdued and withheld. She liked him and felt quite comfortable in his company. They ordered coffee and brandy and began to talk. Generally, at first about where they came from and what he did but with the freedom that being in a strange country for a limited time gives, they soon moved onto personal situations and feelings.

He had set up his own business a few years before as an accountant and it had been very hard going to begin with. His wife had not liked the lack of money coming in and the things that she had to give up. Looking back all the signs had been there. Weight loss, a new hairstyle, a dreamy far away look in her eyes and a gentle glow about her. She seemed much happier and he thought she'd finally lost her post pregnancy weight and had decided to be more supportive, but one evening when the girls were in bed she had dropped the bombshell that she was leaving. She had not wanted custody of the children, which had at least prevented even more bitter fights. Working mostly from home and with some hired help, he was managing to take good care of them and develop his business. Meg told him he seemed to be doing a fantastic job with the girls. He thanked her with doubt in his voice; he blamed himself for not paying his ex-wife more attention.

"I really loved her and just didn't see that she was that unhappy with me and the girls. I kept thinking that once I got a few big contracts everything would be all right. When she announced she was leaving, I was totally shocked. Since then, so many people have told me that it was obvious and that everyone had known about the affair. I still feel pretty stupid."

"Time to move on," said Meg gently.

Tim sighed and then to distract from himself, he asked if she wanted to walk along the beach.

They strolled down by the water's edge and Meg took off her shoes so she could feel the cool foam lapping around her feet and ankles. There were only natural sounds; the sounds that the land had made its whole life before settlers came to farm the olive groves and produce the honey and before tourists.

They passed Melissa's room and Meg cringed at the thought of her malicious comments. At the point where the beach curved, they stopped and sat under a fig tree that leaned out over the sand.

They talked and talked as the night moved on towards day. Tim asked her how she came to be here and she found herself pouring out the radio debacle and then went on to tell him what had happened with Spiro on the phone. She didn't mention Pete. As she opened up, she realised that she had been bottling up all her emotions. She was lost and tired and confused and the tears began to fall. He slipped his arm around her shoulder and she gratefully took comfort in the contact. She wiped the tears away, apologising and trying to smile. He bent his head down to kiss her.

"Time to move on," he whispered. His lips met hers as the dark blue sky began to give way to grey and a line of pink spread across the horizon.

Meg pulled abruptly away.

"No! I'm sorry. This is not what I want."

He pulled her into his chest and reassured her that it didn't matter. She knew she had hurt him. The last thing she had wanted to do. She tried to explain. Make him see that nothing was real when you're on holiday. That she really felt at ease with him, but she had a boyfriend. Didn't she?

They sat and watched the sun rise with the pink taking on an orange glow and then, without speaking they stood and walked back towards their rooms. When they reached her door, she kissed him on the cheek and smiled,

"See you in a couple of hours!"

The tension was broken. He laughed and said, "God, yes. Better try and get a couple of hours before the girls jump on me."

# CHAPTER 10

Another night with very little sleep and she had Spiro to face, but she still surfaced and took up her post at Michael's. A couple of people from up the hill came in and asked her about the boat trip. She said she didn't have details yet but if they put their names up, she would have more idea of what to book. They put their names down and those of the others staying up the hill. Charlotte came in with Elizabeth and James. Elizabeth was already turning a golden brown and her hair was bright with natural highlights from the sun. In her white sun top she had transformed from the pale wan teenager of the first day into a very attractive young woman. She was smiling and happy and Meg wondered if she had seen any more of Gregor. Charlotte put their names on the list and said that they were taking the bus up to Nidri to have a look around.

Eventually, Sandra arrived from the direction of the beach. She looked hot and angry. When she saw Meg, she managed a smile and joined her on the verandah.

"My God what a set up!" she exclaimed. "I've been working in the travel business for seventeen years and never before have I worked with such stress."

"What's been going on? Have I still got a job?" Meg asked.

"Spiro is a nightmare. Everything is so disorganised. The new girl down in Vasiliki has disappeared. She'd obviously had enough but didn't tell anyone. Then all this nonsense with you."

"But I didn't do anything."

"No, I know you didn't. I've just been down there. It seems one of the guys you went to Nidri with is actually Melissa's boyfriend."

"What! Which one?"

"The beefy one. Used to be her personal trainer. Apparently, she is some kind of important business woman, anyway, they started going out. They had a row on the plane because he had invited Aaron for a bit of male company and they weren't talking to each other when they arrived."

"God I didn't think they knew each other."

"Well, no. So Keith, whatever his name is, decided to chat you up to make her jealous. He told her that he had slept with you."

Meg couldn't speak.

"Anyway it obviously worked, they are all lovey-dovey again and she has insisted that they all be moved up to Nidri."

"Bloody hell. Aaron too?"

"Yes," she shook her head and raised her eyebrows, "so, you still have a job for what it's worth and they won't be around for you to worry about. Spiro has taken them up to Nidri and is too proud to come and tell you he was wrong."

Sandra went to the bar to order, leaving Meg dumbstruck. She thought about Tim and went hot and cold. Had she just made the same mistake? She hoped not. She liked Tim and felt he was genuine. Maybe he was just less obvious than Keith. Would he now be bitter and out to get her? She felt a wave of vulnerability and paranoia and immediately shook it off. She had done nothing wrong.

The sun shone innocently down from a clear sky, its rays scattering shadows through the branches of the eucalyptus as it swayed gently in the soft wind.

Sandra returned with two cappuccino coffees.

"I've added a little snifter. Thought we both could do with it!" she laughed.

The aroma of the coffee mixed with the distinctive breath of brandy hit the back of Meg's throat as she took a sip.

"Oh what the hell? Cheers!"

She enjoyed a moment of bravado before feeling her heart freeze as she heard the high-pitched voices of Tim's daughters behind them, calling her. She and Sandra turned as Samantha and Ashley came running up to say hello. Meg introduced them to Sandra and heard Tim behind her.

"Morning!"

His voice was bright. They met each other's eyes and he grinned. The relief made her want to cry, but in a cool voice, she asked how he was and introduced him to Sandra.

"Well, apart from needing about six more hours sleep, I feel fine."

Meg quickly told Sandra that they had stayed up talking very late. Sandra raised an eyebrow at her and Meg made a grimace. Tim sat with them and drank coffee, chatting easily to them both, while the girls played on the beach below. He asked if Meg still had a job and Meg let Sandra tell the story.

"Wow! Just shows you have to be careful who you stay up talking to at night."

He winked at Meg and she felt herself going red. Suddenly a loud car horn sounded from the front side of the bar.

"Ah, my driver awaits. That'll be Spiro. I'm trying to persuade him to get me my own jeep – we'll see!" said Sandra.

Meg asked Sandra to see if she could check on the boat trip for her. Then, with a cheeky grin asked Sandra to give her receipt for the things she had bought to Spiro and gave her two rolls of film to get developed if they went to Lefkas town. They said goodbye.

Meg turned to Tim and began to apologise again. He interrupted her,

"Hey, it's okay. I understand. I'm only here for a few more days, we can have a good time."

"Friends then?"

Meg suddenly felt great warmth towards him. He was so kind, but she did not fancy him at all.

"Friends. We are all staying on the beach today. Come and join us if you are free."

"Well, actually, I was thinking I could come down and organise some games for the children and let you parents have a rest. That way I'll feel that I'm working, not dossing and getting into more trouble!"

A couple of hours later, Meg wandered along the beach. She had spoken about the rooms to Callista, who had shrugged and said that it was fine with her.

'The families', as she called them, were lounging on the sand under the shade of the trees that lined the edge of the beach. With the aid of Mark, she organised various competitions and races and then took them to a shaded area off the beach for them to organise a small show for their parents.

In true, amateur dramatics style, they performed a dreadful version of Cinderella with multiple role swapping, giggling, shoving and loud prompts. The parents loved it and applauded their efforts genuinely. Meg shook Mark's hand, and giving him a quick hug, thanked him.

He smiled and blushed deeply.

Denis opened a bottle of wine and they sat on towels and mats laughing and joking in the sunshine. Meg just had one glass before feeling a little awkward. They had all become close friends in the intimacy and timelessness of sun, sea and escape. She felt an outsider in her capacity as their rep. Despite their friendliness, she felt an underlying expectation from some of the group that she should not be having too much fun.

She explained that she had to check on the boat trip and made her way down the beach alone. She passed the groups from up the hill, and smiled and explained that she was going to check on the boat trip. She passed Charlotte with Elizabeth still religiously sunbathing nearby and James, in a T-shirt in the shade, who seemed to be inspecting some shells and rocks he had collected. Meg smiled and sat down next to Charlotte. Elizabeth raised her head and said hello. Charlotte asked about the boat trip, and Meg said she was going to check. Elizabeth stood up and pulled a strappy sundress on over her costume before announcing that she was just going for a walk. Charlotte nodded and began to ask Meg more questions. Meg watched Elizabeth as she strolled down to the water's edge and then made her way nonchalantly along the beach towards the Taverna. Charlotte was always polite and friendly in a reserved fashion, and Meg felt a little sorry for her being on her own with the two young teenagers. The other guests were always inviting her to join them but on the whole she preferred to be alone. Charlotte asked a number of questions about the island and its history and Meg felt ignorant. She knew nothing about the island and had no references. In the blur of leaving she had not had a chance to go to the library to find out about the place before she came, and she had expected there to be plenty of information available at the resort. She decided she must find out about all the things there were to do on the island to suit different tastes.

Charlotte had done some research and she shared a little of what she knew with Meg. Apparently, there was a castle and a church on the outskirts of Lefkas town known as Santa Mavra, which had also been the name of the island for a while.

Originally connected to the mainland, the Corinthians had dug a channel in the 7ᵗʰ century BC to provide a route North and thereby created the island as it was now. In it's history it had been under the rule of Turkey, Venice, Russia, France and Britain before becoming part of independent Greece in 1864. The island itself was twenty-two miles from North to South and nine miles from East to West. Meg had been down the East coast road from North to South and wondered what was on the West coast. Charlotte said she had a very small unclear map that seemed to show no roads going down the west coast and she thought it must be all cliffs. She said that there were numerous islands off the coast of Nidri and Meg said that she had seen them from the shore. Charlotte was very excited about the boat trip.

"I feel a bit trapped in this tiny village with just a beach and a bar. I'm not really a beach person. Meganisi sounds so pretty and untouched and I am so looking forward to seeing Skorpios Island, the home of Christina Onassis. Did you know that her father and her brother are actually buried on the island?"

Meg shook her head and sighed. So much to find out. She thanked Charlotte for sharing what she knew and promised to let her know what was happening with the boat trip as soon as she had the details. She stood up and brushed sand off her shorts realising that she had been talking, or she should say listening, to Charlotte for ages. She made her way back to the bar and turned and looked back up the beach watching everyone so relaxed and peaceful with the whole beach to themselves. Elizabeth was coming back round the curve from the direction of the taverna. She was walking in the shallow waters at the edge of the sea and had a dreamy, far away look on her face. Her blonde streaked hair flowed over her lightly tanned shoulders in the gentle breeze and she looked quite lovely. What a transformation.

She went up into the bar and Michael told her that Sandra had phoned and she felt immediately guilty for not having been there. She went round to Callista who greeted her with her usual slightly mocking smile and let her use the phone. Sandra came on the line and Meg immediately went into a full report of where she had been. Sandra laughed and said she didn't need to know. She then went on to tell her that a boat trip to an island had been organised for the day after tomorrow. She gave her the cost, time of departure from Nidri and the itinerary.

At last, a sense of organisation and things happening.

Meg immediately drew up a poster to put in the bar making it sound exciting and great value for money. The trip included visiting some caves and lunch in a taverna at Vathi, a fishing village in a harbour on the island of Meganisi. She also made use of Charlotte's information and mentioned that they would be passing the island of Skorpios, home of the Onassis family. She put up the poster feeling more optimistic and went to sit in her 'office' with a glass of wine and watched the people on the beach gather up their things and start to head back to shower as best they could and change for the evening. As each group passed, she indicated the poster and asked them to put their names down in confirmation.

She didn't see Tim and felt a bit panicky about what to do that evening. Nobody had asked her to join them. She didn't want a relationship with Tim, but she liked his company. She knew she should be pleased at the chance of a rest but she was too unsettled to enjoy being alone with herself. She persuaded herself that she needed some space and planned to write some letters, and maybe go and get some bits and pieces from the store. Get a good night's sleep perhaps. Maybe phone Pete. No, she had to wait until he phoned her now. She laughed at herself. She had seen Pete only four or five days ago; he wouldn't even be missing her. She missed him though, as she sat on the empty verandah of the bar. What was she doing here? Why was she always so impetuous? If she'd stayed cool, she would be with him now. What had happened to them? She didn't stop her memories from flooding in.

As her thoughts ran riot almost unconsciously, (about Pete, about everything) she watched the changing colours of the sky and sea. Twilight made silhouettes of the trees and the waning moon sent a few sparkles across the darkening, placid water.

She jumped when Tim tapped her on the shoulder and said,

"Hi there."

"My God! Don't do that."

They both laughed.

"What are you up to?' he enquired.

"Sitting here contemplating life."

She realised that her free running imagination had taken her into dark corners. She felt anger towards Pete. He should have phoned. Why hadn't he stopped her from going?

"Listen. I don't know if you want to. What I mean is I, er, Denis and Sarah have said that they will take the girls out if you want to come out for dinner with just me somewhere. Just friends. I just thought you might want a break from being on duty all the time."

He was nervous and embarrassed.

She immediately said, "Thanks that would be lovely. As long as you are sure it's okay with the girls."

"They are only interested in being with the other kids."

Meg went to change feeling pleased that she had something to do. It would be good to go out with easy company and she didn't want to be on her own.

They took the bus up to Nidri and wandered along past tavernas and bars lit up magically and buzzing with life. They chatted easily and laughed at the waiters trying to catch their attention and draw them in to eat and drink at each restaurant. They chose a small taverna at the end of the street and sat at a table overlooking the beach. Soft Greek music was playing and the sea sparkled on the shore. The waiter came over and treated them like lovers. It was a perfect setting for people in love. She remembered with a pang the year before when she had flown to meet Pete in Athens and they had gone on to tour a few islands. They had walked through tiny streets past pristine whitewashed villas edged with bright blue to a similar taverna overlooking the sea. As usual Meg was swamped by sickening regret as she remembered the holiday. Tim saw the sad look on her face asked her what she was thinking about.

Meg didn't want to think about it or talk about it. She changed the subject and they enjoyed a good meal of freshly caught fish and crispy fried calamari, some average local wine that tasted better and better as the bottle went down and watched with delight as the Greek waiters put on a little show of traditional dancing.

Greek guests got up and joined in and Meg and Tim clapped to the music. Laughing, they looked at each other and Tim leant forward to kiss her. She pulled back and pretending she hadn't realised his intention, pulled him up and into the circle of dancers. Round one way and then the other, faster and faster. They tried desperately to follow the steps. Eventually, they collapsed back onto their seats laughing.

Meg said they ought to catch the last bus back. Tim insisted on getting the bill, "No strings," he said, and she smiled and thanked him. When they got back, she said she had to get some sleep and he politely said good night. She wanted to get away from him. She felt so comfortable with him that she was uncomfortable.

She lay awake. How did she feel about Tim? She enjoyed his company. Was she being unfair to him and to Pete? She didn't like the idea of him spending time with any other woman. Had they missed the moment? Was it all too late? Confused and lost, she finally went to sleep.

# CHAPTER 11

Sandra came over for breakfast in the jeep she had persuaded Spiro to give her on threat of her resigning. Meg congratulated her and gave her the numbers for the boat trip. Sandra then asked if they could go up to the hill accommodation to make sure everyone was happy. When they arrived, they found the children messing about on the verandah, while their parents were still in bed.

Empty wine bottles and dirty glasses lay as evidence of a good night before.

The children showed Meg and Sandra where a little path led through some trees down to a small cliff. The tide was out and by sliding down the muddy slope you could reach a tiny shingle beach about ten feet long. So, they hadn't exactly lied when they described the accommodation as having its own private beach, although from the watermarks the tide obviously came right up the edge of the cliff.

Luckily, everybody seemed happy there. It was a huge relief after the previous group.

On their way back they stopped at the little bakery and had a drink. The owner came out to them and practised his limited English on them, smiling and gesturing, squinting in the sunshine with his tanned, lined face full of character. He managed to convey that he was busy baking for a wedding. He kept pointing up the mountain and saying 'karya and wedding' so Meg presumed the two words meant the same.

Meg asked Sandra if she knew much about the island and both admitted to each other that they had very little information about the whole area. Sandra suggested they explore, so Meg collected her camera and they set off.

They drove up towards Lefkas town and spotted a rough road leading upwards. They took it. It was not well made, but was definitely a well-worn track that had been used by motor vehicles. The vegetation on either side was lush and green, and at various points when it wasn't too high, they could see the rich blue of the sea dotted with fishing boats below.

They came to a fork in the road. There was a small hand-painted sign and with Meg's ability to make out the Greek alphabet, though not always understand the words, she laughed as she saw one way to Lefkas and the other to Karya.

"Oh! Karya is the name of a place! I didn't even know there were villages up here!" she exclaimed.

They followed the steep road twisting and curving until they came to a small house with a couple of chickens squawking in the front. The road began to narrow after that, and worried that they wouldn't be able to turn around, they parked and began to walk. They came around the corner and ahead of them the path was cobbled as it led past a high wall and a row of whitewashed houses with blue shutters and a tiny church with it's open bell tower. It was like discovering a secret. Tiny streets led onto one another and joined in a small market square with tiny shops selling beautiful embroidery and a few souvenirs and a small cafe. There were women dressed in traditional black with lace headwear and a few men in black suits. With their shorts and T-shirts, Meg and Sandra felt like some anachronistic mistake.

Then they heard music. Loud, wild, happy music, and a band of men came into the square, some playing fiddles and others shaking and tapping tambourines. A crowd wearing a mixture of traditional costume and modern dress, young and old people singing, dancing and cheering, followed the musicians. They led a donkey with a glorious, young woman dressed in a fine, white dress, sitting sidesaddle on its back. She wore a light veil and a coronet of flowers on her head. The crowd came past them and round them laughing and shaking their hands and inviting them to join them.

Meg and Sandra found themselves clapping and dancing in the street with the throng until it started disappearing up one of the lanes. They were left in the now deserted square. The bright sunlight reflected off the white walls and the shadows of bougainvillea continued to dance on the square to the fading music.

They looked at each other, both filled with the joy that had filled the air, and laughed. They were hot and thirsty and needed a drink but realised that there was no one in the small open café or in the shop, which had been abandoned with doors wide open. Meg went into the dark, cool interior of the café and took a bottle of water. She left more than enough money on the counter for it, and ran out to Sandra who laughed at her audacity.

They made their way back to the jeep, but neither spoke for fear of losing the magic. Meg had taken lots of photographs and she was excited about getting the film developed so that she could start an album for guests to look at. A sudden flash of the future stopped her thoughts. A brief glimpse of progress and corruption. She wanted to share the experience, the quaint village nestling in the past, but by sharing she was inviting tourism and with tourism, authenticity would be lost. She saw the road widened and laid with tarmac. A parking space cleared in the wild vegetation for coaches. Trendy cafes and overpriced shops selling lace and souvenirs. She shared her thoughts with Sandra, who nodded and said, "It is progress, sad for the tourists who won't see it as it was today but the islanders will see it as a good way to make money and will only realise what they have lost when it is too late. Look down there at the coastline and imagine the line of hotels and villas that will be there. The only saving grace is that the island is prone to earthquakes so they can't be too high!"

"Earthquakes?" cried Meg, now understanding the building structures in Lefkas.

Sandra smiled, "Don't worry they're usually just tremors; the last big one was in 1948."

At the junction of tracks, they went straight across to drive into Lefkas and get some lunch at a café in the main square. Remarkably few people were at any of the bars and cafes that edged the main square.

"It's only ever really busy at the weekend apparently, when Greeks come over from the mainland. They come to buy the olive oil and honey produced here. The thyme honey is a speciality," said Sandra.

They chose a table at random and ordered Greek salads with plump olives and rich, tangy feta cheese. They followed the food with coffee, and Sandra said that she had better phone Spiro before he had another blue fit. She went into the taverna to use the phone and Meg leaned forward to take a sip of her coffee as a cloud passed over the sun sending a dark shadow across the table. Before she had touched it, the cup rattled and the spoon fell off the saucer. She then felt the strangest sensation as if she had been moved without moving, experienced a complete loss of balance and then nothing. She felt her chair to see if it was wobbly and looked around. Everyone else was doing the same. Café owners came out into the square looked around and then laughed and shouted, "Seismo!" to each other before carrying on as normal. It was so fleeting and almost imperceptible that Meg wasn't sure whether she had imagined it. Sandra came rushing out.

"Wow! Did you feel it?"

"Do you mean did the earth move for me?" laughed Meg, but she had that familiar feeling of vulnerability that you can't quite put your finger on, and inexplicable excitement. It felt like there should have been more, something stronger, but it was just the earth flexing its muscles, a subtle reminder of its power.

"I can't believe it. You were just telling me about earthquakes!" exclaimed Meg.

Sandra didn't seem to share Meg's excitement and was quiet and irritable on the way back to Nikiana. Spiro was driving her mad with his demands and his ever-changing mood swings. She didn't go into too many details but Meg knew she was seething. The sky was strangely cloudy and the wind was picking up when they arrived back at Michael's bar in Nikiana.

Nearly everyone was in the bar talking fervently about the tremor. It had been stronger there and

Tim began telling them how they were having lunch inside because it had turned cloudy when the whole building began to shake. A few glasses had fallen off the shelves and it had lasted for much longer than a couple of seconds. Everyone was buzzing with excitement and stories about where they were when it happened. Denis started telling everyone that he had been in the toilet when the whole room had started to shake and he had to hold onto the basin to get his balance. Then he thought he heard a strange whirring, mechanical sound along with some weird music. Everyone was listening, enthralled until he burst into the theme tune to Doctor Who. Everyone groaned and laughed. Suddenly, they were interrupted by loud horns and the sound of music outside. They all went out to have a look. Coming down the street was a column of cars and pick-up trucks. They were all blaring their horns, heads stuck out of car windows shouting, and on one truck, there was a band playing violins, tambourines and ouds. On the back of another was the bride they had seen earlier with her new husband waving and smiling at all the villagers who were lining the road waving and shouting as they went past. Everyone waved back and the children ran up the road following them and picking up flowers that had been thrown to them. When they had disappeared up the hill, Meg and the others returned to the bar chattering and laughing. The atmosphere of excitement in the place was tangible and an impromptu party began – celebration of the wedding, or the only thing to do after surviving a natural disaster. Michael, as usual, was unmoved by the sudden surge in afternoon business. He turned up the cassette player and everyone laughed when an unmistakable track by Shakin' Stevens came on. Everyone danced to Wham! singing 'Freedom' and ubiquitous Madonna tracks, with Denis getting up on a table to dance to 'Like A Virgin' to everyone's great amusement. Meg joined in with the dancing for a while until she was too hot and sticky. Laughing, she went outside to sit with Sandra and Tim on the balcony. At about eight, Callista tapped Meg on the shoulder and beckoned her to go with her. There was someone on the phone for her. An English man. Her heart missed a beat.

It was Pete.

"Hi, how are you?"

Meg was still buzzing from the excitement and the party atmosphere.

"Hi. Yeh, I'm great. How are you? Where are you?"

"I'm at home. I go back to Saudi in a few days, unfortunately."

"Oh right. We've had an earthquake here!"

"God. Are you all right?"

"Yes, yes it was only a tremor really."

"Not like being with me then?"

They both laughed. Meg was hyper from the whole day's activities and from a few glasses of wine. She told Pete about the wedding in the village and then the tremor and excitedly explained that everyone was now celebrating their survival.

"Right" said Pete quietly. "Having a good time then?"

"Well, it's been a bit of a nightmare, actually."

She realised how weak that sounded and couldn't explain everything clearly to him. There was an awkward silence.

"I'd better go; I'm on Dad's phone. Write to me and give me your address. Miss you."

"I miss you too. Take care. I'll write."

"Okay, bye, take care. Watch that retsina and ouzo, remember what it does to you!"

They both laughed but it was strained with the memory of their time in Greece the year before. She didn't want him to go, so she asked him what he'd been doing and they fell into easy conversation about the things he'd done and the people that he'd seen and they reconnected as they always did when they weren't talking about 'them'. They discussed the Band Aid concert, the threat of AIDS and the chances of England winning the Ashes before finally saying their goodbyes and I love yous.

Meg came off the phone elated. He did care and he did miss her but as she went back to the bar and went through the motions of drinking and talking, she played back the conversation and realised that she'd given him the wrong impression again. She resolved to write telling him exactly what she had been thinking and feeling.

The next morning Meg woke to the alarm feeling like she needed a lot more sleep, but filled with anticipation. She was looking forward to the boat trip. Everyone else seemed to be too and they were all waiting for the coach when it arrived with David looking suave in a blue and white striped t-shirt and white shorts. To complete the picture he was wearing a sailor's cap with an anchor on the front. They all climbed aboard the bus chatting and happy as they set off for Nidri quay. The driver pulled up next to the quay and David got off and spoke to an old man with jeans falling down under his rotund belly. Meg could see David getting agitated with the man who was shrugging, scratching his belly with stubby, grubby fingers and vaguely pulling up his trousers. Meg decided to go down the bus collecting money for the trip but David called to her from the door and she stepped off to speak to him.

He was sweating and jumpy.

"The boat we booked has already gone. We have to wait half an hour for another one, possibly."

Meg said she would take everyone to the nearest café and let him sort out a boat as soon as possible. Grumbling, everyone got off the coach and went over to sit at tables and wait. There was nothing Meg could do, but stay with them. Time went on. Nobody wanted to order another drink and there was no sign of David. The children were persistently asking when they were going and everyone was feeling hot and frustrated. At last, Meg saw David running towards them waving.

He did not look so suave now as he wiped his dripping head and called impatiently for her to bring everybody. They followed him down the quayside to an old, wooden, fishing boat. It had a large open deck at one end and a small covered area where the driver stood. There was no proper seating and if you needed the toilet, you were to sit at the back of the boat and aim over board.

Meg acted as if this was expected and smiling at everyone, ushered each one on board. They all managed to fit on and find themselves spots to settle around the deck. The captain, a small, wizened old sea dog with a cigarette hanging out of a toothless mouth, got on without acknowledging anyone and the engine roared, faltered, and then chugged into life. The breeze created by the movement of the boat cooled and calmed everyone slightly, and they made their way slowly out into the sea, past the headland with the tiny island of Madouri on their left.

Meg stood near Charlotte. James and Mark were leaning over the rail talking to each other and Meg was pleased that the two young lads had finally connected as they were of similar ages and both quite shy. Elizabeth was sitting quietly, looking a little bored and obviously wishing that she could have stayed in Nikiana with the chance of seeing Gregor. Charlotte had obviously read up on everything as she showed Meg her map of Lefkas and the surrounding islands. Meg listened enthralled as she explained that they would soon be passing Skorpios, the island belonging to the Onassis family and that there was a beach which could be used when nobody was staying in the house. Sure enough, they went quite close to the flat, green and lush land with a small beach. A couple of small motorboats were floating off the beach and you could make out a small group sunbathing on the sand. They caught a glimpse of the house built into the island and almost invisible from offshore.

Their boat went south past Skorpios and the outline of a much larger land mass lay in front of them. The map showed a huge tadpole floating on the side of Lefkas with a long tail drifting down towards the southeast. This was Meganisi. They made their way down a broad channel with the tree-clad cliffs of Lefkas on their right and the rising dark green of cypress and pine on Meganisi. It was spectacular. The water was clear turquoise and the sky clear azure. Images of Odysseus and other Greek heroes and heroines came to mind. The sun was not too high in the sky and the wind created by the movement of the boat sent a glorious, refreshing sense of freedom through the intrepid travellers.

The boat continued along the coast of Meganisi as the bulk of the island ended in a long peninsula. At the start of the peninsula, they headed inland towards sheer cliffs. There was no beach and no landing place but as they neared, they could see that at the base of the rocks were caves. They dropped anchor in front of a large opening in the rock known as Papanikolis cave. From the boat to the cave was about twenty metres. The water was deep but completely clear, slipping and sliding up against the rocks in ribbons of aquamarine and sapphire. It sucked and slurped at the entrance to the cave and the opportunity to jump in and explore was irresistible. Meg joined those that were tempted.

The water was tremendous, a blast of cold shooting through the body and taking the breath away, completely absorbing the heat from the body. Apart from the water skiing experience, which her inner thighs were still suffering from in hues of purple and blue, Meg had not been for a swim. She had grown up near the sea and she always felt happier near it or preferably in it. Her body seemed to balance out, the weightlessness felt more natural than walking or standing. Cares dissolved as she dived down under the surface to experience the muffled sounds of under water, the eerie peace before breaking for air into chatter and noise. Balancing on a rock and looking down you could see every grain of sand on the bottom as though you were looking through clear but misshapen glass. Inside the vast chamber, said to be the second largest sea cave in Greece, stalactites stabbed down from the roof as the water swelled inwards and outwards echoic and cool.

They were not allowed to stay long as David called them back. Apparently, the boat driver wanted to move on.

They all clambered back on board dripping and laughing. Charlotte told Meg that there was a story that German U-boats had hidden in the cave during the Second World War and Meg expressed due wonder at the story. She went to her bag and wrapped a towel around herself, feeling exhilarated. She looked back towards the fabulous cave and suddenly realised that the boat had turned and was heading west towards Lefkas rather than continuing southeast along the peninsula. They were meant to be going around Meganisi and stopping for lunch in Vathi on the other side.

Meg wasn't the only one who noticed. People started coming up and asking where they were going. Meg went over to David and asked him. He shrugged and said,

"To a restaurant in a harbour on Lefkas."

"But why? The trip is meant to be round Meganisi."

"Because that's where the boat owner is going and it his boat."

"Why didn't you tell everyone?"

He shrugged.

Meg was furious. She could not be heard above the engine if she tried telling everyone, so she made her way around the boat telling each group. She made up a story that the weather conditions were not too good going round the peninsula, although she suspected that the boat owner was probably a relative of the owner of the restaurant they were going to. She received tuts and shrugs even though half of them didn't really have a clue where they were meant to be going.

Then she came to Charlotte, smiled and began to explain. She was bowled over by the reaction. Charlotte went mad. All mild manners had been pushed to their limit. She came out with a barrage of complaints about everything that had upset her since her arrival. Meg was useless, the whole show was a joke and Meg fully expected her to announce that she would be writing to her MP about it. Meg said nothing. She stood there waiting until she had finished and then said quietly,

"I'm really sorry."

She didn't know what else to say and walked away wanting to burst into tears. She really liked Charlotte, and didn't want her to be so upset. She looked at David who was standing next to the captain ignoring everybody. She wanted to slap his smug face.

The coast of Lefkas loomed up ahead. In front of them, the rising slopes of cypress and pine gave way to a small bay. A pebble beach lay between two headlands with a taverna at one end. It was very pretty and the beach was deserted. As they, neared Meg recognised it as the one she had come to on her first night. How long ago was that? Five days.

The boat moored close to the beach and waiters emerged from the taverna. They brought out a long gangplank and set it up resting on the boat for everyone to walk down. They all made their ways unsteadily down the plank of wood and made their way over to the restaurant, which lay prepared for a large group with long tables and chairs. Despite the extensive looking menu, it soon became apparent that they only had swordfish, calamari and even though they had chips - word had gone round quickly - people were frustrated. The service was incredibly slow and people already annoyed by the state of the boat and the change in route were grumbling and complaining to Meg. She ran back and forth to the kitchen to see what was happening, and then trying to sort out wrong or forgotten orders with waiters and chefs who could not be rushed.

Once everyone had finally been fed and watered, still muttering and grumbling, they began to wander off along the beach to swim or explore. Some complained to Meg that the beach was covered in pebbles, so she even showed them how to move the pebbles to make themselves comfortable. Gradually, people started to relax. Then the boat owner started to shout for them all to get back on board the boat. Meg went to David but he said he couldn't do anything. Disgruntled, they all gathered up their towels and belongings and clambered back on board. The journey back was subdued. The sun was hot and there was no shade. The breeze from their movement brought only slight relief and the young ones began to complain. The captain stared straight ahead with a cigarette permanently drooping out of the corner of his mouth; his tanned weather beaten face bore no expression. David stood trying to look cool and avoided catching anyone's eye.

As they made their way back up the channel, everyone struggled with the blazing sun beating down on them with nowhere to hide. Meg looked at the idyllic surroundings, which had enchanted everyone on the outgoing journey, but were now of no interest, and thought how sad it was. No images of Greek heroes came to her apart from the story Charlotte had told her of one Greek maiden, the poet Sappho, who had apparently thrown herself off the cliffs of Lefkas in despair over her love for Phaon. The idea at that particular moment was tempting.

On the coach back to Nikiana, Denis began to make jokes about the day and everyone began to make fun of the 'disastrous' trip and lightened up. Meg felt disappointed and exhausted.

It was mid afternoon when they returned, the all-day boat trip had been no more than a couple of hours, so most people went down to the beach. The young couple, Mike and Elaine went to their room for a late 'siesta' and Meg decided to take the opportunity to write some letters and postcards. She phoned Sandra to tell her what had happened and arranged to meet her in the morning.

She wrote a few quick postcards to her Mum and to her Dad saying everything was fine and humorous letters to friends before trying to concentrate on writing to Pete.

Her third attempt lay crumpled on the floor. It was difficult to concentrate with the siesta couple not exactly sleeping. She had been in her room so little she had never realised exactly how thin the walls were. Writing a loving, open letter was tricky with the sounds of lovemaking practically in the room with her.

She took her pen and paper over to the bar and getting a beer from Michael she sat on the balcony in the shade offered by the trees. After writing down all that had happened with the radio station and why she had taken the job in Greece and what had happened since she got there she screwed up version number four and wrote,

'Love you and really miss you. Where are we now?'

She sealed it, addressed it and went down to the little shop to post it before she could change her mind.

On her way back, Tim called out to her. He caught up with her outside her room and thanked her for organising the trip. She grimaced.

"No, it was excellent. We're all burnt to shreds but if we hadn't known about the changes, none of us would have had reason to be upset. The boat owner was a bit of a dictator but it all goes to make up some great stories when we get back," he smiled. "Don't worry about Charlotte, we all know it wasn't your fault. I think she's just had a tough time of it."

Meg gave a small smile in return.

"Right, a few of us are all going to the taverna we went to on the first night tonight and then tomorrow is our last night so Denis has had the great idea of organising a barbeque for everyone. Perhaps you can advise."

"All right, sounds good."

Of course, Meg had lost track of time. Some were staying for two weeks but most were only there for the week.

# CHAPTER 12

At the taverna that evening, everyone was lighthearted, relaxed and full of banter. The two couples Denis and Sarah, John and Deidre and Tim had become good friends and were planning to meet up in the U.K.

John and Deidre were staying for another week with their son, Mark. Charlotte was there with Elizabeth and James who were also leaving. Gregor wasn't working when they got there and Meg could see Elizabeth constantly looking for him. Charlotte was aware of this too and kept trying to divert her attention. She wouldn't look at Meg. Tim sat next to Meg and was sweet and attentive to her. Meg began to feel uncomfortable with it. She wasn't sure if the others presumed they had something going on and since the phone call Meg's heart was definitely still with Pete. Tim was lovely and obviously liked her and although she really liked him, she did not want a relationship with him.

They all drank plenty of wine and were laughing and joking loudly by the end of the meal. They settled the bill and got up to leave and go to one of the small bars on the way back. Meg went to see Kostos to say thank you and tell him that new people were coming in two days time and could she do the same as last week. He was over the moon, held her wrist with both his big, brawny hands, and shook it up and down.

"Chips," he laughed. "We do chips with all."

When she asked about Gregor, he winked and said,

"Night off. He see Greek girl friend tonight."

Meg was a bit surprised by that information and felt a bit sorry for Elizabeth. As she turned the corner of the Taverna to follow the others, she nearly bumped into Charlotte who was waiting for her.

"Oh, sorry!" exclaimed Meg.

"No, no. I'm sorry," started Charlotte. "Listen, I just wanted to apologise for what I said on the boat. I know it's not your fault, but I was so looking forward to Meganisi and it was just the last straw. Nothing has been as I expected or was told and I have been so worried that the children wouldn't enjoy themselves."

"I am so sorry," said Meg. There really is nothing I can do about anything, except try and point out that it is a beautiful island, the weather is fantastic and Elizabeth and James seem to be having a great time."

"Yes, I know. They are. It's me. It's been so hard since their Dad passed away. Anyway, I wanted to say that I was out of order the way I spoke to you."

"Thank you," said Meg, "that means a lot to me, but I'm so sorry about your husband; that is really sad. It must be so hard for you on your own."

"It's been two years now, but this is the first holiday we've had without him. I really miss him; we used to have such fun times together with the four of us. I'm afraid I'm a bit overprotective of the children."

"You are doing a great job from what I can see. They are really lovely and it must be a hard time for them as well. I am really sorry that the holiday's been a disappointment for you."

"No, it's not your fault and you are right. The island is stunning and the local people are so interesting and friendly. And everyone's been so kind to us." She paused, "Meganisi is where Stan proposed to me. I really wanted to share the memory with the children." Her eyes brimmed with tears. "It's just been a bit cramped with the three of us staying in such a tiny room with hardly any water to wash in. It wasn't how it was described."

Meg was also on the verge of tears when suddenly Charlotte laughed. It was the first time Meg had heard her laugh all week and it was delightful. Meg looked at her, quizzically smiling.

"I just realised I was complaining again! Silly really. I should have known better than to try and recreate the past." Charlotte said.

Meg smiled and admitted that unfortunately she agreed with everything that Charlotte was complaining about. They both walked down the street together, to catch up with the others, and Meg felt pleased. Her natural reaction when Charlotte had started shouting at her on the boat had been to stick up for herself but she had been so surprised that she had said nothing; now she realised that it had paid off. She felt quite proud of herself. They found everyone at a very basic looking bar where the owner and his friends had decided to play ouds and sing to them. Meg sat down in the seat Tim had saved for her and Charlotte sat with Elizabeth and James.

The girls were up dancing with the old Greek guys and ouzo was passed round the table as everyone learned to say 'yamaas!' before knocking it back.

Tim walked with Meg back along the road as the girls danced along in front of them and Denis and John tried unsuccessfully to sing one of the songs they had heard.

"Meg, I don't know how you feel, but I really like you and feel so comfortable with you."

Meg's heart sank.

"You don't have to say anything, but if it's all right with you can I keep in touch?"

"Yes, of course you can keep in touch. I really like you Tim, but probably not in the way you mean. I'm already in a relationship. When you get home this will all seem like a dream. You'll get back to reality and will laugh at all this."

"Well I don't think so, but I can write to you anyway?"

"Yes, I'd like that. I love getting letters!" she laughed and squeezed his arm. What else could she do?

She was in the office the next morning as usual and made a shopping list. She had offered to get all the things for the barbeque that evening as she felt she should.

Sandra arrived and Meg asked if they could go into Lefkas. Sandra agreed but she was very uptight about something. They ordered coffee and Sandra told her about the nonsense going on in the other resorts. They had found the missing rep who had apparently shacked up with a waiter from one of the tavernas, but this had turned sour. Spiro had refused to pay her any money or let her fly home so she had been screaming and crying. Sandra had persuaded Spiro to give her some money and they had put her on a bus to the mainland and from there she had to make her own way.

In addition, they had been organising the next group of people, who were arriving the following day, but they had over booked and there was not enough accommodation for all the people who were definitely on the flight.

Sandra told Meg that she was not to go to the airport but to wait in the bar for her guests to arrive. Meg wouldn't get the list of people and where they were going to stay until they arrived. Sandra was not the cool person that Meg had first met. She was nervy and upset. She indicated her hands and Meg could see dry, red peeling skin.

"Eczema," explained Sandra. "I'm prone to it when I get worried or upset. I just had to leave Spiro to it. By the way, more reps have been employed so you will be getting an assistant in Nikiana."

Meg checked what the plans were for the coach to the airport the following morning and made a couple of notices. She checked her own lists to make sure she knew who were leaving and who were staying. Sandra said she intended to spend the day in Nikiana so they sat on the verandah and spoke to all the guests who came by on their way to the beach and talked to each other about their lives. In spite of the age difference, they got on well. Sandra opened up about her life and revealed that she had just got divorced after over twenty years of marriage. It had been painful but inevitable after drifting apart when the children left home. Meg had been hoping for wise words of wisdom regarding Pete, but Sandra said that the older she got, the less she knew.

"Follow your heart and see where it takes you."

Meg thought she had, but it had taken her nowhere. Suddenly she realised that her heart was following two different objectives. She really wanted her career and she really wanted to be with Pete and the two did not seem to be compatible. Neither was working.

They checked their shopping list with Denis and decided to go at about four after siesta time. Tim joined them for most of the day while the girls played on the beach in front of them. He was easy going and humorous and Sandra obviously liked him a lot. Meg did too, and through the day she kept almost trying to persuade herself to fancy him, it would be so much easier, but it wasn't something you could pretend to feel.

As the sun was going down, they all went round to the back of the chalets and mega chef Denis built a barbeque with bricks and managed to cook burnt sausages and half cooked chicken drumsticks, in true English style.

Meg and Sandra had also made salads using large fresh tomatoes, rich olive oil and onions full of flavour. Everyone staying at the chalet joined them. Denis tried his best to be lively but the air was subdued. It had taken a week to relax into the Greek way of life and now most of them were heading back to England, rain, work and bills. The good summer weather couldn't last much longer. Only the children were blissfully making the most of their time, unconscious of their imminent return to early nights and disciplined routine. About half way through the evening, Elizabeth, who had barely spoken and not touched her food, burst into tears and ran to her chalet. As Charlotte followed, everyone looked at each other with raised eyebrows, apart from her brother, who tutted and continued eating heartily. Charlotte returned embarrassed and flustered without Elizabeth and Tim gave her a glass of wine and put his arm round her shoulders.

"She thinks she's in love with that waiter," Charlotte sighed, taking a large gulp of wine. "And she didn't get the chance to say goodbye."

"We've got it all to come. I suppose," Tim said, looking at his two little girls screeching and giggling as they threw water at Mark and James who then chased them around the outside shower.

"Well that's something I am looking forward to," announced Denis changing the subject.

They all looked at him.

"A lovely hot shower in my own bathroom."

They all laughed, including Charlotte and shook themselves out of their morose frame of mind. They played some games, which got sillier the more they drank and despite plans for an early night, it was two in the morning before they gave in. They all said goodnight and made their ways to bed. Sandra was staying in Meg's room and just as they were about to turn off the light they heard a knock at the door. Meg opened it and peeped out into the darkness. It was Tim holding half a bottle of wine.

"Just wondered if you would like a night cap."

Meg told Sandra, who encouraged her to go. Reluctantly she pulled a sweatshirt on over the T-shirt she slept in and went out. She desperately wanted to sleep. They sat on the bench in front of her room and spoke in whispers. Tim, she soon realised, was quite drunk.

"I really like you Meg. It's not a holiday crush like Elizabeth with Gregor. I'm too old for that. I really want to keep in touch with you and when you come back to England we can meet up and you can follow your dream of working on radio or television and I'll help you."

Oh God! It was all she had wanted Pete to say to her. What could she do? She couldn't force herself to feel differently about Tim. Why didn't she feel anything for him? He was good looking, kind and thoughtful with a great sense of humour. She had to let him down gently.

"Tim, I really like you. I'm just so confused at the moment. I don't know what I want or where I want to be, or who I want to be with. I've known you for one week and what a week it has been for me. Look, let's keep in touch and see what happens."

"Oh Meg."

It was as if she had agreed to marry him. He hugged her and leant his mouth towards her face. She couldn't stop her reaction, as the overwhelming fumes of wine struck her, she jerked away. He carried on moving forward, slipped off the bench and fell on to the ground at her feet. She also couldn't stop herself from laughing as she asked him if he was all right.

"No physical damage," he replied seriously and then laughed as well. She helped him up still laughing and gave him a hug.

"See you tomorrow."

# CHAPTER 13

The next morning all was pandemonium as the coach arrived late from Nidri. David was flapping and waving his arms around trying to get people to hurry onto the bus.

Everyone shook hands with Meg and thanked her. Tim gave her a longing look and a hug before promising to write and climbing onto the bus. As Elizabeth passed her with eyes red rimmed from crying herself to sleep, Meg stopped her and whispered, "Gregor told me that you are the most beautiful English girl he has ever met and he won't ever forget you." Elizabeth looked into Meg's clear blue eyes as her own brimmed with tears again. "Tell him I won't forget him either". She wiped her eyes and smiled as she got onto the bus. Sandra got on last saying she would see her later, and Meg returned to the bar to wait. Sandra had had the photos developed, so Meg arranged them on a notice board with general information about the island and bus times. She also put up a notice inviting people to join her at the taverna for a meal that evening and asked them to put their names down.

John and Deidre came in with Mark for breakfast, so she chatted to them for a while. They wanted to know who was coming, but of course, Meg had no idea. Unfortunately, she had to tell them that they wouldn't be able to keep the spare room, but they were relaxed enough to just shrug. They were going to be lost without the others for company and were more concerned that they would meet more people. She asked Mark about his school, and what he liked doing when he was at home. He was a polite good-natured boy, not like many teenagers of his age and chatted easily and openly.

Meg found herself getting nervous about the new onslaught of disgruntled visitors that she would have to deal with when they saw their accommodation. Michael was busy getting welcome drinks ready in his slow methodical way, so she went outside to see how Callista was getting on with preparing the chalets across the road. She was coming back across the road, everything finished and ready. She grinned at Meg and offered her a cigarette, which Meg refused. She looked very cheerful.

"Why are you so happy?" asked Meg laughing.

"My son come this week."

"I thought Michael was your son."

"Yes, yes but this number one son. He big business man. Very clever, handsome man. You see him," she said and raised the tips of her fingers and thumb to her lips and blew a kiss.

Poor Michael, no wonder he was so hunched and cynical. At that moment the phone in the apartment rang and Callista went in to answer it and spoke for a while in rapid, high-pitched Greek and then went into the back of the apartment and returned with piles of sheets, which she took up the steps to the top floor above the bar. Meg followed her up. Inside was a small living room with a kitchenette. Three doors led to a bedroom with en-suite shower, a bathroom and another bedroom. It was clean and neat with ceiling fans. Luxury.

"People stay here," said Callista.

"Why not before?" asked Meg

Callista smiled, "More money. Spiro not like to pay."

Meg laughed. She had thought Callista was just the cleaning woman but she owned all the apartments over the road and the whole of this building.

They heard the heavy wheels and the squealing moan and hiss of gears slowing as the coach arrived outside and Meg hurried down the steps. Sandra was the first to get off, followed by an olive skinned girl with very dark, big hair. She appeared to be about eighteen or nineteen with lots of make up and wearing a short skirt, a skimpy T-shirt and high heeled wedged sandals. Great thighs were on display to the world and a roll of fat around her midriff escaped over the top of her skirt. Sandra introduced her with a straight face as Meg's new assistant in Nikiana, Lindy. Meg shook the plump outstretched hand and said hello.

"All right? Nice to meet yer," Lindy replied in a strong London accent.

There wasn't time for any more. Meg guided everyone through to the bar and Sandra gave her the list of people and where they were staying, before getting back on the coach and wishing her luck.

"Spiro is on his way," she called as the coach door swished shut.

Meg looked around at the people in the room, preparing to put faces to names and try to remember them all as quickly as possible. There was the usual mixture of shapes, sizes and ages and wondered what personalities she would have to deal with this week. There were only two young children; two girls aged about six or seven.

She introduced herself and indicated the notice board now decorated with photographs, and asked them to sign the lists for dinner that night and boat trips. She also told them that she would be available all afternoon that day but otherwise between eight and ten in the morning or from five to six in the evening to deal with any problems or answer any questions. An executive decision she had made so at least she wouldn't feel guilty every time she wasn't in the 'office'.

Looking down the list, she saw that there were a Dr. Shelley and a Mr. Withers in a group of four. At least having a doctor around might save her from pretending to be some kind of nurse. She called their names out first and the two other names, Alice and Celia Johnson, which belonged to the two little girls. They were bright and lively and jumped up in front of Meg. Dr. Diane Shelley turned out to be their mother, a woman in her forties with short-cropped brown hair and large brown eyes. She had a large, beaky nose and thin drawn lips. Her body was thick and stocky and she shook Meg's hand firmly while looking her up and down disapprovingly. Her partner, Ben Withers strolled across the room from the bar still holding his drink. He was tall and portly. His hair was too long to be short and too short to be making a fashion statement. He had a ruddy complexion and a once good-looking face spoilt now by a puffy double chin. He looked bored but he introduced himself politely in a very well spoken voice to Meg and holding her hand, told her that he was pleased to make her acquaintance. They were staying in the rooms upstairs. There were two more names for that apartment and she hoped it wouldn't be a problem having to share the same entrance.

Simon and Louise made a handsome couple. Both were tall and slim in their early thirties. They came forward and said hello in a friendly easy fashion. She took them all up to the apartment and gave the en suite room to Louise and Simon. At least they couldn't complain about the condition of the room or the fantastic view they had over the beach and sea.

"Is the bar very lively at night?" asked Dr. Shelley.

"No, not usually. It's a quiet resort. You'll have to go up to Nidri if you want discos, music and dancing." replied Meg with a serious face.

Meg saw Ben hide a smirk but Dr. Diane didn't appreciate the humour. Meg changed the subject, and showed them their room and bathroom and made a quick exit reminding them of dinner that night.

The remaining guests were all staying across the road so that was easy. Thank God, the beach villa wasn't being used.
Lindy was sitting at a table on the verandah painting her toenails when Meg joined her and asked her if she wanted a drink.

"Yeh – great! I'll have a coke."

Meg got them both a drink from a now winking Michael. She raised her eyebrows at him. Lindy was very chatty. She was actually only sixteen and the niece of the lovely Athena in North London. She'd just finished school and her Mum reckoned a bit of work experience would be good for her so they'd packed her off to Lefkas.

"Should be a laugh," she said seriously.

Spiro arrived with a big hug for Lindy and greetings in Greek; he lit a cigar and sat down.

"Everything okay here?"

"Yes seems to be. I've just taken everyone to their rooms so they'll be back in about ten minutes with their complaints," said Meg.

Spiro shrugged and grunted, "Right. I take Lindy to her room in the beach villa and then you can explain everything to her."

"Um, Spiro?" Meg plunged ahead. "A few people have asked about mopeds and jeeps. Is there any way we can organise renting them from here to save people going up to Nidri for them?"

Spiro plugged his cigar a couple of times. Blew out a thick cloud of smoke and then said, "Yes. I think this may be a good idea. You find out how many. I know one man, Mike."

"And what about a boat trip this week. Can I organise one? It was a disaster last week."

"Yes, yes, good."

"And can I have a jeep so I can get around easily and check on things?" She'd gone too far.

"Why you need jeep? No, maybe you can have moped for one day."

Better than nothing. Spiro looked at his watch.

"Let's go Lindy."

Meg knew he was trying to avoid meeting any angry punters. As he reached the door, he looked at her notice board and said, "And this week, on the last night we organise barbeque for everybody."

"Great!" replied Meg stunned.

Meg was putting up a notice about jeeps and mopeds when an older couple that she had placed in the chalets came in. They were dressed in long shorts, T-shirts and hiking boots and wished to speak to her. She took them to her table on the verandah and listened as Rod told her that the room was not as the brochure had described and that there had been no hot water. Sylvia his wife sat primly nodding as he spoke.

"We won't be coming to dinner this evening as we prefer to do our own thing. We would really like to be moved to better accommodation, but I don't suppose that's possible."

Meg agreed it wasn't possible and said she was sorry about the water problem.

"We specifically stated that we were walkers and were told that there would be information regarding the many routes around the island. Do you have anything?"

Humbly Meg admitted that she had only started the week before and that no, she didn't have any walking maps but she would try to get some.

"No, we may as well do that ourselves. Thank you. Don't worry, we will be writing and formally complaining on our return." They got up to leave and then added, "And another thing, "It is far hotter than we were led to believe."

They left leaving Meg dumbfounded and she never saw them again until the last day.

Louise and Simon came in next but they just smiled and said hello as they put their names on the lists. They bought a bottle of water from Michael and headed onto the beach. Next, Dr. Diane arrived with the two girls. She sent them on to the beach telling them not to swim without her and to find them a good spot. Then she marched over to Meg and with a swift thin smile sat down. She had no complaints as yet, she informed her and she was considering the dinner and the boat trip but she wanted more information.

Meg told her as much as she could and said that she was thinking of arranging a night boat trip to Meganisi with dinner on the island. She had seen one advertised and it sounded excellent. It also returned at 10pm, which meant it was fine for the last bus back from Nidri.

Dr. Diane then started asking Meg personal questions about how old she was, where she came from and how much experience she had as a rep. Meg answered her openly and honestly but she wasn't impressed by the interrogative manner. Eventually, she looked down at the sea and with a sniff she thanked Meg, picked up her bag, and strutted off to the beach. The girls were playing with Louise and Simon. Meg observed the way they were competing for attention. As their mother arrived on the beach, they stopped and looked at her nervously. They ran up to her and helped her put out her towel. Diane removed her sundress to reveal a full black costume. She neatly folded the dress and put it next to her bag, took out a book and settled herself on her towel. The girls stood silently digging the sand with their toes; their heads hung down until Diane locked up, and with a dismissive wave of her hand told them to go away. They immediately ran back to Simon and Louise.

Diedre, John and Mark came through and asked if they could come for the dinner. Meg laughed and said that of course they could,

"You can help me by telling people the good things about the island."

They went on to the beach and Meg watched as they stopped to speak to Louise and Simon and then settled down next to them. Mark, along with Simon and Louise took the little girls into the sea to play catch with a colourful beach ball. Diane relaxed with a book ignoring everyone.

One of the other couples, Grant and Erica arrived. Grant was tall and wiry with shoulder length brown hair, while Erica was tall and curvy with short, spiky black hair. They both had kind, easygoing natures and Meg immediately liked them. They told her about the water problem, but were laughing about the fact that they had used the shower outside. They said they would come for dinner and were just off for a wander.

The next one to arrive was the guy on his own – Clive. He came and sat with Meg and asked her if she would like a drink. Caught by surprise Meg said that she would. He was a small, thin, gawky man with thin blonde hair and a big moon-shaped face too big for his body. He returned with two beers and proceeded to explain why he was on his own and to tell her his life story.

Meg sat and listened as he told her that he had got married the week before but his wife had left him after the first day. He'd managed to get the deposit back from the honeymoon and so he had booked this holiday at the last minute to get away. He didn't seem to need Meg to say anything as he continued in a very boring voice to tell her that he was thirty-one (she had guessed forty-one) and he had waited until then to get married so that he didn't make the mistake of marrying too young. His wife had left him a note to say she was leaving, but gave no reason and he hadn't spoken to her since. He declared that he was a good man and had a good job and was well equipped to be a good husband. Meg listened and nodded sympathetically.

"And it makes me sick when you see people abusing their good fortune!"

Meg looked at him in surprise and asked, "What do you mean?"

He nodded down to the beach and Meg saw Dr. Diane, now lying on her front, pretending to read as her eyes kept looking up at the verandah watching Clive.

"Do you know them?" Meg asked, baffled.

"Yes. We met this morning; she's a lovely lady, we got talking on the plane when her partner eventually passed out. He's been drinking since before he got on the plane."

He spat out the word 'partner' with contempt.

"Oh," Meg said. It was all she could come up with in response. Clive had finished his counselling session. He stood up and announced he was going down to the beach.

"Just so you know what kind of a person he is," said Clive.
"Thank you," Meg replied.

Clive made his way down to the beach and put his towel down near to Diane. Meg laughed to herself as she saw Diane casually roll over and sit up, push her large breasts out and lean back on her elbows as he approached. She stared out to sea as if she hadn't seen him and turned quickly as if caught by surprise when he said hello and gave him a huge smile with her head on one side.

Later on, Meg set off to go up the road to let the restaurant know roughly how many would be coming that evening. She saw Ben coming down from the apartment looking like he'd just woken from a rough sleep. He was still in the clothes he had arrived wearing. He waved to her and said, "Think the sun's gone over the yardarm," as he headed for the bar. Meg noted that the sun had probably already gone over the yardarm when Ben had his last drink.

On her way back from the restaurant, she suddenly remembered Lindy and went via the beach villa to see where she was. She knocked on the door of the larger room loudly and Lindy's head appeared at the door to the smaller room. Her hair was flattened on one side and she looked sleepy.

"Hello," she said.

"Hello," replied Meg. "Everything all right? Why are you in this room? The other one's bigger."

"I don't know. Spiro put me in here. He told me to go and join you in the bar, but I fell asleep."

Meg moved towards the now open door. Inside she could see a suitcase open with clothes falling out at the edges, more clothes and other bits and pieces lay haphazardly across the floor and both beds. There was a used syringe lying on a pillow and unopened packets of syringes across the top of the suitcase. Meg couldn't help but stare at them in surprise.

"Oh, oh sorry," said Lindy, as she hurriedly threw the syringe into a plastic bag with other rubbish in it and collected up the unused ones and put them inside the case. "I'm diabetic."

"Oh right, right. Are you okay?"

"God. Yeh. Just have to be careful about what I eat and drink. I was gonna 'ave a shower but all the water came into the bedroom. Few things got wet so I just left 'em. In this weather they dry pretty quick."

Meg looked at the damp floor and realised that sure enough, the twenty pairs of shoes, assortment of underwear and tops spread over the floor were wet looking.

"Let's put the wettest things out on the veranda to dry and have a look at the shower," Meg suggested.

Together they moved a pile of damp or sodden items outside. Meg then turned on the shower and watched as the slope of the floor took some of the water down the uncovered hole in the middle and the rest swept on under the door and into the bedroom. She took a towel, and went in and closed the door. Then she put the rolled towel against the bottom of the door and stopped the flow. She turned the shower off and then realised that although it was the solution, she now had to sweep all the built up water down the hole and wring out the towel before she could get out again. She explained this to Lindy and both of them laughed.

"At least you get water for a shower! In the other places there's rarely any water."

She went over the plan for the evening, and told Lindy to get herself unpacked and sorted, and to meet her in the bar whenever she was ready. Lindy looked a bit confused when Meg said about unpacking. As far as she was concerned, she had unpacked.

# CHAPTER 14

At dinner that evening, Meg immediately liked
Simon and Louise, and the other young couple,
Erica and Grant. They were relaxed and easy-going
trying all the different dishes and partaking of the
local wine. The two daughters of Dr. Diane had
latched themselves onto Louise and Simon and
they were very kind and playful with them. Diane
was flirting with Clive by complaining in a posh
voice about the bread, and then the chips weren't
the way they did them in the fish and chip shop
back home, and there really was too much olive oil
with everything, and why did they insist on
putting olives with everything, and Alice sit still,
and Celia stop picking, between glares at Ben with
little huffs that received sympathetic smiles from
Clive. Ben ate and drank copious amounts without
paying much attention to anything else.

There was a family of four also there and they
seemed quiet and unassuming. They had not made
any complaints and sat together on Meg's right of
the long tables set out. The mother, Janet, was a
good-looking woman with long, straight, brown
hair, wearing a pair of tight, white trousers and a
sexy halter neck top. She was very quiet, while the
husband chatted away to John and Deidre on their
other side.

All was going fine. Meg was up and down checking on everybody. Lindy had managed to become friends with Gregor very quickly. She spoke Greek of course and so she was beyond help with Gregor's charms and no help to Meg during the meal.

As everyone was finishing she stood up to make a little speech about what there was to do next. She had already decided she wasn't taking them to the disco, so she explained how easy it was to get there and back and that there were other little bars and of course Michael's. As she sat back down, she jogged her untouched glass of red wine, which was unbalanced on the join of the tables. She tried to grab it but was too late. It fell and red wine leapt across the plastic tablecloth and onto Janet's trousers.

"Oh my God! I'm so sorry," Meg cried as she offered napkins and tried to mop up the still dripping table, "I'm so sorry. Are you okay?"

"No! I'm not bloody okay," Janet hissed. "Look at my trousers you stupid clumsy cow! Well you can bloody well pay for them to be cleaned. This is the last straw. Come on Kevin, boys."

"Hey, come on love," tried Kevin.

"Listen I am really sorry. Of course I'll get your trousers cleaned," Meg insisted.

"Oh don't bother. This whole bloody set up is a disaster."

She stood up from the table and stormed off. Kevin told John and Deidre that they were going back up the road so they too decided to leave without really knowing what had happened. Meg sat back down mortified. Janet hadn't shouted so much as spat, so as she looked to her left, Meg realised that only Erica and Grant had noticed the outburst. She wanted to cry. She felt clumsy and useless, but she kept smiling.

"Hey, that was a bit unnecessary," said Erica as Meg sat down.

"Yes. Are you okay?" Grant asked.

Meg gave a forced laugh and said she was fine.

"Where do you usually go now?" continued Erica.

Meg smiled and admitted there wasn't really a usually as she had only been there a week. Grant ordered another bottle of wine and they stayed there, while everyone else made their way off. Lindy came over to Meg and said she was tired and asked if it was all right if she went to bed.
Meg sat with Grant and Erica, and they chatted about where they came from and what they did and Meg told them a few of the things that had happened since she arrived.

When they had paid the bill and walked back up the road Erica said they were thinking of going to Nidri the following afternoon and asked Meg if she would like to go with them. Meg said that would be great, as she needed to go and book boat trips. As they passed the track to the beach villa, she saw a tall, slim silhouette disappearing into Lindy's room.

At Michael's, Grant and Erica went in for a nightcap, but Meg decided she needed a reasonable night's sleep. Pinned to her door was a small note, which told her Pete had phoned.

Her disappointment at missing his call was exaggerated by the outburst from Janet and too much wine, and she began to cry. She went to bed exhausted, thinking of Pete and wanting him. She thought back over all their time together.

# CHAPTER 15

*September 1980*

Music pulsed, coloured lights flashed and flickered turning sweaty bodies and faces eerie shades of blue, green, red and yellow as students danced or hovered around the edge of the dance floor in the smoky dining hall of the university hall of residence. The room was crowded with young men and women drinking, smoking, dancing self-consciously, each of them trying to find a place to fit. Meg entered the crowded, noisy hall with two girls from her corridor. Drawn together for security not necessarily for lasting friendship they made their way to the crowded bar and fought to get drinks before moving to the edge of the dance floor. Meg felt nervous and shy as she looked around. Numerous people came up trying to make conversation and she had just answered the mandatory questions, 'Where are you from?' What A levels did you do? 'What are you studying?' for the millionth time when she caught sight of a tall guy in jeans and a collarless grandpa shirt leaning casually against a wall watching the room. A jolt of electricity went through her; she liked the look of him and positioned herself to watch him. He ran his fingers through a thick mop of dark hair as he calmly surveyed the room with a relaxed attitude that contrasted with the almost frantic behaviour of other freshers desperate not to be lonely.

One of her companions suddenly pulled Meg onto the dance floor to get away from a very drunk young man asking the seemingly requisite questions followed by the offer of 'a shag' in a slurred voice as he slopped his beer on the floor and down his shirt. Meg began dancing and glanced over at the tall guy. A very pretty girl had joined him, and as she passed him a pint of beer, he put his arm around her and leant in to kiss her. 'Fast worker,' Meg thought and turned away, throwing herself into dancing to one of her favourite bands, The Jam playing 'Strange Town'.

Fresher Week was an onslaught of information, mixing, mingling, and sorting out the people you wanted to spend time with, what you wanted to join and what your timetable involved. A plethora of events including concerts, discos, barn dances and a large number of people wanting to sleep with as many people as possible. Some were virgins, sex starved and repressed in their previous life and others were taking full advantage of the over zealous determination of young men and women to lose the last bastion of innocence. It was a frenetic time of tears, vomit and glory.

Pete was one of those who threw himself into drinking excessively without recourse as often as possible and was quite obliging whenever a girl offered him her body. Meg was not interested in either the excessive drinking or the wanton sex. She had been in a long-term relationship up until a few months before which had come to an amicable end when they were both heading to different universities. She wasn't interested in playing the field, but she was interested in having fun. She gradually relaxed and became lively and sociable and made friends with a wide range of people from ranting political activists to dope smoking bohemians who had no plans other than to get stoned for three years, neither of which she subscribed to, but she loved getting to know different people.

She could be found dancing on tables in the Student Union bar, taking part in stage productions, playing squash for the university and occasionally reading in the library. Amongst the wide ranging social demographics was a small group of hard working, hard playing engineering students, one of whom was Pete.

After the initial attraction, Meg had decided he was not her type, but they saw each other on a daily basis for meals in the dining hall and would say hello when they passed each other in the corridor. They had got talking when he was in front of her in the queue for breakfast. He had put a kipper on his plate and she had asked him what it was. She had actually never seen a kipper before. She said observantly that it looked like fish but she couldn't imagine anyone eating fish for breakfast. He told her that it was sausage rolled flat in the shape of a fish and was really tasty. She frowned at him in doubt.

"You know scotch eggs look like eggs, but are made with sausage?"

"Yes, but they have got egg inside. What's this like? Has it got a minnow in the middle somewhere?"

He laughed and she put a portion on her plate to try it anyway.

He then waited for her so that he could sit with her and watch her eat. She was quite flummoxed when he pointed to an empty table and said, "Do you want to sit here?" She could not help the strong attraction to him, despite not wanting to pursue it. They sat down and when she tasted the kipper she screwed up her face in disgust and he burst out laughing. She looked at him in horror and then realising how gullible she'd been, she laughed with him.

They became friends, visiting each other's rooms for coffee and talking and talking, sometimes long into the night about anything and everything. At weekends when there were no meals provided and they were both at a loose end they would cook meals together. Or to be correct, he would cook lovely meals and she would help. She would mock him for chasing women and he explained that he planned to work hard and play hard and not get involved with anyone. She enjoyed his friendship and carried on doing her own thing with other friends, but deep down she knew that she was beginning to really like him. Beyond the drinking and playing around he was incredibly kind, funny and thoughtful.

Then one afternoon when he'd popped into her room for a ccffee, she mentioned that she was going down to London at the weekend with a guy she'd got to know on her course. After he left, something clicked in him that he was jealous. He went back to her room that night and asked her out. She was completely taken by surprise and elated.


Cue 'Perfect Day' by Lou Reed and shots of the happy couple eating lots, drinking lots, studying together, going on camping holidays around the country in his tiny car, too small for him but all he could afford; picnics in their rooms as they spent hours in bed; walking across fields and through woods near his Uncle's house in Devon; splashing in the sea; making love in the back of lecture theatres and other normal undergraduate behaviour.

Meg was lively and outgoing with loads of friends, Pete was sociable and fun-loving as well, but only had a few good drinking buddies that he would go out with and get wrecked. He loved her naivete and guilelessness. She was a bit ditzy, always losing her keys, falling off her bike in strange and hilarious circumstances, or burning toast, but she was bright, loving, independent and kind to everyone. Too kind sometimes, always wanting things to be fair and just, she was forever attracting waifs and strays and inviting them out to make them feel wanted and involved. He was practical and down to earth while she was sensitive, a romantic dreamer. While he balanced her out with practical and sensible advice, she taught him how to love. She had made him wait before she would sleep with him and it had been well worth waiting for. He told her that she was the loveliest person he had ever met. She loved the fact that he could cook, he made her laugh and she felt safe and protected when she was with him. Everyone knew them as a couple and by the end of their first year they were deeply in love. Meg was full of the love of life. She loved her course, she loved all the things she was able to do and most of all she loved Pete. She went home for the summer radiant.

Over the summer break Meg's world, as she knew it, disintegrated when her Dad left her Mum. Her Mum fell apart and everything Meg had taken for granted was swept away. They had been her rock; supportive, dependable, always there for her, and suddenly her Mum had disappeared into a shell of depression and her Dad was with another woman who was pregnant with his child.

She went back late for her second year, missing fresher's week, having stayed to be with her Mum for as long as possible, but eventually she had to leave. Her two brothers lived nearby; they would be there for Mum and keep Meg posted. She was full of worry and sorrow and at the same time desperate to be with Pete as she got on the train to go back. He met her at the station with a card saying he'd missed her and that night they went for a drink in the students' union with a crowd of friends. A girl walked in, obviously a fresher. Meg saw the look she gave Pete and Pete's reaction. She saw his friends shuffle with embarrassment and look into their pints.

When she asked him, he denied he knew her, but when she said that she would go and ask the girl, he admitted he had walked her home a couple of nights before, but nothing had happened. He loved Meg. Didn't she know that? She thought she knew he did, but a shard of glass dug in deep and already off balance from her parents' split, she felt insecure. They began to have arguments and silly fights. She had trusted him without ever a thought before, but now she was never sure.

She worried constantly about her Mum and felt guilty; she thought she should have known something was wrong, that she'd been too wrapped up in her own world to notice things were not right. She went home as often as possible to support her brothers and help deal with her Mum who was in the depths of depression, but refusing to get help. She felt angry with her father, angry and rejected and she projected that anger and fear onto her relationship with Pete. She began to be suspicious and jealous of everyone, convinced that he was going to leave her. So-called friends who were envious of their relationship saw the chink in the armour and began to stir up trouble. Odd comments here and there about what Pete was doing and where he had been. Male friends who took him out drinking and persuaded him to have one more and one more and one more so that he arrived late at Meg's and drunk or didn't turn up at all. Filled with suspicion and doubt she'd looked through his drawers one day and found a card and a letter from two different girls. There wasn't anything definite to say that he'd been unfaithful, but they'd obviously enjoyed his company at some point that she hadn't known about. One girl he'd met on a course and the other was a friend of his cousin, but Pete insisted that nothing had happened. Meg was lost and confused. She felt like she was going insane, wanting to believe him but not knowing if she really did. She finished with him, but it didn't last and missing each other badly, they got back together.

They continued for a while splitting up and then getting back together again in painful repetition as Pete tried not to lose her, but he still wanted to play the field and she fought with him to understand what love meant, having lost all sight of what it meant herself. She lost all her confidence and Pete tried his best to support her but he was looking for the old Meg that he had fallen in love with and she needed more from him than he knew how to give.

It wasn't working and Meg finished it again. This time Pete began going out with a new girl. Meg felt desperate pain and wandered around in a daze for a few days until she walked into a tree and the graze she had on her nose, brought her back to her senses. She met the new girl in the library one day, who said,

"I hope you are all right about me and Pete."

"Oh God! I'm fine," replied Meg.

The girl gave Meg a small, patronising smile, "I'll tell Pete that he must be nice to you and stay friends."

Meg smacked her in the face - hard.

She didn't really, but the exchange made her angry enough to stop moping. She started going out again and having fun. Gradually she regained her lively, friendly nature and began to laugh again. She had a host of admirers, and Pete heard about it and came to reclaim her. They talked for hours about anything and everything, but despite wanting him more than anything, she said no. He continued to ask and finally towards the end of their third year, she said yes.

So they started and finished university together and it seemed as if they had overcome all the ups and downs. When Pete got the engineering job in Saudi on bachelor status she was pleased and excited for him. Jobs for art students were scarce and Meg had decided to stay on for another year to get a marketing diploma in the hope that an extra bit of paper might help her get a job.

The following year was romantic and exciting, with long distance phone calls and loving letters, between visits back when Pete had leave. Meg missed him so much when he was away and constantly worried that she would lose him again now that he was earning so much and could go wherever he pleased. The relationship strengthened despite Meg's underlying worries and insecurities and the following summer Pete called to say they needed to talk and they arranged to meet in Athens.

As the trip neared, she began to read different things into his need to talk and her old insecurities took over as she began to imagine that he wanted to finish with her. Her flight was to land in Athens in the early hours of the morning about six hours later than his flight and so she had said she would get herself to the hotel. Secretly she thought he would come to meet her. When she arrived at the airport very late at night, he wasn't there, and so she had fought with taxi drivers to get one to take her to the hotel without over charging her and made her way to the hotel a little disappointed, tired and nervous about what was going to happen.

She carried her scruffy bag into the extremely chic reception of the hotel, and feeling very self-conscious she made her way across the shiny marble floor to the desk and asked for a key to his room. He was in bed sleeping when she got to the room, which made her even more anxious, but she put her bag down and leapt on top of him to wake him up and he laughed and held her in his arms. He got up and said there was champagne in the mini bar. Together they went onto the balcony of the hotel with the champagne and sat down on a wicker lounger overlooking the swimming pool lit up from below the water making the turquoise surface flicker with gold. Pete opened the bottle and it popped and sighed. He poured the sparkling bubbles into the glasses and handed her a glass. They clinked glasses and grinned.

"Better than a tent," Meg smiled looking around at the elegant furnishings and remembering their camping holidays as students. He turned to face her and began by saying that they had had their ups and downs. Meg panicked and instead of just letting him speak she responded by saying that there had been lots of downs and reminded him of some of his bad behaviour. She had meant it light heartedly, but Pete went quiet and sipped his champagne thoughtfully and changed the subject by asking her what she wanted to do in Athens. They made a plan to go to the Parthenon the next day and then he took her by the hand and led her to bed.

Two weeks of island hopping, lazing on beaches, playing in the sea, eating, drinking and partying with other travellers ensued. They had fun, they had a few adventures, they had walks along narrow, winding, cobbled streets and romantic dinners in tavernas overlooking quaint harbours, but 'the talk' never happened. It was as though they were dancing around each other. On the surface they were like any couple on holiday together, underneath they were both unsure, watching, waiting; each of them wanting the other to lead the way. When it was time for them to get their separate flights Meg finally said, "You said we needed to talk, but we haven't really, have we."

Pete responded by saying that everything was fine as it was and they should just carry on as they were."

The pain of parting was as always wretched, but this time Meg felt deep sadness. Her stomach lurched and her heart ached with longing. She wasn't really sure what had happened, it was as if she'd been unconscious for the previous two weeks, the heat, too much alcohol, and anxiety. There but not there. Something had shifted but she didn't know what.

She found out on Pete's next leave in the autumn. Staying with him at his Uncle's house, she ran out of film for her camera and he told her there was one in his bag upstairs. Feeling around in the holdall she felt a small square box under the material on the bottom. She realised there was another compartment underneath and reached in. Instead of feeling cool cardboard she pulled out a small velvet box.

Her whole body was shaking as she opened it and stared with her heart racing at the most beautiful diamond solitaire ring. The script in the lid of the box was in the charming swirls of Arabic and she found it hard to breathe. She sat on the edge of the bed as her legs lost their purpose, and just stared at it in shock. Had he had that when they went to Greece? Was he about to propose? Had he meant her to find it? Her stomach churned. She felt excited, nervous, pleased. She wanted him to propose more than anything else.

But he didn't ask. The two weeks went by with Meg being loving and attentive, enjoying his company and waiting. She decided to put the past behind her, see what was in the here and now, and she wanted a future with him. On his last night she asked him where they were and he said everything was fine as it was. Should she stay quiet and let things continue? In a whisper she told him that she had seen the ring. He calmly told her that he had bought it as an investment; gold and diamonds were really good value in Saudi. She knew it was a lie.

She went with him to the airport, both of them quiet. It was always hard saying goodbye. Just as he was about to go through the departure gate they hugged and she said, "Please don't give the ring to anyone else."

The year had gone by with an underlying tension. And here she was now, still in love with him, both unwilling to let the other go, but unable to move forward either. Meg had thrown herself into work, trying to survive on pitiful wages and desperate to get a permanent job at the radio station. Nothing in her education had prepared her for this. She was always waiting for Pete's next leave and trying to see as much of him as possible when he came back.

She suddenly realised that maybe subconsciously, she had come away to show him how it felt to always be at home, missing him and waiting for him to say when he was coming back. It was not a well thought out plan. If only she could find the right words to tell him how she felt without pushing him away.

# CHAPTER 16

Sandra came over first thing in the morning. Her eczema was getting worse and she had developed an abscess on one tooth, for which she had some strong medicine. Meg gave her the lists for who wanted jeeps and mopeds and for how long and they phoned Spiro to organise those by midday. In Vasiliki, Spiro had not booked enough accommodation for the number of people and two families had had to wait until six in the evening to be finally put up in Nidri; not much good when they were there for the windsurfing. Naturally, Sandra had had to take care of dealing with them not Spiro.

Meg told her about Janet's outburst and said she wanted to go and see her but didn't want to cause more trouble by going to her room and waking her. Sandra advised her to wait.

They sat on the verandah by the steps going down to the beach and ordered some breakfast from Michael. Dr. Diane came past with her daughters who waved and shouted hello as they ran forward on to the beach on their skinny, already tanned legs. Meg gave Diane a big smile, and said good morning. In return, she received a thin smile and a polite good morning, as Diane had a good look at Sandra and checked what Meg was eating before taking a seat at a table on the terrace next to the beach and ordering coffee.

Louise came into the bar wearing a floppy brimmed sun hat and a magenta sarong tied up above her bosom over a matching bikini. She was asking for a bottle of water and some sandwiches to take onto the beach, when Simon came into the bar. They both came over and said hello. Meg asked them if everything was all right. Louise glanced at Simon and he said that everything was fine. They could not help their eyes flitting down to where Diane was now sitting with Clive, who must have gone straight down the side steps.

"I'm sorry about putting you next to young children. Are they a bit noisy?"

"The girls are fine. They are really lovely."

Again, Louise and Simon swapped looks and Simon changed the subject. "We put our names down for a jeep, can you let us know when it'll be here."

"Yes. They are coming about midday - Greek time! I'll come and find you when they get here."

"Great. See you later."

They made their way onto the beach where they were greeted by squeals of delight from Alice and Celia. The little girls flung their arms around

Simon's legs and he swooped them up, one in each arm, and swung them round smiling.

Meg and Sandra chatted for a while. Sandra was unhappy with Spiro, the whole situation and set up and it was affecting her physically with the inflamed eczema and toothache. She warned Meg that she might not stay much longer. Then she went onto the subject of Tim.

"He really likes you, you know. And he's a lovely man."

"I know he's a lovely man, Sandra, but I only met him last week. I don't know him at all. It's being on holiday, everything seems magical and special and removed from reality."

"I got a letter from him yesterday asking me what you thought of him and asking me whether he should write to you or not."

Meg sighed.

"Of course he can write to me. Maybe we can get to know each other through letters and maybe when I go back, I'll meet him for a drink. But I certainly don't feel undying love for him at the moment, so would it be fair to write to him?"

Suddenly she found herself telling Sandra all about Pete and her Mum and Dad.

"Sounds like you are trying to recapture something that's gone past its sell by date. You're afraid that you won't meet anyone else. You feel that because you have put so much time and energy into the relationship, you can't give up. He's the one that lost your trust, but you took him back without forgiving him. He's the one that's confused. He made stupid mistakes, probably because he was young and didn't know the meaning of trust. Many men never learn. They are often brought up to think it's okay or even expected of them to mess about as long as they don't get caught. What they don't realise is that women nearly always know. Some shout and scream, so the men feel justified. Others stay quiet; others leave, but either way they've both lost the full and complete love that a woman will give to a good man and visa versa. So, in the end nobody wins."

Meg was stunned by the torrent of words and sat silently listening as Sandra continued.

"You have to decide whether he truly loves you now and has learnt from the past, and you must see that past as a good thing that made you stronger and more sure of each other. If you are not completely sure that he won't hurt you again, then you have to move on and look for someone better."

"Gosh! I don't know," replied Meg, "Sounds like you're talking from personal experience."

"Believe me. You're young and still free. I was married when it happened to me. I kept quiet. I thought it must be my fault. I tried to love him better and I couldn't complain about the way he treated me. I tried to persuade myself that as long as he was lovely when he was with me, then I shouldn't complain. But, I couldn't pretend that I didn't know when he was lying to me. That I knew when something wasn't quite right. I tried to talk to him but he always lost his temper so I stopped. We had two children and we carried on as a happy family for the outside world, but I moved away from him in my heart. It's funny how your life can get caught up in daily chores and routines and before you know it, twenty-five years have gone by, your children have left home, and there's nothing left between you and your partner because you never dealt with problems right from the beginning. I could have confronted my husband, I could have investigated my suspicions and found out who and when and where. The truth is I kept hoping he would realise that I was the only one for him. It worked. About three years ago, he changed. Maybe he got too old to mess about any more, maybe he couldn't attract women in the same way. Maybe someone hurt him. Anyway, I knew I'd got him back and it was too late. I'd stored up the hurt and I started to feel contempt for him. The number of times I'd cried over him. The number of times he'd got angry when I asked him anything he didn't want to answer. The number of times he'd managed to avoid taking me with him to places when I suggested it. It was all there stored under 'Mrs. Angry' in the recesses of my brain and it ate away at my heart until I couldn't bear to be with him anymore.

He honestly thought he'd got away with it and now his lovely successful wife was there to look after him, as he got older. When I left, he was shocked and baffled. When he first asked me why I was unhappy, it all came out. I didn't even realise I'd stored it all. Dates, times exact situations all came out like regurgitating a list of historical quotations that you've learnt for an exam. Why hadn't I said anything? Why didn't I stop him?"

She paused and exhaled heavily before adding,

"You don't know all the ins and outs of your parents' relationship. Just know that they love you and don't feel that you are responsible for their lives."

"God, I'm sorry, I'm going on. This job was me running away and it's not the answer. My body knows that. Look at my bloody skin."

They both laughed.

"I had no idea. I know I'm not the first person to have parents who split up but it just came as such a shock," said Meg. "I'm sorry, I feel quite pathetic."

"Not at all. Nobody knows what's in store. I'm fifty this year. I'm trying to rebuild my life and I don't want to be bitter. To be honest it was an incredible relief to say it all, get it all out."

"Well, you don't look that old. Sorry, I don't mean old."

"Yes, you do.' she laughed. You are in your early twenties, thirty seems old to you. You are bright and full of energy and you want it all right now. You don't have to have Pete. Give him love and see if he responds with love and honesty. You know when he's lying, so if he lets you down again and can't give a good explanation, don't make excuses for him. Don't destroy yourself in fear and jealousy. Dump him. Take control. I lost over twenty years of my life because I thought I had no choice."

Meg tried to take it all in.

"You do know that you are very attractive?" continued Sandra.

Meg scoffed, "No, I'm not! I'm okay. All my girlfriends at school and university were pretty, beautiful even. They'd have all the boys chasing after them with tongues hanging out. I grew up with brothers who always criticised the way I looked. My bum's too big and my boobs are too small! I was a tomboy, preferring to play football and climb trees rather than play with dolls so I am easy in the company of men. I've always had as many guy friends as girl friends"

Sandra laughed.

"I'm fairly straight forward, and usually too trusting. Often to my detriment," she grinned, "Tim likes me because I listened to him and he's lonely. Keith just tried to use me, did use me, to get to chignon Melissa."

Sandra nodded, "Don't underestimate yourself. Just remember, some people find it very easy to lie to other people and to themselves to get what they want. Lecture over. I have to make a move and sort out Nidri. I'll see you for the barbeque if not before," she said. Sandra rose hurriedly, embarrassed by her outburst and her eyes slightly watery.

"Thank you," said Meg. She wanted to say something useful, but she was unable to find suitable words, "See you tonight."

# CHAPTER 17

Meg was left analysing what Sandra had said and trying to apply it to Pete. But she was trapped by her conviction that he was the one. She made excuses for his bad behaviour, ignored the fact that too often she felt upset, or insecure. She blamed herself for being too needy because of what had happened to her Mum. He loved her, she loved him and the sexual attraction was incredible. She couldn't let go; she'd invested so much time and emotional energy.

Suddenly, she realised it was ten thirty and there had been no sign of the lovely Lindy. She decided to go and find her. As she went out onto the road the heat already shimmering across the tarmac, she saw Janet coming from the direction of the chalets. Meg could have continued, pretending not to see her, but she held her head up and walked towards her. She was greeted with a huge smile and Janet said,

"Oh, I was just coming to find you!"

Taken aback Meg smiled, but said nothing.

"I'm so sorry about last night. I lost my temper and I feel really bad about it. It was the travel and then the accommodation was not what I expected. I was so disappointed when we first arrived. It's not your fault I know that. I shouldn't have shouted at you."

'Wow' thought Meg and then said, "Listen, I'm sorry if you were disappointed. I will get your trousers cleaned for you."

"No, no. God. It's only a pair of trousers. Don't worry about them."

"Okay, if you are sure, but listen, do let me know if there are any problems. I'm afraid a lot of things are out of my control but sometimes it's better to get them off your chest," she said. She bit her lip as she thought of what Sandra had just been saying.

"Thanks, but it's okay. It is what it is and we'll be fine," Janet replied. She gave Meg a small smile and hurried off across the road with her head down, leaving Meg feeling unsure about whether she deserved an apology or not.

She went to her room to use the bathroom and when she came out again, she bumped into Kevin, Janet's husband. He was wearing a T-shirt with 'No Sex Please we're British' on the front and short black shorts over white hairy legs.

"Good morning!" he said.

"Oh, hi!"

"Have you seen Janet?"

"Yes, she just went over to the bar."

"Right. I hope she apologised to you about last night. I'm afraid she was completely out of order."

"She did, but I think she was just a bit upset about everything."

"Nonsense. No need to make such a show of things. I hope she didn't upset you too much love," he said His eyes moved up and down her body, making her fold her arms.

"No, no, it's all part of the job," she smiled.

"My lads, Bruce and Darren, are still sleeping. Went off to that disco in Nidri and came back very late," he laughed and winked at her. "What time is our jeep arriving?"

"They're being driven over at lunchtime. If you are on the beach or in the bar I'll come and find you."

"Great stuff. Cheers."

He headed manfully off to the bar. On the back of his T-shirt was 'OK, if you insist.'

Lindy was still sleeping when Meg knocked on the door. Sleepily, she opened the door from her bed and mumbled,

"Ugh, what time is it?"

"It's nearly eleven."

"Oh, right. I'd better get up then."

As she moved the covers back, a used condom slipped onto the floor. Lindy bent down to pick it up, dropped it casually into an empty plastic bag used as a bin and went to the bathroom.

"Bit of a one, that Gregor," she laughed as she closed the door.

Meg felt herself getting really angry. She waited outside on the verandah where the wet things from the day before lay dry and crisp where they had put them. Lindy eventually came out grinning.

"I was thinking of getting some yoghurt and honey for breakfast. Greek yoghurt is just the best. Do you know where I can get some?"

Meg didn't know whether to laugh or slap her.

"Listen, Lindy. Are you getting paid to be here?"

"Bloody right."

"We start at eight. There may not always be things to do but that's the job."

"Right."

Lindy's head went down and she kicked the ground with her wedged sandal. Meg started walking back and Lindy shuffled behind in a sulk. Meg was exasperated. She couldn't think of anything that Lindy could handle on her own. When they reached the road Meg showed her the little shop where she could buy most things and then she told her about the bakery up past Michael's.

"Why don't you go there and get us both some yoghurt and honey and then I'll go through what's happening?"

Lindy immediately brightened and began chatting about her boyfriend back in London.

"We was engaged but my Dad wasn't happy because he's West Indian and said at sixteen I was too young. That's part of the reason for being sent here. I ain't exactly going to forget about him just like that am I?"

Meg was shocked to discover that Lindy was only sixteen.

"I don't know, what about Gregor?"

"Hah, just a bit of fun. Ed ain't gonna know about it, is he? Here, don't go telling Uncle Spiro."

"Not as long as you don't piss me off," Meg said smirking at her. Suddenly, Meg felt responsible for her.

"Right. I won't." Lindy laughed nervously.

They reached the bar and Meg pointed her in the direction of the bakery.

Lindy was never late again. She could not take responsibility for anything, but she chatted to everyone and was quite artistic so she got to do all the notices.

# CHAPTER 18

Meg sat in her usual spot on the balcony and watched as the different groups met and got to know each other in the rising heat under a cloudless blue sky. A group of ladies sunbathed and chatted away on the sand in high cut bikinis or one piece costumes, while the men in short boxer swim shorts jumped around in the sea with the children. Moon-faced Clive was deep in conversation with Dr. Diane on the terrace. They leaned into one another in a conspiratorial way. Every so often Diane's eyes would dart to their room above the bar.

Grant and Erica came in for a late breakfast; they sat with Meg for a while and made arrangements for the afternoon. They were laughing about the other couple who nobody had seen since they arrived the day before. Apparently, they were having a marathon sex session for all to hear. Grant and Erica went off for a swim and the lads, Bruce and Darren, came in and tried to order an English breakfast.

"Bloody hell!" said Bruce.

Meg winced and prepared herself to say something.

"What kind of place doesn't know how to do an English breakfast?"

"A Greek place," replied Michael unfazed.

Meg smiled to herself.

The boys ordered sandwiches and acknowledging Meg with a brief hello, went down onto the terrace making jokes about the food. Their conversation soon moved onto the talent from the night before and when they started eating their sandwiches both declared them to be 'fucking tasty' for Greek stuff. Meg presumed they were talking about the sandwiches. It was getting hotter, the sun shone down relentlessly and the noise of splashing and laughter carried from the calm sea. Meg longed to dive into the cool water and go for a swim.

Lindy returned and so as not to insult Michael, they went outside and sat on the bench outside Meg's room to indulge in the delectable, creamy yoghurt sweetened by pure runny honey.

You're right it is the best!" said Meg.

Amazingly, at ten past one, just as Meg was beginning to worry, Spiro arrived in his car followed by two young guys in jeeps and an older, handsome man with jet-black hair and a rough black beard driving a pick up truck with mopeds on the back. The older Greek introduced himself in a loud laughing voice as Mike and then shouted at the young guys to come and get the bikes off the truck.

Meg went to round up those who had booked. They were all waiting in the bar and murmurings of impatience had just begun. She collected money from them, and they trooped outside.
Meg headed for Mike with the money but Spiro pulled her to one side and said,

"It's okay, I will do the money."

His eyes flicked sideways as he took the money and shoved it into his pocket before turning to Mike who was busy explaining how the gears worked.

Meg watched with trepidation as people sped off or puttered and stuttered off on the mopeds. Fat legs dangled down close to the exhaust pipe. Louise and John looked too tall and gangly for the small machines as they wavered off up the road, gears screaming and jolting, their knees jutting out to the sides. Grant and Erica had hired a jeep and had driven up the road and back down again grinning.

Freedom to explore.

Meg watched Spiro talking to Mike and handing over a much smaller wedge of cash than she had given him. Mike departed with a wave and a smile and Meg went over to Spiro to tell him that she was going to Nidri that afternoon to book a boat trip.

She wasn't going to be caught out again. He was so relieved that she wasn't confronting him about the money that he smiled broadly and told her she was a good girl. Meg was just relieved to be able to go without feeling guilty. She didn't give a damn about any money deals he might be making.

At that moment, Lindy came over and she and Spiro started talking away in Greek. Meg listened, picking out enough words here and there and reading body language to be pretty sure that Lindy was complaining. She took a gamble and interrupted,

"It's okay you can tell me what's wrong to my face."
They both stopped and stared at her. She hadn't understood everything, but it meant that from that moment on, they could not turn to Greek with any confidence, if they wanted to talk about her in earshot.

Lindy bumbled and burbled, "No, I mean, it's just that..."

"Remember you are here to work!" said Spiro in a stern voice, and Lindy shuffled her chubby feet together and bit her nails.

Meg still found herself feeling guilty about going up to Nidri with Grant and Erica. She had planned to spend the rest of the day with them hiring a motorboat to go to one of the islands and exploring. She had placated Lindy by saying she could have the night off, but by the time they reached Nidri, she was feeling so uncomfortable that she told them that she would just book a boat trip for the following evening and then get the bus back. Both Grant and Erica tried to persuade her that she was entitled to some free time, but she felt she couldn't risk causing any more trouble.

In Nidri, they made their way down the beach to Niko. He was still there under his tree, tanned, and relaxed. Grant asked about hiring a boat.

"Why not? First, have a beer. You British – always feeling you have to be doing something quickly. Relax."

Grant laughed and looked at Erica, who nodded. They all accepted a beer and sat down on the sand next to Niko's low deck chair. Grant asked Niko how long he had been renting out the boats and Niko needed no more prompting to tell his story.

Five years earlier, he had been working in Athens as a very busy, hardworking businessman. One day he decided he'd had enough. Long hours, parties, dinners, meetings, trips abroad – all very exciting for a while and good money – but no time for him, for his wife, for his children. He sold his house and bought a small place in Nidri and the boats. Now, he spent nearly everyday on the beach, water-skied, went night fishing and still partied, but with his wife and a few friends. Not with business people pretending to be his friend;

wanting something from him. His eyes twinkling, he described going out fishing at night, the peace and the glorious phosphorescence sparkling around the wake of the boat. Meg, Grant and Erica were mesmerized by his ease and charm as they sat listening, sipping the cold beer in the shade of the old tree. The hot sun dappled and shimmered across the white sand. Taking a last swig of beer, Niko said, "Right you want a boat then."

Meg quickly said, "Yes, they do and I just want to arrange a boat trip for the people down in Nikiana."

"Okay. Let me get these two off and then you and I can do business."

Niko led them down to one of the little boats with an outboard motor and oars. Meg waved them off laughing as the boat bobbed and rocked in the shallow water. Grant was knocked down a couple of times by the waves as he pushed it out beyond the breakers with Erica shouting instructions from her seat in the boat. Niko was also shouting instructions and shaking his head as Grant eventually clambered in and began pulling the starter cable. The motor coughed and spluttered into life and they whirred off towards the headland.

Niko and Meg walked back up the beach to Niko's spot. He got out a little book and efficiently wrote down what time the boat would leave, how many people would be coming and what time they would return. He said he would arrange for the restaurant on Meganisi to expect them, and told her the price per head. As soon as that was done, he resumed his lazy attitude and offered her another beer. She declined and immediately regretted it. She liked Niko and his easy way. She felt she wanted to talk to him, and that she would be able to learn from him. For all his charm and twinkling eyes, she felt safe. Maybe it was the way he talked about his wife and children. You just knew they were the most important people in his life. Maybe it was the feeling that he'd lived and learned.

"Why do you have sad eyes?" Niko suddenly asked. "You always smiling and laughing but your eyes are sad. You are too young to have sad eyes."

Meg baulked at his perception. She looked at him, wanting to confide. She couldn't tell him. She smiled and said, "I'm just a bit tired. Thanks Niko. See you tomorrow."

"See you," he replied, leaning back in his chair and opening another beer.

Meg plodded up the beach, past dormant bodies shiny with oil and raucous children. The restaurants were getting quieter as they finished lunchtime and chefs and waiters went off for siesta. She browsed along the shop fronts and looked in the window of one boutique selling unusual but stylish clothes; a change from the usual shorts, hats and 'No Problem' T-shirts. She would have to try to save some of her measly pay to buy anything though.

On the bus back, she felt she had made the right decision. She needed to get going on posters and informing people about the boat trip and the barbeque. She was tired. Although setting office hours controlled things a bit she was still working all day and night answering people's questions, checking accommodation problems and constantly smiling. It was more stressful having Lindy than nobody at all and of course Spiro did nothing about any complaints.

She got off the bus with the sun still beating down and went to find Lindy. She was not in the bar and Michael hadn't seen her since Spiro left. She wandered down the beach smiling and waving at everyone and stopping to tell them all about the boat trip and the barbeque. They were all interested and said they would sign up. She saw Mark wandering aimlessly along the edge of the sea and called out to him. He smiled brightly when he saw her and blushed red.

"I expect your missing the little ones this week aren't you?"

"I am in a way," he said quietly. He kicked the sand at his feet and then said,

"Meg, can I ask you something?"

"Yes of course you can," laughed Meg.

"Well, it's just that, well, I really like someone and I don't know what I should do."

"Well it is difficult, but you know if you don't ask, you will never know, and even if you get turned down it's better than always wondering and even missing the chance. Is it someone at your school?"

"No," he said. He paused, embarrassed. Then he looked at her shyly and added, "It's you. Would you go out for dinner with me?"

Meg reeled inwardly. This was not expected.

"Oh Mark, I am so flattered."

"It's okay; I knew you'd say 'no'," he said with disappointment.

"Mark, you are great, and if I was ten years younger or even eight I would be jumping at the offer. But I'm way too old for you."

Mark wasn't convinced. He looked totally dejected.

"Honestly Mark. You'll meet someone your own age and it will be much better."

"But I don't want anyone else. I love you."

He spoke with determination, his eyes shining and his face burning. Meg's heart went out to him; she was completely out of her depth; she didn't know what to say without hurting his young heart.

"I can't go out with you, Mark. I'm so sorry. You're a lovely guy."

"Can I write to you when I get back?" he asked. "Maybe when I'm older you'll change your mind."

Meg wasn't sure, but she felt that it would do no harm to say yes. She was sure that it was a crush and that he would soon meet someone else.

"Yes okay. You can write and tell me about all the lovely girls you meet back home."

She wrote her address on a piece of paper and gave it to him.

"Thank you. I'll never forget you."

Having not known how to ask someone out he suddenly wasn't finding it difficult to say all the right things to win someone over. She smiled at him and said, "You're going to be very popular. I promise you!"

Mark walked away glowing with pleasure, he clutched the piece of paper, reading it as if it was a love letter. Meg hoped she'd said all the right things and felt both flattered and flustered.

# CHAPTER 19

She arrived at Lindy's room and was about to knock when she heard grunting, heavy breathing and squeaking bedsprings. Meg was so angry she nearly burst right in. Then she decided she really didn't want to see Lindy in mid-bonk, or whom she was with.

"Bloody hell!" she murmured to herself and missed Pete.

Just as she was walking away down the path to the main road, Lindy's door opened behind her. She turned around to see one of Janet's sons adjusting his Bermudas and slipping round the side of the villa back to the beach. Janet and Kevin had hired a jeep for the day. He'd obviously decided not to go with them. Meg went back up to Lindy's door and knocked.

"Hang on. Just a sec," came the rough London accent. Lindy opened the door with one towel wrapped round her head and another held up around her body.

"You're back early. I was just 'avin a quick shower before goin back. Bin chattin' an' sortin' fings out all day."

"Right," said Meg. "I'll see you up at the bar. Oh, don't forget to put that in the bin will you?"

"What?" Lindy turned to see what Meg was pointing at. It was a used condom tied in a knot, hanging from the bedpost. She turned back to Meg with her mouth open, but Meg was already walking down the steps.

"See you in a minute," called Meg laughing to herself.

In the bar, Diane came up to speak to Meg about the boat trips and the barbeque. She wanted to know what time the boat would return as Ben would be taking the girls to give her a break. Meg told her it would be around eleven in the evening by the time they got the bus back from Nidri.

"Oh well, they're on holiday. It won't harm them to stay up late."

Meg felt it would have been all right if she'd said four o'clock in the morning. She wondered what Diane was planning to do.

Diedre, Mark's mother, came in from the beach. Meg smiled brightly and was about to say something, when she saw the look on her face. She hurried towards Meg with something in her hand, and a look of agitation. She came up to Meg and sat down saying,

"What is going on?"

Meg looked blankly at her and asked her what she meant. The closed hand opened and she revealed the piece of paper with Meg's address on it. All around the address were little red hearts and the letters M+M.

"What do you mean by exchanging addresses with my son? He's only sixteen for God's sake! First you mess about with that oaf, Keith, then you have Tim running around after you, but Mark – he's just a kid."

She looked ready to burst into tears. Meg wanted to cry too. She started to speak as John came in. He immediately interrupted.

"Diedre, calm down. I've just spoken to Mark. Sorry Meg. Diedre found the paper and we over reacted."

"I'm sorry. I think he has a crush on me, but I didn't do anything to encourage it. I promise. He asked if he could write to me and I gave him my address to make him feel better," Meg explained. She felt incredibly guilty and looked at Diedre beseechingly, but Mark's mother still looked doubtful.

"She's telling the truth Diedre. I'll tell you all about it. Come on. Sorry, Meg," John said, embarrassed. Diedre wanted to protect her little boy and Meg was devastated that things had gone wrong again. She was left feeling very lost, confused and lonely.

Meg stayed in the bar and by the end of the evening, she'd seen everyone, and got all the bookings. She had kept up a smiling face, while feeling like her stomach was going to digest itself and her throat was going to choke. She was strained and exhausted by the pure mass of changing emotions and lack of sleep. Grant and Erica came in about ten. They looked sunburned and very merry. They came over to join Meg and told her about their day in shared outbursts, cutting in on each other to correct the story. They'd had a great time on the boat and then they had sat talking to Niko for a while until the sun was setting. Then, Niko had asked them if they wanted to go out on a boat to see the phosphorescence. They could barely contain their excitement. It was amazing, the most beautiful thing they had ever seen. Meg enjoyed their happiness and spent the rest of the evening in their company. They were easy with each other and with her. She felt warm and cared for. She didn't need to spoil their mood by telling them what had happened. She just let herself be cheered up.

The following morning, Sandra came over with some letters for Meg. She was so excited to get post. She scanned the writing on the four envelopes recognizing the sloping scrawl of her Dad, the small curves and high upward strokes of her good friend, Tony; the small, neat rounded curves and open vowels of an old friend from home, Rachel; a dirty postcard from Tom with only a couple of lines and – her heart gave a little leap – Pete's so familiar script. She put his to the bottom of the pile to save for last.

"Go on over there and read them. I'll get coffee," Sandra said kindly.

Meg went over to her usual table and quickly scanned her Dad's short note wishing her luck and hoping she was well. She felt a little knot in her stomach as she thought about him all loved up with his new family and no care for the devastation he had caused. Tony's letters were always humorous and full of news and jokes about people they both knew. She opened Rachel's letter with a smile. They had known each other since they were little girls in primary school together. They had gone to different secondary schools but had always kept in touch. Sometimes they wouldn't hear from each other for months on end but then one or the other would make contact and it would be as if they'd spoken to each other the day before. She liked and admired her and they always got on really well. She always thought of Rachel as one of those 'perfect' people. She was very tall and slim with long auburn hair that always looked sleek and shiny. She always looked immaculate, and while Meg was scatty and impetuous, Rachel was always organised and seemed to be in control of her life. She had gone into personnel work after 'A' levels and had a great job in London. The last time Meg had seen her, was when she'd come to stay with Meg, when Meg was at university. Rachel had been unusually down as she had been caught sleeping with her flatmate's boyfriend, and had to look for somewhere new to live. Meg had been in a squash tournament on the Saturday afternoon, so she'd left Pete to show Rachel around. In the evening, they'd gone out with a crowd of friends and suddenly Meg remembered feeling a little uncomfortable by how much attention Pete had paid Rachel, and they'd rowed about it, but she hadn't thought about it again until now. Rachel wanted to come over and stay with Meg in Greece, as she needed a break. Meg wasn't sure she wanted anyone to see where she was. She felt a failure, conscious that nothing she had planned had worked out in any way. However, it would be good to have someone who knew her well to talk to about everything. She decided to write and tell her how to book.

With anticipation and trepidation, Meg slowly opened the envelope containing Pete's letter. She felt slightly sick as she thought about all the romantic letters that she had received when he first went away. Some days two or three would arrive together as they'd been caught up in the post from Saudi Arabia. She had felt such joy on seeing the pale blue airmail envelopes lying on the carpet by the door. She would keep them unopened, while she made a cup of tea and then settle down on her bed to savour the loving words and funny, intimate lines. Now she was never sure what he might say.

Inside was a simple card, no letter. There was a picture of a penguin standing on an iceberg and the words 'I feel so ice-olated without you. Love always.'

Inside he had written 'Cold and lost without you and it's 50 degrees outside.' Her stomach did strange things. She felt relief and warmth mixed with confusion and shock and an inability to trust the words. She realised that before she'd opened it, she'd thought he might be telling her it was over. In many ways that would have been easier. She'd have been heart broken, but she'd have known where she stood and could move on. Now she just felt that if they were true, why the bloody hell was she where she was and he was where he was. She read and re-read the card wanting it to say more. By the time Sandra came over with the coffee she'd managed to convince herself that 'Love always' was something you'd write to anyone you knew well, like family or a long-standing friend.

"Bad news?" asked Sandra looking at Meg's face.

A soft breeze fluttered across the balcony. The sun, only beginning to warm up, filtered through the trees.

"No, good. I think," she replied and laughed. "I don't know, a bit confused," she added. She had told Sandra nearly everything so she showed her the card.

"Try and see it from his point of view. You're the one who suddenly got on a plane and ran away.

Maybe he's a bit confused. You're both dancing round each other saying 'I love you one minute and then playing it cool the next, you're both afraid of looking stupid. What do you want? Do you want him to propose?"

Meg paused, trying to be honest with herself, and said, "Yes."

"Then you have to make him feel that he can."

Meg knew she was right. If that was what she really wanted, then she had to put all her doubts and hurt away and love him.

Sandra changed the subject. "I got another letter from Tim. He asked again, if he should write to you."

"Oh Sandra. I would love to keep in touch, but I don't want to give him the wrong idea."

"Just keep in touch and see what happens."

Meg felt that Sandra would prefer to see her with Tim and forget about Pete. If only it was that easy. She knew that if Sandra met Pete, she would love him. Everybody liked Pete.

They discussed the boat trip and barbeque and arranged the bike and jeep bookings.

# CHAPTER 20

Meg gathered everyone to go up to Nidri on the bus for the night boat trip. There was a general buzz of excitement and Meg prayed that it would go smoothly this time. Louise and Simon were there; Ben was on his own with Alice and Celia. Grant and Erica had decided to do their own thing and explore the island, and the only others missing were Clive and Diane. Mark smiled sheepishly at Meg, but he was hustled away from her by Diedre.

Niko was as good as his word and led them down the jetty to where an attractive, wooden boat with an upper and lower deck waited for them. It was old but it looked freshly painted clean and comfortable. There were plenty of seats under cover and a large open deck at the back.

Men, women and children clambered on board in ungainly fashion and chose their spaces. A young skipper with greased back hair and tattoos covering his arms and bare back welcomed them on board, smiling and charming. He winked at Niko and saluted him as the rope was untied and then he steered the boat out of the harbor and across the bay. The late afternoon heat fell pleasantly on the skin.

The boat made its way slowly past the headland and headed towards Meganisi over calm water.

Meg sat on the open deck allowing the breeze from the movement to blow through her hair and across her face relaxing and cool. Ben discovered that the skipper had a supply of cold beer for sale and was happy. Alice and Celia ran unchecked from one side of the boat to the other, screeching in delight. They received a few disapproving glances from other guests so Meg went over to settle them down in one spot. She stood between them at the side of the boat spotting for fish in the clear, dark water.

The little bay that they were heading for came into view out of the steep rocky mound of Meganisi. It was like a bowl cut out of the rock with no beach. The water went right up to a wall that had been built onto the natural rock. At first, it looked like there was no way out of the bowl apart from the sea. Sheer, grey rock formed the back and one side, while the rocks on the other side sloped more gently upwards covered in trees and vegetation. In the middle of the flat, dusty floor was one taverna. Long tables had been laid out and rows of lanterns placed around the edge of the clearing stood waiting to be lit. Meg thought that access could only be by boat, but then she saw that there was an old pick-up truck parked at the rear of the building and wondered how it had got there. She looked more closely at the rock faces and realised that there was in fact a track leading up the sloping side. Everyone was intrigued and entranced. Waiters suddenly appeared out of the low wooden taverna and greeted them like family as the boat tied up and everyone disembarked.

Kevin and Janet's boys went off exploring and came back exclaiming that there were steps leading up the side of the cliff. One of the waiters told them that it was tradition to eat and then climb the steps to the old church at the top. Older members of the group groaned and the waiter grinned, adding that there was a longer but easier route following the track round.

"But first, you eat!"

Menus appeared and orders were taken. Lamps on the tables and the lanterns around were lit as the sun began to go down streaking the skyline with reds and gold, before making way for the moon and stars. Greek music filled the air along with chatter and laughter from relaxed, appreciative guests.

Meg helped with the orders and chatted to everyone, but their surroundings and the characters of the waiters made her work easy. They brought plates of grilled fresh fish, steaks, skewers laden with peppers, mushrooms, tomatoes and onions, bowls of salad with feta cheese, pita bread and chips.

After eating, Kris, one of the waiters, took people to the bottom of the cliff and led the way up the very steep, stone steps lighting lanterns as he went, which he placed on pillars. Meg watched as his shadowy figure glowed in lamplight up the steep steps. Then he came back down the winding track lighting more lanterns until the mountainside was twinkling and glowing through the trees.

The first of the intrepid explorers returned gushing with excitement about the beautiful, old church perched on the top of the hill. It was out of sight from their position, but it faced out to sea. Camouflaged by trees and bushes during the daylight, at night it was lit up as a beacon.

Meg, Louise and Simon decided they had to go and see for themselves. They gamely headed for the steps, which were very steep and seemed to go up for ever. They made their way up, laughing at their level of fitness as they reached the top with calves screaming and pulse rates racing. They gasped and stopped to catch their breath before looking around. The steps joined the narrow road and they followed it around passing returning guests, who all told them how wonderful it was. Suddenly, looming up ahead, bathed in bright up lighting, they saw the quaint church. It was painted in bright, fresh white paint with a bell tower outlined in blue. The vibrant lights made it seem to glow eerily in the dark. It stood alone and tiny on the top, staring out to sea, and a huge bell hung silent inside the open belfry. They looked out over the black, black water. Lights flashed and glittered in the distance indicating the existence of land and small fishing boats. They lingered for a while, taking in the enchantment of the setting, before they meandered back down the rough track to the restaurant. The pretty lamps sent flickering shadows across branches and cicadas gossiped around them in the balmy warmth.

Back at the bottom, someone turned up the music and the waiters started to dance and the Retsina flowed. Men in black trousers and bleached, neatly pressed shirts stamped their feet and clicked their fingers in unison; their arms waved and their hips swayed rhythmically to the beat; all perfect in their knowledge of the steps and movements. Then, to everyone's amazement and cheers, Kris bent down to an empty table and gripping the corner between his teeth, he lifted it clear off the ground.

Everyone applauded and he repeated the spectacle. Then he invited anyone in the audience to try. Laden with the arrogance of alcohol a few brave souls tried and failed pathetically and painfully, while onlookers cheered them on and laughed at their futile efforts. The dancing resumed and all around people stood up and joined in. Forming a large circle, they began following the traditional steps of Zorba's dance; faster and faster they whirled as the tempo increased. They finished giggling and puffing as they collapsed back into their chairs.

All too soon, it was time to board the boat and head back. Meg rounded everyone up and counted heads. Then, waving and shouting goodbye, the boat moved away from the glowing basin and they watched it fade into blackness, as if it had never existed. Only the church remained in sight as if hanging in the black sky.

The journey back felt much longer. The sea was still calm, but the air was cold and it picked at the skin. Not many had thought to bring jumpers; they were never needed on land. Alice and Celia fell asleep on a pile of ropes, exhausted. Ben came over to where Meg was sitting on the deck with her back up against the side of the boat. He was holding a bottle of wine and, slurring, he offered her a swig. She accepted out of pity more than any desire for a drink and started talking to him. He sat down heavily on the raised wooden hatch. He seemed so lost. He began to tell her about his marriage. Diane was his second wife and the girls were hers from her first marriage. "It was good in the beginning," he assured Meg and himself. "Suppose it always is… in the beginning. Then I lost my job and I haven't been able to find anything else that makes the same money as before. Diane started going on and on about money and how useless I was, and I suppose I just turned to this. He held the bottle up a little too quickly and lost his balance momentarily.

"I love thosh little girlsh though, really love them," he sighed and took another swig, "But she won' lemme near them mos of the time. Ha! She has tonight though hasn' she? So she can be with tha tosser," he took another swig, "Wha do I care?"

"Maybe she's just trying to make you jealous. Make you show her that you care," Meg ventured.

He looked at her and Meg saw a flash of something she couldn't quite discern pass across his eyes. It frightened her. Then he laughed, a soulless laugh, and took another drink, only just managing to hold the bottle to his mouth. Meg leant back into the side of the boat away from him. He didn't pay any attention.

Around the boat, nobody was talking. They huddled close together for warmth, wanting to get back to shore now. Only the sound of the chugging boat could be heard. Meg rested her head against the wood and stared up at the sky. Clear and black, more stars than she had ever seen before stared indifferently back. She made out The Plough as she always did. It was her link to Pete. They always said that wherever they were, they could always look up at the sky and know that they were both looking at the same stars. She lost herself in the universe; she felt huge and significant as a being to herself, and yet totally tiny and insignificant in the whole scale of things. Ever since she was a child she had spent time looking up at the sky through her bedroom window. She could make herself seem gigantic, the focus of all the stars and then turn it around and become a tiny speck in the never-ending universe. On the one hand she knew she didn't matter and on the other something screamed inside; a burning in her soul to achieve great things, but she didn't know what she was meant to do.

They arrived in Nidri and everyone roused themselves, they were drowsy and thirsty, but still in good spirits.

Louise and Simon picked up Alice and Celia and carried them off the boat and Meg went over to where Ben had slumped. His bottle rolled empty across the deck, so she picked it up and threw it in a bin. His head lolled to one side. He was snoring and dribble slid down his chin out of his open mouth. She called to him and gently shook his shoulder. He grunted, opened his eyes blearily and suddenly swore and swung his arm out, violently. Meg jumped back in surprise and fell against the edge of the hatch. The skipper ran over and started shouting in Greek at Ben. Everyone on the quayside looked around as he hauled himself to his feet. Faced with the strong, young man, Ben, though big and stocky, became a baby.

"Okay, okay," he burbled, barely able to stand. Meg calmed the skipper down and between them they helped Ben off the boat. On dry land, he shrugged them both off and insisted he was fine.

Meg led the way to the bus stop and went to buy bottles of water to pass round. Everyone ignored and avoided Ben. Alice and Celia, just awake, clung to Simon. On the bus, Meg handed out the water and the chatter and laughter resumed as most talked about the enjoyable trip.

# CHAPTER 21

Meg sat in the bar eating an egg sandwich in peace. She was reading and re-reading Pete's card, drawing as much love from it as she could. At half past eight Lindy appeared.

"Blimey! You're up early," Meg joked.

Lindy didn't laugh, "Yes, my aunt is coming." she announced in a sullen voice.

"Who? Athena, from London? Why? How? The flights don't come in until tomorrow."

"She came by boat via Corfu last night. She wants to know why she's been getting so many complaints. Please don't say anything bad about me."

"I won't," Meg promised. "When is she coming here?"

"I don't know. Spiro phoned last night. She's in Vasiliki with him and Sandra. He was having a blue fit as she didn't tell anyone she was coming."

Meg laughed, "I bet he was."

"Shall I get some yoghurt and honey?" Lindy asked sweetly. Meg said that was a good idea and watched her waddle away in her high wedges, shorts clinging to her rubbing thighs, folds of smooth flesh protruding out of the tight T-shirt. She did have the most beautiful tan.

Meg looked at her card again, thinking how to respond.

Nobody sought her out and she was able to eat her yoghurt and honey in peace, savouring each glorious mouthful. Those guests she had seen had all thanked her for the boat trip, so she was feeling quite relaxed. She went over to her room to get some writing paper. Suddenly, there was an urgent knocking on her door. She opened it and found Clive standing there very agitated and hopping from one foot to the other.

"Hello," said Meg.

Without a word, he shot out his hand and revealed a small scrap of paper.

"I just got this note. What are you going to do about it?"

Completely taken aback, Meg took the note and read it. Written in a scrawl of babyish words she read:

*'Ben hurted my arm and said he was going to break your legs. Can't see you'*

Meg was appalled. She looked at Clive, who said, "So what are you going to do about it?"

Meg looked him straight in the eye and said, "I'm not going to do anything about it."

He blustered and puffed, "But this is a threat! I have it in writing. I can sue him!"

"You can do what you like," Meg stated calmly. She was fuming. 'Who were these people? These adults? Diane was a qualified doctor.

Clive stalked off, affronted. Meg went back into her room and sat on the bed. Two minutes later, there was another knock.

Meg opened it and saw that it was Diane, who immediately looked past Meg to see what her room was like.

"Hello, Diane," said Meg stepping forward and closing the door.

Diane looked at her and said, "Clive's told me that you are not going to do anything."

"I thought you couldn't see Clive," replied Meg.

"Yes, well, he had to come and tell me."

Meg was getting fed up with the nonsense and hypocrisy.

"I'm sorry, but who were you with last night?"

"Clive kept me company while Ben was off gallivanting, but..."

"So, is Ben right to be a little upset?" she asked softly.

"Huh! Don't think I didn't smell your perfume on him when he came in!"

"What?"

"You know exactly what I'm talking about!" she spat.

Meg felt it was all getting out of hand.

"Right, come and see me in the bar in half an hour."

She leant against the door with a sigh and then headed back over to the bar to sit and think for a while before they came.

Louise and Simon were on the terrace having a late breakfast. She went over to talk to them and asked if everything had been all right in their apartment the night before. They both looked at each other and then Louise said, "Look it's none of our business, but perhaps you should know. When we got back, Clive was in the apartment with Diane. Ben put the girls to bed and then he went berserk and threw Clive out. He didn't hit him or anything, just told him to leave. Then we could hear Diane and Ben arguing. Diane accused Ben of being with you and told him she could smell your perfume. To be honest she managed to turn the whole thing away from her and Clive, and as you know Ben wasn't in the best state for defending himself."

"Those poor little girls," said Meg and Louise and Simon nodded.

Meg went back to her 'office' table on the balcony and watched Clive's gangly body stride towards her. He sat down full of self-importance.

"I'm going to sue him! How dare he threaten me?"

Meg kept her voice steady and low, "You can do whatever you think is necessary when you get back to the UK. For now, aren't you forgetting the two most important people in all of this?"

"Oh, Diane and I will be fine. We're going to see each other in the UK," he announced this proudly, completely missing her point.

"I wasn't talking about you and Diane. I was talking about two little girls, on holiday, listening to and watching you adults fighting and screaming."

"Oh."

"So whatever you do is up to you. But try and consider them and their feelings in all of this."

He stammered and faltered, and looked at Meg dumbfounded, "So you're not going to do anything, then?"

Meg ignored him and said quietly, "Could you ask Diane to come and talk to me?"

He left hurriedly, glad to escape. Diane came in with her back straight and a haughty look. She sat down facing Meg who suddenly felt as if she was somehow caught in an absurd Harold Pinter play.

"I hope you are going to have a word with Ben."

"I'm just here to try and help people have a good holiday. I'm not a marriage guidance counselor or a lawsuit solicitor, but as you have involved me, I will say my piece. I'm very upset about comments insinuating that I was 'with' Ben, which you and I both know is rubbish. For starters, I don't wear perfume. Perhaps I should sue you."

Dr. Diane looked taken aback and was about to say something, but Meg continued, "You're a GP aren't you?"

"Yes, I am."

"Well, I hope you show more care with your patients than you've shown your own children in the past week."

Diane looked ready to hit her.

"Look, I don't want to fight with you. It's fairly obvious that Ben has a drinking problem and is very unhappy. You're obviously not happy either. He must care about you to be threatening to break someone's legs. Perhaps you should use your skill and knowledge to sort out your relationship with him before rushing into the arms of the first man that pays you a compliment."

Meg shocked herself. She didn't really know what she was saying, but she was so incensed by the behaviour of these people in their forties behaving like school children and totally fed up with being accused of being 'involved' with various males. She expected Diane to shout at her, but to her amazement, Diane lowered her head and simply said,

"Yes, perhaps you're right. Thank you."

With that, she stood up and walked away, rummaging in her bag for a tissue.

Meg sat staring after her. "This can't be real' she murmured to herself, and felt herself beginning to shake.

# CHAPTER 22

Meg didn't have long to contemplate the actions or reactions of the scenario as Spiro and Sandra arrived with Athena. Lindy trailed behind like a puppy. Spiro looked as if his blood pressure was about to erupt through the top of his head. Athena was stern faced at his side. Meg suddenly felt nervous and defensive. Without any form of greeting, Spiro told Meg to show Athena the accommodation.

"Of course. I won't be able to show you inside any except mine and Lindy's, as people are staying in the others," she said politely to Athena.

Lindy's eyes nearly popped out of her face in horror. To her relief, Athena said she didn't need to look, she just needed to know what was wrong. Meg looked at Sandra who raised one eyebrow.

"Well, to be honest," started Meg, "We are starting to get things settled here. There are trips and people can hire jeeps and mopeds so they're having a good time. The accommodation is all right, it's just very basic. As long as people were told that before they came, I don't think they would mind." Meg said plainly. She was having a great day for speaking her mind.

Athena glared at her and then spoke very rapidly in Greek to Spiro. Spiro replied and Meg understood that he was telling Athena that Meg could understand Greek. Athena glared again and took Spiro outside with Lindy following.

Sandra groaned and sank into a chair, "What did Athena say?"

"Not a clue!" Meg said smiling. She went over to the bar to get some coffee from Michael. He was never very cheerful, but Meg seemed to have developed an understanding with him and she was upset when he didn't give her his small smile of acknowledgement.

"Are you all right?"

He looked over the bar at her and said in his slow, deep voice with his shoulders drooping,

"Too much nonsense and my mother is going crazy."

"Callista? Why?"

"Spiro is giving her a hard time about the water in the chalets and of course Alexander comes today," he said. He raised his palms facing outward in a gesture of surrender.

Meg grimaced sympathetically.

"Don't worry. I bet he's not as handsome as you."

Michael snorted and shook his head. Meg took the coffee to Sandra. She looked terrible. The skin on her hands and arms was flaking where rough red patches of eczema covered them. Her face, though tanned, had a grey tinge to it and dark shadows circled her eyes.

"You don't look well."

"No, this abscess on my tooth is getting worse so I'm going to the dentist in Lefkas this afternoon. God, help me!"

"Oh God, Sandra!"

"I'm afraid I've had enough."

"Please don't leave me," pleaded Meg.

"You don't have to stay either. I have never worked with such terrible people in all my life."

"I suppose it's not so bad for me hidden in Nikiana. I don't see that much of Spiro, although Lindy is driving me to distraction! At least Athena might make some positive changes."

"Don't be so sure. They're only interested in making money. They haven't heard of customer service or gaining loyalty. Next year they'll just change the name and start again."

Spiro, Athena and Lindy returned and Spiro magnanimously suggested lunch. They all sat around one table, barely talking. Lindy sat with her head bowed, biting her nails on one hand and twiddling her hair with the other. She looked like a chastised child. Sandra couldn't eat anything and was in obvious pain. Athena picked at a salad with her freshly manicured, red fingernails. Only Spiro ordered a huge meal, which he put his full concentration into devouring.

When the plates were cleared, Meg gave Spiro the money she had collected for vehicle hire after paying Mike and asked about the barbeque. To her amazement, it was all organised and planned for six o'clock. He said he would take Sandra to the dentist and return with the food and wine. He lit a cigar and stood up followed by Athena and Sandra. Just as he reached the door he turned and said casually,

"Oh, by the way, you must move in to Lindy's room. We need your chalet for tomorrow's arrivals. Meg stared at him in disbelief, but he didn't wait for a discussion.

Meg was horrified. She looked at Lindy who shrugged innocently.

"Come on then, Lindy. You can help me."

Together they went over to Meg's room, collected up her meagre possessions, and traipsed down the road in the searing heat to the pit. Meg tried to open the doors to the other rooms in the old villa, but they were firmly locked.

Lindy thoughtfully moved all her things from the spare bed and the surrounding floor by gathering them up in her arms and dumping them on to her bed.

Meg was so fed up that she didn't bother to unpack. She didn't want to stay there, so she told Lindy she was going back to sort out the next day's departures and to let everyone know what time the barbeque started.

She walked up the road blinking back tears of frustration. The little old ladies sat in their chairs crocheting and talking; watching her as she walked past. She smiled and waved as she always did and received blank expressions in return. She felt hot and sticky and hated the sun for beating down so cheerfully from its clear blue haven. The lads, Bruce and Darren walked towards her, so she smiled automatically and asked them how they were.

"Great thanks," replied Darren. "Where's Lindy?"

"In her room," Meg informed him.

Darren grinned and nudged Bruce. "Oh fuck off!" came the charming response.

She continued past them and heard Darren calling after her, "Nice legs."

Callista was outside the chalets about to go in and clean Meg's ex-room.

"You move, eh?"

"Yep."

"That Spiro is a pain here."

She pointed to her backside and Meg couldn't help but laugh.

"My son come today with his cousin. He sleeps now. You see him later." She smiled with pride.

Meg couldn't wait to see the legendary first born. She went into the bar and busied herself with lists of departures and arrivals. She put up posters with the latest information and organised the latest batch of photos to go on display. Michael was busy laying up tables outside and a large barbeque grill was delivered to the terrace. Spiro returned with the food, and Sandra, with a very swollen cheek, could barely speak. Meg couldn't look at Spiro, but he came over and told her to go to the bakery to collect the wine he had ordered. Glad to get away, she walked up the road seething. She didn't know that the bakery sold wine and she presumed someone would help to carry it back.

The cheery baker, Papandrou, greeted her and led her to the back of the kitchen to a large storeroom. Inside were crates and crates of wine stacked up to the ceiling. He picked out four large bottles; two red and two white and handed them to her in a cardboard box.

"Is that all?"

"Yes, this is the order."

She clunked back down the road and lugged them onto a table.

"Where is the rest?" she enquired innocently.

"This is all. We have juice for the children as well," stated Spiro, annoyed.

Meg bit her tongue. She couldn't see the wine lasting or people being very happy. The barbeque was on and Michael, with the help of two local boys, was starting to cook. Meg nipped back to her room to shower and change. She hoped that she wouldn't find Lindy entertaining Bruce and Darren. When she got there, Lindy was dressed demurely in jeans and a long T-shirt and ready to go. Meg sent her on ahead and had a little time to herself in the not so sumptuous bathroom. At least the water was hot.

She tried to wash the tension out of her, but she felt strained and miserable. Maybe she should leave with Sandra, after all. It was nearly two whole weeks since she arrived.

# CHAPTER 23

Meg kept her mind on trivial practicalities to stop her self from bursting into tears. She found the least creased of her clothes and took the time to hang the others on the back of her bed. She was running out of clean clothes and had only managed to hand wash her underwear and a couple of her T-shirts. In the time she had been there, she had got away without ironing, but she was sure Callista would lend her an iron if she needed one.

When she returned to the bar, the BBQ was in full swing. The distinctive and inviting smell of grilled meat filled the air and a queue of people were handing in tickets and accepting white plastic cups with barely more than a splash of wine in them. Meg helped herself to a cup and gulped it down. She smiled and said hello to everyone and made small talk. The atmosphere was happy and relaxed. She looked more closely at the table of food and noticed there were only chicken drumsticks, bread rolls and a manky looking lettuce and tomato salad. Michael had stopped cooking. Glancing around, she realised that only about half the people had arrived and there wasn't going to be enough.

Sandra, Athena and Spiro were standing together away from everybody, like an elite clique too good to mix with the guests. There was no sign of Lindy. Spiro puffed away at a cigar looking very pleased with himself. On the wall next to him stood a bottle of wine, from which they were filling their cups. It had a different label to the four Meg had collected from the bakery to share between everybody else.

Meg went over to them and without thinking, blurted out.

"There isn't enough."

"Of course there is, if they're not greedy," responded Spiro nonchalantly.

"For the price, they will want more than this," continued Meg.

Spiro ignored her. Meg looked at Sandra for help, but she didn't respond. Meg moved away.

More people began to arrive, and Meg stood back listening as the grumbles began. The wine was getting low and people who presumed they were due more than half a cup were refilling. People started to come over to Meg to complain and, agreeing with them, she went back to Spiro.

"We need to get more wine. You'll have a riot."

Spiro shot her one of his evil looks and drew heavily on his cigar. He called over one of the waiters, who promptly left the bar area and returned five minutes later with more wine. It saved the day as far as the punters were concerned.

There were murmurs of discontent, but the wine flowing more freely meant most people forgot about the food.

Meg, tense and upset, drank too quickly and accepted a couple of refills without question.

She chatted to Grant and Erica and ignored the mafia bosses behind her. She noticed Clive standing alone and looked around for Diane. To Meg's surprise, she saw her sitting on the steps next to Ben. His hand was on her knee and he was drinking coke. Alice and Celia were eating and giggling on the step below them. Meg caught Clive's eye, but he immediately looked the other way. She was pleased that Ben and Diane seemed to be working things out, but she felt sorry for Clive.

She was about to go over and talk to him when someone touched her shoulder and she turned to see Michael standing there, gangly and stooping, beside a short, well built man with short, thick black hair cropped close to his head, black eyes and a large nose and another muscular, lean, straight-backed man with very little black hair and angular unattractive features.

"Meg, this is Alexander," said Michael indicating the lean man with little hair.

Meg nearly choked. This was not who she had imagined.

"Pleased to meet you," she said brightly.

"And I am pleased to meet you," he said in a good English accent

He turned to the other man, "This is our cousin and good friend, Marzun."

"Hi!" said Meg extending a hand to him.

"Hello," he replied. He shook her hand, while his eyes roamed over her body.

Michael disappeared and she was left with the famous brother and his cousin. They both spoke excellent English and despite an air of arrogance about being successful businessmen in the city, they were polite and easy to talk to. She accepted another glass of wine and then someone interrupted the conversation, so she excused herself. She got caught up in answering questions about departure plans and gradually people began to leave. Meg went over to Sandra feeling quite calm and relaxed.

"You, young lady have too much to say!" Spiro snarled.

It was too much. The events of the day, and the wine, took their toll.

"How dare you! It would have been a disaster. You are just ripping people off. This whole set up is a joke!"

"And you are drunk," Spiro fired back. "You are sacked! Pack your bags you silly girl!"

"Fine!" Meg snapped and walked away.

There was nobody left. She went into the bar and asked Michael for a large brandy. She took it and walked out to sit on the balcony out of sight. Her head whirled. Sacked for the second time in two weeks. She was so upset with herself for losing it and furious with Spiro. It was partly the wine but she wasn't drunk – yet. Now she decided to get plastered.

Sandra found her. "Spiro is waiting for me, so I can't stay. He says he will forgive you. You can stay if you want."

Meg looked at Sandra and shook her head. "Oh my God. I don't know."

"I'll see you tomorrow," Sandra said patting her shoulder. She looked distraught and in pain.

"Thanks, Sandra. Hope you feel better. See you tomorrow."

Meg stared out into the night, the brandy numbing her brain.

"Mind if I join you?"

It was Marzun. He sat down and gently asked what was wrong. She found herself talking freely to him about everything that had just happened. He ordered more brandy and in her desperation and by now reasonably drunk, she found him easy and kind. In his perfect English with the slight Greek inflection, he was very soothing.

"The family, they have a little boat. Maybe tomorrow you can take some time and I will take you for a picnic. I know a beautiful beach, very private."

The thought of getting away, having some space and time to herself was too appealing.

"I can't tomorrow but maybe the next day. Thank you, yes, that would be excellent."

She didn't even know if she was going to stay or go, but if she was staying, she was going to have free time. She finished her brandy and said goodnight, realising that she was starting to feel far too relaxed. She checked herself.

"It's very kind of you. Can I just check that it is just as a friend," she didn't want to be making the same mistake.

"But of course!" he replied with a broad smile.

"Sorry. Just making sure there's no misunderstanding."

She laughed nervously and felt the sway of alcohol. She managed a straight line to the door and called out goodbye to Michael. He had his head down cleaning the bar and he looked up and raised one eyebrow as he said goodnight.

'Oh God, he thinks I fancy Marzun' she thought, and then couldn't think about anything important as she concentrated on getting down the road and into bed in her lovely new abode. She brushed her teeth, set the alarm and fell into a coma beside the snoring Lindy.

# CHAPTER 24

She woke, not because of the alarm, but due to Lindy moving around. It took her a few moments to remember where she was and then the events of the previous day swept over her with sickening ferocity. She reached for her bottle of water and drank half a litre in an attempt to re-hydrate. She looked through bleary eyes at Lindy about to ask her why she was up so early and then noticed she was packing her things.

"What are you doing?"

"Aunt Athena is taking me back to London. I'm leaving."

"Oh," was all Meg could manage. "Are you happy to go?"

"Spose so," she said quietly. She didn't sound convinced.

Rousing herself, Meg tried to say something kind.

"I'll miss eating yoghurt and honey with you."

Lindy smiled shyly at her.

"Shall we have some now?"

"Great idea."

Meg got dressed, desperately tried to get the stale taste out of her mouth by cleaning her teeth for the third time, and then helped Lindy heave the heavy suitcase up the road.

They sat on the roadside consuming creamy yoghurt mixed with honey before the first departing guests began appearing with their luggage.

Meg wasn't going to the airport. The night before seemed like a crazy dream and she decided, for now, to forget about it. She knew she wasn't ready to face going back home, so when the bus arrived, she stood by the door as they all boarded. Louise and Simon thanked her and wished her luck. She hadn't got to know them very well but they had impressed her with their complete togetherness and non-judgmental care of Alice and Celia. Clive got on without looking at her, but she touched his arm and wished him luck. Janet went in after him, and then Kevin, who pushed the boys in front of him and winked at Meg as he stepped up. The old couple, Sylvia and Rodney, said goodbye politely, and without smiling Rodney added,

"There are some lovely walks all over the island. The one to Nidri waterfalls is particularly beautiful," and continued onto the bus.

'Waterfalls! Where?' thought Meg astounded.

Diane came next with the girls, and said a very quiet, "Thank you," and nearly smiled. Ben, looking fresher than he had all week from a night off the pop, gave her a warm handshake and a huge grin. John and Diedre gave an embarrassed goodbye but Mark waited behind and said,

"I will write," and smiled hopefully.

"You take good care," replied Meg and squeezed his arm. He blushed and got on the bus.

Thank God she didn't have to go and wait at the airport.

Athena shook her hand firmly and with tight lips, informed Meg that she would be in touch. Lindy straggled behind, so Meg gave her a huge hug and wished her luck. The doors swished closed.

# CHAPTER 25

It was the usual chaos. The new crowd arrived tired, but expectant. More faces and names for Meg to try to remember. Spiro took two families up to the hill. There were mostly couples apart from two older women in their mid-forties and one more family, Mr. and Mrs. Patel, with three beautiful, dark skinned children including a six-month-old baby.

'Oh my God!' thought Meg looking at the young family with a baby, 'Where are they supposed to go?'

There were also three young and trendy single girls in their late teens. They were wearing high waisted tapered trousers with baggy T-shirts tucked in and held in place with belts. One also had braces attached to the trousers and a thin scarf wrapped around the top of her head and tied in a bow. All wore their hair in deliberately messy styles with blonde streaks. Their appearances, combined with striking eye make-up and bright red lipstick, made them perfect Bananarama lookalikes. They didn't look impressed as they glanced around the bar and at the other guests.

Meg took everyone, apart from the Patels, to their designated spots and returned to chat to the remaining family, until Spiro returned. He eventually arrived full of charm and gusto and piled them all into his car. He made no mention of sacking her the night before, as Meg had known he wouldn't.

"Where will they be staying?" Meg asked casually.

Spiro indicated with his cigar up the road towards the beach villa. Meg stared at him in horror.

"No, no, this wonderful. No complaints here."

Meg went to her 'office' and one by one people came through with the usual complaints. She distracted them with information and photos of the island and persuaded them to book jeeps and mopeds.

Spiro did not come back, but Mr. Patel did.

He was very polite, but very distressed. His head nodded wildly on his neck, and his hands waved around, as he tried to tell Meg what was wrong. Meg needed to see where they were, so she told him she would go back with him to check for herself.

They walked down the road past the little shop and then he turned to the left. Facing the sea were the new apartments set back from the road with little balconies. Compared to anything else they looked like luxury. Meg followed him up some stairs and into the flat. It was clean and white with an en-suite bathroom off the main bedroom, a sitting room with a sofa bed and a small kitchenette. Ceiling fans provided some relief from the heat of the day. Meg felt like showing them the other rooms. What was it that made people always find something to complain about?

She smiled and greeted Mrs. Patel who was sitting on a chair breastfeeding the baby. She did not return the smile. The little boy and girl stood and stared at Meg with large almost black, melting eyes.

"We were promised air-conditioning," stated Mrs. Patel and Meg almost choked.

"There is no cot for the baby and no fridge in the kitchen."

"I'm so sorry. As far as I know there isn't anywhere on the island with air-conditioning, but I will speak to Spiro and get him to bring you a cot and a fridge," she said. She sounded efficient, she felt helplessly deficient.

Mrs. Patel glanced angrily at her husband and he felt compelled to say more.

He went on and on about how they had been promised all of these things and how expensive the holiday was and how they would never have come with a young baby if they'd known. Meg edged to the door as he repeated the promises he'd been given, and she repeated her apologies. In her head, she cursed Spiro and wondered again, why she was staying.

She finally managed to escape and phoned Spiro immediately. She managed to get hold of Sandra who was up to her eyes in all sorts of problems down in Vasiliki, but she promised to tell Spiro.

Meg waited all afternoon for Spiro to make an appearance. She watched as the new arrivals came down to the beach and gradually relaxed in the undoubtedly glorious setting. She could see them marvelling at the clarity of the blue water and the vast expanse of unsullied sand.

Spiro did eventually arrive, angry and blustery. How could these people complain? These were the best apartments. Athena had found them. He rushed off to try to sort it out. Amazingly, he managed to find a cot and promised them a fridge would be coming. The fridge never came and Mr. Patel never stopped asking.

# CHAPTER 26

The evening welcome meal went smoothly and the three girls, who had been a bit dubious about the attractions of Nikiana, were smitten with Gregor, who arranged to meet them all at Michael's later with some of his friends.

Meg was sitting with Grant and Erica outside Michael's bar when the three young studs arrived. Dressed in jeans and tight fitting T-shirts they swaggered and joked around the girls and with Gregor leading, they were soon persuaded to go for a moonlit stroll along the beach. Gregor offered his arm to the prettiest.

Alexander and Marzun made a brief appearance in the bar and Meg felt quite at ease when she accepted the repeated offer to go out the following afternoon. She asked if Alexander was going to join them but he said he had to head back to Athens.

In the morning the two ladies, Brenda and Mary came down early for breakfast and chatted to Meg before going down the steps and taking a table on the terrace. Brenda was tall and well built, with short, brown hair. Mary was smaller and plump with medium length black hair. They both seemed to be conservative, twin-set and pearl ladies, who obviously knew each other very well. When they were talking, they nodded and agreed with one another. They were in the flat above the bar and quite happy.

After they had eaten, Mary went for a swim and Brenda took a novel out of her bag. Every so often Meg noticed that she looked up from her book and watched Mary, as she swam with confident strokes out to sea. Then she would look up at Meg and smile.

After the fourth time that Meg had politely smiled back, Brenda got up and came to sit at Meg's table.

"I hope she doesn't go out too far. I hate it when she does that."

"She seems to be a strong swimmer."

"Oh yes, she is," Brenda replied proudly.

Then she looked at Meg and said, "You have such pretty eyes."

Meg was flattered and said thanks. Brenda continued to ask Meg why she was in Greece and where she came from. Meg answered without giving too much information and they chatted lightly.

Mary emerged from the water and wrapped a towel around her body as she walked up the beach. She came onto the terrace and giving Brenda an odd look she sat down at their table and pulled out her own book from the bag.

Brenda calmly said, "See you later," to Meg and went down to join her friend. They chatted briefly and then Brenda picked up her book again and the pair of them both began to read and sat engrossed in comfortable silence as more people began to turn up.

Meg took bookings for jeeps and mopeds and a boat trip and everyone either settled at the bar or made their way to a spot on the beach, while others went off to explore.

At half past one, Meg watched Marzun appear out of Callista's apartment wearing a T-shirt over skimpy, tight speedos revealing his stocky, muscular, hairy legs and bulging credentials. It was not a particularly attractive sight. He was carrying a picnic hamper and a towel and he smiled and greeted Meg with a kiss on both cheeks.

He seemed shorter in the light of day and there was an arrogant confidence in the way he told Meg to follow him, but Meg felt quite at ease and was looking forward to getting away. They made their way down to the water via a path through the trees, which obscured that end of the beach from the bar.

A small boat with an outboard motor lay silently on the calm water, shifting dreamily in the soft wake. They set off and Meg felt relaxed and free as she sat back taking photos of the beach and the bar. They headed out of the bay along the coast towards Nidri, passing the Hill accommodation on their right. The boat cruised round a large outcrop of rock and back in, to where a tiny beach lay in front of a wall of thick trees. The tidemark showed that the sea came up to about halfway on the white sand. Marzun cut the engine and jumped athletically into the shallow water. He took a large pole from the boat and jammed it into the sand, before tying the boat to it with rope. Meg followed him, carrying the hamper up onto the hot, soft grains and they laid out towels. It was perfect. The tiny cove was hidden and virtually inaccessible by foot. A secret beach. All Meg could see was the sea expanding in front of her and tall trees behind their spot. Meg exclaimed in pleasure. It was delightful.

Marzun opened a bottle of chilled wine and revealed cold chicken, bread and salad.

"Cheers!" said Meg when he passed her a plastic glass filled with wine.

"Yamaas!" replied Marzun and Meg laughed as the cold wine slipped refreshingly down her throat.

They ate while Marzun told her stories about Michael and Alexander's father teaching the boys to fish and bringing them to this beach. He had grown up with them and often came for holidays or short breaks with or without Alexander, he was very close to them all.

Full and totally relaxed, Meg lay back on her towel and closed her eyes. "This is wonderful. Thank you so much. This is just what I needed."

The sun beat down, warming and comforting; soothing her skin and relaxing her tense body and taut soul. If only she were here with Pete. How perfect, how romantic. She imagined his long, strong body, his skin on her skin and began to drift into erotic fantasy.

The light on her eyelids went momentarily dark, and she opened them to see a fluffy white cloud drift past the sun. Marzun pulled his towel close to hers and lay down. The renewed brightness of the sun, as it emerged from behind the cloud, made Meg close her eyes again, but Marzun's proximity made her feel slightly uneasy.

She leant up casually, leaning on her elbows and said, "Let's go for a swim."

Marzun lay on his side, leaned over her, and brushed a hair from her face gently, "Not yet. I can think of a way for you to say thank you."

Her heart froze as he caressed her shoulder and traced a lazy line down her arm with his fingertip. She shuddered inwardly and felt panic rise as she tried to think of some other 'way' than the one that had obviously occurred to him. She was stuck on a beach with no means of escape. Her feelings went from total trust and calm to complete and utter disappointment. She was wildly thinking of the best way to handle the situation.

"Oh Marzun, I really like you," she began in a soft, kind voice with a strong feeling of déjà vu. "But I thought we were clear that we were just friends."

"Oh come on," he urged. "It will be good."

He turned on his best Greek charm, "A sharing of our bodies under the sun. It is only natural to want this. We are not doing anything wrong."

Meg wanted to be sick. She knew she had to protect his ego but she didn't quite succeed with, "You are a very handsome man, but I'm sorry I don't want to sleep with you."

*'Sleep! – Ha!' She didn't want to have sex with him. She didn't want his hairy body anywhere near hers. How dare he!'*

"But why?" he almost wheedled, keeping his voice low.

"I have a boyfriend," she told him pathetically, "I hope you can respect that."

"Huh! What do you English girls care about respect and faithfulness?" He was losing his gentle approach.

Meg remained outwardly calm. She had to get back to Nikiana. He kept on. His hand moved onto her thigh.

"Come on Meg – you know you want it. Why not?"

"Because I don't fancy you," she finally said. It came out softly enough.

He threw his body on top of her, pinning her arms to the soft relenting sand. She was now terrified, as he pushed his weight onto her. She looked straight into his dark eyes defiantly and saw the black brows meeting in the middle. He stared back with dark and violent eyes, and then swore loudly and stood up. He began to pick everything up and head for the boat. Meg followed. She was not going to be left stranded. He didn't stop her from getting in and they set off.

It was a long, silent journey back. Meg huddled as far away from him as possible in the small craft wanting to cry, needing to cry, but refusing. "Was it her fault?" she asked herself repeatedly.

She had felt safe because she knew his family. Was it naïve and stupid of her to go out on a boat with this man that she really barely knew and not presume that he would expect sex? All she concluded was that if that was true, how very, very sad.

When they got back, Meg thanked him without smiling and made her way quickly over towards the bar. She couldn't fight with him; he was so close to Callista and Michael. It seemed as if all the guests were there, and they were all watching her. She didn't care; she was actually pleased and relieved to be back with them all. Whatever they might be thinking. She smiled and said hello to them all and managed to laugh when one called out,

"Wouldn't mind your job! Swanning around on a boat all day."

"Just doing some research and getting photos," she replied, holding up her camera.

Marzun came up behind her and with a mean glint in his eye he called out "See you later, Meg," and winked at her, for everyone to see.

"Thank you for your help," Meg called back, but the damage had been done.

She somehow managed to get back to her damp, musty room before breaking down in tears.

She took out the card from Pete and let huge salty drops fall onto the page causing the ink to fatten and blur. She pulled out the card she had managed to find for him. A little bear sitting on a swing and the words *'Lost without you"* which mirrored the penguin's message in the card he'd sent to her. She grabbed her pen and quickly wrote.

*'I miss you so much. All not going well. I just want to be with you."*

She sealed it, stuck a stamp on it, and after splashing her face with water and sticking a pair of sunglasses on to cover her red eyes, she headed for the post box. She stood in front of the post box and held the envelope on the edge of its mouth unwilling to let go. 'Should she say more? What good would it do?'

There was something about putting letters into post boxes. It was that letting go. Once it had fallen from your fingers it was literally out of your hands. Whatever had been written would now be read. Nothing could stop those words from being there, undeniable. Meg thought about the hundreds of job applications she had written. Time spent agonising about finding the right words, praying you'd said the right thing to persuade some anonymous person that you were who they wanted. Each one had been posted with that moment of hesitation before a passive red mouth swallowed it without question. Then the wait. The excruciating time pretending not to think about it, but jumping every time the letterbox in the door rattled. Rushing to pick up the post and find the envelope with the tell-tell company logo. Slowly opening, pretending you don't really want it, eternal optimism rising – this is going to be the one – and then stomach buffeting destruction as the familiar words of a standard letter tell you, thank you, but no thank you.

Meg remembered with a grimace about the time she had mixed up letters and envelopes. One written very formally had gone to a friend of her aunt. The other chatty and very informally introducing herself as the niece of someone he knew had gone to a radio station. She received an amused reply from the radio station saying he was sorry he had never met her aunt and no, they didn't have any vacancies. (Not for scatter-brained dodos thought Meg.)

The other letter did result in a phone call from the aunt's friend to tell her that he thought she may have mixed up letters but was intrigued to know how she had his address. When she explained the full story, he had roared with laughter and offered to meet her to see if he could help with work. He obviously remembered that Meg's aunt was incredibly beautiful and was interested in checking her out. They got on very well, but it soon became apparent to her that he couldn't actually help her and after a few dinners without getting into her knickers, he lost touch. Meg sighed at the memory and let go of the card. She heard it flutter against other letters waiting patiently inside for the next stage in their journey and exhaled.

She lay on her bed trying not to think about what could have happened with Marzun. Great tears slid down her cheeks as she ached for Pete to come and rescue her.

She went down for evening office and Michael asked her if she had enjoyed the boat trip. She couldn't trace any irony in his voice.

"It was fine," she responded blandly. Then added, "I was right. You are much better looking than either of them."

He raised his eyebrow and actually smiled.

She dealt with the innumerable inane questions from guests on automatic pilot, but noticed that complaints about the actual accommodation were few. Most of the questions were about where to go, what to eat, when they should do things, what they should wear and what the weather was going to be like. Others began to search her out, not to complain, but to tell her about their personal problems and ask for her advice. It seemed she had become nurse, advisor, confidante and meteorologist. She barely had a minute to herself.

# CHAPTER 27

Meg stayed in her 'office' in the bar and, between interruptions, wrote some letters to friends and family. Callista came in beckoning to her urgently. Meg was immediately embarrassed. Was she going to be told off? Did Callista know that she had upset number one son's best friend and her favourite nephew?

"Telephonee – quick!"

Meg jumped up and rushed round to the little apartment. She stopped short of the door. She did not want to see Marzun. She went in quietly and picked up the receiver.

"Hello."

"Hello – it's me," came the familiar voice.

"Hello you."

Her heart was doing strange things. She had not expected Pete and she was so pleased. Then despite all her thoughts and the words in the card, she found herself telling him everything was fine. It was partly because she didn't know whether Marzun was listening, and partly because she was afraid that if she started to say how she really was, she would burst into tears.

She let him tell her everything he was doing, and they clicked into easy conversation talking about all kinds of nonsense and making each other laugh. She felt the love in his tone and they both kept the conversation going each time it seemed to be stopping, neither wanting to finish. When it finally came to say good-bye, he whispered "I love you" and she replied with a heartfelt "I love you, too."

She came off the phone flushed and happy, but as she turned to leave, she saw a shadow by the kitchen. She turned back and saw Marzun move across the living room and go out of the patio door. She felt a shiver of fear, but thought of Pete and smiled. At least he knows I wasn't lying about a boyfriend she realised.

'Good timing for once, Pete.'

Grant and Erica took her out for dinner and after a few wines, she plucked up the courage to tell them what had happened. She was embarrassed, feeling it was her fault.

"Was it stupid of me to go?" she asked.

"Bloody hell no! What an arrogant and selfish bastard!" exclaimed Erica.

Meg looked at Grant.

"Yes, maybe," he muttered, thinking.

"Rubbish!" cried Erica. "She told him the score before they went and even then when she said 'no' he should have accepted that with good grace."

"He was an arse for not accepting 'no', but you should have known that that was what he was hoping for."

"I didn't," Meg said, sadly. "It honestly did not occur to me."

"Well, look. You're fine, nothing bad happened. At least he didn't rape you." Grant said trying to make light of it.

"I know. I thought he was going to," she said. Tears pricked at her eyes.

"Well, I don't agree with you, Grant. I think Meg did nothing wrong. But let's forget about it. Meg, come with us tomorrow. We're going over to Meganisi on one of Niko's boats.

Mike arrived with mopeds and jeeps just before midday. Meg checked that everyone had collected and paid for their vehicles and then she was free to head up to Nidri with Grant and Erica.

She booked a boat trip for the following week and they hired a small motorboat from Niko and set off bobbing and laughing across the waves. Once past the headland and away from the water skiers zipping up and down along the length of the bay, they aimed for the crouching hulk of Meganisi. With no one else around, Meg and Erica took off their bikini tops and rubbed sun cream into their bodies, while Grant pretended to lose control of the steering and shouted

"Lucky me!"

The girls told him to shut up and concentrate on where they were going as they made themselves as comfortable as possible, leaning their heads back against the end of the boat and soaking up the heat. Suddenly Grant yelled,

"Look, look!"

Meg and Erica sat forward in surprise at his outburst, looking around to see why he was shouting. Ahead of them, Meganisi loomed up out of the sea. Greenery stretched up over the top of the mass and clusters of red rooftops could be seen peeking out here and there across the visible landscape. At sea level sheer grey rocks stood relentless against the marauding waters. They could see the clearing and the small bay with the taverna. However, this was not why Grant was exclaiming. He pointed to the open sea to the left of the island and as they strained their eyes, the fins of two dolphins suddenly appeared. Delicately they emerged and submerged, a shimmer of smooth grey, the water catching the sun and glinting around them. Then one after the other they leapt completely out of the water in sweeping arcs giving a brief show before disappearing once more. The three in the boat stared and stared at the spot and looked al around trying to catch another magical glimpse, but they had gone. They whispered to each other, afraid to spoil the moment with normal voices, and decided to head for the bay all the while looking out for more dolphins.

As they got closer, Meg enjoyed their excitement as Grant and Erica saw the basin cut into the rock by some bizarre freak of nature, and realised that there was a taverna in the middle.

They tied the boat up on the jetty wall and clambered out onto the dusty floor. There was no one around, and the taverna sat forlornly in the middle of the bare, flat clearing. In the unforgiving daylight, it looked shabby and deserted. Tables and chairs were stacked on top of each other under the veranda. They walked towards it and saw that the truck was there, so they wandered around to the back. Three men were sitting at a table eating from plates of bread and salad. They were wearing black trousers and white vests. When they saw the three explorers, they jumped up in welcome.

"Are you open?" asked Grant hopefully.

Meg realised one of the men was Kris, the table eater, and at the same time he recognised her and leapt over to give her a huge hug. Without another word, the Greek men ushered them round to the front and set up a table and chairs. The obligatory blue and white tablecloth appeared along with cutlery and glasses. Water was poured out and a bottle of Retsina was opened.

"No menu," apologised Kris, "We have some fresh fish and salad. Is okay? Everyone come evening time. Not so pretty in the day!" he said, waving his hand around.

They sat, ate, and drank in their private restaurant, laughing and joking with the waiters. Meg insisted that they climb up to the little church. She wanted to take some photos in the daylight. It was very hard going in the heat of the day and Erica begged them to stop three or four times on the way up. But, with the help of alcohol spurring them on, they made it to the church. Not as magical in the daytime, it was still charming, and the view over the sea back to the coastline of Lefkas was breathtaking. They practically fell back down, and drank plenty of water before accepting a bottle of wine on the house.

"What shall we celebrate?" asked Kris.

"My birthday!" blurted out Meg.

It wasn't anywhere near her birthday, but it was force of habit in this situation. She and friends often declared it was someone's birthday and the whole bar or restaurant would join in singing 'Happy

Birthday' and if you were lucky, sometimes a free cake or drink would be offered.

"When is your birthday?" asked Kris.

"Oh, it's next week," laughed Meg. She presumed Grant and Erica knew she was joking.

"So, that is it then. Happy Birthday to a beautiful lady!"

They clashed glasses and drank.

Time moved very quickly, as it does on a drunken afternoon and they realised that they ought to get back. They paid and left, shouting thank yous and promises to return as they clambered very unsteadily back into the boat. Grant pulled over and over at the starting rope and fell backwards onto the floor of the boat as it finally burst into life. Grinning stupidly, he regained control and they waved to the waiters lining the jetty.

Elated and full of good humour, they didn't notice the change in the water. The sky lay smooth and blue above them and the sun still shone down brilliantly. They were mid-channel when the swell increased and the little boat smashed against oncoming waves, which threw them up in the air and dropped them down again with a heavy smack. Suddenly, the engine cut out and they were at the mercy of the currents, as Grant tried desperately to restart. The rocks of the headland drew them in.

Meg and Erica paddled pathetically with the oars. They all sobered up very quickly as the boat floundered and was thrown around relentlessly by the sea, ever nearing the jagged edges. The engine shot into life and, just in time, Grant steered the craft away from the hungry rocks. The boat rose and crashed, soaked by spray for what seemed like hours, as they battled to get past the jutting rocks of the headland and into the calmer water in the bay. With total relief, they rejoined the lazy world of pedalos and lilos; water skiers gliding over the glass like surface, all oblivious to the angry sister waters beyond the headland.

Niko was standing at the water's edge waiting for them with concern. He knew the sea and he had seen the signs for rough water out to sea. He was angry with them for going so far. Any longer and he was going to send out a search party, he told them. Humbled and apologetic they pulled the boat up to him. He saw their faces and laughed. "Never under-estimate the sea, my friends. I think you learn big lesson."

# CHAPTER 28

Meg got back just in time for evening office hours. She didn't have time to shower, so she did what she could to improve her bedraggled, salty appearance in the toilet at Michael's, and went to sit in her usual spot with a cup of coffee. She hoped Marzun wasn't around.

It was quiet. A few people sat on the terrace still in beachwear, but most were either out exploring, or they had gone to change for the evening. She felt very relaxed. It had been a great day out and she had only had loving thoughts of Pete, missing him warmly, not with the aching fear that he didn't love her anymore. She gazed into space wondering what he was doing. A small cough behind her broke her reverie. She turned and Brenda was looming over her, looking very disconcerted.

"Hello" said Meg cheerfully.

"Er, hello, could I have a quick word?" Brenda looked behind her in an odd way as she spoke.

'Of course – sit down."

Brenda sat down nervously on the edge of the chair next to Meg. Her eyes kept darting to the door as she spoke.

"Listen, I'm really sorry about this. Mary's got a bit of a problem."

Meg immediately thought that she might have to organise another hospital trip and sat forward concerned. At that moment, they were interrupted by loud voices outside. The door of the bar opened and the jolly lady from up the hill came rushing in looking wildly around for Meg. When she spotted her, she called for her to come quickly. Brenda told Meg that she could wait, so Meg hurried outside.

At the edge of the road, a small crowd had gathered around one of the three girls, Laura. They had hired mopeds and Laura was crying and holding her leg. Meg rushed over and asked everyone to stand back, dreading what she was going to see. The inside of Laura's leg had a bright red patch spreading down her calf. She had brushed it against the exhaust sitting on the back of the bike. Meg had seen this before on previous trips to Greece; it was a common injury and she thought she remembered what to do. She looked at it carefully and was pretty sure it was only superficial. It was obviously very painful and Laura was certainly letting everyone know that. She got a bucket of water for Laura to put her leg in to take away the heat, then she dried it carefully before bandaging it lightly with gauze that Callista had given her. Her friends then half-carried the limping Laura to her room. Meg returned to the balcony with everyone saying well done. She was pleased she had been useful. She looked around for Brenda, but she had disappeared. Then she saw that she was down below on the terrace with Mary, so she went down to apologise for the interruption and find out what was wrong. As she neared their table, she caught Brenda's eye and took in the almost imperceptible shake of her head.

"Hi," said Meg taking the hint and changing tack, "I was just wondering if you'd be interested in the boat trip I've organised."

Mary gave her a strange look and then looked straight at Brenda.

"Oh I don't think it's really our thing. Thank you."

At that moment, Gregor appeared with his two friends at the top of the steps looking around.

"Hi Meggie!" he called when he saw her.

They had become good friends. Meg teased him about his Casanova attitude, but always chatted to him when she went to the taverna to let them know how many people would be coming and jokingly told him when new girls arrived. She waved and smiled.

"Good looking boy, that," commented Mary. "Aren't you interested in snapping him up?"

Meg burst out laughing and said, "Oh no! Not my type at all."

"No, I didn't think so," Mary said flatly, and gave Brenda a knowing look.

Brenda raised her eyebrows and sighed.

"Right, well have a think about the boat trip. It takes you right around one of the beautiful islands. Have a good evening," Meg said and moved away feeling very confused and embarrassed by Mary's coldness.

She went over to Gregor and told him about Laura. A girl needing sympathy. How perfect for him. They laughed together with Meg teasing him for being such a flirt.

"I heard that you have a Greek girlfriend."

"Oh yes!" he smiled. "She is beautiful girl. Girl I will marry."

"So what are you doing with all these girls on holiday?" asked Meg, shocked.

"Just some fun before I settle down and make my mother happy. I am young man and these girls... I am making their holiday a good time. They go home and say good things about Lefkas." He smiled the smile of an angel.

Meg shook her head and laughed, "Ah! So it's just good for business?"

"Good for business, yes. Nice work, if you can get it. Is that how you say?"

They both laughed and Gregor gave her a hug, "Only you good girl, Meggie."

The girls arrived soon after, with Laura hopping and resting her arms on her friends' shoulders dramatically. Gregor winked at Meg before rushing over to assist and to find out what happened with charming concern.

Meg returned to the balcony and Grant and Erica joined her for the rest of the evening. Meg mentioned Brenda's strange visit, and Grant and Erica burst out laughing.

"You mean the two ladies who are here together?"

"Yes," Meg said.

"Well you realise they are *together*?"

"What do you mean?" Then her jaw dropped. It hadn't even occurred to her.

"No! Are you sure?"

"We overheard them the other day having a little tiff about you"

"What do you mean – about me?"

"Mary is jealous of you and she thinks Brenda fancies you."

"No!" Meg cried, aghast.

"Afraid so."

"But they saw me go out with Marzun on his boat."

"They also saw you come back and could see you were not happy."

"Did you really hear them saying all this?"

"Yes, we thought it was highly amusing."

"Why didn't you tell me?"

"Didn't think it mattered."

"Yes, I think Brenda is a bit old for me," she said in a serious voice.

They both stared at her, unsure what she was saying.

She laughed at them.

"I've got a boyfriend actually."

She told them a bit about Pete. She'd not mentioned him before. It was too confusing and she thought it would be too boring for a couple so obviously happy and together.

Erica spoke first. "We've all been there. Grant and I split up for three years before getting it together."

"Yes. I was an idiot and nearly lost her."

Erica smiled gently at him and reached for his hand, "Actually it worked out for the best. I became more confident and independent, more in control of my own life and feelings. After the initial hurt, I was much stronger when Grant came back for me. We were both absolutely sure that we didn't want anyone else. Bit older and a bit wiser. Sometimes you have to let go to see if it is meant to be."

Grant continued, "I thought I was doing the right thing when I left Erica, thought there was more out there, all those women I was missing out on. Soon found out that the reason I felt so confident about myself was because that's how I felt with Erica. There were plenty of women, but it was never as comfortable and exciting at the same time. If you know what I mean."

Meg thought she understood what they were saying. She had thought that she was taking control when she came to Greece, but she felt more lost than ever. It had not had the desired effect on Pete and yet he was still there saying he loved her but not committing. They had split up before and got back together. He had been working away for nearly two years and they still loved each other. Was he still thinking that something better might come along?

Meg went to bed thinking about Pete's strong, lean body, legs too long for the average bed, his thick, dark hair receding slightly at the temples above his soft brown eyes. And his gentle, caressing hands. She was aching for him, despite all her own efforts, when she finally slept.

# CHAPTER 29

The next day, Sandra arrived to tell Meg that she was leaving and a new girl was arriving to help run Nikiana. Things had got worse in Vasiliki. With two flights coming in a week for that resort they were getting in a mess working out accommodation, and it was the height of the season. Sandra had done her best to control and organise bookings but they had continued to send people over without any actual accommodation for them. Spiro had been running around persuading local people to rent out rooms. He was in a permanent state of explosion and Sandra was a nervous wreck.

Meg remembered the cool, serene lady she had met just a couple of weeks ago and compared her to the lady in front of her shaking, worn out, exasperated and on the verge of tears.

Sandra suggested that Meg leave as well, but Meg knew she wasn't ready. Something told her to stay. She couldn't keep running. Although, given the circumstances she wondered whether she just wasn't a good judge of when to give up on certain things.

She was so sad to see Sandra go. She was losing an ally as well as a friend. Sandra reached into a bag and brought out some letters and a small blue packet, which she gave to Meg. Meg put the letters on the table and held the delicate packet looking at Sandra questioningly.

"Open it. It's just a small gift to say thank you."

Embarrassed, Meg opened the paper wrapping and saw something glinting inside. She pulled out the most exquisite silver dolphin, the length of her fingernail, attached to a fine chain.

"Oh, it's lovely! I love dolphins."

"I love dolphins too. It's going to be the name of my company when I get back home."

Meg looked up in surprise.

"Yes, this has been an awful experience, but I've decided anyone can do better than this and I don't want to work for anyone else, so I'm going to start my own travel agency. Keep in touch and when you get back, I may have a job for you."

Meg was stunned, very pleased and felt quite emotional.

"Of course I'll keep in touch. Thank you so much. I wish I had something to give you."

"Just keep in touch. Remember you're a wonderful person. From the way you've handled things here, you can cope with any job. Believe in yourself."

Meg's stomach gave a little jump. Nobody had ever said that to her before. She didn't think she was so wonderful at all. She hugged Sandra and told her to write with an address as soon as she could. They walked outside and Meg waved her off with a burning in her chest. She wandered back inside with that empty, lost feeling that she always got after saying good-bye to Pete. The letters were lying on the table where she had left them, so she sat down to read them and distract her self.


There were four. One was from her brother, Chris, chiding her for leaving him to deal with their Mum. She knew he was joking. In fact, Mum was fine. She'd eventually got over the shock and depression and had found new life in all sorts of strange hobbies. For the last year she had had barely any time to see any of her children as she began life anew. It was almost as if she blamed them for taking away the best years of her life. Her latest interest was rescuing stray dogs which she'd taken a bit too seriously and apparently she had taken a dog home from the park that actually had good owners desperately upset by their little Sammsy's disappearance. The letter cheered her up and she moved onto the next envelope smiling to herself and shaking her head. She didn't recognize the handwriting and it turned out to be from Tim. He had written four sides of foolscap. It was light and humorous to begin with and she felt relieved until she reached the last page. He wanted to see her when she got back and he wouldn't ever forget the wonderful time he had with her. It didn't make her feel good. She felt under pressure, and guilty. She folded the paper carefully and put it back in its envelope with a sigh.

The third letter was from Rachel. Meg had written giving her all the details, half-hoping that she wouldn't actually come, but the words told her that Rachel had booked and was coming out the third week in September. Meg found that she was pleased. It would be good to see her. She just hoped she wasn't sacked again before then.

The last letter was from Pete. She had kept it for last as usual. The opening words made her heart jump and her tummy twirl as they told her how much he loved her and didn't want to lose her.

"Good morning!" A cheery voice interrupted her reading. She looked up to see Brenda and Mary looking over her shoulder. She quickly folded the letter and pushed it under the other envelopes.

"Oh, hi. Good morning. How are you?"

Meg saw Brenda looking intently at her and Mary still with that slight scowl. Meg took her opportunity.

"Sorry. I was just reading my letters. One from my boyfriend," Meg said casually. Brenda breathed in sharply and then smiled in relief and winked at Meg. Mary shifted uncomfortably and looked very taken aback. Meg carried on in uncharacteristic chatter.

"Yes. Oh, it's so good to hear from him. I miss him so much."

Mary started to become very interested and friendly, "How long have you known him, dear?"

Meg answered with exaggerated enthusiasm and gave a picture of total happiness and plans for the future. She was here while he was in Saudi saving up for a house. Mary seemed satisfied that it was all true and softened her approach now the threat of the younger woman was gone.

"Well, good luck. Brenda, I'm just off for a swim. Order us both some coffee, love."

She strolled off to the sea without looking back and Brenda smiled. "Thank you," she said to Meg.

"No problem," Meg laughed.

Brenda went off to order breakfast from Michael and Meg picked up Pete's letter thinking if only what she had just said to Mary was true. She read the opening lines again, letting her hopes rise. His words continued.

*"Seems you want to travel and see the world and that's great. You do what you have to do and I'll be able to come and visit you wherever you are in the world."*

Her heart sank to the depths of her body. She didn't want to travel the world, not alone, anyway. What was he thinking? What message was she giving him? Oh God!

# CHAPTER 30

The next boat trip went well. Niko had organised everything and he waved them off from the dock. They went around Meganisi and stopped at the most charming and picturesque bay of Vathi; a deep inlet lined with small houses right on the waterfront, with fishing boats bobbing gently on the water. Rich, green vegetation spread over the gently sloping hillside and more white washed houses with their red roofs dotted up the mountain between the trees. The whole area was, as yet, visibly untouched by tourism. The water was crystal clear and they were welcomed at the taverna by friendly, kind, hospitable people and mouth-watering food. (For those who dared try.) It was glorious. Everyone also appreciated an unscheduled stop at the Onassis island of Skorpios where each tried to get a glimpse of the house built into the landscape behind a well-disguised barrier of electric fences.

The final day for many of the guests, including Erica and Grant, arrived. Spiro had not suggested a barbeque, surprisingly enough, so Meg was wondering what she should organise for a farewell bash. She put up notices about the coach departure time but decided to go round and speak to everyone personally and get some idea of whether they wanted to do something that evening. She walked down to Mr. Patel's room and then back along the beach, round the chalets and then up to the Hill accommodation in the searing heat. She asked if anyone wanted to meet in the bar and then go for a final meal together and was met with complete indifference. They all seemed to have their own plans. Meg was quite relieved and went to see if Grant and Erica wanted to do something with her.

They were a little embarrassed when they told her that they had decided to go up to Nidri for a final romantic dinner on their own. Meg quite understood. Why on earth would they want to spend it with her? She said she hoped they had a great time without any qualms and headed back to her room to shower. She was hot, sweaty and grimy after all the traipsing around.

She decided that after the evening office she would take it easy and write a few letters. It would be the first evening all to herself since she arrived. Then she pictured herself in her musty, grotty room and didn't feel so happy. Maybe she would risk staying with Michael and Lorraina. Marzun must have gone back to Athens by now. She persuaded herself that it would be great to have some time to get her thoughts in order. She walked along the beach to the office refreshed and clean. The air was just starting to cool and the sand felt warm between her toes. The gentle sea lapped at the shore and a sweet breeze ruffled the leaves. She noted as she did everyday how absolutely beautiful the island was. And she mulled, as she did everyday, over what she could say to Pete. The beach was completely deserted; there were usually a few who stayed until the sun went down. The bar too was empty. She presumed they were all packing or changing to go out early on the last night.

She sat quietly on the balcony with not one visitor coming to the 'office'. She ordered a glass of wine; her personal signal that she was not officially on duty any more and remained sitting at the table watching the blue sky slowly change as the sun began to go down on the other side of the island. The trees were gradually thrown into black silhouette and the sea turned from bright blues and greens into black oil. A few bright stars became visible on the darkening azure. She became entranced by the natural peace and beauty of the view contrasting greatly with her inner conflict as she tried to think clearly and make sense of her life so far. The flame of ambition burned inside. Her desire to be with Pete burned inside.

She had always felt that she was meant to do something important, had never had any doubt, and now the feeling was physically painful as she felt so lost and unimportant and without direction.

She had read interviews with successful people who made comments saying they'd always known that they would be successful and that things had just fallen into place. Maybe everyone felt that way, but unless they did become successful, they never got the chance to say those words. How many people were there in the world, who had this feeling, but were left thinking 'what is this about?' when nothing seemed to be working out? So far, all her burning ambition had achieved was a cold iron bed, a job that was heading nowhere and a fucked up relationship. She wasn't thinking bitterly, just honestly assessing her situation and seeing if she could see a way forward, a way to change things. She wanted to get things back on track without doing anything rash or impulsive. Again.

She thought about Pete's letter. A niggling thought occurred to her. Whenever he was in Saudi, he was loving and attentive but as soon as he got leave, he was off doing his own thing and fitting her into his plans when it suited him. She looked at the pattern. Whenever she tried to finish it, he came running but as soon as he made sure that she was still madly in love with him he'd take her for granted again. She really didn't know how to play the game properly. Nothing she ever did or said was part of some greater plan. She had watched girls at school and university 'catching' their man with words, gestures and actions and Meg didn't think she could do that. Did that mean that she would always struggle? Her brain hit a wall. She was about to order another glass of wine, her stomach in its own knots when Erica came in. She was still wearing the same shorts and T-shirt as earlier.

"Hi Erica. I thought you were off to Nidri."

"Oh yes we were just packing up first. Listen Meg. Can you just come over to our room? Grant's back is playing up and I can't lift the case off the bed."

Meg immediately agreed. She didn't see Erica wink at Michael as they left. Grant and Erica's room was in the second block of 'Tenco', away from the road. As they passed by the outdoor shower, Meg was met with a huge cheer. Everybody staying in Nikiana seemed to be there sitting around tables. Meg was astounded and then mortified as they all burst into 'Happy Birthday' and Brenda came up with a cake alight with candles. Meg was going to protest and say it wasn't her birthday, but when she looked at all the faces so pleased at their surprise, she knew she couldn't. Brenda proposed a toast to their special rep, who had looked after them all and turned what seemed like a disaster on arrival into a great holiday. Meg cut the cake and handed it round, genuinely thanking everyone. She was delighted but had an overwhelming urge to laugh hysterically. When everyone was drinking and talking amongst themselves, she took Erica to one side.

"Erica this is wonderful, but I've got to tell you it's not really my birthday. I thought you knew I was joking on Meganisi."

Erica laughed. "Grant and I knew. Don't you remember talking about horoscopes? Yours didn't quite match up to the date. It was Brenda's idea to have a party and I just happened to mention someone might be having a birthday."

"Do you think I should tell them?"

"God no! They're really pleased with themselves. They got the baker to make the cake and he supplied the tables, and the wine. Cheers Birthday girl!"

They both giggled like little girls.

"Careful, all these birthdays will age you."

"I feel like I've already aged twenty years since I got here."

Meg got merrily drunk allowed them to give her the bumps and got up on the table with Erica to dance. What the hell! They were all leaving the next day. She fell into bed some time later and into a deep sleep.

Next morning was a more subdued farewell. Grant and Erica gave her their address and wished her luck before boarding. They were both bronzed, their hair streaked blonde from the sea and sun. Grant gave her a big hug and ruffled his hand over her curly hair.

"Take care and call us if you're in the area."

"Yes, make sure you do!" added Erica and she too hugged Meg.

"Thank you," replied Meg, from the heart. "You've been really good to me."

"And watch out for lecherous Greek men!" Grant added as his parting advice. Meg felt sad saying goodbye, but everyone that said goodbye that morning had had a great time and they all thanked her, so she had a good feeling as she walked back inside wondering who would be arriving next. Sandra had told her a new girl was coming. She prayed she was more useful than Lindy.

# CHAPTER 31

Meg busied herself with the notice board and checked with Callista that all her rooms were ready. The little lady, still as kind and bossy as ever, was coming over the road with a large bag of dirty linen almost as big as she was. Meg ran over to help but Callista ignored her offer.

"You think I not manage?"

"No, no. Just seeing if I could help you. Fine, I won't bother."

Meg raised both hands in surrender and walked away.

"Okay, okay. Maybe you help me take upstairs."

Meg helped her carry fresh linen to the top apartment and Callista brought up the subject Meg had been dreading. Since Alexander's visit with Marzun, Meg had been relieved that Callista treated her in exactly the same way as always.

"So, you like my boy?"

Meg smiled and truthfully said that she did; she'd barely met him.

"I know he very handsome, charming man. And Marzun, maybe you like him. He bad with the ladies you know? They both bad with the ladies," she chuckled proudly and added, "You no be hurt. My boys save themselves for Greek girls."

"Oh that's great!" exclaimed Meg sounding a little too pleased, "They will be very lucky girls," she added quickly.

Callista smiled broadly, "Yes, yes. You never mind. You find nice Engleesh man. This man he phone? He sound good man."

"Yes, I think he is," Meg said wistfully.

"You make him chase. This the way. Slowly, slowly catchee monkey."

And then she started to laugh to herself.

"What?" asked Meg.

"I just thinking. You the monkey."

Meg laughed too, remembering Callista's first description of her. She went back to the bar where Michael was laying out glasses and jugs of Buck's Fizz.

"Ready for the next onslaught?" asked Meg.

Michael gave his usual shrug. His lanky body leaned over the table as he wiped a glass and replaced it on the table.

"You okay?" he suddenly asked.

He had caught her staring absently at the glasses. She snapped herself out of her trance and smiled,

"Yes, apart from being completely knackered."

She had been thinking about Pete. There were no plans and she didn't see how they could have a future the way they were communicating at the moment. Why had she come to Greece? She'd wanted Pete to stop her from going. Now his latest letter showed that he thought that she didn't want to settle down and be with him. And he would soon get her letter. Why did they keep misunderstanding each other? How could they ever get it right?

Her thoughts were interrupted by the familiar drawn out whine and high-pitched yelp of the coach braking and pulling up outside. She pulled herself together and went out to meet and greet with a ready smile.

As usual, the pale complexions of new holidaymakers made their way off the bus in anticipation. Daveed stood at the top of the steps in the coach checking off names on a list. When the last of the guests for Nikiana had alighted, Daveed came out follcwed by two girls about Meg's age.

"Ah, Meg. How are you today?" he asked her in his cheap seductive manner never quite meeting her eyes. "I have brought these beautiful ladies who are going to work with us."

He ushered the first one down the last step, holding her hand to help her down. His eyes never left the well-exposed, large bosom.

"This is Holly," he announced proudly, almost as if he was responsible for the magnificent breasts.

Holly giggled and fluttered her eyelashes at him. "Such a gentleman, David," she said in an ever so sweet voice.

She was attractive, with perfectly styled, smooth, brown hair. She was wearing a flowery sundress, cut low, with buttons down the front; the last few had been left undone, so that her thighs flashed as she stepped off the bus in high-heeled sandals. She looked like she was ready for a fashionable garden party. She held out a well-manicured hand to Meg and limply laid it in Meg's firm grip and gushed.

"David's been making us laugh all the way here! Haven't you David?" she said, lightly slapping his arm and flicking her head to one side.

Meg winced and looked for the second girl. She too was good looking with very long, straight brown hair and very little make-up. She looked slightly built but it was difficult to tell much more as she was wearing a baggy T- shirt and loose cotton pants. David managed to take his eyes away from Holly.

"Oh and this is ..." he paused too long.

"Hi, I'm Becky. Good to meet you," she said. She spoke in a strong Australian accent.

"Right," David said, "Becky is staying here with you, and Holly will be based in Vasiliki. We'll leave you to it. Here are the names of the new guests and where they are staying."

Before Meg could say anything, David had his hand on Holly's backside as he guided her helpfully back onto the coach.

The last thing Meg heard her say was "Oh David, you are so funny," followed by a giggle.

Meg and Becky looked at each other and both raised their eyebrows but said nothing. Meg smiled at her and quickly explained about the welcome drink and then taking people to their rooms. She told Becky to relax for now and said she would explain everything later. They hurried inside to where everyone was quite happy enjoying their drinks, looking at the notice board and chatting.

Meg listened to people getting to know each other discussing the weather in England, the terrible situation with football hooligans and what should be done about it before next season and if they'd seen the film "Back to the Future'. She gathered them together and went into her routine welcome speech, explaining everything that was available, when and where she or Becky could be found and asking them to put their names down for the first evening meal. She then took them to their rooms with Becky following, so that she could get her bearings.

Meg soon discovered that the group for up the hill were still with her and kicked herself for not checking that before David had left. There was no sign of Spiro, of course. She suddenly remembered that there were a couple of jeeps that had been returned and were waiting to be collected. Checking that Becky could drive, she decided to use those. They loaded one with luggage and the other with people all sitting on top of one another – totally unsafe – but they all thought it was great fun.

Gareth and his wife Sandy and three children were very happy with the accommodation, but soon realised that they were a long way from the main resort. Gareth immediately asked if he could hire one of the jeeps. Meg didn't see a problem. She asked him to come down to the bar when he was ready to arrange payment. His wife Sandy was a voluptuous woman with a smiling, cheerful face surrounded by auburn hair. She said that they would definitely like to go for the dinner that evening and go on the boat trip. Meg promised to put their names down. Sorted.

Meg and Becky gave Gareth the keys to one jeep and they left in the other jeep.

"Good job we've got our own transport with the accommodation so spread out," Becky said.

"Unfortunately, we haven't got transport. I just borrowed them because the people had been dropped off at the wrong place."

"Jeez. So how do we get up here? Walking?"

"Yup."

Becky began to ask lots of questions, which Meg answered plainly. Becky soon began to get a clear picture of what she'd come to.

Meg said, "We'd better get back to our office, there will be people complaining about their rooms already."

"That'll be right. Load of whinging poms. Met quite a few of them in London."

"Yes, well, in this case some of them have got a point. Don't worry, once they wind down and realise how beautiful the place is, they stop complaining so much."

Surprisingly, there was nobody waiting when they returned, except Spiro. He greeted them with his customary grace, not even lulling the new girl into a false sense of security. He had lost faith in all his staff and didn't see that it could be anything to do with him.

"Where you go? What you do in jeep?" he shouted at Meg.

"We took the jeeps to deliver guests up the Hill. They have kept one because it's so far from the village."

"What!" His eyes nearly popped out of his head. "They pay, yes?"

"I think you should give it to them for free. He's quite a big bloke and he looked very angry."

Spiro gasped and spluttered, "He can have discount."

"Okay. He'll be here in a minute, so you can discuss it with him."

"No, no. I have to go. Very busy. You take the money. Don't pay Mike. You keep and give to me. Understand?"

Meg understood perfectly that he was charging more than Mike did.

"Where's Becky staying?" asked Meg.

"She stay in chalet one. You tell to her everything. I go now."

Spiro waddled off at his fastest rate and drove off in his old white car, without looking back.

"Wow. Great welcome," said Becky.

Meg was fuming. Chalet one was her old room. She didn't tell Becky this when she took her to it. Becky looked around unimpressed and Meg quickly said that she had better go back to the balcony office. She told Becky to take her time and come over when she had freshened up; she forgot to warn her about the water situation before heading back to the bar feeling very pissed off.

Meg waited in the bar and sure enough, guests gradually came through. They had a few questions but nothing too staggering. Most of those who came to see her were more interested in getting to know her. She had added a few words about the accommodation in her opening speech. She decided that it was better that they have the right expectations rather than a huge shock and it seemed to work. There were a number of comments, but because she had already told them, they were mainly just to agree with her. She had, of course, made the rest of the island sound so wonderful that they were all reasonably satisfied and even excited. Gareth and Sandy were very pleased about the discount.

"We'd have hired it in any case," laughed Gareth. It was a loud, free booming sound that made his chins wobble and his stomach move up and down. "The rooms are fine. Shower's a bit dodgy, but what do you expect in Greece?"

"You have no idea how refreshing it is to hear someone say that," replied Meg.

"Oh, right. Some people will always find some reason to complain. They wouldn't be happy in Buckingham bloody palace. Don't let them worry you love," he laughed again. The booming, resounding sound filled the air and it was infectious.

Becky came over complaining about the cold shower.

"Oh, yes. Sorry, I should have warned you about that. It's great first thing in the morning and sometimes in the evening if you get in before any of the other guests."

"Where are you staying ther?" Becky asked suspiciously. "S'pose it's one of those posh flats where we put that snotty couple, is it?"

"I'll show you, if you like," said Meg. "Shall we grab a bite to eat first? Michael makes the best sandwiches."

Meg introduced Michael to Becky, and he went off to get their food.

"God, he's a happy soul."

'Look who's talking,' thought Meg. "He's fine once you get to know him," she laughed.

She asked Becky about how she got the job and Becky explained that she was travelling around Europe for a year. She'd been in London and had a couple of jobs, saw the advert, and decided to get away from the wet and miserable England. (Meg frowned thinking that the weather in England was fantastic at the moment). Becky continued saying she planned to go grape picking as soon as the season started. She said that she wasn't impressed with the set up and Meg told her that things were much better than when she had first arrived. They carried on talking and Becky began to calm down. Meg decided her moaning was because she'd just arrived. She was bright, witty, and very down to earth. Meg thought they might actually work well together. When they had eaten, Meg took Becky down to show her the 'posh' room in the old villa and Becky was suitably gob smacked.

"Jeez! You must have done something to upset the boss."

"A couple of things, apparently. It doesn't take much. I think they've gone through so many staff now he's given up sacking me."

She told Becky about the first couple of weeks.

"Well, I wouldn't have bloody well stayed," she exclaimed and Meg didn't even try to explain.

# CHAPTER 32

It turned out to be great having someone her own age with a bit of initiative to work with. Becky still managed to complain about just about everything, but she was quite amusing with her descriptions of characters and what they had said or done to piss her off. There was nowhere near the same number of complaints since Meg had sorted out jeeps and mopeds, meals and trips. In her opinion, the guests were great. The types of people coming over did seem to be changing. There were more groups of young single guys and girls, who tended to be more self-sufficient. After a couple of days, Becky managed to persuade Meg that they could sunbathe and swim on the beach next to Michael's; something Meg had never felt comfortable doing in front of the holiday makers.

"Sod 'em. We are entitled to time off, you know. And it's a bloody free beach."

As they stretched out their towels on the sand beneath a bank of overgrown bushes, Meg realised she had not even been for a proper swim in the sea at Nikiana since she arrived. There were not very many people around and they moved a little way along from the bar and nearer to Meg's room in relative isolation. Becky flung off her clothes to reveal a very slim body with a little paunch of a stomach. Above this were the most enormous breasts. She took off her bikini top and they seemed to cascade out of their holdings. Meg couldn't help but stare.

"Bane of my life," stated Becky, obviously used to this sort of reaction. "Sends men wild though."

Meg looked down at her own little peaches in comparison to the watermelons that Becky possessed,

"Same here."

They both laughed and lay face down on their towels for a while, soaking up the heat and not speaking. The sun penetrated their skin and gently heated them until the sweat streamed out of their pores and they could stand it no longer. Putting their bikini tops back on and leaping up, they ran down to the water with Becky using one arm to hold her swinging pendulums. They dived under the waves, the water cold and breathtaking and so refreshing. They floated around for a while and then Meg set off swimming. With strong sure strokes she sped across the water parallel with the shore and then turned and swam back. Oh it felt good.

"Good swimming," remarked Becky, "I couldn't swim across a goldfish bowl."

Back on their towels, the water droplets evaporated quickly in the intense heat of early afternoon.

"Gregor's a bit of a dream," remarked Becky casually. "He's got a bit of a thing for you, hasn't he?"

Meg laughed. "Gregor is absolutely gorgeous, we get on great. But no, he's too young for me and only interested in the holiday girls that I can introduce for a quick fling."

She paused, "Oh God! Does that sound like I'm some kind of Madam?"

She laughed, but Becky didn't respond and Meg realised that she had fallen for him. Meg asked Becky about London. She began talking and it soon emerged that Becky had had an intense relationship with a guy she'd met there. She had thought it was something special until she caught him with her flat mate. It was then she had seen the advert for the job in Greece and had taken it. ('Both of us running away,' thought Meg.) Becky gazed off into the distance morosely and then changed the subject abruptly.

"Did you see that couple from Manchester? What are they called?"

"Amanda and Stephen?"

"Yeh. They couldn't keep their hands off each other and they disappeared very quickly at the end of the meal."

"Maybe they've just got married."

"Or they are having an affair. She's wearing a very tidy diamond on her wedding finger. Can't see anyone coming on this kind of holiday with that sort of money."

Becky went on analysing everybody. She didn't have a kind word for any of them. Eventually, they decide to pack up and get changed. They headed for Meg's room. The bathroom had leaked again and the room was sopping wet.

"Listen," Becky said magnanimously, "there are two beds in my room. Why don't we share?"

Looking at the cold grey walls of her cell and the huge puddle spreading across the floor and under her iron bed, Meg jumped at the offer. Together they gathered up her things and went down to chalet one, laughing and joking about Spiro and the company.

In the evening, they sat in the office taking bookings for mopeds, jeeps and boat trips. Amanda and Stephen came in. They were the only ones still looking pale. Since their arrival, they had barely left their room and people had noticed. There had been others like them, thought Meg. They sat together on the terrace and Meg noted that while they looked very much all over one another, Amanda quite often had a glazed expression, barely listening to Stephen.

Becky announced that she was going to get something from the room and a minute later, Amanda passed by Meg on her way to the toilet. She smiled at Meg and Meg asked her how she was. Amanda looked at her for a moment; she was very pretty with big brown eyes and short, shiny black hair.

"Yeh, great," came the response, not whole hearted.

On her way back from the toilet, Amanda glanced down at Stephen with his back to her and sat down next to Meg. She crossed her slim legs and looking at Meg with innocent doe eyes, she said,

"Listen, about this boat trip," she had a faint Manchester accent compared to Stephen's broad twang.

"I was wondering. Does it go from Nidri?"

"Yes," replied Meg. "We catch the bus up the road and get the boat from the harbour there."

"I've got to tell someone or I'll explode and maybe you can help me. Do you know someone called Malcolm Drewer?"

Meg shook her head, "Sorry, never heard of him."

She looked at Amanda questioningly.

"He's my husband," she said this in a hushed voice, leaning forward, "God. I know this is going to seem awful. We're separated. He caught me having an affair with Stephen. Well, he was always away on business. I got lonely. But, I still love him and I want him back. I found out he was in Nidri, He's got a cruiser docked there. I booked this holiday so I could find him."

Meg couldn't help herself, "But you're here with Stephen."

"Yes, he's not meant to be here. I booked the holiday on my own and when I got on the plane, he was on there too. He'd seen my ticket and booked for himself as a lovely surprise. He doesn't know my real reason for being here."

"I don't mean to be funny, but you seem pretty much with him now."

Amanda gave a little grin. "Yes, well, he's great in bed. Can't say no to great sex, if it's on a plate. Have you seen his body? But that's all it is. Stephen's got no money. Malcolm is a different class and I don't want to lose the life style I had with him. I'm thirty-eight next year,"(Meg was shocked at this. She looked ten years younger.) Amanda continued, "Could you put me down for the trip? I'll come on the bus with you and then I'll go off and look for Malcolm."

"What about Stephen?"

"Oh, don't worry. I'll take care of him. He won't be interested in a silly boat trip. I'll wear him out before I go," she smiled knowingly.

Meg was irritated. Why did she have to be involved?

"Just if he says anything, don't tell him I wasn't on the boat."

"I won't if I can help it, but why don't you just tell him the truth?"

Amanda stared at her as if she was mad, "I don't want to end up with nobody, do I? I'll let you know what happens."

She glanced over at Stephen who was looking around for her, and she waved and gave him a big smile. He smiled back and watched her with admiration as she sauntered back to where he was sitting. She massaged his shoulders as she passed behind him and slid into the chair next to him. He leant forward and they kissed and looked into each other's eyes holding hands. Meg was impressed and horrified at the sheer duplicity.

Becky eventually returned and they had a couple of drinks up at the bar with Michael before heading back to the room for bed. Becky chattered away about the punters, complaining about the whole set up and the inane questions she had been asked. Meg just wanted to sleep. She coped with the guests by listening, smiling, and not thinking too deeply about any complaints she could do nothing about. Compared to the first couple of weeks, everything was very calm, but she couldn't explain that to Becky. She asked Becky where she had been for most of the evening and Becky said, "Oh, I was er, down at the phone trying to make a call home." And that, luckily, was the end of conversation for the night.

They both went on the boat trip and it was good for Meg to share the burden of responsibility and have someone to talk to. Amanda had come along and then disappeared as soon as they reached Nidri. On the boat she and Becky came up with a moneymaking scheme to make printed T-shirts. All the little shops and stalls were selling 'No Problem' vests. Why not make company tops for all the holidaymakers. It was a great idea; they just needed Spiro to help.

The trip went without incident. The weather was perfect; bright blue skies, dazzling clear water and a relaxing stop in the little bay of Vathi on Meganisi, where the taverna was all geared up for twenty or so visitors wanting mainly chips.

Lazing on the deck on the return journey, Meg tried to take time to think about Pete, and what she was going to say to him. At the other end of the boat a man called Barry was reading palms. He was staying with his wife and five young children in the apartment above the bar. His wife a silent, timid woman had not come out on the boat. The children were also very quiet and well behaved. Barry had jet-black hair and piercing blue eyes that seemed to look straight through you. He was softly spoken and had an air of supreme confidence. He had made Meg feel quite uncomfortable when she had first met him. He had asked questions in his soft, almost hypnotic voice and stared into her eyes as if reading things written there. Someone had mentioned that he was a psychic and listening to the burr of his voice as he read people's fortunes in their hands to gasps of wonder, Meg wondered if he could tell her where she was going.

They arrived back in Nidri about four. There was no sign of Amanda and so, partly to protect Stephen's feelings and to protect herself from having to deal with questions from Stephen, she told everyone that they could stay in Nidri to shop and look around or take the next bus back to Nikiana. The idea was for people to make up their own minds, but they asked what she and Becky were doing. Meg said they were going to catch the five o'clock bus and everyone nodded in agreement and went off.

Becky was aghast at the pathetic nature of the holidaymakers and went on and on about it until they reached a stall selling T-shirts. A young Greek salesman came over to practice his English flirting vocabulary and they persuaded him to show them how the T-shirts were printed. It was incredibly simple with the use of a small, manual printing-block.

They made their way back to the bus stop and found everyone waiting for them. There was still no sign of Amanda, but Meg couldn't hold everyone up. Luckily, they didn't see Stephen when they got back. Becky and Meg showered and changed, all the time talking excitedly about T-shirts and how they could persuade Spiro to help them.

"If he thinks he can make money, he'll be keen," stated Meg.

They went over to their 'office' and Meg stopped off at Callista's to ring Spiro. His dulcet tones came down the phone.

"What?"

"Hi, Spiro. It's Meg."

She heard him draw in breath as if expecting trouble, "Yes, yes, what is it?"

"We have an idea to make money."

A sharp intake of cigar. His voice was calmer, suspicious, but interested, "What idea you have?"

"We thought we should make T-shirts for the company."

He blasted, scoffing down the phone, "What! How you think we do this?"

Meg thought the 'we' sounded promising, "We just need a simple print block, some paint and some plain vest tops. If you come here, we can explain. It's really easy and we could sell lots to the guests."

The line went silent for a few seconds and Meg could hear him sucking on his cigar.

"Okay, okay. I come later."

The phone clicked dead. Meg smiled to herself.

She went to tell Becky that it looked very hopeful. She was sitting down on the terrace with two girls on holiday together called Katie and Sharon. Katie was Gregor's latest conquest and he arrived with a friend to take the girls for a 'romantic' walk along the beach. He waved up at Meg before holding court with the girls, including Becky, giggling at his every joke and hanging on every word. Meg was just wondering about Amanda when she walked into the bar. She grinned at Meg and rushed over.

"I've found him!" she gushed.

"What did he say?"

"I haven't actually seen him yet, he was out on his yacht, but I left a message and he'll know where I am. Oh, I can't wait to see him!"

Stephen came in behind her. His firm muscles rippled underneath the tight shirt and he walked over to the two of them confidently.

"Better go," said Amanda as she saw him.

He put his arms around her waist and she smiled sweetly up into his adoring face. Stephen said hello to Meg without really looking at her, and Amanda gave her a wink as they turned towards the beach steps. To anyone, they looked like a young couple, completely in love.

Gregor and friend left with their partners and Becky came back up to join Meg. She didn't look too happy, but before Meg could ask, Callista popped her head in the door and ushered Meg over.

"Spiro outside," she said in her brusque voice.

"Why doesn't he come in?" asked Becky.

Callista shrugged and disappeared. Meg and Becky went outside to find Spiro slunk down in his car in a cloud of cigar smoke. Meg realised he was too frightened to meet anyone. Quickly they explained what they needed and to their amazement, he agreed.

"I supply everything, you give money to me."

"Yes, of course," replied Meg, "But we'll take a cut for making and selling."

His eyes narrowed, "Okay, we see."

Then he drove off without another word. Becky looked at Meg with disgust written on her face and Meg shook her head. They went back into the bar and sat with Michael and Lorraina. They came up with more and more elaborate plans for their T-shirt empire as the evening went on and the metaxas went down.

# CHAPTER 33

Sure enough, Spiro returned the very next day with a very basic wooden print set up, red paint and a pile of pastel yellow and pink vest shirts. Judging by the colours, he had obviously got the cheapest he could find.

"I keep count of shirts, you give me money." Then he added quickly, "Holly will come with lists for this week's flights.

Becky and Meg exchanged looks, but before they could ask anything, he was off.

Forgetting Spiro and Holly, they started looking at the equipment they had been given and tried to figure out how it all worked. A few curious guests came to see what they were doing and between them, they set up the wooden block so that the T-shirts could be held in place while a roller of paint could be pushed across the top of a stencil. They made the stencil and then through trial and error and a lot of red paint everywhere, they found the most effective method of printing cleanly across the chest of the shirts.

It was slow and strenuous work, but they had great fun doing it and set up outside their chalet on the roadside where they attracted a lot of attention and soon had orders flooding in.

The gaudy combination of colours seemed to sum up the whole view of the company and people were buying them for their humour rather than in admiration.

"Joke T-shirts for a joke holiday." As one person put it.

Someone asked if they could make them a T-shirt with the popular 'No Problem' slogan on it and they made up a new stencil. This became more popular than the company name that nobody really wanted to advertise. Meg and Becky enjoyed themselves thoroughly, and despite the continuous demand on their attention for the most mundane of questions, Meg realised that the madness of the first two weeks already seemed a long way away. For the first time, she was glad she had stayed. Becky might moan a lot but she was hard working and full of energy and it was good to have someone to talk to about all the nonsense.

Holly arrived late in the afternoon when they were clearing up red paint from the road. She and Daveed drove up in a jeep and she stepped out of it like a 1960's film star with her hair neatly swept up into a scarf and her red high heeled shoes. She removed the scarf and with a little shake of her head, each hair fell obediently into place.

"Hi girls!" she called.

Daveed put an arm round her waist and Holly trotted over in little white shorts and a low cut top. She viewed the printed T-shirts hanging to dry from the verandah and exclaimed,

"Oh, very good. Haven't you been busy? Well done. You'll have to let me have some to sell."

"If we have any spare. These are all spoken for, I'm afraid," said Becky, trying her best to stay calm.

"Here are the lists," continued Holly without listening. "Call me if you have any probs."

"How's it going in Vasiliki?" Meg asked, trying to keep things light.

"It's a breeze. Course, I had to get Spiro to give me new accommodation. I couldn't even plug my hair dryer into the dump he first gave me. I'm sharing with Daveed in Nidri now, much more central."

"Everybody happy down there?"

"I guess so. The first day was a nightmare. Nothing but complaints, so I just don't show my face too often. Best way. Spiro has put me in charge of all the resorts, and arrivals and departures. Don't know what the woman before me was doing, it's a right mess."

"Right. Thanks for these lists. We'll call if there's anything," Meg replied, trying not to sound too abrupt. She just wanted Holly to go.

"Okey dokey. See you later."

Oblivious to the fast freezing atmosphere, Holly twirled around and set off towards the jeep with Daveed following. He gave Meg and Becky a smug smile before turning and patting Holly lightly on the bottom as she stepped into the jeep and tied her scarf back on her head. The jeep burst into life and they sped off down the road.

"Call me if you have any probs," mimicked Becky. "She must have given Spiro a blow job."

"And Daveed," added Meg.

They both burst out laughing.

"Bloody hell! We're doing something wrong," announced Meg and they both went quiet.

"Let's get on and sort out tomorrow's flight," Meg said trying to sound lively.

There was no formal farewell-do for the few who were leaving. The ones who had been there for a week had made the bar at Michael's their local for the week and it had become quite a lively meeting place each night, with Michael using Meg's compilation tapes to provide background music.

Meg went over early to do the 'office'. Becky was in the bathroom as she went to leave. Standing in her bra and pants she was spending a long time carefully putting on make-up and complaining about spots on her chin.

"See you over there," Meg said, opening the door.

"Right, I'm going down to the shop to get some bits and pieces. Do you need anything?" Becky asked, putting another layer of mascara on.

"Just some water if you could, thanks," replied Meg.

"Have fun," called Becky sarcastically.

Meg strolled across the road in the late afternoon light. The air was still hot from the August sun. The bar was quiet when she arrived, so she sat up at the counter to talk to Michael and Lorraina. She was gradually building up a good relationship with the pair and would end most evenings having a nightcap with them. Lorraina's English wasn't as good as Michael's, so they had amusing conversations with Meg's limited but increasing Greek, Lorraina's complete mix of English and Greek words and a lot of sign language.

Meg had guessed that they had lived in the apartment above the bar before Spiro began renting it. She wondered how they all managed in the tiny apartment below. She finally asked them how it worked. Lorraina laughed and explained that beneath the bar there was not just the cellar, but also three bedrooms and a bathroom. Meg smacked her hand against her forehead. Because there were no windows below, she had assumed there was only a cellar. It was strange to imagine no windows.

"Too expensive," Michael explained, "and no point. Hot in summer and cold in winter. We only sleep, wash and change, so why have windows?"

Of course, it made sense, but Meg thought it would be very claustrophobic not having any windows at all. She took her place on the balcony. She sat alone watching the calming sway of the sea in the light evening and whispered to a lone star wishing someone would tell her what she was meant to be doing with her life. From the bar the sweet voice of Rose Royce echoed her thoughts singing 'Wishing on a Star', one of her favourites from a much simpler time in her life.

People started to come in. A few came over to ask general questions and she got some orders for T-shirts. Some came in to meet up for a drink before going out for a meal. Others ordered snacks and settled down for an evening in the bar. She watched Barry come onto the terrace below her and look around. He moved slowly, confidently, with his back straight and his chin up. Casually, he glanced around the terrace and then stood staring out to sea. Suddenly, he turned and looked up to meet her gaze, and she felt as if she had been caught out, and he had known that she was watching him. She smiled at him and without smiling back at her he made his way up to the balcony where she was sitting.

Very politely, he asked if she was well and sat down. He asked her a few ordinary questions about the flight the next day in a soft melodious voice, and then he stared at her for a while without speaking. His light, almost translucent blue eyes penetrated her darker blue, which she held steady. She could feel goose bumps rising on her arms and at the back of her neck and then he spoke.

"Don't worry, but be careful. This is the calm before the storm. What you want is not what you want. There are surprises in store. Your smile hides many tears and there will be more before you find happiness. Your smile makes jealous people angry, but don't stop smiling. You see but you don't see, you hear but you don't hear, let go and the answers will come."

He stared at her a while longer and Meg waited for him to say more, but he stood up, "Good night," he said with a small nod of his head and walked away with his hands held behind his back.

Meg sat rigid, then shook herself and gave a little snort of disbelief. She went over what he had said in her head and decided he hadn't said anything useful, he was just guessing and full of himself. She felt angry then, how dare he come and speak like that, without her asking? She thought about the palm reader she had gone to before she came and another one for fun at a garden fete the summer before. He had told her that yellow was lucky for her and that there would be a chance for love and commitment in the late summer. She laughed at herself as she remembered going out and buying a whole collection of yellow clothes before meeting Pete for their holiday. It certainly hadn't brought her love and commitment. Then with a jolt she realised there had been the chance of love and commitment. A chance she'd blown. Maybe there was still hope for the gold ring and life in the Middle East. She shook her head and asked Michael for a drink before looking around the bar and terrace. Suddenly, she saw Amanda run down the steps and onto the beach. Meg put her drink on the bar, went outside, and walked over to where Amanda was sitting on the sand staring out to sea.

"Hey, what's happened?" Meg asked softly.

Amanda looked up, her eyes were red and her cheeks were smudged black with wet mascara. She handed a piece of paper to Meg, without speaking. Meg read silently. The note was short and brutally to the point. *'I never want to see you again. You are nothing but a cheap tart. Stay away.'* Meg handed her back the note, not knowing what to say. Amanda filled the silence. She stood up, brushed sand off her shorts, and wiped her face with a tissue.

"Bastard wouldn't even see me! Well, we'll see what my lawyer has to say. He won't know what's hit him. He'll pay dearly for this."

She gave Meg a self satisfied, wicked smile and headed back across the beach with long, determined strides.

# CHAPTER 34

The atmosphere was light and relaxed back at the bar. Katie and Sharon came onto the terrace and called hello up to Meg and she decided to go down and join them.

Where's Becky?" Katie asked Meg.

"Oh, we decided to take it in turns to be on duty in the evening, so she was going to come down a bit later. I thought she'd be here by now, though."

The terrace and the bar filled with people. Tina Turner sang out 'What's Love Got to Do With It'. The sky, clear as ever, twinkled up above. The waves continued their persistent stroking of the shore and the air reached the perfect ambient temperature where you don't even notice it.

"How's Gregor?" Meg asked.

Katie and Sharon grinned at each other.

"What a dream," laughed Katie.

"Not love then?" Meg joked.

Katie and Sharon burst out laughing.

"No, not love but a bloody great shag and he tries to sound sooo romantic. He's sweet."

"Thank God for that," said Meg. "All the others have been tearful wrecks by the end of the holiday."

Too late the words were out. Katie and Sharon looked a bit miffed.

"Oh shit! I'm sorry, that didn't come out right at all."

"And he told me I was the only one for him," Katie sighed melodramatically.

"I'm sorry," repeated Meg.

Katie and Sharon burst out laughing again.

"Don't worry, just messing. We know their type. We haven't fallen for either of them. Makes the holiday though, doesn't it, a bit of romance?" Sharon told her.

"Having a shag, you mean," said Katie and they both laughed loudly again.

At that moment, Becky appeared at the top of the steps. Meg was surprised at her appearance. Considering the time she had spent getting ready, she looked slightly disheveled. Her hair needed a brush and she had smudged her make-up. She came over to join them.

"Are you all right?" Meg asked quietly.

"Of course I'm all right. Why shouldn't I be?" Becky fired back.

"Fancy a drink, girls?" Sharon interrupted. She called Lorraina over and ordered a round of drinks. She raised her glass and said, "Here's to a good holiday and our wonderful reps!"

Meg laughed and said, "Thank you." Becky barely managed a smile and Meg carried on, ignoring her, "So, have you enjoyed it?"

"Have to say that when we first arrived we were not impressed. The accommodation was a bit of a shock and the night life isn't exactly what we were hoping for."

"Yeh," joined in Katie, taking a long drag on her cigarette, "we thought we'd go home brown, but bored. But, actually, it's been really different and we've had a great laugh. We went out with those two lads, Ray and Joe on their mopeds yesterday. What a laugh! Thought we were going to die going along some roads. We went to the most fantastic beach, didn't we Shaz?"

"Yeh! Never thought you'd catch me on the back of a moped. It was hairy! The beach was fab though."

Meg presumed they'd been to Vasiliki.

"Did you have a go at windsurfing as well?" she laughed.

"No, we didn't see no windsurfers."

"Wouldn't have tried, if there had been!"

"God, no!" they both laughed in loud shrill peels.

Meg was intrigued to know which beach they were talking about. There was still so much to discover, she hadn't found anyone to tell her about any waterfalls either.

They all stayed on the terrace until midnight with various people coming and going. Becky relaxed a bit after a few drinks and when they went to bed, they were on good terms, but Meg felt a bit wary about something being wrong.

Katie and Sharon left the next day along with a few others, including Stephen and Amanda. Holding tightly to Stephen's arm, Amanda smiled sweetly at Meg and thanked her for all her help. New guests arrived without too many problems, and generally, compared to the first manic weeks things were becoming relatively smooth. She and Becky had a good routine going and the T-shirt business made a steady little profit. They continued to collect money for mopeds and jeeps, and boat trips, but they never saw Spiro to give it to him. Meg gave Mike the amount he wanted and kept the rest hidden among her things in her room, ready to give it to Spiro as soon as he demanded.

Even things with Pete seemed to have reached some kind of balance. He was phoning nearly every week, although always a day or two later than he said he would, and a couple of humorous cards had come through the post. They talked easily about everything apart from their future and Meg didn't know what to do apart from accept it for what it was, but the ache in her guts was a constant reminder that things were not right. Becky continued to moan about most things, but Meg liked having someone around to share the burden of the demanding, bad tempered guests that came amidst the lovely, friendly ones each week.

Feeling bright and at ease one morning Meg opened the bar door and called out hello as she walked in.

"Hello."

It was a familiar voice, but she knew it wasn't Michael. Startled, she stepped inside and turned to see Marzun sitting at the bar sipping coffee. He smiled broadly at her as if she was his best friend in the entire world and she responded with caution.

"Hello, I wasn't expecting you. How are you?" she asked politely.

"I just arrived. a surprise for Callista's birthday as Alexander couldn't make it."

"Oh, I didn't realise. I must get her something."

"Would you like a coffee?" he asked.

Meg really did not want to be near him, but she felt she had no choice.

"Yes, thank you."

He moved a seat out for her and she sat down moving it back a bit as she did so.

"Still here then," Marzun remarked.

Meg felt it was slightly scathing but she smiled warmly and said, "Yes, can't leave Michael at the height of season."

He nodded and then coolly asked, "Do you want to go out somewhere this afternoon, have a break?"

Meg could not believe he was asking her. She could feel her stomach bubbling warning signs and thought quickly.

"Oh, I'm sorry. I have to go to Lefkas to get some things," she blurted. It was a lie but she couldn't think of anything else in the moment.

"I can give you a lift," he said in a friendly voice. He was not letting go.

"No, it's okay thanks," Meg tried to sound as gentle as possible, but she did not feel comfortable.

Marzun's face went blank. His lips squeezed tightly together for a second, he looked at her intently with sheer hatred, and then he rose and walked off without another word. Meg felt scared. She wanted to talk to someone, but she couldn't tell Michael, and Becky didn't know him, so it would just sound like nonsense. She kept it to herself.

That afternoon when all was quiet, she and Becky went down to a quiet stretch of the beach to laze in the sun for an hour or so. They laid out their towels, smoothed on sun cream and lay on their bellies with the hot sun beating down on their backs. They chatted for a while and then the heat made them sleepy and they began to doze.

A sharp pain in the back of her leg, a kick, roused her, but she didn't move. She just knew it was Marzun. She lay still, wondering if there would be more. Her pulse raced but she didn't look round. Nothing. Still she waited. She heard a branch crack further up the beach and raised her head slightly; her eyes caught the back of him as he disappeared into trees up by the old villa. Becky dozed beside her, droplets of sweat trickling down her brow. Meg felt sick; she was truly frightened. She nudged Becky.

"Someone just kicked me."

"What?" Becky asked drowsily.

Meg tried to explain about Marzun.

"Bloody hell! Are you sure he kicked you?"

Meg realised it sounded mad. She couldn't explain how she'd known and why she didn't jump up when it happened. She looked down at her leg where there was a red mark, but it didn't look like much.

"Are you all right?" Becky asked.

"Yes. I'm fine. Bloody nutter!" she didn't think Becky believed her, so she dropped it.

When they went back to the bar, a bit later, Meg was really worried. There was no sign of Marzun and when Michael came over with drinks, he told her that Marzun had gone.

"Back to Athens?" asked Meg, amazed.

"Yes, said he had an urgent phone call telling him to go back immediately. He left in his car a while ago."

Meg was so relieved, but the fear of his return at any time would not go away.

That evening they'd decided to organise an informal trip up to Nidri. The idea was for Becky and Meg to go up on the bus with anyone that wanted to come and then leave them to entertain themselves before meeting to get the last bus back. However, when they got off the bus everyone started to follow Meg and Becky like a flock of sheep down the street. Meg stopped and pointed to all the restaurants and the rows of shops.

"There are loads of places to eat and a few nice shops. Just go wherever you like and we'll see you all later."

One determined lady said, "Oh no, we want to know where you are going to eat. You must know the best places."

"See you later," Becky whispered to Meg, and without waiting for a response, walked away, across the road.

Meg didn't have time to stop her. She led everyone down the street and found she could do nothing except arrange a group of tables in a quiet restaurant for everyone. She had no idea if it was good or not, but it had space. As it turned out there was good reason for it not being busy. The food was sloppy and greasy; stodgy moussaka and withered stuffed vine leaves swimming in oil, and the service was very slow. Meg found herself apologising and trying to keep people amused, while they complained, oblivious to the fact that they could have gone anywhere else, if they'd chosen. At the end of the meal, Meg was bored and tired of the continual moaning and her fixed grin began to ache: she fumed inwardly at Becky for abandoning her. She quickly told everyone that she was going to do a bit of shopping and that she would see them all back at the bus stop. She left before anyone could demand to go with her.

She breathed in deeply as she wandered back down the row of restaurants full of relaxed, happy holidaymakers in strappy sundresses, shorts and T-shirts. She stopped at a gift shop and bought a present for Callista. She felt guilty that Marzun had not stayed for the birthday and thought it might be her fault. Then she saw Becky laughing and joking with Ray and Joe at a bar. She went to join them. She was already annoyed with Becky but when Becky said,

"Oh, here's muggins. What have you done with them? Led them all into the sea and left them to drown, I hope."

Meg was furious. "Thanks a lot Becky. Where were you?"

"Oh come on, we're not bloody baby sitters!"

"Girls, girls!" interrupted Ray. "Have a drink Meg and sit down."

Meg realised there was no point in having a fight. She sat down and gave them a comic rendition of the ghastly meal and how she had escaped. Ray and Joe laughed but Becky was sulking. Ray ordered more drinks and he and Joe chatted away about the holiday. Becky joined in with them but wouldn't look at Meg. They were first year university students, they'd worked in a pea factory all summer and grabbed a last minute holiday. It wasn't the rave they had expected, but they were making the most of it. They were laughing about Shaz and Katie and their antics with the Greek guys.

"Man eaters!" exclaimed Joe. "But good fun. They were hilarious on the back of our mopeds in their high heeled shoes."

"Oh yes, they told us, and said you went to a fantastic beach."

"Yeh, we've found the most amazing place. Why don't you two come out with us tomorrow?"

Meg and Becky agreed and they arranged to meet the following lunchtime. Becky asked for a lift home on the back of Ray's bike and Meg went back to the bus stop to meet up with the other guests. When she got back to their room, Becky was already in bed and didn't respond when Meg said 'goodnight.'

The next morning Becky was still ignoring Meg and stomping around getting ready. Meg couldn't bear the bad feeling so she broke the ice.

"Sorry about having a go last night," she said, as they walked over to the bar.

"I should think so," Becky replied brusquely.

Meg was astounded and hurt. She had expected Becky to say sorry too. They were both stressed and tired, but Becky obviously felt she had done nothing wrong. Meg wondered if she had been wrong expecting Becky to help, maybe she was the stupid one for feeling responsible for the guests. She felt hot, frustrated and confused. She had wanted to clear the air, but now she felt foggy and hurt.

In the middle of breakfast, Callista called Becky to the phone. She returned to say that she was moving to Nidri. Holly had done a runner. They were both shocked, but the rift between them hadn't had time to heal, so neither could honestly say they were upset. They sat in awkward silence for a while.

"When have you got to go?" started Meg.

"Spiro is coming to get me in an hour or so."

"You'd better go and pack up then."

"Yeh," Becky said without emotion. She finished her coffee and went off to the room.

Meg sat not knowing how to feel. She was relieved in many ways. Becky was an oppressive roommate and she'd been getting moodier, but they'd had some good times and Meg hated the bad feeling. When Becky reappeared with her rucksack, Meg made conversation,

"God, I wonder what happened to Holly."

She expected Becky to make a sarcastic joke but instead she replied,

"Good on her. I'll go up to Nidri today, but I'm not staying in this pathetic dump much longer. You're a mug for putting up with it."

Meg didn't have a response. She'd been starting to enjoy it until the events of the day before. Now she wondered if Becky was right. When they heard the familiar sound of Spiro beeping his horn, they both went outside.

"Good luck," said Meg. "See you on the airport run."

"Yeh, guess so," Becky said. It was a cold and stiff parting and Meg was sad. Though not completely like-minded, they'd shared a lot and told each other secrets. Meg wondered if she'd missed something else for Becky to be so bitter.

Ray and Joe came over at lunchtime and persuaded Meg to come with them on the mopeds. She'd got everything under control, so she decided she would. She climbed on the back of Ray's moped with towels and water packed into the tiny basket at the front. She kept her calves well clear of the exhaust pipe and placed her hands lightly on his waist as they set off.

She expected them to head left towards Nidri and then onto Vasiliki, but instead they went to the right in the direction of Lefkas town and she wondered where they were heading. As far as she knew, the beaches around the town were near the port and not very pleasant.

To her surprise, they turned up the side of the mountain on the road where she and Sandra had discovered the wedding village of Karya. At the crossroads, they turned right again following the road back down to Lefkas. Suddenly, Joe swerved to the left up a rough sandy, donkey track heading upwards. It was hardly a road and as it wound up and round the mountain, the flat land with Lefkas town sprawling across it came into full view below. The mopeds screamed with the effort of going up and Meg felt the thin tyres struggling to grip the gravelly surface. She gripped onto Ray who shouted, "It's okay!" back to her.

They carried on up and the road went inland a little so that there was no view through the rocks on either side of them. Out of nowhere, the sandy track turned into a perfect tarmac road that swung downwards to the left and disappeared round a bend against the rock face. The open sea spread out below, and only a tiny barrier separated the road from a sheer drop. They followed the road around the bend and the most stunning view revealed itself. The clear water glistened; bright turquoise merged into aqua marine, navy blue and azure depending on the depth. The road led straight down to a tiny fishing village shrouded in lush greenery with only a few buildings. A long beach of pure white sand lined the edge of the sea beneath the sheer cliff. Meg held on for dear life as Joe and Ray raced down the hill. Sheer fear mixed with awe as she tried to take in the spectacular beauty. How could she not have known about this?

The road ended in the tiny village consisting of a few small houses and a café on the edge of the beach. Past the houses a steely mass of rocks tumbled into the sea, blocking any further progress around the island.

Meg stepped off the moped, slightly shaken but exhilarated. They parked the bikes and made their way down to the virgin sand. A wizened old man cleaned empty tables outside his café and nodded at them, but otherwise there was nobody. It was unbelievable. Meg filled with the untainted joy that only nature can induce. It felt like a privilege to be there and she almost cried when she saw, out to sea, dolphins playing.

"Isn't it fantastic?" exclaimed Ray. "We couldn't believe it when we discovered it."

"Yeh, and you nearly made us go back," laughed Joe.

"God, yes! Joe went off up that first sandy track and as we started to go up and round, I thought the bike was going to slide right off the edge. But he just kept saying 'one more corner, one more corner' and then we came round the top there. Hope we didn't frighten you coming down the hill. Now we know the road we can't resist going as fast as possible."

"Not at all. I was only terrified."

The three of them laughed and lay down their towels at the top of the beach before flinging off their clothes and charging into the surf. Like small children they buried each other in sand, and made a huge sandcastle with a moat and sat on top as the tide came in and stole it from under them. Then they sat outside the café and drank beer, chatting and laughing.

After that, Meg joined the two lads most evenings and thoroughly enjoyed their easygoing characters and sense of fun. At the end of the week, Ray and Joe joined Meg for breakfast while they waited to go to the airport. They gave her their address in Nottingham in case she was ever up that way and wished her luck with the rest of the season. "Don't let the bastards get you down!" laughed Ray.

Unsurprisingly, when the coach arrived for the airport changeover, Becky was on board and she told Meg she was leaving.

"Can't wait to get out of here," she said, not caring who heard her.

"Take care," was all Meg could think of to say and smiled warmly.

"Always bloody smiling," muttered Becky, shaking her head, "See you."

She spoke in a hard, flat voice and turned away as the coach doors swished shut and the coach hissed and grumbled into life. Meg felt hurt and sad.

# CHAPTER 35

That evening, at yet another first night dinner, Gregor was working and, as usual, he was sussing out any potential lovers. Meg went over to talk to him. She hadn't seen him for a few days and asked him where he'd been. He grimaced and said he had been in trouble.

"What do you mean?"

"Becky. She is gone now, I think."

"Yes, she left this morning - why?"

"One night she come to restaurant, early evening. She say she need to talk to me and take me to beach," Gregor told her. He pointed to a group of trees blocking the view of the sea, "And then she say she want to have sex with me. I tell her I am working. She take off her top and start to kiss me. I push her away and say it not good."

Meg was shocked but couldn't help laughing,

"That's not like you to say no, Gregor."

Gregor grinned but then said seriously, "No, this not good. She work here, she not on holiday wanting good time. It will become too problem. Already I have problem with Lindy. Should be like you. I tell her this and she shout and swear. I try calm her but she run away. Since then I hide from her."

Meg suddenly saw everything very clearly.

"She's gone now Gregor. You take care. Maybe this is a lesson for you not to mess around too much."

"I know, I know. What to do?" he said rolling his eyes. He gestured towards two girls glancing over and fluttering their eyes at him.

Meg slapped his arm and laughed as he hurried over to serve.

New people came and went and she fell into a steady routine. Pete called every so often. She missed him like crazy in between calls and managed to get herself into a state about where they were going, but every time they spoke, she found herself unable to find the right words, so the conversations were light and easy and she gave him the impression that she was having a great time. They always finished with miss yous and love yous but made no plans for see yous.

In fact, she did start to have a great time. The guests seemed to be more easygoing and not so bothered about their accommodation. She didn't know if Athena had made changes to the advertising or whether it was because she had organised everything to be a bit more inviting. She rarely saw or spoke to Spiro and no new reps arrived.

She organised a few barbeques herself with the help of Gregor and his boss, Kostos and Papandrou from the bakery/wine store who always laughed and asked her when her next birthday was going to be. She made sure she introduced people to the 'other' beach and enjoyed the reactions of first timers coming round that bend on the mountain and never failed to be impressed herself at the amazing beauty of the crystal clear water and the varying shades of intense and spectacular blue below.

August melted into September, the guests were a constant flow of different characters, many feeling the need to share their lives and problems with Meg. A family of four with loud, uncontrollable children managed to disrupt the peace and quiet of the resort until Meg managed to get them moved up to Nidri where they were much happier; a couple in their seventies celebrating their first wedding anniversary like young lovers decided to give Meg explicit details of their sex life. A gay couple, Quentin and Justin, who were loud and extrovert, kept everyone amused with their outlandish behaviour. They organised makeshift karaoke evenings getting everyone to sing along to songs by Culture Club, The Pet Shop Boys, Village People and Wham! During the day they would sunbathe religiously and when they saw Meg they would give her advice on her hair and clothes. The days were still hot but the evenings became cooler and sleep without air conditioning became easier.

With three weeks to go before the end of the season, Ralph arrived. Meg was in a rush and threw on the last unworn item of clothing; a pale lemon, cotton dress with short sleeves and a cut out back that without realising it, showed off her golden skin and flattered her slim body. She hadn't worn it before as it was quite smart and Meg felt it didn't really fit in with the casual beach atmosphere. Busy welcoming everybody and explaining everything, she noticed Ralph quite objectively as the most beautiful man she had ever seen and was conscious that her dress needed an iron. He was quite tall and lean, pale and composed with perfect bone structure, an aquiline nose and short blonde, slightly wavy hair. He stood alone, apart from the others and Meg judged him to be in his late twenties.

He was in the 'hill' accommodation, staying for three weeks, and Meg spoke to him briefly when she took him and two other couples to their rooms, using jeeps available. He had a soft, refined voice and was polite and reserved. He told her that he wouldn't come for the dinner as he was going to rest. 'Beautiful but boring' Meg decided, but there was something gentle and mysterious about him. She didn't see him to speak to for the rest of the week, but every morning he jogged down to Michael's for breakfast wearing a scruffy T-shirt and fashionably short running shorts revealing long, strong legs. He had a Sony Walkman in his pocket and headphones over his ears as he listened to Dire Straits' latest album, 'Brothers In Arms'. He sunbathed, swam and read all day without speaking to anyone other than Michael to order something to eat or drink and jogged back up the hill in the early evening. They always smiled at each other, but he didn't join in any activities or mix with anyone else.

By the end of the week, he was even more handsome; with a golden tan he resembled, ironically, a Greek God. Meg admired him and was intrigued by him as he seemed sad but serene, but she was too busy to give him much thought and Pete still had the monopoly on her romantic thoughts.

The following week, Rachel arrived. Meg was looking forward to seeing her. She wanted to talk to someone who knew her well and she felt more confident now that she would have a good time. As luck would have it, Spiro came by in his usual frantic state of panic and gave her the list of arrivals without where they were staying. Meg sorted it out and she put Rachel in the best flat, down past the shop with the sea view balcony, and decided she would move in with her for the week.

Rachel looked as good as ever and Meg groaned as she unpacked the perfect set of mix and match summer outfits, while Meg shook out her crumpled, slightly grubby, sun faded collection.

They both laughed and Rachel said that Meg could borrow anything she liked.

There was a great crowd of people, a new couple who were now sharing with Ralph up the hill had persuaded him to come out for the meal that night and they were lively, funny characters determined to have a good time. Kostos was almost caught short as people ordered all sorts of previously unpopular and unusual dishes from the menu wanting to try new things, but he was delighted at the opportunity to show off all his Greek specialties.

After the meal, they all headed back to Michael's and the bar stayed busy until the early hours of the morning. Meg introduced Rachel to a group of five students who she had spent a lot of time with the week before and they spent most of the evening with them. Others had found friends and Ralph sat with the couple, Jason and Caro, and Belinda, a girl about Meg's age from Canada, who lived in London and had come on holiday on her own.

Rachel had spotted Ralph, and on their way back to the flat, she commented on how good-looking he was. Meg agreed but said he seemed to be quite boring and they went on to discuss the other people there.

Rachel got up with Meg in the morning and they strolled down to Michael's along the quiet road. The sea glistened through the sparse trees and undergrowth and the sky like a pale blue canopy stretched over them.

They passed the little shop and the bars with their shutters still down and made their way up to the bakery for some yoghurt and honey.

Papandrou welcomed Meg with a beaming face and when she introduced Rachel as her friend from England, he was overjoyed. He took both her hands in his and repeated, "Welcome," over and over until Rachel and Meg were both laughing.

They hadn't had a chance to really talk, but as they sat outside the bakery relishing the creamy, cold yoghurt sweetened with delicious honey, they began to catch up on each other's lives. They strolled back to the bar and Rachel went to the beach to wait until Meg had finished sorting out jeeps, mopeds and T-shirts and answered everyone's questions. Finally she got the chance to join Rachel on the beach and they talked. Gradually they filled each other in on all the details of their lives over the past few years, which letters and postcards had not included.

Rachel was in love. She had met a guy at a conference in Geneva and they had kept in touch for the last year and now he was coming to work in London. The only problem was that he was married.

She told Meg that they had been writing and calling for over a year now and they were in love so it must have been meant to be.

"Has he left his wife?" asked Meg.

"Well, Jeff is still with her at the moment. He doesn't want to hurt her. But now he's going to finish it properly before he comes to England."

Meg just nodded.

"What about you? What happened to Pete?

"Oh we're still together," Meg laughed self-consciously and told her how she and Pete had got back together and that up until the year before they seemed destined to be together. It felt good to confide in someone who knew her well and who had met Pete. She knew she was trying to justify why she was hanging in there and as she spoke, her doubts began to grow again. She wanted to ask Rachel about the weekend she had come to stay but she daren't, probably because she didn't want the answer.

She realised, as she spoke, that Pete had let her down many times. There was the girl at freshers. The girl who had sent him a card thanking him for a great night, the letter from a girl he'd met on a course, both of which he'd hidden from her. There had been the troublemakers who had hinted at indiscretions. He'd denied anything happening with all of them and she'd believed him, thinking that what they had was special, but underneath she held misgivings.

"The course of true love, never did run smooth" was what his Nan told her when she went to visit. She was a wonderful lady and Meg liked to visit her and be close to someone who knew Pete well, since he'd started working abroad.

Rachel listened and Meg finished with, "What do you think I should do?"

Rachel paused and then said, "Only you know the answer. Get on with your own life, Meg. See what happens, but don't put your own dreams on hold waiting for him to make up his mind. That's what I have been doing."

Meg knew she was right, but she didn't know what to do about her own dreams any more. She thought about Rachel with her career mapped out. Everything was under control and her man was coming to be with her. She felt the familiar stab of failure and shook it away.

"They don't prepare you for any of this at school, do they? I was so sure that I'd be firmly ensconced in a career with a great future ahead of me by now. Instead I've got barely two pennies to rub together and no clue what to do about it. They push you along a production line telling you to get your O levels, get you're A levels, go to university. Apart from Pete of course, very few people I know are in jobs that use their degrees. The most successful people from home are the ones who left at sixteen or even eighteen and went straight out to work and built up experience. Look at you. You definitely made the right decision not to go to university."

"I didn't know that. I just couldn't face any more educational establishments and no money."

Rachel laughed and asked Meg what plans she and Pete had for the future and Meg found herself pathetically saying that they were going to wait and see.

"I still want to get my career going. I'm not really ready to settle down," she said trying to persuade herself as much as Rachel. She sounded cool and confident, but then she frowned.

"I had such mixed messages growing up," she went on. "I can always remember overhearing my Dad saying that my brothers had to go to grammar school but it didn't matter which secondary school I went to; there was no point in me going to university, because all I was going to do was get married and have children."

Rachel rolled her eyes, "So much for the sixties and women's liberation!"

Meg frowned, "I know. I think I've been trying to prove him wrong, ever since. But now my career plans have gore down the pan, so do I give it all up to be with the man I love?"

"Get your head sorted. Don't be put off by what happened at the radio station. It's a difficult line of work to get into. You can't let one little knock stop you. And let Pere come after you."

It sounded so obvious, so why did Meg's stomach clench and throat constrict?

They wandered back up to the bar for Meg to do her work and Rachel joined Jason, Cara and Belinda on the terrace. Meg joined them and they had bar snacks and drinks with the crowd that came in. There was no sign of Ralph.

The following day, Meg organised a BBQ for the evening. She went into Lefkas to buy the food and Papandrou supplied the drink. She and Rachel set up at the back of the now unused Beach Villa and did the cooking together. There was a calm, relaxed atmosphere as everyone ate and drank watching the waves lap while the sun went down.

Meg had one upset to deal with as one guy in his fifties with a much younger wife questioned her about the cost in a loud and boorish voice. Meg made a very small profit on the event depending on the right numbers showing and she got very good deals on all the food and drink. He was obviously showing off in front of his partner, so she took him to one side to speak to him.

Quite calmly, she said she was sorry if he thought it was expensive and asked him if he would like to organise the next one himself and see if he could do it for less. He blustered a little bit and said that, no he wouldn't. She smiled sweetly and walked away. The man walked over to his wife with plates piled as high as possible with food and led her up the beach away from the crowd. Meg went over to join Rachel on the verandah. Ralph was there with Jason and Cara and to her surprise he came over to join Rachel and herself. He spoke to Meg looking clearly and directly into her eyes. It was the first time they'd really spoken and Meg felt herself getting hot and her cheeks growing red and it wasn't the proximity of the grill. He was incredibly handsome and his voice was soft but powerful. Without realising it, they fell into easy banter; he was intelligent and had a delightful quick wit and droll sense of humour.

Meg found herself pleased that he wasn't just a pretty face. He told her that he was an economist in London and Meg asked him if he was responsible for the present state of the economy. He laughed a genuine, gentle laugh.

Rachel spoke and he turned his attention towards her.

'Of course!' thought Meg shocked at how deflated she felt. 'He was talking to me to get to Rachel.' She watched in amazement as her practical, kind friend transformed into a floppy, eye fluttering, giggly girl. Mind you, she could understand the effect Ralph would have on any female. He was very polite and didn't leave Meg out of the conversation, but Meg decided to leave them to it and not play gooseberry. She said she ought to check on the others, moved away and began chatting brightly to everyone else.

The light began to disappear as the sun sank down in the sky, and a few stars flickered in the twilight. People started making their way back down the beach towards Michael's, where the evening continued, somewhat raucously. Tequila shots were suggested and Meg woke the next morning very dehydrated with vague memories of dancing on tables and staggering home arm in arm with Rachel singing 'Yesterday', not very prettily.

# CHAPTER 36

She left Rachel sleeping and set off to get down to her 'office' on time, even though she was sure she wouldn't actually be needed. Michael poured her a coffee. He looked tired but not hung over and grinned at her struggling to cope with a very fuzzy head. At least with Michael she never felt the need to speak. She sipped her coffee, slowly coming back to life. A breeze rocked the soft branches of the trees and ruffled the surface of the sea. A few clouds shifted across the ever-blue sky and as usual, she appreciated the peace and beauty of the setting and recognised the signs that summer was coming to an end. Her brain felt muffled in cotton wool and she couldn't think too deeply about anything but thoughts of Pete floated across. She noted dully that he hadn't called for well over a week. He never called when he said he would, always made her begin to worry, but he hadn't left it so long before. She tried to work it out, but it was too difficult. Feeling restless, she decided to walk up to the bakers for nourishment.

The sun was moving up and she felt the heat on her skin but the breeze comforted and cooled her. Papandrou greeted her warmly and served her water, yoghurt, honey and freshly baked cheese bread. She ate and drank greedily to replenish her dehydrated brain and body before making her way back down the road. As she revived, her thoughts became sharper. It had been eleven days since Pete had phoned. They had agreed it was better for him to phone because he never knew when he would be offshore and it would save her money. She had received a card a few days earlier, funny and loving, but from the postmark, it had taken two weeks to arrive. The feeling that something was wrong gnawed at her. She decided to phone him later.

She went back down to the bar where a few heavy eyed guests attempted breakfast. Rachel popped in and told her she was going to Nidri with Ralph, Belinda, Jason and Cara. Meg was a bit taken aback, but remembered that Rachel was on holiday and so she said that she would come and find them as soon as she could.

It was early afternoon by the time she'd finished everything. She felt much better and was looking forward to a refreshing swim. Mike had left one spare moped with her. He'd said, "You keep. Maybe you rent her or maybe you need it," and winked kindly at her. She had grinned and thanked him. The locals were all so kind to her. In their eyes, she was a 'good girl' and they helped her in any way they could.

She whizzed down to the apartment to get her beach bag and set off to Nidri feeling a little bit guilty like a school student playing truant. The wind whipped her hair and kept her cool in the searing heat as she wound her way along the coast road. The thick forest swept up to her right and down to the sea on her left.

She parked and chatted with Niko for a while, briefly checking that the boat trip was still on for the following evening.

Rachel and the others were easy to find on the uncrowded beach. They were playing volleyball near the water's edge. She strolled towards them feeling shy, but as soon as they saw her, they waved and called and as she got near, Jason threw the ball to her.

Rachel looked fantastic with her long slim legs and flat tummy, her skin already turning honey brown. Her hair was pulled back off her pretty face and tied back in a neat ponytail. She and Ralph went for the ball at the same time and crashed into each other. Rachel fell dramatically and Ralph put out his hand to help her up. She took it and then half way up, he let go and she fell back down. She got up laughing and slapped him playfully on the arm. He seemed relaxed and happy for the first time since he'd arrived.

Meg felt a strange tingle of annoyance, but removed the feeling and joined in with the game. They continued to play for a while and then Meg announced that she needed a swim.

"Let's swim to the island," Ralph said, almost as a challenge. He was pointing to the tiny rocky island just off the end of the headland.

"Okay," replied Meg. She was a confident swimmer and it didn't look that far.

"Oh yes, let's!" cried Rachel.

"Not me," stated Cara, and Jason and Belinda quickly said that they would stay and keep Cara company.

The three dived over the waves and began swimming. The distance was deceptive and as much as they swam, the island didn't seem to be getting any closer. Rachel called to the other two.

"It's too far. I'm going to turn back."

"Okay," said Ralph. "What about you, Meg?"

"I'm all right," she replied, with determination.

"Come on then. See you later, Rachel."

Rachel started back for shore and Ralph and Meg swam on, neither wanting to give up. Ralph tapped her shoulder and they trod water. The island was now clear in front of them. It was a mass of uneven grey, with boulders around the base and a small area of smooth flat rock.

"Ralph pointed and shouted, "Race you to that rock!" and immediately started swimming away from her.

Meg put her head down and chased after him; she caught him easily and swam past him to reach out for the edge of the rock. As she was pulling herself out, he grabbed her ankle and pulled her backwards. He then pulled himself out quickly and sat on the rock.

"Too slow," he said, calmly smug.

"You cheated!" spluttered Meg, laughing and pulling herself up to sit on the rock beside him.

They sat on the rock ledge breathing deeply, looking back to the shore and the tiny people on it.

"You're a bloody good swimmer," he said.

"You too," replied Meg. "Not quite as good as me, but well done."

He laughed. They sat for a while getting their breath back and comfortably fell into conversation about London, jobs, life in general. Why she was there, why he was there. Neither gave away too much. She told him briefly about the radio not working out. He said he'd been working incredibly long hours and needed to get away as he was burned out.

Meg was conscious of how attractive he was and how easy she felt in his company but he obviously fancied Rachel, and she loved Pete, so she didn't take her thoughts any further. Their conversation took them onto likes and dislikes, honest points of view without trying to impress.

She felt quite at ease when she asked him if he had a girl friend. He looked down at his feet dangling in the clear water and then out across the bay. He didn't look at her as he said, rather too flippantly, "Been too busy to think of romance," he said in a quiet voice. Meg interpreted his gaze across the bay as thoughts of Rachel just as she'd suspected.

He told her he was thirty-one and she laughed at him for being so old. For her in her early twenties, thirty was a milestone, way off in the future when she would be a successful and settled grown up. He laughed and said, "It comes quicker than you think, and when you get there you don't feel particularly grown up or settled."

His eyes glazed over and she saw the sadness she had seen before and knew that someone had broken his heart.

"Rachel's lovely isn't she?"

She immediately regretted being so obvious.

"Yes, she is," he replied, punishing her. "Come on. Time to go back."

They slid back into the cool, delicious water and swam back slowly; still talking lightly about the island and the magical quality it had because it wasn't too commercialised.

The others clapped as they emerged from the waves staggering and pretending to be exhausted. Rachel gushed excuses about getting cramp. Meg said she had to go back to Nikiana and Cara and Jason said they were going to stay and have dinner in Nidri and the others including Rachel agreed to do the same.

"Okay, might see you later. Have fun!"

She walked back along the beach feeling a little bit dejected and lonely, but she reminded herself once again that they were all on holiday and she was working. She rode back, salty and sandy and looked forward to a guaranteed hot shower.

In the bar, feeling fresh and clean, she took bookings for the boat trip and chatted to the other holidaymakers. They were mostly young and relaxed, out to have a good time and not to moan and groan.

Everyone went off to shower and change and go to one of the tavernas and she was alone. She thought about Ralph and the swim. It had been lovely. He was sensitive, intelligent and mature. She smiled to herself as she thought about how comfortable she had felt talking to him. Her thoughts quickly turned to Pete and she reminded herself that she was going to phone him. Like a fist slamming into her chest, it hit her. She tried to calm herself as she did the maths. Pete was due leave. He hadn't mentioned anything about his next time off and she had lost track of time. Again she worked it out, he should have been due leave a week before. Shaking and feeling slightly sick, she set off to the shop to use the phone. On the way, she tried to make excuses. Sometimes his leave was delayed if he had a big job on. She made her way to the back of the little shop and as she dialled the number, she stared at a packet of washing powder, Pow! And a shelf lined with insect killer, Zap!

The number rang and rang and rang emptily. Then she heard the click and a muffled voice came down the line. Her heart raced, her palms were moist.

"Hello?"

Masculine tones crackled faintly down the line. She recognised faint music in the background as Tears for Fears singing 'Shout'.

"Hello, Pete?"

"Hi there! It's not Pete, Pete's not here."

Meg willed herself to sound cheerful.

"Oh. Hi! Do you know where he is?"

"Yeh, he's on leave."

"Oh, right of course! Where's he gone this time?" She spoke casually, brightly, a knot forming in her stomach.

"I think he's gone to Malaysia with one of the other guys. Yeh, I'm pretty sure that's where they've gone. Went a good few days back."

"Oh wow! That will be good. Any idea when he'll be back?" she struggled to keep her voice light.

"Couple of weeks I guess. Can I take a message?"

"No, it's okay, thanks, bye," she managed to say. Her voice cracked a little. She hung up quickly. Zap! Pow!


Rick hung up the phone and turned to Pete, "Sure that's what you wanted me to tell her?"

"Yes. It'll be more of a surprise when I see her in England."

"I'm not sure telling her you've gone to Malaysia will make her very happy."

Pete just grinned, "Well, I am going to Malaysia first. Got to have a bit of fun, before I tie myself down. Then I'll see her when she gets back to England in less than a couple of weeks."

"Not sure you've got the right idea about love, mate," Rick said scratching his greying beard.

"Meg's a great girl. She's having a good time in Greece. She'll have men running around her. Every guy I knew at uni fancied her."

"How did she end up with you then?" Rick asked mocking him.

"Because of my natural good looks and charm, of course," Pete said laughing. "To keep 'em keen, you've got to treat 'em a bit mean."

"That may work in the beginning. You may think I'm a silly old fool, but I haven't stayed married for twenty years in this work by treating my wife mean. I can tell you that for nothing. It might work in the early days but then you've got to have trust and honesty. You've got some learning to do, mate."

"She's the one. I don't want to lose her."

Rick stood up and went to the door.

"What happened last year? You told me you were going to ask her then; you showed me the ring."

"I didn't ask her. I didn't think she was ready."

"Cold feet eh? He turned to go and then turned back, "She was upset, she tried to hide it but I could hear it. You're pushing her the wrong way, I reckon, but hey you know her better than me. I'm off to bed. I've got a chopper to catch at the crack of dawn. Good luck."

Pete leant back in his chair and ran his fingers through his hair. The sound of Judy Tzuke singing 'Stay With Me Till Dawn' floated across the room. It was one of 'their' songs. He didn't know how to understand her. Suddenly, he missed her so much it hurt.

"I need you tonight, Meg. We'll get it right."

Meg forced a weak smile as she fumbled in her purse to pay for the call. She handed over the money and politely said, "Eferisto. (*Thank you*)" to the shopkeeper.

"You okay?" he asked her.

"Yes, yes. Thanks. Bye," she said quickly.

She gave him a bright smile, hurried outside in a daze and began walking towards the bar. Her eyes began to blur and she felt wild and lost. She turned around and made her way back to the apartment, breaking into a run to get inside and close the door on the world. She stood in the barely furnished room looking around desperately at nothing, clenching and unclenching her fists, not knowing what to do with herself. The tears came and she sank to the floor, her mind was blank, her body incapacitated. The pain in her gut spread through her, across her chest and gripped her throat. She wanted to be sick. She began to breathe, deep intakes of air. She did not understand. She did not understand. There was no excuse. She had not missed any phone calls; he hadn't mentioned his leave. Why would he do this? Just when she was starting to think they might be on track. The tears stopped and a cold hardness filled her. She decided she had to go back to the bar or she would never move again. She dragged herself to the bathroom and stared at her red eyes. She splashed her face angrily and then carefully applied make-up to disguise the crying.

She walked back along the road; a vigorous breeze swept through the trees and whipped her hair about her face. It cooled her burning face. Unusually dark clouds scudded across the evening sky. She didn't think about anything. She just felt empty. She walked into the bar, which was getting busy, and smiled and nodded at everyone automatically, as she headed to the bar. She smiled weakly at Michael and asked for a large brandy. He made a small frown and poured her a Remy instead of the usual cheap Metaxa, and said, "Storm coming. Summer nearly over."

She took a large gulp and let the warmth hit the back of her throat and tingle down to her stomach.

It didn't dissolve the lump stuck in her chest, and beneath her composure, tears welled. She took another gulp, breathed deeply and smiled at Michael before turning to face the room and watch the small groups chatting and laughing. She heard a Sade track come over the speakers, 'Hang On to Your Love' and her heart felt as though it was ripping.

She stood still and then went out of the door and down the steps to the terrace. The wind was gaining energy and the supple eucalyptus trees waved their branches in protest. Even the ever-calm sea was beginning to clamour. Waves bobbed against each other, gathering excitement as they rushed to the shore in a shout, and the sky turned velvety grey.

One of the holidaymakers, Eddie, called to her. He was with his girlfriend, Lucy and another couple, Robert and Sophie. They had just graduated from university and from their accents were very posh. Their voices were rich and plummy; they found the holiday a 'hoot'. Not having hot water and using an outdoor shower was an hilarious novelty. They were kind, friendly, and enjoying 'living rough'. There was obviously no shortage of money between them and they were generous with it.

Eddie insisted she join them for a glass of champagne that they had brought with them. Michael didn't mind; they spent plenty at the bar.

She downed the rest of her brandy and sat down with them, determined to hide her pain.

"Didn't expect this sort of weather. Jolly blustery! Think there may be a storm?"

"I've never seen it like this. Michael says it's a sign that summer's nearly over."

"Oh! I love storms. Thunder and lightning, how exciting!" exclaimed Lucy.

Suddenly the wind stopped. The air went completely still as if the world had suddenly held its breath. Heat buzzed around them.

"It's still bloody hot," remarked Robert.

A deep rumble came from above, followed seconds later by a flash across the grey. A few heavy drops of rain splattered onto the table and then it came, hard and fast. People reacted in an automatic rush for cover. They stood beneath the balcony feeling exhilarated.

Another deep roar tumbled across the heavens and a bright white streak forked, crackling across the sky. The trees swished and swayed erratically and the sea rose in a bubbling, chopping mass, sending white horses crashing onto the sand.

Then it stopped. Almost as suddenly as it had started. A brief reminder of the forthcoming weather of autumn and winter.

Everyone stood still; looking out at the dark, wet sand. Stray leaves and pieces of eucalyptus bark were strewn across the terrace. The trees restored their composure as if nothing had happened. Only the glistening leaves remained as evidence, reflecting on the grey clouds and creating a purple hue. The sea still bobbed and rushed, slower to react and the air felt fresh and clear.

"Let's swim!" cried Sophie.

Robert and Eddie looked at each other and with a shout of 'tally-ho' charged onto the sand and raced into the water. Sophie followed and Lucy nudged Meg and said, 'Come on!"

Meg didn't stop to think as she ran down with the girls and some other lunatics and they all leapt, fully dressed, over the waves, laughing and splashing. The more sensible ones stood on the terrace cheering and shouting as they emerged, spluttering and giggling, their wet clothes clinging to their skin.

As Meg came up the beach she saw Rachel standing on the steps and she waved, surprised to see her. Rachel shouted hello and came towards her.

"Thought you might be lonely!" she grinned and Meg felt touched that she had thought about her.

Ralph came down the steps from the bar with Belinda.

"Thought you might need this," he said smiling. He handed her a brandy. "You look a bit cold."

Meg was beginning to shiver in her wet clothes. The T-shirt clung to her slim body and cold nipples pressed outward, almost visible. She hugged herself and sipped at the brandy, smiling. She had really enjoyed the swim and another brandy and the fact that Rachel had thought about her, warmed her. The pain still hung inside her and every so often the memory of the phone call would send a wave of heart- wrenching nausea sweeping through her. More than anything, she felt humiliated and didn't want to tell Rachel that she had failed.

"Did you get caught in the rain?" asked Meg.

"Yes. It was so funny!" said Rachel.

"We left Cara and Jason in Nidri and got the bus back. When the first flash of lightning came, the driver stopped the bus, got off and disappeared into a little house. He didn't say anything. There were only a few of us on the bus and we just sort of looked at each other and waited. He didn't come back so we decided to walk. Of course then there was more lightning and then the rain bucketed down. We ran under a fig tree, praying we wouldn't be struck by more lightning. We barely got wet at all because Ralph held his towel over us and we all huddled together."

Meg laughed, again feeling that odd twinge of annoyance, and then sneezed.

"Bless you!" said Belinda. "Listen, shall I lend you some clothes?"

Meg thanked her, and they walked over the road to Belinda's room. Meg hadn't really had the chance to speak to her properly. She was quiet and self-contained in the group. Now she chatted away in her soft Canadian accent. She told Meg how she always travelled on her own. She didn't like being fixed to someone else's agenda and could meet new people more easily. Meg admired her independence, forgetting that she had also come alone. Belinda handed her a tracksuit, which swamped her and they both laughed.

"Sorry. I'm a bit larger than you," Belinda stated in a matter of fact tone.

"It's perfect," laughed Meg. "Those damp clothes were becoming uncomfortable, not to mention embarrassing."

They both laughed and went back over to join Rachel and Ralph who were sitting side by side on the balcony, chatting.

"Don't they look cosy?" Belinda said and Meg caught jealousy in her voice.

As they came up, Ralph instantly moved his chair to allow them to bring in more chairs. Rachel swiftly brought two more chairs and sat back down next to Ralph again.

"That looks very chic, darling," she said to Meg.

"Why thank you," Meg replied, doing a twirl, before sitting down.

"Ralph and I have ordered a load of picky bits to eat," added Rachel looking at Ralph.

"Oh great! I'm starving!" Meg said enthusiastically, ignoring the gnawing in her stomach, which wasn't due to hunger.

They ate and drank, and laughed at Eddie and his crowd, still in their damp clothes, playing drinking games with forfeits. Every song played from Meg's own compilation tapes stirred up memories. Lou Reed's 'Perfect Day' and all the picnics they'd shared in the sunshine; Eric Clapton's, 'Wonderful Tonight', Pete's song for her, and Bonnie Tyler's, 'Total Eclipse of the Heart' which reflected exactly how she felt about him and many more that had defined their university days of partying, loving, fighting, crying, laughing. Alcohol numbed Meg a little, but the burning lump in her chest and throat would not go away. She watched without emotion as Rachel leaned towards Ralph and laughed at everything he said. She didn't care. She was aware of Belinda's rising antagonism towards Rachel. They were both competing for Ralph's attention. It all felt pointless, a futile game. She joined in with the conversations, laughed at the right moments, even made a few jokes herself, but she just wanted the evening to end.

As early as she could, she announced that she was tired and needed to go. Ralph asked her if she would be all right and offered to walk her back. Meg refused, said she'd be fine and would see them all the next day.

"Some of us have to work!" she laughed.

She set off down the unlit road, where a couple of bars still had their lights on. Locals sat around tables, watching football on the television, smoking, drinking, and chatting behind the glass. Tears rolled down her cheeks as her leaden legs plodded her forward. She got back to the apartment, brushed her teeth and fell into bed with a sob. She had held onto herself all evening and now she was ready to cry with abandon, but the alcohol and exhaustion took over, sending her crashing into a deep sleep.

She woke wondering where she was, and then as her mind clicked in, everything flooded back with resounding painful force. She looked over to Rachel's bed half expecting it to be empty, but the mould of her body lay still under the sheet. Meg got up and dressed quickly and quietly. She left a note for Rachel and left.

# CHAPTER 37

The sun shone down from a clear blue sky; all signs of a storm had disappeared. Everything was as before, the fig trees rustled gently and the air felt soft and dry. Outside all was constant; inside her everything had radically altered. She went through the motions of checking, organising, smiling. Rachel came down later and joined her for a coffee and a sandwich.

"Have a good time, last night?" asked Meg.

"Yes, it was a good laugh wasn't it?"

"Did you stay late?"

"No, not really, we were all a bit tired. I wasn't long after you, but you were out cold."

"I completely crashed as soon as I got into bed. What have you got planned for today? I'm going to stay around here. The boat trip's tonight and I've got some orders for T-shirts."

"Oh, right. Well, I'll stay around here with you then," said Rachel.

Meg was surprised. "What are the others up to?"

"I don't know. Thought they might be here."

Meg thought no more about it. After lunch, they set up to print some shirts.

"You seem to be getting on well with Ralph," remarked Meg.

"Oh, he's all right," replied Rachel, nonchalantly. "I'm really missing Jeff, actually."

"Not long until you can be together."

"Yes," Rachel tried to sound enthusiastic.

Meg couldn't be bothered to pursue it. They both spoke very little as Rachel helped her complete the T-shirts and pack away the printer and paints, then they both headed for the beach, hot and sweaty. They went in the sea to cool off and then lay on the sand lost in their own thoughts as the sun beat down. They headed back to the apartment making small talk and got showered and changed.

Everyone was going on the boat trip. It was the last one of the season. Meg was a bit worried about the weather but Niko confirmed that it would be fine and she trusted that he knew.

It was breathtaking as they set off with the sun going down behind the mountain in a blaze of orange and pink. The sea was calm and the air warm and salty.

As usual, the boat filled with awed gasps as the bay came into view already twinkling and shining with lamps and candles. The lively group bounced off, excited and wanting to explore. They had seen the photos and read Meg's information sheets so they wanted to see the church at the top of the cliff.

The waiters performed superbly and it was a lively, fun atmosphere. They all found places at the carefully laid tables with the candles flickering in glass holders and Meg checked orders and went around talking to everyone.

When she finally went to sit down, Rachel had saved her a seat beside her. Ralph sat on Rachel's other side. Ralph leant forward and told Meg how fantastic the place was. Meg was about to reply when Rachel interrupted, "We must go up to the church," she said to Ralph.

As she spoke, she completely turned in her chair to face Ralph, so that her back was to Meg and she blocked her from Ralph's view. The movement shocked Meg, but at the same time quietly amused her. She ignored it and began talking to Belinda who was sitting opposite, next to Jason and Cara. Belinda raised her eyebrows. She too had spotted Rachel's manouvre. Meg didn't mind, after all she wasn't interested in Ralph. She only had eyes for Pete, however confused she was feeling.

The food was delicious and the retsina added to the general bon-homie. Kris did his table trick, lifting the table with ease and speed cleanly up off the ground to tremendous applause and Robert and Eddie were first up to attempt the same, ending up in crumpled heaps on the dusty floor with everyone laughing. The dancing began and all joined in with their attempts at Greek dancing. At various points in the evening, people headed up the mountainside and returned mesmerized and enchanted. Meg declined, despite Ralph trying to challenge her. She was putting on a good front, but she had no extra energy.

On the boat on the way back, Eddie and Robert led a chorus of rugby songs and the journey sped by. Meg watched the flickering lights fade while the church beacon remained like a lantern hanging in the black sky, and realised it was the last time she would go to the magical bay.

Rachel huddled up to Ralph saying she was cold. Belinda turned away and chatted to Jason and Cara.

The next day, Meg suggested Rachel and the rest of the group go over to the 'Other' beach. Ralph knew the way so the five of them went off in Jason and Cara's jeep and Meg rode over later on the moped. As she came round the bend, the emerald, turquoise and sapphire water flashed below like a mass of precious stones. The crystal-clear water created miracles of colour on the rock and sand below and despite her pain, the view had a soothing, deeply touching effect on her troubled soul.

It was Rachel's last day already. The rest were all staying for another week. It was still hot but a breeze offered cool relief and you could feel the shift in climate as September progressed.

There were a couple of other people from Nikiana but otherwise the vast expanse of beach was theirs. The waves danced onto the shore flashing their frilly white underskirts shamelessly.

Meg didn't want to sunbathe. She didn't want time to think. She urged them to play volleyball minus a net in the sea and splashed and jumped around, refusing to be anywhere but in the present moment and enjoying it. She hadn't told Rachel. She didn't want to talk about it. Didn't know what to say. As much as she tried to relax, she was restless. She didn't want to be on the beach watching Rachel flirt incessantly with Ralph, while Jeff waited for her. She didn't know where she wanted to be. Anywhere, but with her thoughts.

Everyone had agreed to meet in Michael's for drinks with those on their last night. Meg and Rachel changed and went down early together, so that Meg could make sure everything was set for the next day's departures. It remained quiet in the bar, so she and Rachel had a salad and a couple of ouzos on the terrace and watched as twilight shifted shadows and silhouettes. They chatted lightly. Rachel said that she'd had a great time and invited Meg to come and stay with her when she got back to London while she sorted out what she was going to do next.

It hit Meg with a shock. Rachel, ever practical and thinking ahead. There was one more week left to the end of season and she had no clue what her plans were. A wave of panic washed over her. Suddenly, she wanted to tell Rachel about Pete. She started awkwardly, not knowing how to say it. Then it all came out in a burst of tumbling reality. She tried to sound matter of fact, but admitted she felt hurt and stupid. Then she tried to make excuses for him, find a reason that made it possible to have some hope. She paused and waited for Rachel to back her up, encourage her to stay cool. Tell her she was over-reacting, that there was still a chance.

Pat Benatar singing something about love being a battlefield floated out faintly from the bar across the terrace. Rachel took a sip of cuzo and said, "I think there is something I should tell you."

Meg could feel the pulse in her neck pumping violently as she looked at Rachel.

"When I came to stay with you. You remember Pete looked after me when you had to go somewhere. I can't remember where, but anyway."

Meg nodded. Part of her wanted to tell her to stop, change the subject. Her guts roared, but she said nothing as she waited for Rachel to confirm her worst fears about that weekend.

"I know I was not in a very good place, but you were all over the place. I'd never seen you like that before. You were always so upbeat and confident. Nothing got you down and you didn't take any nonsense, but that weekend you were anxious and edgy and I could tell you were jealous of Pete paying me attention. I don't really know what was going on with you two then but when you told me later that you had split up with him, I wasn't surprised. The truth is he told me how much he loved you but that he was struggling. You reacted so badly to your Mum and Dad splitting up and he didn't know how to deal with you. I know I haven't got a very good track record, but nothing happened. I want you to know that. I did enjoy his attention; you know what I'm like. "

Meg felt sick. She wasn't sure if she was relieved or not.

"I'm sorry, Meg. I was jealous. I've always been jealous of you."

"What!"

"Listen. You've always had steady relationships, long term. You always get on easily with men. You're funny and you're lively. You do the most ridiculous things and you laugh them off. I can't bear to make mistakes, so I'm always careful, practical, except when it comes to men and I just seem to fall for bastards."

Meg stared at her astounded.

"At school you had Andy; lovely, dependable, Andy, while I was in and out of relationships, always with the wrong guys. When you were with Andy, I was having an affair with my biology teacher."

Meg was truly astounded. "Never!" she exclaimed.

"Yes, I thought it was real. That he was just waiting until I finished school, but it was just an ego trip, and I wasn't the only one. Then you went off to university and within no time you met Pete, happy and stable again."

"Hardly stable," muttered Meg, and then continued, "But why, Rachel? Why do you go for unavailable men? You're great looking, bright, confident. I've always been jealous of you. You're always together, you always look immaculate, always know what you're doing. A crowd turns up unexpectedly and you create a delicious meal. I might manage to open a bag of crisps or peanuts but even then I end up dropping them on the floor or something."

"You make great cheesecake... Oh, I don't know Meg. I want to prove that I'm attractive, that I can get them into bed. Of course, then I realise they only want the excitement, they don't actually want me."

"You've got Jeff."

"Have I? He keeps promising to leave his wife, but I'm not sure that he will."

"Is that why you're flirting with Ralph, even though you love Jeff?"

"Partly, and also just to get his attention. I love the chase. I'm on holiday and he's gorgeous."

She smiled ruefully.

"Look Meg, I don't know enough. I'm sorry about what happened with Pete. That was a long time ago, you split and you got back together. Maybe you're meant to be or maybe you're both chasing what you had in the beginning. His behaviour now is what counts. See what's right under your nose instead of chasing lost dreams. Ask yourself, does he make you happy. You are better now than when I saw you then, but you've lost all your old self-assurance. I know what happened at the radio hasn't helped but maybe you didn't get that because deep down you don't believe in yourself. Or maybe you want to be with Pete so much that you're not really committed to your career."

Meg didn't know whether to punch her or hug her. Her mind raced, her stomach churned.

She realised it was true. She had been practically obsessed with Pete in the last year. She had worked hard at the radio, but she had been overwhelmed by finding a decent place to live, working long hours waitressing, dealing with rejections and all of the time wondering what she had done wrong last summer to stop Pete from proposing. She felt out of control in every area of her life.

"A-ha!" A loud and pompous voice interrupted them.

"Drinks, girls?"

Eddie came towards them with his friends following. He held a bottle of ouzo, a bottle of water and glasses. They were all very merry and in high spirits. Meg and Rachel accepted drinks and raised their glasses in a chorus of 'Yamaas!'

Robert and Eddie chattered away about their moped escapades and Meg went to the toilet. She sat down on the seat in the tiny cubicle and put her head back with her hands covering her face. She began to run her fingers back through her hair melodramatically and failed as her nails caught in a knot of curls and jammed sending a sharp pain through her scalp. She struggled to get her fingers free angrily, and then hit her head on the edge of the sink in front of her. As she rubbed her head, she caught sight of herself in the mirror and couldn't help but laugh at the pathetic reflection. She couldn't even be upset in a cool way.

It wasn't until about ten that Ralph arrived with Jason, Cara and Belinda. The bar was full by then and the last nighters were making the most of it. Ralph came over. He was chatty and friendly and asked Rachel if she was packed and ready to go. Eddie put a new cassette in the player and turned the volume up. Dancing ensued as 'A Town Called Malice' by The Jam, roused everyone in the bar and was followed by tracks by Madness, Adam and the Ants, U2 and other lively bands. Meg and Rachel joined in with the general mayhem as Eddie and Robert ordered rounds of strange cocktails for everyone and Meg tried not to react to the lyrics of The Clash playing 'Should I Stay or Should I go Now'. Michael put his foot down and called last orders at one a.m. He had to be up early.

There were a few groans, but most had had too much to know what time it was. Rachel said her goodbyes with promises to keep in touch via Meg. She and Meg set off down the road to the apartment without speaking. Rachel finally broke the silence.

"He likes you, you know."

"Who?" asked Meg.

"Ralph."

"Yes. Right." Meg, did not believe her, but was surprised at how it had made her heart jump a little.

"Why can't you see what's right in front of you? He's spent all week trying to talk to you. Can't you see how jealous Belinda is?"

"I think you'll find Belinda was jealous of you monopolising him all week!" Meg laughed.

They went quiet again and reached the flat in silence.

"Would you like a coffee?" asked Rachel quietly.

"Yes, okay," said Meg.

They took their cups out onto the balcony. The star filled sky looked on. Meg looked for The Plough out of habit and her eyes filled with tears. Rachel put her arms round her.

"We've known each other too long to let stupid men come between us."

Meg wiped her eyes and smiled.

"Yes. You're right. Bloody stupid men and lack of commitment."

"I'm scared Meg. Scared that Jeff won't come or won't want me when he does."

"I'm scared too," admitted Meg. "Scared that Pete won't call me and scared that he will call and say he loves me and I won't be able to say no."

They looked at each other and sighed.

The following morning, Rachel hugged Meg as she was about to board the bus and said she'd see her soon.

"It's been great having you here," Meg smiled.

Rachel smiled, "I'm really glad I came. Take care and good luck with everything."

"I'll call when I get back. And I really hope it works out with Jeff."

# CHAPTER 38

She returned to the bar realising that this was it – the last week. England seemed so far away. The first weeks of being on the island seemed a long, long time ago but she'd only been there about nine weeks. Now she was going back to start again. It hadn't exactly been the break she had imagined.

The bus came back with only a handful of end of season holidaymakers so accommodation was easy: Four girls together, two lads and a young married couple. Meg gave the couple her lovely apartment and moved back to her old room. There were no complaints. She gave them all the information she could and told them about the meal up at Kostos' restaurant in the evening. She had put up a notice inviting everyone who was still there to come as well so that they could all meet, and it would be more fun with a bigger group.

Ralph and Belinda came in to the bar at lunchtime and asked her if she wanted to come to the other beach with all of them. She refused the invitation saying that she felt she should be around for the new arrivals and was hoping to see Spiro about final arrangements; she hadn't spoken to him for over a week. She felt pleased that they'd asked her though, and said she'd see them at dinner.

What she really wanted was a few hours on her own. Now it was time to start thinking and planning.

In the early afternoon, when all was quiet, she wandered down the beach and laid her towel on the sand. She stripped down to her bikini and smoothed suntan cream all over her now, very brown skin before walking into the sea. The sun beat down with less intensity and the water stung cold and salty. She ducked under, allowing the bracing chill to shiver through her body before she acclimatized. She swam strongly out to sea. Her arms and legs powered her through the water as she swam as hard and fast as she could for about fifty meters, turned and swam back just as hard and fast. She stopped and trod water, breathing hard and looking back to shore. The white washed building of Michael's bar peeped, half hidden through the trees at one end. The bay curved round, edged with vegetation and fig trees to where the old villa sat quaint and pretty from a distance. Further along, you could just see the taverna between the trees. "What a place to have a house.' thought Meg. She took in the tranquility and natural beauty of the setting with the mountain reaching up behind. She rolled onto her back and floated, staring up at the sky flecked with wispy white clouds.

She was glad Rachel had come. Things were becoming clearer. She was glad she had been wrong about Rachel and Pete, but it made her realise how jealous and insecure she had become. It was that, and many other things that were not right with Pete. The seed of mistrust had been planted by the girl at Freshers and there were the other women who had raised her suspicions and made her insecure leading to them splitting. When they got back together it had seemed right, but she wasn't sure he had changed his ways or whether she just couldn't stop looking for things to be wrong. He always denied anything, just as he had with the estate agent in Devon and she always let it go because she wanted to believe in him. She had been wrong about Rachel so was she wrong in her other suspicions. After all, she enjoyed the company of other men without it meaning anything. Maybe deep down, she was just unable to trust him completely?

Her nerves clenched in her tummy. She did love Pete with a passion for all his good qualities, but without trust, there was nothing.

She realised that apart from odd moments she had been in a state of panic for well over a year. Worrying obsessively over her relationship with Pete. Continually knocked by her failure to get a good job, worrying about money, where to live. Where had the confident bubbly schoolgirl gone? Everything had seemed so easy then. She had thought she knew everything, was so sure of her successful future. Seemed as if she still had a lot to learn. She needed to relax, take stock and start again. Suddenly she smiled, turned over and began swimming slowly back to shore. She had just remembered going to a yoga class, years before.

"Imagine you are floating on a calm sea, the sun is shining in the blue sky, fluffy clouds float past and you are supported by the gently bobbing water."

And here she was. She wondered what they told you in Greek island yoga. "Imagine you are on a busy tube packed with people in suits, bad body odour mixes with Chanel No.5 and you are on your way to your fantastic job in the city where you are highly successful, respected and incredibly well paid."

She pushed through the surf to the soft beach and adjusted her bikini, before treading across the fine sand and flopping down onto her towel. She tried to think clearly about her and Pete. Maybe there was nothing to think about. Pete had already made his choice. Why had he sent all those lovely messages only to go on leave to somewhere like Malaysia on a boys' holiday without telling her? What had he said about coming to see her wherever she was in the world? Was this Pete taking the easy way out to finish it? She just had to face the fact that it was over.

She turned her thoughts to the future, and thought about what to do as soon as she got back: To go to London and find fame and fortune? Crowded tubes, black snot and grubby fingernails were all that came to mind. She pushed those images aside and thought BBC, Covent Garden, theatres, shows, museums, art galleries, parks and pubs. That was where she would go. She started to feel optimistic again. She felt ready to start sending out applications all over again. She would survive for about a week in London on the money she'd saved. She could do shop work, waitressing, anything, while she applied for something better. She should forget about love and concentrate on her career.

A twig cracked in the bushes behind her. Her heart froze as the soft thud of feet landing on sand reached her ears. Marzun, mean and aggressive flashed across her mind.

She braced herself and dared to turn and look. Standing over her was a very hot and sweaty Ralph swigging water from a large bottle. He took his headphones off and placed the Walkman down on the sand next to her.

"Hi there! Sorry, didn't mean to startle you."

She was so pleased to see him.

He offered her the bottle and said, "I need a swim, coming? I can see from your rat tails you've just been in."

Meg self-consciously felt her hair, which hung in damp ringlets and laughed. She jumped up and started running towards the sea. Caught by surprise, he dropped the bottle and chased after her. He reached her at the edge of the water and shoved her lightly forward so that she tipped into the breaking waves.

She came up coughing and spluttering, "You bully!"

"Hardly touched you!"

"Didn't you go to the beach with the others?" she asked.

"Yes, but I got a bit restless and decided to run back.

Meg stared at him.

"My God! It's miles!"

"It was quite tough, but once I'd started I had to keep going. Once you get into a rhythm, you don't even notice. It's very relaxing and it's not really that far."

Meg looked very doubtful.

He splashed water at her and they began splashing and dodging each other. Meg was definitely coming off worse so she eventually ran out of the water and up the beach, laughing.

"Chicken!" he yelled after her and then he dived into the water and swam for a while.

He emerged shining. His bronzed skin glistened with water and Meg sitting cross-legged admired his long, firm legs, slim hips widening out to broad shoulders, as he made his way towards her. She felt a tingle of desire and enjoyed the sensation.

He sat beside her with his forearms resting on his knees and said, "Rachel get away all right?"

"Yes, yes she did."

"Everything all right? You seemed very quiet last night."

Meg was surprised he had noticed.

"No, fine, bit tired and realising that at the end of this week I don't really have a clue what I'm going to do," she said. She gave a little shrug and exhaled sharply, then quickly changed the subject, "Expect you'll miss Rachel, won't you?"

He chuckled softly and said, "Not really. She's a nice girl, but not what you're thinking."

"I wasn't thinking anything," she said with mock innocence, smiling at him with her eyebrows raised. 'Could Rachel be right? Does he like me?' The thought excited her.

"Actually, there is someone I like."

She felt disappointed.

"Ah, Belinda, she's lovely."

"Yes, I like Belinda, she's great, but no, that's not who I meant. I meant you. From the first time I saw you in that beautiful yellow dress, actually."

Meg felt a jolt. All summer she'd had people saying that to her, and it had made her feel annoyed, embarrassed, or guilty, but this time she realised she liked it. She stared at him, shifting sand nervously between her fingers.

"But I thought, Rachel... I mean. Oh!"

He laughed and reached one hand out and covered hers, looking intently at her with his strong, shining blue eyes. She was amazed at his ease. She could feel warmth spreading through her, melting her. His touch sent a shock of pleasure right to her heart. A million thoughts raced through her head, emotions crashed and jingled, but all she could really think about was kissing his beautiful, sensuous lips, and wondering what it would be like.

"Oy, oy!"

They looked round and saw Eddie and Robert shuffling across the thick sand towards them. James was holding a bottle of wine and some plastic cups. Meg and Ralph looked at each other and smiled.

"The girls have gone for a nap so we thought you might like to join us for pre-dinner drinks,"

Eddie said, flopping down on the sand next to them. His milky white skin was red and peeling, sweaty and freckly. Meg realised Ralph was still holding her hand and she liked it.

Robert sat down in front of them and proceeded to pour out the wine and hand it out.

"Rather cheeky little number, I think you'll find," announced Robert, screwing the top back on the bottle.

They all said 'Cheers!' and tried not to grimace too much as they took the first sips.

"Aaaah – not quite the best claret," proclaimed Robert. "Still, when in Greece…"

"Do as the Romans do," laughed Ralph.

"Exactly, old chap. Exactly."

They sat and listened to Eddie regaling their day. He managed to turn everything into an adventure and was an hilarious storyteller. Ralph moved closer to Meg as they cried with laughter and she felt tiny electric shots fly through her each time his arm brushed against her.

They began telling awful jokes and Ralph told the story of the wide mouth frog. Meg had never heard it before and she roared with laughter, partly because she loved silly jokes but mostly because of the ridiculous expressions on Ralph's face as he told it. This was a completely different man to the silent, sullen recluse that she had first met.

The four of them sat working their way through the disgusting wine as the sun began to go down and the sky developed a mauve tinge. A call came from the direction of the bar and Sophie and Lucy stood waving.

"Ah, the wenches await!" announced Robert, and Meg suddenly realised she ought to be in the bar meeting people.

"Oh dear! I'd better go and change."

"You look fine to me," said Ralph, admiring her slim, golden body.

Meg pulled on her T-shirt and shorts and said,

"Thank you, but not quite suitable for a rep of my standing."

Together they made their way along the beach.

"Thanks for the wine," Meg said to the guys. "See you in half an hour."

"Righty ho," said Eddie.

Ralph walked across the road to Meg's door. She suddenly felt shy, but he remained calm.

"I'll come back down with the others, see you in the restaurant. Are you sure half an hour is long enough for you?"

She looked at him indignantly and saw that he was laughing.

"You'd be amazed what I can do in half an hour," she retorted

He brushed one hand softly down her arm and said softly, "I'll see you in a while."

Then he grinned and walked away.

She didn't have time to mull. She showered in tepid water and towel dried her hair. Soft and clean, it fell in shiny waves over her shoulders. As she quickly applied a little make-up, she was aware of a tiny buzz inside. She thought about Pete and felt angry.

# CHAPTER 39

A small crowd made its way down the road to the taverna with Eddie and Robert entertaining the new people. They were all laughing at his stories, which he told with great panache in his powerful, plummy voice.

Ralph was already there with Belinda, Jason and Caro and they all greeted her warmly. Meg went over to see Gregor who was rubbing his hands with glee at the sight of the four young women. Meg told him off, laughing.

"We go to disco tomorrow night, yes?" He asked, smiling with a twinkle in his eyes.

"Actually, that's a great plan," replied Meg. "I'll see who wants to go."

She checked everyone was fine with their orders and went over to sit in the chair Ralph had saved. He handed her a glass of wine and raised his to everyone.

"Yamaas!"

Everyone echoed him. A cool breeze swept across the tables and the sea whispered beyond, a lively evening began.

Ralph was open in his affection for her. When he naturally placed his arm on her back and gently tickled her neck mid-conversation, she was completely mortified and looked up at Belinda and the others to see if they'd noticed.

Belinda met her eyes and smiled with approval. Jason and Cara made no reaction. It was as if everyone knew something she didn't. His touch created goose bumps over her whole body and she felt like she wasn't really there. Faces around her were smiling, laughing, opening and closing to speak words she didn't hear. She thought of Pete and for a moment wished he was there. Slowly she relaxed and started to enjoy herself. "Sod Pete," she whispered to herself.

The meals were finished, and Eddie started rounding people up to go back to Michael's. A merry troupe set off down the road. Meg watched with amusement as Gregor swooped in on the girls and arranged to see them in the bar.

Meg thanked Kostos and promised to come back for a final meal before everyone left.

"Which one is it to be, then Gregor?" she asked as she passed him clearing a table.

"We'll see. We'll see," he said winking, "and you? Who is this man? I am very jealous."

Meg blushed and shrugged with a huge smile on her face.

Ralph waited for her and they followed behind the rest, with his arm linked through hers.

"You okay?"

"Yes. Yes I am."

He stopped and turned her face towards him in the moonlight and bent his head down towards hers. She lifted her face, and his lips touched hers. Her lips melted into his and then she didn't know whose lips were whose as everything fitted, everything blended in an exquisite kiss. He pulled her closer with his arms wrapping her up and she moved her body into his wanting all of her to be touching all of him. She slid her hands up the back of his T-shirt feeling the heat of his smooth skin and could feel her own heat and desire.

They came apart slowly and he held her face looking into her eyes with such caring that she thought she would cry. Something held her back from wanting to go any further and he recognised it.

"Great swimmer and a great kisser."

She smiled up at him and hugging her with one arm round her shoulder, they walked on to the bar.

She was so grateful that he had read her mind. Such sensitivity, such gentleness.

They joined the others in Michael's and Gregor came down with two friends in tow. The two English lads had moved in on the four girls and Meg saw them puff themselves up at the sight of the Greeks. Meg watched, worrying that there might be trouble, but luckily, the girls made the decision. Two stood up and went to the toilet. They walked past Gregor and his friends eyeing them up as they walked by. On their return, they paused to let Gregor start chatting them up and left their two friends to the English guys. Meg relaxed and wondered which of the Greeks would lose out. She was stunned when Gregor came over alone to say goodnight. Meg raised her eyebrows at him as he approached and he shrugged and held his hands out, palms up, as if to say he didn't know what happened. Meg knew it must have been his choice.

Belinda said she was going, and Jason asked Ralph if he wanted a lift. He accepted and Meg wasn't sure if she was pleased or upset. They all walked outside and Ralph said he was just going to walk Meg home. It was only across the road but Caro quickly took the hint and said she needed the loo and nudged Jason who jumped and said quickly that he did too and they went back inside.

Ralph and Meg walked over to her door and kissed long and hard, every cell in her body crying out to be touched and loved, but still not ready to give herself away.

"Not yet," he whispered. "See you tomorrow."

Meg floated into her room. She went to sleep remembering the kiss and filling with anticipation. She refused to think beyond that.

The next morning, Ralph came into the bar and had breakfast with Meg. He said he was going to Nidri and they arranged to meet as soon as she could get there. She could hardly wait for Mike to come and go with the vehicles. She raced up to Nidri with a feeling of great lightness, which she realised she hadn't felt for so long. She found them in the usual spot, lazing on the beach and drinking beer. Meg offered to get everyone a drink and Belinda said she'd go with her. They sauntered up to the nearest bar and as soon as they were out of earshot, Belinda said,

"You and Ralph are so good together!"

Meg looked at her to see if she was being honest and Belinda laughed.

"Don't worry. I'm not jealous. I really like Ralph, but I feel more like a sister to him. I'm sorry to say this, but I was worried that he was going to fall for your friend, Rachel."

Meg felt protective towards Rachel but she said, "I did too. I didn't even consider that he liked me and I didn't realise how much I liked him."

"You are joking. Well, it was obvious to everyone else and he went way up in my estimation when I realised he had seen straight through her."

Meg didn't know what to say. She felt sorry for Rachel.

"Look I know she's your friend, but she knew that he liked you and she did everything she could to stop anything happening between you."

Meg suddenly felt incredibly protective.

"No, no. You've got her wrong. Rachel is a good person, she's a great friend of mine. I think she sometimes gives off the wrong impression but she just likes to flirt, and it's not as if I had anything going with Ralph."

Belinda looked a bit taken aback but then she smiled.

"Hey, I'm really sorry. I was completely out of order. Maybe I did misjudge her. Well, you've got something good going now. Enjoy!" she said.

Meg grinned at her, "We'll see!"

They returned to the others with the beers.

"Took your time!" called Jason. "People dying of thirst here."

They handed out the beer and Ralph suggested a game of boules.

Meg felt confused; she didn't know what was real anymore. Here they all were, relaxed, on holiday, drunk with sunshine and beer. Who were these people that she had only known a couple of weeks? She remembered those first few days when she had first arrived and how she had told Tim that nothing was real when you were on holiday. The sun, sea and sand definitely had a lot to answer for.

"Penny for 'em" said Ralph, putting his arm round her. It felt comforting and exciting. 'Shut-up, Meg,' she told herself. 'This is lovely – enjoy.'

"Worth more than a penny, I'm afraid."

She laughed and picked up a ball, "Right let me show you how to do this."

She rolled the heavy blue ball with no finesse whatsoever and it rolled about ten yards past the jack. They all laughed.

On her next go, she took more care and it came to rest a few inches away.

"Wooo!" Jason shouted and then proceeded to knock her ball right out of the way. Ralph came next and skillfully knocked hers back into play right next to the jack while his own ball careered off to the side Meg gave Ralph a high five and Jason held his head in shock. It was the only time Ralph did that. Jason went on to win every game.

"County bowls champion," he admitted when they'd had enough of him smashing their balls to left and right. They threw sand at him until he ran into the sea and they all followed to cool down and refresh.

Ralph swam up behind Meg and encircled her with his arms, letting her legs float out in front as she leant back into his chest. Meg closed her eyes enjoying the feeling of his strong arms around her and her whole body relaxed. She hadn't realised how uptight and heavyhearted she had been until the feeling of total release came. It was as if she'd been pushing against a huge rubber band stretched to capacity and she had let go and been flung into the air flying free. She didn't know where she might land and at that moment, it didn't matter. She was filled with what the Greeks call 'ke fi', the desire to sing and dance with happiness.

"Come on, love birds!" shouted Jason. He sent a huge splash over their heads. "Time to go."

They'd planned to get a bite to eat in Nidri before going to the disco but Meg had to go back to Nikiana to meet people there and bring them.

Ralph said he would go back with Meg on her moped.

Ralph drove and Meg put her arms tightly around his waist and pressed herself up against his back. The wind blew over them and she felt safe and relaxed.

As they came round a sharp bend in the middle of the journey, a strange guttural noise erupted from the engine. The exhaust coughed unhealthily a few times and the bike slowed and then stopped. Ralph tried to start it, to no avail.

"Oh God!" he laughed. They both clambered off and he shook the bike with his ear next to the petrol tank. There was no comforting swishing sound.

"Out of petrol, I fear."

"Oh. Shit!" exclaimed Meg, "I forgot to check."

"Think we'll have to walk."

"Sorry," Meg said weakly.

They set off with Ralph pushing the bike. Meg felt stupid and annoyed with herself. The sun was still quite strong and the air was hot. Ralph turned and saw her crestfallen face.

"Hey. This is great. Now I get to see every leaf in the trees. Hear every bird and insect singing in the branches. Oh, look!"

He propped the bike up on its stand and crouched down pointing at something on the verge.

"What is it?" Meg asked, coming closer.

"Shhh," he whispered.

She edged nearer and knelt beside him.

"I'm not sure but..." he put on a David Bellamy voice, "I do believe we may have come across a rare breed of 'lipsomus kissamus'."

Meg leant closer still trying to see anything other than dry grass.

"Where?" she whispered, worried that she might squash a rare and exotic creature. Ralph plucked a blade of grass and held it up between them so that their heads were touching.

"Lips-oh mus, kss.." he said slowly and clearly. He looked at her with a twinkle in his eyes and his lips pursed. She laughed and laughed, kissed him quickly on his lips and pushed him backwards. He lost his balance and fell back onto the grassy verge. He grabbed her and they laughed and kissed at the side of the road.

The sound of an engine came from the other side of the bend and they quickly stood up and waved down the small, white truck that appeared.

"Kalispera," (*good afternoon*) Meg said to the driver, and the old man dressed in the traditional black trousers with braces over a white vest and wearing a black beret, nodded at her.

She pointed to the bike and told him it had no petrol. His thick tanned skin was grooved with the deep lines of working in the sun all his life. He had strong muscular arms and, without a word, he picked up the bike and put it in the back of his truck between boxes filled with olives. He nodded for them to get in the front. Ralph went to go in first and the man grunted, shook his head and pointed to Meg. Ralph and Meg looked at each other. Meg shrugged and got in first and slid across the bench seat. Ralph got in beside her and put his arm around her protectively.

The Greek driver sucked in his cheeks and set off towards Nikiana. Throughout the journey, he stared at Meg's legs and body. He hardly watched the road at all as he sped around bends, beeping his horn on blind corners, but not slowing down. Meg and Ralph exchanged glances and Meg clasped her hands tightly in her lap, praying. He screeched to a halt outside the bakery and Meg and Ralph almost fell out in relief. The old guy lifted the bike out with ease and stood it on the ground. Then he went into the bakery and came out with bread. Papandrou followed him out and shook his hand, smiling and laughing. Meg and Ralph said, "Efaristo, efaristo." (*Thank you, thank you.*) to the old man. He nodded briefly as he got back into his truck and drove off.

Papandrou laughed and shook his head at Meg and went back inside his shop. Meg and Ralph burst out laughing.

"Bloody hell! Didn't think we'd make it out alive then."

They decided that Meg would take the bike down to her room and Ralph set off at a jog back up the hill to his. They arranged to meet in an hour.

Meg pushed the bike along giggling to herself. Eddie and crew (as she referred to them) came screeching up behind her on their mopeds.

"You okay?" called Sophie.

"Yes. Ran out of petrol," Meg said sheepishly.

They all laughed.

"We'll sort it out. We'll get a can from the garage."

"Oh, thanks!" called Meg. "See you in a while."

# CHAPTER 40

The sky was losing its light; slowly, imperceptibly dimming. Meg missed evening office for the first time and she didn't care. None of the guests cared. They all found her when they needed her and everyone met up in the bar in the evenings anyway. Meg felt good. She was relaxed and bright from feeling wanted.

As she came out of her room, washed and changed, Callista's door opened and Callista stepped out. Meg noticed the dark shadow of a man pass behind her inside the apartment but didn't have time to think about it as Callista shouted to her.

"Meg! Meg!"

Meg went over to her.

"Yassou, Callista. Ti karis?" (*Hello, how are you?*) Smiling at the frenetic, little lady.

"Spiro call. He very upset."

'Typical,' thought Meg, 'The only time I'm late,' she felt herself becoming tense.

"What about?" she asked.

"He not tell me. Something about flights. He come in the morning."

Meg sighed and said, "All right. Thanks, Callista. I'll wait for him."

She went to walk away and Callista held her arm.

"And, other call," she said, looking intently at Meg, "Your friend, I think."

Meg's heart somersaulted. She was completely thrown, "Oh," was all she could manage in reply.

Callista raised one eyebrow, but said nothing.

"Thanks, Callista," Meg finally added.

She looked imploringly into the wise, ageing face. She didn't want Callista to think badly of her, but what must she think.

Callista pressed her lips together in a thin line.

"I know you good heart." She indicated her own heart with her fingertips, "You be careful. Sun do funny things to monkey."

Meg smiled at her and continued into the bar with her stomach beginning to go into the usual knots. She was angry at the reaction the phone call generated. She wondered where Pete was calling from and then made a conscious decision not to think about him.

She soon got caught up in the general banter in the bar. Ralph was having a lighthearted political discussion with Eddie about Margaret Thatcher and Ronald Reagan, the Cold War and high unemployment and he was running rings around Eddie with his knowledge.

Around half nine, after grabbing a bite to eat, they all headed up to the disco in Nidri on the bus. When they arrived it was surprisingly full and very lively. With the steady, strong beat of Duran Duran's 'Wild Boys' resounding off mirrors and walls you could barely hear yourself speak, let alone anyone else. Meg stood in a circle with Ralph, Jason, Caro and Belinda. Eddie and Robert were flinging Sophie and Lucy around the dance floor paying no attention to the rhythm, and the four girls were gyrating in front of a handbag on the floor.

Meg spotted Gregor with a crowd of his Greek friends. She waved and he came over with one of them. Jason and Caro turned to face the dance floor and Belinda attempted to have a conversation with Ralph over the sound of the blaring music. Gregor tried to say something to Meg but she couldn't hear. He laughed about something and then moved away speaking to his friend. Suddenly, Meg felt someone shove violently against her back. The music faded from one record into the next as Meg turned her head and came face to face with Marzun. A strobe sent flickering white light in flashes across the room putting the dancers into slow motion as they moved to Michael Jackson's "Wanna be Startin' Something'. The music seemed to grow louder, throbbing, pulsing. Meg smiled automatically. Marzun moved to her side, grabbed one arm and twisted it up behind her with sharp force. He pressed the back of her hand between her shoulder blade sending shooting pain through her upper arm. His hot breath whispered harshly in her ear, "Don't smile at me, you bitch."

Meg tried to pull away, but he held her firm. She looked wildly around. Belinda and Ralph held their heads close together, as they attempted to hold a conversation. Jason and Caro were still facing the dance floor, their bodies rocking to the beat.

"Don't try anything, nobody can hear you. You are a tease, a user. You use people to get what suits you."

He spat the words into her ear pressing her arm into her back.

Meg's shoulder screamed with pain. She couldn't see his other hand and she became convinced he had a knife. She filled with sheer terror. Suddenly, Marzun let go of her. She saw Gregor put his arm round Marzun's shoulder and pull him away to one side. Gregor hugged Marzun tightly, smiling and asking him how he was. As he did that, he put himself between Meg and Marzun. He moved him away and then whispered something in his ear. Marzun scowled with a look of sheer hatred but backed off and slunk away. Gregor went back to Meg.

"Malaka," he stated. "You okay, Meggie?"

Meg stood quite still holding her arm. She was in total shock and her body began to tremble uncontrollably. Ralph turned to her, laughing. He took one look at her face and full of concern grabbed her hand and asked her what was wrong. Meg stared at him unable to speak. Ralph glared at Gregor, but Meg shook her head. She touched Gregor on the arm and mouthed 'thank you', then she steered Ralph towards the bar.

He ordered her a brandy and asked again, what had happened. Meg didn't know what to say. It had happened so quickly and Ralph knew nothing about Marzun. How could she explain what it had felt like? How scared she had been. She couldn't stop the shaking.

"I- I'm fine. I-I – can't speak," she stuttered.

She waved her hand in front of her face, breathing deeply and trying not to cry. She glanced across the room and saw Gregor exchanging angry words with Marzun. Marzun pushed Gregor's shoulder and immediately six or seven Greek lads formed a line behind Gregor. Gregor said something else to Marzun and with a black scowl he turned and barged through the throng and out of the disco.

Belinda, Jason and Caro came over to the bar oblivious of any problem.

"Drink anyone?" shouted Jason above the music.

"I'm just going to take Meg home. She's not feeling very well," Ralph shouted into Jason's ear.

He bought a bottle of water and handed the waiter some money saying to get Jason and the others whatever they wanted.

"Oh, Okay. Hope you feel better, Meg," Jason said in a concerned voice and kissed her on the cheek.

Meg managed a small smile and Ralph took her hand and led the way, pushing through the mass of dancing, sweating bodies to the door. Meg was suddenly petrified that Marzun might be waiting outside. Her body still shook and her knees could barely support her. There was no sign of Marzun and no taxis so Ralph led her to sit on the tree stump. He knelt in front of her and put his arms round her and she burst into tears. He stroked her hair saying, "It's okay. You're safe."

She cried from release of tension. She cried for Pete, for her non-existent career, for all the broken, troubled people she had met in the last three months, for lack of sleep, and for this beautiful man, who made her feel so special and yet she knew that there was no future for them.

Great sobs wracked her until she was too exhausted to cry anymore. Ralph held her and soothed her until she finally pulled back and searched for a tissue to blow her nose. She looked up at him with red eyes and breathed deeply.

"Sorry," she gasped.

He shook his head and handed her the water just as a taxi came up. Ralph said simply, "Come on, let's go."

They climbed into the back of the taxi and Ralph leaned forward and said, "Nikiana" to the driver. He sat back and put his arm round her. She squeezed his hand and slowly got her breath back and calmed down. He kissed her on the top of her head as she tried to explain what had happened.

"God, I didn't even see him. I'm so sorry," Ralph said, annoyed with himself.

"It happened so quickly, but I was so scared. I really thought he was going to kill me. I really don't know what I did to upset him so much. He said I was a user, but all I did was refuse to have sex with him."

He held her tighter. "Hey, you did nothing wrong. He's an arrogant wanker with a bruised ego. You are the loveliest person I have ever met."

He looked away out of the window and she knew the words were straight from the heart and he was worried he had said too much.

They were coming to the top of the hill, so Ralph leant forward to ask the driver to stop outside his accommodation. He paid the fare and led Meg without speaking down the steps and into his sparse, whitewashed room. He switched on a dim bedside lamp, which illuminated the book he was reading, 'This side of Paradise' by F.Scott Fitzgerald. She sat on the bed and he sat beside her with his arm around her and she began to cry again, apologising and sniffing and he just held her in his arms. She stopped crying and looked at him and tried to smile. He passed her a tissue and soothed her and told her everything was going to be all right. They lay down on the bed with Ralph holding her from behind and he nestled his head against hers.

Meg felt a curious fullness. She realised that she was relieved that he wasn't going to make love to her. That neither of them was ready, but she felt so comfortable and safe. She kissed Ralph's hand and sighed deeply.

"Penny for'em," he whispered.

"Worth more than a penny," she replied.

# CHAPTER 41

Meg woke a few hours later, freezing. She slipped quietly off the bed and stared down at his handsome sleeping face. She pulled the cover over him and kissed him softly on the cheek. Quietly she left the room and made her way back down the pre-dawn road. Birds chirped 'wake-up', 'wake-up!' and the rising sun streaked pink and grey across the sky above the sea.

When she reached her room, there was still a long time before anyone would be up and about. She was too wide-awake to sleep, so she put on her bikini under a T-shirt and took a towel across to the deserted beach.

The sea lay before her like a sheet of shimmering silk. She strode in, dived under the cold, clear, calm surface, and swam in long leisurely strokes. The feeling of fullness hadn't left her and she dared to think. She thought about Pete and felt deep sadness but this was followed by a sudden, warm sense of nostalgia. She smiled in fondness at all the good memories and she realised that they had both been hanging on; they'd both been trying to find that first happiness, not realising it had gone. It didn't matter why or how anymore. She had to accept it had gone and let it go. She flipped onto her back and floated on the surface of the water, allowing her body to lift and fall on the undulating waves.

Suddenly she filled with calm and then an intense sense of joy shot through her like a jolt of electricity. For the briefest of moments she felt connected to the sea, to the sky, to everything and it was as if she understood everything with complete clarity. Then the moment was gone. She tried to recapture it, to remember what she had understood, but all she had was a memory of the joy.

She thought about the future and realised she had no idea and it didn't matter. She thought about Ralph and that feeling of fullness swept through her once more. She felt they couldn't possibly have a future, but it didn't matter. He had reminded her how to feel. Love. She emerged from the sea and for some reason said, "Thank you," aloud, to the sea, to the sky, to God.

She showered, changed, and made her way over to Michael's with all her accounts in order and money for T-shirts and profit from vehicle hire ready to give to Spiro. She worked out how much Spiro owed her, as she hadn't seen him for so long, preparing to argue if necessary. To her surprise, Spiro arrived at eight-thirty. He burst into the empty bar with his usual elegance and charm, red-faced and shaking.

"Come outside!" he demanded.

Meg followed him out to the road, where his car stood still running.

"We have problem. Too many people for last flight."

Meg looked at him.

"We get numbers wrong. Some book one week, two weeks. We forget three weeks. Now too many. You can not fly on Wednesday."

"So, when can I fly?" enquired Meg.

"No more flights after Wednesday. Airport close."

Meg waited, her mind racing.

"You go by bus overland."

Meg felt a burst of panic, her mind raced and she tried to persuade herself that she would quite enjoy travelling through Europe. She had friends in Germany she would love to visit. With her newfound sense of freedom and clarity, nothing was going to be a problem.

"And you will pay for this?"

"Yes, yes. I will pay."

He was getting impatient. He obviously hadn't thought anything through. Meg actually felt sorry for him.

"Look, Spiro. I have money here for the mopeds, jeeps and everything and you owe me my wages."

"You keep this money, keep this money."

He was nearly jumping up and down in his agitation.

"And money for travel?"

"Yes, yes! I give you after. But, no flight. Okay?"

"No, I'm not okay. But I guess unless you leave one of the holiday makers, I have no choice."

She felt strangely calm, but she wasn't going to tell him that.

"You good girl. I see you at airport," he said quickly, and then he got into his car and drove away, fast. She was in shock after he'd gone, shook her head in amazement and tried to think positively about travelling back through lots of different places. Apart from anything, it postponed her step back into reality.

She told Ralph when she saw him and he was furious for her.

"Let's just enjoy the rest of your holiday," Meg said, smiling into his eyes. She was silently growing in turmoil, but didn't want to spoil the few days they had left.

She realised that this man made her feel everything at once. Each time she saw him she was surprised by how gorgeous he was and felt an ache of desire but in his company she felt relaxed and uninhibited, completely natural.

They did enjoy the last couple of days. They spent time eating, drinking, swimming with the others, and when they found time to be alone, talking. Gradually they discovered more and more about each other's lives, thoughts and feelings; opening up their hearts freely. He finally revealed the sadness she had seen in the first days of knowing him. He had split up with his long time girlfriend. She had wanted him to commit to marriage and he had not felt ready, so she had finished with him. He had been deeply upset and had thrown himself into work until someone had made him take a holiday because he was getting ill. Meg did not miss the irony. On the last night, they sat huddled on the beach below Ralph's room as the September chill crept across the island.

"It was my boss who practically booked the holiday for me. He told me that he was sick of seeing my pale face and that if I didn't take a break and get some colour and rest, he would fire me. I wasn't looking forward to it but, well, here I am, and here are you. You've taught me how to feel again, Meg. Thank you."

He stroked the back of her neck, and she could feel his pain. "No, thank you. I think we've helped each other," she said quietly.

They sat staring out across the black sea streaked with a golden path of light from the moon. Then they leaned in towards each other and rested their heads together. Meg breathed in the now familiar fresh smell of soap, shaving foam and shampoo. They held each other close, not saying anything.

"Here and now for each other," he said and she understood.

He walked her back down the hill holding her hand. Neither spoke. At her door, they kissed tenderly in the cool night air.

"See you tomorrow."

"Yes, see you tomorrow."

Meg went into her little room and sat on the edge of her bed. She didn't know what she expected from Ralph. She felt he had released her from the chains of irretrievable love that bound her to Pete, but she didn't know if she wanted or expected to have a relationship with him. It was all so surreal. Beautiful, but surreal, and she had to try to find her way home across Europe first.

In the morning, she went over to the bar and Michael made her breakfast. "On the house."

"Are you staying on the island?" she asked him.

"No, we shut up here and go to Athens for the winter in a week or so. My mother and father stay."

"I think I'm going tomorrow. Is it all right, if I stay one more night in my room? I want to say goodbye to everyone before I go."

"Yes, of course. No problem."

He pointed to his T-shirt, one of her creations and smiled. Meg laughed.

"Where's Marzun?" she dared to ask. She hadn't seen him since the disco and she wanted to be sure that he wasn't around.

"He go back again. My mother very upset. He say he stay for two weeks then he suddenly say he go."

Meg was relieved, but she didn't give anything away. "Can you tell Callista I'll be back after I've taken everyone to the airport."

People started coming in asking questions and Meg was caught up in the general hubbub of departures. People thanked her and gave her their addresses, insisting she call on them anytime she was in their area. Ralph came in with Jason, Caro and Belinda. Meg checked names off her list. She went out to get all the vehicles lined up and the keys. Ralph came to find her.

"All set?" she asked him.

"Yes, all set," he replied, and held out a small package with an envelope attached. She took them looking at him quizzically.

"Just to say how lovely you are."

"Oh. Thank you!" Meg was touched. "Is it okay if I open them later?"

"Yes," said Ralph simply, "Right, I'll be inside. I've just ordered a bite to eat."

"Fine. Let me get everything organised."

He bent and kissed her quickly before returning into the bar.

Two people were missing. Meg rushed over to their chalet and discovered them finishing their packing, nursing hangovers. As she crossed back over the road, the bus was coming. It drew up and Spiro leapt off.

"Meg! Pack your things. You are on the flight."

Meg looked at him, aghast.

"Quick! Quick!" he urged.

Now she really did feel panic. No time to think or question, she rushed into her room and gathered all her things together. She stuffed all the money for the mopeds, jeeps and T-shirts into her purse. She left her unread novel lying on the bed and hurried out of the door. Everyone was on the coach waiting for her.

Meg ran inside the bar and hugged a surprised Michael,

"I've got to go. I'm on the flight. Please say good-bye and thank you to everyone!"

She rushed back out looking for Callista but she was nowhere to be seen.

"Come on!" shouted Spiro. He bundled her onto the coach.

She made her way down the coach and flopped down next to Ralph.

"I'm flying!" she said, not knowing whether to laugh or cry.

"That's great!" Ralph exclaimed, "I was really worried about you."

Callista came running into the bar, "Where is Meg?" she asked Michael.

"She has gone. Spiro got her on the flight after all. She asked me to say thank you and good-bye. Why?"

"Phone call. He miss her again. Funny little monkey."

Callista went quickly back out to tell Pete that Meg was flying to London. Michael continued to wipe glasses at the bar.

They arrived at the airport and everyone got into a queue to go through the little customs and passport shed. There were busloads of people arriving for the three flights that marked the end of the summer. Meg suddenly felt herself go hot then cold. She had far too much local money on her. She had told people all season not to carry too much foreign money out of the airport. What if they stopped her? She arranged for Ralph to go through first. She would give him her purse over the fence and then go through herself. She waited by the low fence that demarcated the departure area.

Belinda came through first, followed by Caro and Jason. They all came over to the fence to wish her luck and she said that she would see them in a minute. Ralph came behind them and she gave him her purse with a grin and rushed round to join the queue. When she got into the shed, Spiro summoned her over to where he was talking to a couple of officials. "Give me passport." Without thinking, she gave it to him and he bustled off to talk to official looking men in uniforms. She sat down and watched him. Now she was worried. The first flight was ready to leave with Ralph on board as she waited anxiously while Spiro continued to talk to different people. He turned and strode towards her sucking on his cigar furiously.

"You no go this flight," he announced flatly. "Maybe next one. You sit and wait there."

He indicated a low couch in the corner. She was completely flummoxed; she had no way of letting Ralph know. She sat down, watching and waiting with her heart pounding. She was stuck. Now she was worried about what she was going to do. She heard the sound of the airplane taking off.

She waited and waited in the stuffy, run-down shack, as the queues of people dwindled.

Spiro came over and said, "No flight. You go by bus."

It suddenly hit her. She had no money. Ralph had it all. She hadn't even said good-bye.

"You have money for me?" she asked, her voice rising.

"Yes, yes," said Spiro unable to look her in the eye, "Wait here."

Meg didn't trust him, but there was nothing she could do. He disappeared out of the shed. The second flight took off and she continued to sit and look pleadingly at the officials, her palms sweating and her heart beating fast.

The last lot of passengers went through for the third and final plane. Meg sat motionless, her mind racing. Where was Spiro? What if he'd already gone? How was she going to get anywhere without any money? Her mind was in a whirl. She could deal with most things, but no money was a big problem. Her passport! She suddenly remembered Spiro had taken her passport. She stood up, her heart was racing and she could feel sweat running down her spine. She went over to a lady at the desk, and tried to ask her in Greek where her passport was, but the lady just frowned at her. Someone tapped her on her shoulder. She twirled round. A young Greek man in uniform held out her passport to her. "Go now, you take this flight."

She grabbed the passport and gathered up her bags. She followed his pointing arm out of the shed and across the field to the waiting plane in a blur of relief.

Completely shell-shocked she wandered down the aisle. An air steward shoved her rucksack into an overhead compartment for her and she squeezed past a large man with a red, peeling nose and collapsed into a seat by the window. She sat staring out of the window trying to collect herself. The plane took off and she watched as the little island turned into a patchwork quilt of greens and browns in a blue surround. She said a silent goodbye and felt sad that she hadn't said good-bye properly to any of the lovely people who had been so kind to her.

The plane rose and Meg looked out on the beautiful field of clouds, a floating world of snow and ice. "What next?" she asked herself. Suddenly she remembered the gift Ralph had given to her. She reached under the seat in front and pulled her leather satchel out and onto her lap. She rummaged for the solid, strangely shaped package and the envelope. Tearing off the paper, she revealed a small, china frog with a wide gap for its mouth to make it a moneybox. It was covered in Greek phrases for 'good luck' and different greetings. She smiled as she remembered Ralph telling the joke about the wide mouth frog, with his beautiful face contorted into ridiculous expressions. She opened the envelope and took out a scrap of paper, folded in half. On the folded outside he had written, "You are lovely, know that". She unfolded it and read the poem by Laurence Hope that he had copied.

*For this is wisdom, to love and live*

*To take what fate or the Gods may give*

*To ask no question, to make no prayer*

*To kiss the lips and caress the hair*

*Speed passion's ebb as we greet its flow*

*To have and to hold and in time let go*

She filled with emotion. He had touched her soul. They had met for a reason and she felt deep down that this meant good-bye. He would send her purse to her. They might meet for a drink or two. Maybe she would never see him again. She knew she wasn't completely over Pete and suspected Ralph wasn't over his lost love. They had rebounded into each other and provided ethereal solace in the magical beauty of sun soaked coves and sighing seas. In the cold light of England she thought it would prove to be exquisite but ephemeral.

It seemed like a million years since she had got on the plane heading to Greece but it was only ten weeks, a brief hiatus from the real world, though hardly the respite she had envisioned. She suddenly realised that while for her the past two and a half months had been a full on roller coaster of events and emotions, for Pete it had been a normal two months away at work. A sudden shock twisted in her stomach. Reality slapped her face as she suddenly understood. She had been fighting for a fairy tale, unwilling to admit that life wasn't perfect, grieving for her Mum and Dad when in fact they'd moved on. She had been confronted by all these people, all these different experiences but not relating them to herself as she held onto the innocent dream of happy ever after. It was over.

The plane landed in Gatwick and Meg went through the motions of passport control in a daze. She had a few pounds that she'd kept in her rucksack, enough to get a coach to her home town and call one of her brothers to meet her, or walk if necessary. She had left with nothing and returned with nothing. Nobody would understand what she had experienced in such a short time.

She thought about all the different characters she had met: the kind and the angry, the content and the discontent, the carefree and the serious, the bitter and the sweet. So many different life stories. She had met with anger, even hate, but she had received so much kindness and friendship and she felt a strange overwhelming love and gratitude for all the people that had come into her life, if only for a brief encounter. What had she learned? That life was a series of ups and downs. That you shouldn't judge people too quickly. You never knew what they had been through, what pain or difficulties they might have experienced. Unchecked tears slid down her cheeks. This was her starting again, hopefully a little bit wiser.

She pushed her trolley into the gangway lined with people waiting to meet friends, family, loved ones. Their expectant faces moved quickly past her to see if the next person through was 'the one'. She stared at the floor in front of her and tried not to feel sad that nobody was there for her. When she came to the end of the barrier she pushed her trolley out into the jostling mass of people and looked around for signs to the coach station.

"Meg!"

She vaguely heard the name but didn't connect it to her.

"Meg! Meg!"

She turned to see where the voice was coming from and froze in disbelief.

Ralph stood there grinning and holding out her purse.

"Purseful for 'em," he said.

A few feet away, standing by a pillar, Pete saw Meg fling her arms around the neck of a good-looking guy. His hand clenched around the small velvet box in his pocket and he turned and walked quickly away.

# EPILOGUE

Meg finished checking her e-mails, leaned back and stretched her arms up with a deep satisfied sigh. She went to the kitchen, loaded the last cups and glasses into the dishwasher and turned it on before pouring herself a glass of wine. She took the wine out onto the verandah in the warm balmy night air of Abu Dhabi where she had been living for the past five years. In a few days she was going on holiday to celebrate her twenty-fifth wedding anniversary. Two children were asleep upstairs. Her lovely husband was also upstairs sleeping. Twenty-five years. It made no sense to her. How had they got there so soon? She sipped the wine and let her thoughts drift. They were going on holiday in a few days; it was going to be a wonderful trip to a villa in Greece with the children and a few friends to celebrate the big day.

The wine relaxed her and she mentally listed things she had to do to get ready for the trip and then her thoughts drifted back over her life to the mad, emotional turmoil of her twenties. She'd been so young, and yet at the time she remembered feeling so old. She'd wanted everything, and she'd wanted it instantly. She thought about the crazy summer she'd had working in Greece all those years ago.

She had seen a few of the people she met there including Eddie and Robert who turned out to be

Viscounts or Earls or something aristocratic. She'd stayed with Rachel for a while, who was a very good friend to Meg as she got into London life and work. Sandra did start up her own tour company and Meg worked for her for a while. By chance she had bumped into one of the men Meg had met on her arrival in Nikiana who had been particularly loud and scathing about the set up. She'd asked him if he had ever complained. He had burst out laughing, "One of the best holidays we've had. So much fun winding everyone up! We've been dining out on it ever since."

Ralph had watched as all the passengers from the second flight came through with no Meg and had continued to wait until the third flight arrived not knowing if she would be on it or not. He took her to the coach station and they promised to keep in touch.

With the harsh October winds swirling across the country and the dark nights closing in, the balmy summer sun and romance of Greece had barely seemed real as she contemplated the next chapter in her life from the comfort of her Mum's house. When she counted the drachma in her purse she realised that she had a few hundred pounds. It wasn't a fortune, but it made her feel safe to start again with renewed determination.

She spoke to Pete once more and he still made her heart jump with desire, but he didn't tell her about the airport and they couldn't find the right words to move forward, so they finished and, though it broke her heart, she cut off all contact.

She headed up to London to find work knowing that the streets were not paved with gold. Life had continued, sometimes full of joy sometimes very tough. Things had worked out well for her, on the whole. It hadn't always been easy. She had learnt the hard way to enjoy the good times, never knowing when life would throw a curveball to knock her sideways.

She hadn't heard from or of Pete for nearly thirty years, but a little part of her would always love him. If you really love someone it never goes away. What ever hurt and pain you might go through, the love remains.

'Where was he now?' she wondered as she sipped her wine. How ironic that she had ended up in the Middle East. The flash of a memory came to her, a fortune-teller in Camden town. She gasped and wondered, as she had many times over the years, what had happened to the ring? This was followed by a familiar twinge of sadness that Pete had changed his mind and decided he didn't want to marry her. She didn't know why it stayed with her. Despite a fair share of life's ups and downs, she was happy.

Since the advent of social media she'd occasionally thought about looking him up but had always decided against it. Now, she was overwhelmed by a sudden, strong urge to find out how he was and decided to see if she could find him. She went back to her computer and put in a search. It was almost too easy. There he was on Linked In, there was no photo but where he had studied and worked was all there. She looked up his company and there was his name listed on the company profile as a top executive with an e-mail address. It suddenly occurred to her that it was his birthday in a few days. Without stopping to think about it, she sent him a message.

*Happy Birthday Old Man!*

*Meg*

She clicked send and went back to sit outside with her wine. A slight breeze ruffled the eucalyptus trees lining the wall of the garden and the memories came flooding back. Sweet and aching nostalgia surged through her, along with the familiar question of 'What if?' as she thought about the ring.

Suddenly, she felt a hand softly stroke her short, dark hair sprinkled with a few greying strands and tickle the back of her neck gently. She turned and looked up into the face of her husband, his hair tousled like a small boy. He smiled and came to sit next to her saying, "Penny for 'em."

She told him about sending the e-mail and he took her hand.

"Still yearning for that lost love? What is a man supposed to do?" he asked in mock desperation.

She grinned at him and said, "Guess you'll just have to try harder."

Ralph pulled her up and said, "Come with me."

The following day she received a reply from Pete. 'Is that the one and only Meg?' They exchanged a few e-mails telling each other where they were living and what they were doing. It was so strange to be in contact with him again. Pete told her that he was with a different oil company based in Houston and Meg told him she was in Abu Dhabi but flying to Athens on Thursday night. Pete sent a mail saying he was travelling for a few days, wished her a happy holiday and said he'd be in touch when he got back. She laughed thinking that he hadn't changed and she probably wouldn't hear from him for ages, if at all.

Everyone set off from the house for the flight at midnight. Laughing and joking they checked in and went through passport control and the security check, and headed towards the bar in the departure lounge. Meg was walking along chatting to one of her friends when she became aware of a tall man with a shock of dark hair flecked with silver-grey coming straight towards her. She looked at him and then stopped in her tracks as she realised it was Pete. Laughing, she ran up and gave him a huge hug. It was the loveliest moment. All the past pain and hurt that had always lurked in the recesses of her heart seemed to disappear in an instant. It was so good to see him. When she'd e-mailed him he had actually been in Abu Dhabi on business. He had checked what flight she must be on and as his flight was a bit later that night he had got there early to surprise her. He stayed and chatted to her and her family briefly and promised to keep in touch. She felt serenely happy that she'd seen him again.

A few months later he messaged to say he was in Abu Dhabi again and they arranged to meet for lunch. It was exactly as it had always been. They clicked into easy conversation and talked about everything and anything. They laughed when they both reached for glasses to read the menu. He filled her in on aspects of his life. He was of course, extremely successful and very wealthy. He'd made wise investments and was as practical and down to earth as ever in his outlook on life. He had a partner and children, but he had never married. They chatted about old friends and their families and then Pete suddenly said,

"I'm really sorry that I hurt you."

Meg's stomach twirled as she nodded acceptance of this apology and shifted awkwardly in her seat.

Then she looked at him and asked quietly,

"What happened to the ring?"

"Well, there's a story about that…"

Up until just a few months before, the ring had been in a safety deposit box and the bank called to say that he needed to come and take his box as they were closing the branch. He went with his partner, and she had opened the box, found the ring and claimed it for herself. The next day she was out in the garden, and she'd looked down at the ring and realised that the solitaire diamond had fallen out. She'd looked everywhere, but she couldn't find it.

Meg looked at him and with a rueful smile said,

"That's because it was my ring."

And he answered, "Yes."

He took a long, slow swig of beer, set the glass carefully down on the table and looked at her with his hazel brown eyes. She waited.

"Would you have said yes?" he finally asked.

She stared back at him and breathed in deeply.

"Yes," she said quietly, "I would have said yes."

## About the Author

Sian Williams Nixon is a writer of plays, pantos, short stories and screenplays. She writes bespoke scripts and stories and whatever else comes into her head. This is her first novel.

Other titles by Sian M. Williams:

The Camel Lot and the Knights of the Desk

Rapunzel II: Back to the Tower

Cinderella

Snow White & the Vertically Challenged Excavators

Rumplesillyskin

Journey to the End of the Rainbow

The Forgotten Wish

The Hive that Lost Its Purpose

The Man with the Disappearing Strawberry Blonde Hair

Email: sianscriptsinfo@gmail.com

Printed in Great Britain
by Amazon